W•CLARK
PUBLISHING
60 Evergreen Place, Suite 904
East Orange New Jersey 07018

UNDER PRESSURE

A YOUNG ADULT NOVEL BY

RASHAWN HUGHES

Wahida Clark Presents Young Adult
60 Evergreen Place
Suite 904
East Orange, New Jersey 07018
973-678-9982
www.wclarkpublishing.com
www.wcpyoungadult.com

Under Pressure
ISBN 13-digit 978-1936649402
ISBN 10-digit 1-936649-40-3
Library of Congress Catalog Number 2011920896
1. Young Adult, Urban, Street Lit, Hip-Hop, Gangsters, New York, African American, – Fiction

Cover design by Nuance Art nuanceart@gmail.com
Interior book design by Nuance Art nuanceart@gmail.com

Printed in United States
Green & Company Printing and Publishing, LLC
www.greenandcompany.biz

WAHIDA CLARK PRESENTS

UNDER PRESSURE

Y.A.
YOUNG ADULT

A YOUNG ADULT NOVEL BY

RASHAWN HUGHES

DEDICATIONS

*Dedicated to Carlos Guevara—until my heart stops,
I will work diligently in your honor.
Because of you, I have learned about my purpose and
how to make a commitment to that purpose.*

*I cry out with my whole heart
—Psalms 119:145*

ACKNOWLEDGEMENTS

First and foremost all praises due to ALLAH.

To our ANCESTORS, for paving the way for us to follow.

To my mother Claudette Mayers (RIP), you are my greatest source of inspiration. There is no doubt that your presence is surely missed. My world is an emptier place without you. Miss you much.

To my most precious jewels...My daughters; Shanaja & Lexus Hughes. You two have been and will always be my greatest work. Thank you for holding me accountable and know because of you two, my life will forever be anchored in love.

To My Friend, My Lover, My Queen—My Everything. Love is too weak to define what you mean to me. However, on a basic front, the beauty of our relationship is that it challenges us to grow on so many levels. Since we met, you have provided me with a purpose beyond me. I am convinced that you love me, you complete me, and you hold my heart in your hands. For that, I am truly grateful and want you to know there is nothing that can tear "US" apart.

To my sister Sasha—thank you for holding the family together. We are all so very proud of you for being the first in the faculty to get your Masters. How real is that? The things that you've done and do will be forever etched in my heart. Do know I am on my way to lighten the load and help you take the whole tribe to new heights, I love you.

To my brothers' Charles & Charlton—the Twins, the time is now! Let's put the pieces to this thing together so we can lay down a path for our children. What more motivation do we need? (Give both Martine and Lisa my love). Vonn Pierre, aka "V-Dub" —What's good Big Bro? If it's only by a thread, we must keep holding on. We're both on deck, and when our numbers play there will be no turning back. Love will be the light and forward will be the motion.

To my Nieces and Nephews—Cheyanne I love you girl. Thanks for your input on the book. We will write your story when I get home. Amanni & Amari, Jahvar, Ashanti & Nasir, Bri-Bri & Jaden, I want you all to know I do this for you. If you ever need me—I'm here. Love you all, Uncle Rah.

To my Newark NJ family—Lenie and all my sisters I love & miss y'all. Kenny, Charmaine, we will get together in a minute. To David (RIP), you will live through the whole team.

To Sloan and Brian Daughtry—thank you for raising our daughters during these trying times. Continue to grow in love.

To my mentor who has provided me with unlimited awareness, wisdom, and understanding— K. "King Allah" Dove. Your influence has opened up a door of endless possibilities. I appreciate all you've done and when we finally link up again, we will move the immovable and do the impossible.

To Jamal "Chick" Fowler and family-my extended faculty, I love you all thank you for all your support over the years. I can't wait until we are all together.

To my comrades whose bodies are confined but minds are free— Fruquan aka Money Mark, A. "Concrete" Brodie, E. "Easy" Diaz (You made the book kid, I didn't forget about you.), Ramel (I put you and Tiff in the book also.), J. (Gangsta J) Goolsby, R. "Robo Just" Townsend, Travaughn "Tee" Hall (this will only make us stronger—still we rise), True & Shaq (My Domincan Brothers…Que lo Que), The God Intelligent (Lets change the game my brother.), Kenneth "Nut" Christian (Thank you for all your input. When I make it, I'm bringing you with me.), Kemet Allah (Peace God, I know it's been a second, but I had to do some things for me. The love is real.) There are so many other brothers who I failed to mention, if that's you, charge it to my memory, not my heart.

To my Gino Green Team, Talib and Prince; I always knew you two would do your numbers. Continue to rise and don't stop 'til we get that Microsoft money. We'll definitely get together and take it to another level in a second. P.S. Ta thank you for being there from day one, you are the one brother I can always count on and that will never be forgotten.

To Elizabeth Morgan a true leader, educator and most importantly a women who strives for perfection and teaches by example. Your work with YouthBuild is remarkable and Smart Kidz University Daycare should be the future of all our children. Continue to rise and forever walk in beauty.

To those Natural Trend Setters—Simone and Yanique "Tru" Hylton, you two sisters have made the whole posse proud. Continue to rise and forever walk in beauty.

To my Comrades on the outside: Dennis Holloway and family, Mervin Bennett and family, Big Head Born (John Henry). Natequan, Talu, Torry, and Demetri—Get your weight up youngins', YouthBuild! I will see you all soon.

To my Long Island faculty, Big Zeus aka Glenn Augustave (Sak Passe), Larry De'Roche, Rocky, Paul Caputo, D. Carter, Aquan, I-God, E. "Notch" Moore (Holla at your boy), Marc "Riv-o" Rivers, Kev Denmark (RIP), Kenyatta Capers, Rick Miller, Guy Pyle, Sheldon Price, Rob Isley (I didn't forget about the kid. You still singing?), Big Hans stack that paper homie, Unique and Shaborn, Mike Tolliver, David "Kaiwan" Smith (You have been there from day-one. How real is that?) Lisa Crawford De'Roche, Roneve, Jamala, Nanette, Lisa Otero, Tonya Adams, Zanika Franklin, Susan Carmen, Pinky, and Patricia Cochran. The Whole 516 Stand up...Your boy is back!

To my comrades at Bard College...failure is no longer an option. It's not about where we are today, but where we want to be tomorrow. Rise Up!

Finally, to our next generation...this is for you...Carpe Diem.

I AM WE!

ONE

As Quentin, Torry, and Chase rode in QB's truck toward Shea Stadium, they could barely contain their excitement as they bounced and sang along with the hook on Neyo and Fab's single *"You Make Me Better."* Torry and Chase had never been to a professional baseball game. They were clowning around like children instead of the grown men they claimed to be. QB was just as excited because he was able to give them an opportunity to experience something other than hanging out on the block. Today was a special day; they were celebrating the hard work and sacrifice Chase and Torry put into achieving their General Equivalency Diploma (G.E.D).

Once they entered the home of the New York Mets, both Chase and Torry looked around Shea Stadium in amazement. This was the Mets final year of playing in this stadium. The organization had finally invested in a 21st century stadium with all the amenities to make it more fan-friendly and more importantly, profitable.

This place is huge, Chase thought. The smell of roasted peanuts, hot dogs, and buttered popcorn wafted in the air.

Families were busy trying to find their seats. Happy faces, exciting sounds of children, and laughter generated throughout the stadium. Children ran around like they were hooked on caffeine.

Torry tapped Chase on the arm. "Yo, peep shorty right there in the Apple Bottoms."

"Yeah, I'm on her," Chase replied. After a quick glance he thought, *My family never did things like this.*

<u>UNDER PRESSURE</u>

QB yelled out to them, "C'mon, I want to get y'all something." He led them to the concession stand to purchase some memorabilia. Both Chase and Torry wanted a Mets 'fitted,' which QB learned was slang for a baseball cap. QB was thinking more along the lines of an autographed photo or maybe an autographed bat.

Both Chase and Torry had enough hats, but this was their day so he purchased the fitted's for them. Torry picked out an oversized black and blue Mets fitted, with the orange N.Y. symbol stenciled on the front. Because of the color blue, Chase changed his mind and selected a black Chicago White Sox fitted. It matched his brand new Gino Green pullover that he'd just copped a few days ago. Gino Green Global was the hottest clothing line to hit the set since Sean John.

QB purchased both hats for the boys even though he knew Chase selected the black Sox cap because it matched his gang colors. QB didn't want to ruin the day with an argument about that so he held back what he wanted to say. Instead he led them both to find their seats.

As usual the boys walked with a hip-hop swagger, which caused a few people to stare at them. Whether they were admiring their style or reinforcing their own stereotypes, it amazed QB how young black men were perceived. QB knew from experience that because of their unique way of doing things they were looked at with suspicious eyes. *Misunderstood should be the epitaph tattooed on the faces of Black and Latin youth,* QB thought.

They sat three rows behind the Mets dugout along the first base line. They could hear the players in the dugout talking, laughing, and getting ready for the game. QB looked around noticing how well the grounds people kept the field. Even the dirt was manicured. *I have to get these groundskeepers to do my lawn,* he thought.

Ten minutes after they sat down, Chase pulled out his BlackBerry and dialed his man.

"Yo, speak."

"What up, B? This Chase."

What's good, my dude, where you at?"

"We're laid up in Shea Stadium right now checking out the Mets."

"Yeah right," replied B.

"Turn on your television, kid."

"What channel?"

"I don't know, try UPN or that ESPN station," Chase answered.

"Hold up, let me find it." There was a pause as B channel surfed. "I got it. The Mets, right?"

Chase looked for the television cameras. "Can you see us?" he asked.

"Nah, they got two cats on the screen talking about the game. Where y'all niggas sitting?

"Right behind the Mets dugout. I got that black fitted on. Plus it looks like we're the only niggas in the building. It shouldn't be hard to spot us."

"I'll check for you when the game starts," B said. There was an unusual pause. B was contemplating whether or not he should tell Chase what was being said about him since Chase was his boy. "Check it, my dude, I don't know how to tell you this but Showtyme told niggas' last night to wash you up. Something about you pressing him about wanting out of the Henchmen," he said.

"Who me?"

"Yeah nigga, you."

"When he tell y'all that?"

"I just told you … last night."

Perspiration began forming on his bald head. Chase sat there in disbelief. There was another pause. During that awkward moment Chase felt his safety net of being in one of the most notorious gangs in New York begin to unravel.

"You there, Chase?"

"Yeah man, I'm here. Let me ask you something, B. Where do you stand?"

UNDER PRESSURE

"What kind of question is that? Where the hell do you think I stand? I wouldn't be telling you jack if I was gonna get at you."

"I hear you."

"My dude, on some bull, make sure you keep my name out of this. I don't want to get caught up in this drama. You should lay low for a minute so I can try to work things out."

"C'mon B, you know how I get down."

"No doubt. Yo, you hear me though. Someone is banging down my door right now. It's probably this hoodrat chick that wants me to crush it. Hit me up when you get back around the way."

"A'ight, B, I'll holla," Chase said, ending the call. He didn't know what to make of the news, but he knew craziness lay before him. He sighed, thinking how being in the Henchmen was madness, but getting out was as dangerous as a landmine.

After B hung up the phone, he took a couple of pulls on the hydro he was puffing, and when he became nice and paranoid he called Showtyme. Unfortunately, it wasn't to try to straighten things out.

After hitting the end button on his phone, Chase sunk in his seat and buried his head in his hands as if he had a headache.

Torry, too busy checking out how the players walked, stretched, and prepared for the game, didn't notice Chase's change of attitude. Torry sat there with his mouth and eyes wide open as if Beyonce and Alicia Keys were mud wrestling on the pitcher's mound.

"Look, there's Willie Randolph," Torry said, pointing to the Mets manager who was struggling to hold on to his job. He was talking with a few fans behind home plate.

QB smiled. *I hope he weathers this storm, for it's good to have a black manager representing in the Big Apple.*

Torry turned to him. "I know what you're thinking, QB."

"What's that, little bruh?"

"I know you're feeling the Mets having a black manager."

QB smiled. "Who the hell do you think you are, Cleo?" QB was amazed at how his students thought they knew him. The truth of the matter is some actually did, which was a good thing. Hopefully, some of his ways would rub off on them. "You got that, and you know what?"

"What?"

"It's long overdue. They should have been hired a black—"

Cutting him off, Chase turned toward QB with his mouth twisted up. "C'mon QB—not now with that black mess."

QB looked at him like he was crazy. "What you say?"

"I don't want to hear that right now, QB."

With a raised brow QB looked at him and tightened his grip on his chair. He took a few deep breaths, a tactic he learned from his wife to prevent saying something he would later regret. He noticed that something was bothering Chase since he made that call. QB possessed the ability to read the attitude and body language of his students like a closed captioning for the hearing impaired. However, that was no excuse for Chase to come at him like that and more importantly it was no excuse for him to undermine the importance of hiring a black man in a profession that was historically biased. He exhaled and wondered to himself, *When will these kids get it?*

Torry looked at Chase and shook his head. He attempted to change the subject. "QB, you really came through with these tickets. That's what's up and I just want to thank you. It's definitely a good look," he said.

QB turned to him then glanced at Chase. "It's nothing. I promised you guys that I would do this if you passed your G.E.D. and you guys stepped up and did it … Now that's a good look. When you put in work, as you both like to say, your efforts will be rewarded." QB's cell phone rang. He looked at the caller-ID and decided not to take the call. Looking out toward center field, he continued, "That's what this is all about—putting in that work because the only place success comes before work is in the dictionary," he said.

Young Adult

Torry thought about that for a minute, then reached out to give QB a pound. "Ain't that right, Chase?"

Chase, lost in his own thoughts stared out into the clear sky, thinking about what he needed to do in order to get up out of the Henchmen.

QB noticed the worried look on his face. "Chase, what's up with you? Is everything all right?" he asked.

In an attempt to hide his concerns, Chase looked down avoiding QB's stare. "Yeah, QB, it's all good."

QB knew he was lying, so he continued to probe. "You sure?"

Chase looked up and put on as much of a smile as his face could muster. He knew he was wrong for coming at QB like that. "I'm good, QB. I just have a few things that I have to handle. I didn't mean to come at you like that; you know you're my nig ..." Chase tried to stop at the last second but it was too late.

QB threw his hand up like he was stopping traffic. "How many times do I have to tell you that I'm not your N-word? You act like you purchased me at an auction or something, because that's where N-words were sold." QB looked at him with disapproval, and then continued, "Chase, do you know where that word comes from?"

"Yeah, QB, I know. It comes from the Latin word Niger, which is actually a country in West Africa. For West Africans the word simply meant the color black, but somewhere around the 1800's it became a symbol of white racism.

"If that's the case, why do you keep using it?" Chase didn't respond. "You need to understand that that word was imposed on African American people by whites because they wanted to make us feel inferior; less than them so they could justify using us for our labor. White people, during that time, knew that in order to make people of color feel subservient they had to not only make us feel different, but make us see ourselves as less than worthy. The N-word, whether it's spelled with an 'er' or an 'a', is the term they used and here you are in 2010 using it like it's some kind of term of endearment." QB shook his head in disgust. "It's crazy."

Neither of the boys said anything. This was one of those arguments where they both knew they had no wins.

QB looked at them both. "Do you two know how important a name or title is? Don't you two understand how easy it is for you to hurt or kill somebody you call the N-word? Don't you see the connection? The N-word is akin to worthlessness, and this makes it much easier for you to get at someone who you consider a N-word."

Torry glanced at Chase. "Why did you get him started?" he whispered.

"You damn right he got me started. Think about it. It is much more difficult for you to hurt someone you call your brother. Listen to how it sounds. 'Let's ride on those N-words,' or 'Let's kill that N-word is much easier to say or do as opposed to Let's kill that brother.'" QB paused to let his words sink in. "It's a big difference—right?" Neither of the boys replied. "You guys better know that how you see yourself will determine just how far you both make it in this world."

"You got that, QB," Chase said.

"Yeah, I know I got that, the problem is you getting it." QB looked him directly in his eyes. "I'm going to give you a pass this time, but don't get it twisted, I can still break one of you young dudes down like a shotgun." QB playfully shot a quick, hard jab into the air startling the middle aged white man sitting in front of him. QB apologized. They all had a good laugh. "Chase, seriously though, if you need to talk or need me for anything know that I am here for you, all right?" QB added.

"I know, QB," Chase said, feeling guilty.

"Let's get something to eat," QB said, wanting to break the tension.

"Can we get some beer, QB?" asked Chase.

QB looked at him. "Yeah, something is definitely wrong with you. You know that's not happening. Your grandmother would kill both of us if she knew I was out here letting you drink."

UNDER PRESSURE

Chase sucked his teeth as he looked for the vendor. "C'mon, QB, she's not going to find out."

Even though QB wouldn't mind a cold beer himself, he knew doing the right thing was a full-time job, especially when dealing with the youth. They were always looking and watching even when you thought they weren't. "You heard what I said?" Now, if you want some popcorn and sodas you better call that vendor over here before she heads the other way."

"Damn, shorty is hot," Torry said, eyeing the vendor.

"Where?" asked Chase.

"Over there," he said, nodding his head toward the beautiful young lady who stood about five and half feet tall. She had her hair pulled back in a ponytail accentuating her pretty brown, oval shaped eyes. *She's a natural beauty*, thought Torry.

Chase was hypnotized. *She has to be mixed with something, maybe some Indian or something. Nothing should be that good-looking*, he thought. She was a caramel complexion, with a body, and a smile that read 'enter here and find your way to heaven.' "That's definitely wifey material," Chase said.

Chase and Torry watched her make her way down the aisles of the stadium. QB watched the boys as they looked open like a twenty-four hour deli. He tried to remember if he acted like that over women when he was their age.

"Popcorn, peanuts, soda and cracker jacks. Get your popcorn, peanuts, soda and cracker jacks," yelled the young lady in a voice that melted Chase's troubles away.

"Excuse me, miss, over here," Chase yelled, standing and waving his hand creating way too much attention.

She stopped twice before making her way over to them. "What would you like, sir?" she asked, showing off a smile that cut through all of Chase's player instincts.

Chase returned her smile. "What's up, ma? I'll take some popcorn and directions."

"Excuse me?"

"I would like some popcorn and directions."

She blushed. "Directions where?" she asked.

"To your heart," Chase said, licking his lips like he was LL Cool J.

QB and Torry simultaneously burst out laughing.

The smile on the young lady's face told Chase that he had a shot. "I doubt you could find my heart if I led you there by your hand."

Looking into her eyes, Chase extended his hand. "Try me. My name is Chase." He peered down at QB and Torry. "Ignore these guys; they don't know how to act in the presence of someone as beautiful as you. And you are?"

She twisted her glossed lips, giving him a well-deserved smirk. "If you were really looking to get to my heart," she said, pointing to her name tag pinned directly above her heart, "You would know my name is Lexi."

"Aaahhhh, she got you there, playa," said Torry.

Chase shot daggers at Torry. "Why are you hatin' on the kid?"

"Look! I work on commission so I don't have time to waste."

Chase cleared his throat. "Trust me, you're not wasting your time, shorty."

"Excuse me—first of all, my name is not Shorty, it's Lexi," she said, rolling her eyes.

"My bad, Lexi," he said with a smile.

Silence settled between them two. QB decided to intervene. "Pardon my little brother. He refers to all women as shortie."

The young lady smiled at QB. "It's okay." She then looked at Chase. "Maybe one day he'll learn that there is a difference between the two."

QB smiled, and then nodded at Chase. He ordered three popcorns, some peanuts, and three large sodas. "That'll be fourteen dollars," Lexi said.

UNDER PRESSURE

Chase reached into his pocket stunting like he was going to pay for it. As the young lady spoke with her next customer, QB gave Chase a 'stop fronting' look. QB momentarily thought about letting him pay for it, but he didn't want to embarrass him in case he didn't have the money. He winked at Chase. "I got it, Chase, you paid for breakfast." He then handed the young lady a twenty. "Here you go."

After QB got his change, Chase extended his hand. "It was nice meeting you." With his number palmed he shook Lexi's hand. "Make sure you call me with those directions. I'll forever be lost without them."

Lexi smirked at his corny line. "I'll think about it." She put the piece of paper in her pocket and smiled then headed up the rows of fans, with what seemed like an extra bounce in her step.

After she was out of earshot, Torry placed his head on Chase's shoulder. "I'll take some popcorn and directions to your heart." In between laughs, he added, "That was the lamest line I've ever heard."

"Not to mention the most embarrassing one," QB added.

They were cracking up. Even Chase couldn't help but laugh, but he immediately started singing Maino's new single "Hi Haters'." People around them started laughing not really knowing what they were laughing about, proving that laughter is contagious.

Regaining his composure QB interrupted them. "A'ight you two, chill-out. That's enough. They're about to sing the *National Anthem*. Take those hats off and stand up."

"What? C'mon, QB why we gotta stand up?" Chase questioned. "This country has no allegiance to us nig—I mean, brothers. So why should we pledge our allegiance to it?"

QB was shocked by his response, but seized the moment. "That may very well be true, but right now I'm asking you to stand out of respect."

Chase put his soda down, knowing QB meant business. They both took off their hats and stood up. QB whispered, "Chase, do me a favor … be easy with that black stuff." They all smiled.

TWO

Chase and Torry had major respect for QB. He was the director of U-Turn, a New York City program for at-risk youth. QB began as a volunteer and worked his way up to become the top-dog. From the first day QB was hired he demanded respect. He was from the streets and everybody at U-Turn learned without delay that QB was about his business. When he was first hired he came in and encouraged everybody to put their cards on the table face up. During the initial meeting with the youth, he gave them the opportunity to voice their concerns and complaints. Prior to QB, that was unheard of–U-Turn was a dictatorship. What the counselors told the youth to do they did, or risked getting kicked out the program. For many of the students, this meant hitting the block, going to jail, or ending up pregnant for most of the females. QB promised every teenager in the program that they would be respected by staff, and in turn, they would be expected to respect all employees, from the maintenance men to the C.E.O.

With the hiring of QB there was a chance to start all over again. Every student would begin from a position of good standing. It was up to them to lose ground and the respect being extended.

The students at U-Turn tagged him OG, which stands for Original Gangster. Initially, he didn't approve of the handle because of its negative connotation, but he let them get away with it hoping he could change their perception of what a gangster should be.

QB had a style about himself that crossed those barriers that existed between youth and adults. The staff at U-Turn, up until QB came aboard

Young Adult

was having a difficult time getting through to the teenagers. Most of the counselors had simply given up. Seeing this, QB called a staff-only meeting and gave out harsh ultimatums. Either the counselors would have to rise to the challenge or resign, because as he had to remind them, U-Turn was in the business of elevating lives. QB thrived when it came to challenges. However, to call the drama QB inherited at U-Turn a "challenge" is an understatement. Put it this way, if David had walked by U-Turn, he would have tossed his Goliath-slaying slingshot to QB and said, "Good luck with this one, homie."

QB was straight up with both students and counselors. He kept things real and this is why the youth respected him. If a student was right, QB would have their back, even against other counselors. It took a couple of years, but QB single handedly slid a blanket beneath the old ways of doing things at U-Turn and yanked the whole operation into good standing.

So there they were standing in Shea Stadium with the players and thousands of fans listening to a sister sing the *National Anthem* like they had never heard before. She had a soul-stirring voice that injected a sense of patriotism into the entire crowd.

"Shorty blew that," Torry said at the completion of her performance.

Chase, without realizing it, was applauding and whistling wildly along with what seemed like everybody in the building. People were clapping as if they were catching the Holy Spirit in a Southern Baptist Church. "What's shorty's name, QB?" Chase asked.

QB smiled. "The woman's name is Deniece Graves. She's an opera singer."

"Get the f—" started Torry, until QB shot him a look. "I mean, get outta here. I never heard of a black opera singer. I thought only white people sing opera."

"There's a lot of things you've never heard of—instead of always telling me to get off my Malcolm X swag, you both should be learning more about your history. Do you two know who Marian Anderson is?"

"Who?" they both asked.

"We know who Pamela Anderson is—you know shorty with the big ta-ta's," Chase added while cupping his hands in front of his chest.

QB smiled, and shook his head "You're a fool," he said. "Marian Anderson was once said to have a voice that came around once in a lifetime. However, because she was black, in 1939 the Daughters of the American Revolution refused to permit her to sing in the Constitution Hall in Washington D.C., but Harold Ickes, the secretary of the interior at that time arranged for her to sing from the steps of the Lincoln Memorial. I'm telling y'all, her voice was so good that she broke racial barriers. In fact, for the inauguration of President John F. Kennedy in 1961 they finally asked her to sing "The Star-Spangled Banner." They couldn't help but to get out their own way. That's how good this sister blew. I'm telling y'all she put birds to shame. What about Paul Robeson? I know you two heard of him."

They were looking at QB as if he was speaking German. They both admired the fact that QB knew so much, plus he would get busy if he had to. It was that kind of balance which made the youth gravitate toward QB.

"Come on, Paul Robeson was a black actor and entertainer. He played Othello on Broadway in 1943." QB turned toward them to see that they both were attentive. He enjoyed expanding their minds beyond the 'hood. "It's important that we study our past, this way you will know who and what you are instead of letting other people define you." He exhaled. "And another thing, you both should stop referring to women as shorties. Do young ladies respond to that?" He looked at Torry. "Does Naysia answer to shorty?"

"Hell to the no. Nay don't play that QB, she got that boy on act right when he is around her," Chase said, laughing.

"What's a shorty anyway?" asked QB.

"What you want to know about shorties for? Mrs. Banks got your butt on lock," said Chase.

Young Adult

UNDER PRESSURE

Torry laughed and gave his boy a pound.

QB smiled. "I see you got jokes." He settled into his seat thinking about his wife. *Five years and this love thing is still going strong.* Up until Reyna he never thought anyone would be able to touch him in that kind of way. He grinned, thinking about how she melted the ice from around his heart, and now with Nia, their two-year-old daughter, his whole world changed. They both became his reasons for living. "Yeah, she got a fella on lock and you know what ... I'm cool with that. You know why?"

"Why?" they both asked in unison.

"'Cause she makes me better," QB said, belting out the Neyo song they were singing on their way to the park.

Chase and Torry stared at each other with that 'you've got to be kidding me' look.

Torry turned to Chase. "Come with me to the bathroom, yo."

"A'ight."

As they walked up the aisle toward the rotunda of the stadium, Chase turned to Torry. "What's up for the night?"

"I don't know, I'm supposed to be swinging by Naysia's spot after the game. She said she has something important to talk to me about. I don't know what, but you know how it is up in the club."

"Nah kid, I don't know how it is up in that club. I don't love 'em, I hit 'em. Crazy in love ... I'll leave that up to you and Naysia," Chase said.

"I hear you," Torry replied as he looked back to make sure QB was not following them. "What's up with you? Why you come at QB like that earlier?"

Chase pushed his hands into his pants pockets. "It's nothin', soldier. I had some stuff on my mind."

"Oh yeah. Well, what about that gang mess?"

Chase spun his fitted to the back. "What you talkin' 'bout?"

"You know what I'm talking 'bout. You wanting the black fitted. You don't think QB caught on to that?"

Chase looked away. "What you want me to do? You know what it is, I can't do blue."

"C'mon, Chase, when you gonna leave that bull alone? Yesterday QB asked me did you talk to Showtyme about getting out. I told him yeah, that you were making moves. You better not be playin' games, Chase. You gave him your word."

Chase looked around. "I know, son, but this stuff ain't easy. Showtyme on some bull and he is not trying to hear about me pulling back without paying in blood. He told me if I keep coming at him with that, I'm done. We got into it the other night about this and when I spoke to B earlier he said Showtyme told dudes to wash me up. That means it's on, Torry. I was thinking about that punk Showtyme. That's why I snapped at QB. Showtyme got me mixed up. He thinks there's something soft about me. I can't trust none of them, not even B ... I'm tellin' you, homie, they won't catch me sleeping. It's goin' down. Real talk."

Torry pulled his fitted down and gritted his teeth. "Forget Showtyme! Let's get at that fool. If he wants to pop, then let's pop." He paused, not really understanding the magnitude of the situation or his words. All he knew was that Chase was his best friend and that he would do anything to help him. "He can get it, too. That clown ain't bulletproof."

Chase stopped walking, turned toward Torry and gave him a pound. He then pulled Torry into an embrace right there in middle of the stadium. People walked by looking at them with a kind of curiosity that showed they were not used to seeing straight men hugging each other in public. After the brief show of love, Chase said, "You know I can't let you get involved in this. You got too much going for yourself. Plus Naysia and your moms would kill me if something ever happened to you. I'd rather go to war with Osama and the damn Taliban before

Young Adult

having to deal with them two. This is something I have to handle on my own, soldier. It was me who decided to climb into bed with the Five Seven Henchmen, nobody else, so let me handle this … I'll be a'ight."

Torry pushed open the bathroom door, walked up to one of the mirrors that was above the sinks lined up along the far wall. He maneuvered his fitted until he thought it was sitting just right on his head. He smoothed out his shirt and checked out his look. Torry was six foot three, brown skinned, and still growing. Everybody said he resembled Tyrese, but, of course, he thought he looked much better. "Let's talk to QB about this. He'll figure something out. He may step to Showtyme by himself."

Chase unzipped his pants and stepped up to a urinal, "I don't know about that. This is strictly for the streets. I don't want him to get involved. Trust me, Torry, I got this. You know a brother could hold his own and if it gets ugly then I'm just gonna wash these dudes up." He flushed the urinal, washed his hands, and checked himself out in the mirror. He then added, "Yeah, Showtyme gets busy, he has put in major work, but I get busy too. I'm not afraid of his gangsta. He got guns, I got guns too. If he wants to make a movie then we could do it whenever, wherever. You know what it is, action!"

Before they returned to their seats Torry turned to Chase. "I'm with you kid. No matter what, I want you to know I'm gonna ride or die with you."

***

The sun blanketed the majority of the crowd with hell's own heat. Everybody who was not in the luxury boxes was perspiring. It had to be at least ninety-five degrees with the humidity and smog of NY. The sun set the air to dancing—it literally moved up and down before QB's eyes. He looked at Chase and Torry who both seemed to be melting in their seats. Since the game was out of reach—the Mets were winning eleven to one—and it was already the bottom of seventh with Johan Santana still throwing strong. QB talked the boys into leaving early. It didn't take much persuading. Baseball games were definitely too long for the impatient. Being teenagers and from the fast-food era, both Chase and Torry's patience were unbelievably short. QB was glad they didn't put up any resistance. He wanted to beat the crowd and avoid the inevitable traffic they would have to contend with if they waited until the end of the game.

As they left Chase scanned the stands for Lexi. He did not see her, but was confident that she would call. On the way to QB's truck the boys were debating about who was going to sit in the front. They both wanted to stunt in his pearl white Cadillac Escalade. The truck was fully loaded, sitting on twenty-sixes, and had a shine that made the sun blush. QB was not really into pimping his ride. The only reason he had twelve thousand dollar rims on his truck was because his brother Amari gave them to him as a present for his birthday. QB was a simple man, even though there was nothing simple about owning an Escalade. QB fell in love with the truck at first sight and other than his home it was the one thing that he was proud he had purchased.

Chase won the argument, since Torry sat in the front on the way to the game. He didn't have to put up that much of an argument. QB, minding his business, was proud to see them settle their disputes without much conflict. He could remember a time when simple debates like that would have led to blows.

As they pulled out the parking lot Chase reached into his knapsack and took out his iPod and connected it to QB's Kenwood docking station. Mims' "This Is Why I'm Hot," remix filled the truck just as QB's cell phone rang.

"Hello," he answered, turning down the music.

"Hey baby," Reyna retorted.

"What's up, beautiful?"

"Nothing. I just called to see what time you're coming home?"

"We left a little early to beat the traffic. I'm going to take the boys to get something to eat, drop them off, and then I'll head home. Why, you missing your king?"

"You know I do."

"Where's Ladybug?" QB asked, referring to Nia.

"She's out in the back yard playing with the little girl from next door." She paused looking out the window in the kitchen, then added, "Baby, can you bring us something to eat? I really don't feel like cooking tonight, it's too hot."

"Not as hot as you, sexy," said QB, trying to score some points.

"You're so cute," Reyna replied, knowing exactly what he was up to, but not feeding into it. "I'll see you soon, love ya."

"Love you more." QB clicked off the phone, smiling.

Chase mimed putting his finger down his throat as if he was going to vomit. They were not used to seeing QB all mushy. QB enjoyed hanging out with his students, but he lived every moment for his family. Reyna and Nia were his heaven right here on earth. He turned toward Chase. "What do you two have planned for the evening?" he asked.Chase immediately started mocking him in a girlie voice. "Not as hot as you, sexy." They laughed. Unfortunately, because of Chase's silliness none of them noticed the black Honda Accord with four Henchmen conspicuously following them.

Torry said, "I got to go to Naysia's, so you could drop us off in St. Albans if that's no problem."

QB nodded. "No problem, but I expect to see you both bright and early Monday morning. We have to work on those college applications. Getting your G.E.D. was just the start, now the real work begins."

"We there, QB—early," Torry said. He began thinking how his plans were finally falling in place. *A college degree is going to be a good look. I could see my mom's face as my name is called to receive my degree. It's all good; I just have to work on my jump-shot so I can make the ball team as a walk-on.*

Chase turned the music back up and sank in his seat. He was knee-deep into his own thoughts, but they were about something totally different. He was putting together a plan to get at Showtyme. He also knew it was time for him to get his life together. That's one thing he admired about Torry—how he was focused. Chase wanted to follow in his footsteps, but he first had to get out of the Five Seven Henchmen.

As they pulled to a stop at a red light on Northern Boulevard, the black Honda Accord whisked around them, blocking them in. Three men with dark shades and hoodies pulled tight around their heads jumped out with guns in their hands. They surrounded the truck and with a knowing nod, they began dumping bullets into the Escalade. QB, who didn't realize what was happening until it was too late, ducked, and hit the gas pedal.

The truck jumped forward and slammed into some park cars. He continued pressing the gas, but the truck was stuck. Windows shattered as bullets penetrated the metal and glass like a hot knife slicing through butter. The people on the block ran for cover as the frightening sounds of automatic gunfire tore through dreams of living. It sounded like a full-fledge war. The smell of gunpowder filled the interior of the truck after the sixty-second barrage finished.

As the Henchmen lowered their guns, except for QB's horn, there was an eerie silence. Then suddenly you could hear police sirens whining in the distance. The Henchmen immediately scrambled back to the Accord and sped off. The smell of tire-rubber and fear was left behind. It was mixed with the strong stench of death that permeated the drug-infested neighborhood.

Young Adult

THREE

QB opened his eyes from what he thought was a nightmare. Blood slowly trickled down his face which caused him to blink his eyes. He struggled to move his arms but was unable to. His ears were ringing and the pain he felt trying to move was unbearable. He attempted to lift himself up off the seat and was met with a feeling that felt like a thousand needles being stuck in his body at one time. His head throbbed. It slowly registered that he was hit—how bad remained to be seen, that is, if he made it at all. He heard sirens in the distance.

Then he heard Chase say something, but it sounded like he was under water, "QB. Torry. You guys a'ight? QB, get up, get the hell up!" His ears were ringing. *Maybe this is why Chase sounded so far away*, he thought.

With very little strength and a wounded voice, QB said, "I'm all right. Are you hit?"

Chase looked into the back seat and saw Torry's fitted on the floor. "Nah, I'm not hit, but I think Torry is. He looks bad. We gotta get him to the hospital," he said, panicking as his eyes filled to the brim. "Torry, get up … move if you can hear me, man."

"Get in the back seat and see if you could help him," QB struggled to say. Blood and glass were everywhere. QB felt death waiting around the corner, but he pushed that thought out his mind. He was more concerned about Torry's health than he was about his own. Then thoughts of Nia and Reyna filled his mind and his fighter instincts kicked in. *Reyna would kill me if I die on her especially after all she's sacrificed for me.* He could hear her now, *You better not leave us; man up, Quentin!*

Chase jumped into the back seat and held Torry in his arms. He cradled his head. "Hold on, Torry, don't die soldier. You can't die on me!" Chase could see and feel the blood soaking though Torry's clothes. Tears rushed down Chase's face.

People hesitantly made their way toward the truck. Some were on their cell phones calling for help. Torry's breath was shallow and his eyes kept rolling up into his head.

Chase was frantically screaming for help, "Get an ambulance. Somebody call an ambulance!" He couldn't believe what was happening. He thought, *Why couldn't I be the one who got shot?* He noticed the blown out windows, the bullet holes in the truck's door panel, and the blood that was now on the seats. He lowered his head then looked up at the slowing traffic and vowed to himself to go after Showtyme. He swore revenge and suddenly felt his strength increase, fueled by an anger that he had never experienced before.

QB felt his door open and heard someone asking if he was all right. *"Senor, tu estas bien?"* He passed out when he tried to respond. His last thought was, *Why does trouble always seem to find me—especially when things are going right?*

***

Quentin Banks had always been a fighter, even though it always seemed as if he was holding on to life by a thread. Since he was a child he had been running headlong into the abyss. His life had been held hostage by a darkness that no child should ever experience. At the age of seven he was molested by an uncle, who himself was molested when he was younger. Because of this abuse, QB's reserve around most people bordered on reclusion. His trust level for people became non-existent and it destroyed most of his relationships with other kids. QB was a bright child, and attracted people to him because of his curiosity. He always asked questions about events he witnessed. Unfortunately, his curiosity about the world and his lack of trust in others conflicted with each other. The molestation continued until QB decided that he wasn't going to be a victim any longer. One day when his uncle crept in his room late at night, QB pulled a butcher knife from under his pillow and threatened to kill him if he ever touched him again. His uncle could tell by the look in Quentin's eyes that he was serious and had it in him to carry out his threat. Grudgingly, Quentin never told his mother, in part because of fear, but more so, out of embarrassment. He buried his experience of molestation inside and for most of his life he blamed himself. It became something he never wanted to think about, much less talk about. He just went on living—broken, trying to put it behind him.

His family was the epitome of dysfunctional. His mother, who did what she thought was best, struggled to raise him, along with his older brother, Amari, and their younger sister, Shai. She worked two jobs for the majority of her life just to get by. His father left when he was three years old. Shai's father was most likely a one-night stand and was never discussed. His brother Amari, until recently, was knee-deep in the streets and considered himself a natural-born hustler. Growing up, Amari and their mother argued incessantly. To Quentin it seemed like they fought every day, until finally, she kicked him out of the house. Their mother had a bad habit of saying that he was going to either die in the streets or go to jail for the rest of his life. She vowed not to lose her younger son to the streets, so she was very strict about Quentin's whereabouts.

This meant QB spent the majority of his childhood in the house, which ultimately caused more harm than good. Quentin literally had to raise his little sister. His mother taught him how to cook just so he could make dinner for Shai and himself when she was not home. He also had to learn how to braid hair, and do all the things a mother should do with her daughter. He was forced to become a man well before he understood or enjoyed childhood. He never understood why his mother wouldn't allow him to be like all the other children. As a young man, he promised that if he ever had children he would never do that to them.

The weight of having to become an adult before his time had caused him to have some serious issues with responsibility and maturity.

While all his friends loved their mother's, he grew up resenting his. What confused him the most was why his mother was so mean? QB wanted a loving relationship with his mom, but found himself wondering if a child could love a mother who showed very little capacity to love him in return. For years this question went unanswered. His only relief came when he went to sleep and dreamed. At night he would cry himself to sleep and get lost in dreams that always took him to places that were fun, far away from his home. QB had begun to literally count the days in which he had until he could leave her house.

Once he left, there would be no coming back. All he wanted was to be able to do the things other kids do; go to school, have some nice clothes, videos, to be able to go outside and play with other kids. His mother claimed that the playground was the devil's workshop.

Quentin, one day mistakenly said, "I don't see any devil out there. All I see is kids having fun." His mother whirled around and gave him what she called the "M". That was her name for a quicker-than-your-eye-can-see smack. If you look on the inside of your hand the lines form the letter "M", hence, the moniker. She had smacked him so hard that day that he thought he saw the "M" imprinted on his face. However, the physical scars were the least of his pain. It was the pain in his heart and the hurt engraved in his spirit that cut much deeper.

When his mother was home she always seemed to be in a bad mood. She always brought home the stress and problems from her job. This caused her to complain about everything: Why isn't the kitchen clean?' 'Turn down the T.V.' Blah, blah, blah. The only time things seemed good was when she was getting her drink on, and that was because on those nights they usually ordered Chinese food, or Quentin's favorite, pizza pie with extra cheese for dinner. But even on those nights when the liquor ran out, Quentin was blamed for any and everything that went wrong. His mother was like a roadside bomb; one

Young Adult

wrong step and she was going to blow up, literally killing the innocence of his childhood. A beating with an extension cord could happen at any given moment. Wounds and scars for him was something that became normal. Unfortunately, Quentin learned at a very young age that when roots bleed the grass is no longer green.

Ironically, it was Quentin who ended up going to prison. Quentin's mother died of a cancerous tumor while he was doing his bid. Of course this devastated Quentin. Thinking that she died from a broken heart, he blamed himself. His only comfort was the fact that he and his mother mended the fences before her untimely departure. They did this by communicating, being open and honest. For QB, it was about him understanding the fact that his mother was not always his mother, that she had her own set of issues to deal with. He had to come to terms with the fact that she was a human being, not just his mom. As an adult, Quentin realized they both made their share of mistakes and was glad they were able to bridge that generational gap. Living with himself would have been next to impossible if they had not cleared the air before she returned to the essence. During her many visits in prison, he promised his mom that he was going to rise to another level and lead their family out of the cycle of mediocrity. She always said that she believed he would and now that promise meant so much more to him.

***

At age twenty, Quentin was convicted of murdering a man who robbed his girlfriend while she was four months pregnant. During the robbery the assailant beat her so badly she lost her baby—his baby—their future. Quentin cried for days. Even though for the majority of his life he felt isolated and alone, he had never felt pain like the loss of his child. Seeing his girl in the hospital and hearing her speak of the emptiness she felt inside pushed him over the edge. QB was more than angry; he was confused, tumbling quickly in a downward spiral. He left the hospital four days after the incident with one thing on his mind— revenge!

It took Quentin a little over a week to find out who tore his family apart. The streets were talking and because QB had a reputation for getting busy everybody was anticipating some get-back. The kid responsible for the death of his child was supposed to be laying low, or so he thought.

One night while QB was about to head into the barbershop he spotted the chain he gave his girlfriend hanging from the neck of this kid who was built like a linebacker. He couldn't believe it. The punk that robbed his girl stood right outside of his car. He grabbed his equalizer, a .44 Bulldog, from under his car seat. Not caring who witnessed it, he stepped out of his Audi GT and walked right up to the beast. It was almost seven o'clock in the evening, and the streets were packed with people getting their hair and nails groomed for the weekend. Anger clouded Quentin's judgment. The hoodlum rocking his chain spotted him a little too late. The Bulldog was centered on the cat's face.

No words were needed, yet, Quentin whispered, "Why?"

The man tried to say something, but QB unloaded the mini-cannon, putting all five shots into the murderer, literally blowing his head off. When the cylinder emptied, Quentin walked to the corpse and bent down and took his chain from around what was left of his head. In spite of the chaos, he got up devoid of sympathy, turned, and calmly walked away.

Oddly, Quentin didn't really understand what it was he was feeling. He was numb during the entire episode and during the eventual trial. He knew no matter the outcome he was going to survive. For his unborn child, he could do the time. Revenge was bittersweet. Yet, he found a way to justify his actions in his own mind. His girl and her family supported him in the beginning. In fact, he wifed his girl before he went Up-North. She vowed to stand by him, but after three years of traveling to prisons, the constant pressure from her friends to hang out, and the many lonely nights, she decided to leave him for another man. Quentin felt betrayed and abandoned by the one person who he put before his own self. The thought of her with another man crushed a part of him that he never thought could be healed. He'd never forget the day he received that *Dear John* letter. He sat on the edge of his bed, dropped his chin to his chest and cried for the first time since seeing his girl in the intensive care unit. When all the tears dried up and he decided to take off the mask of being weak, gullible and stupid, Quentin moved further into his shell, but he also began the process of getting his life back on track.

***

"*Papi, no lo muevas mucho porque se la hace peor. Acuestalo en el asiento de atrás.*" Chase looked at her like she was crazy. In broken English, she said, "No, no move. Lay he down."

She grabbed QB's wrist and began checking for his pulse. After a few seconds she found it and then stepped out the truck and went to the back seat to check on Torry. Finding his pulse was much more difficult. It was faint, but a pulse nonetheless. "Gracias dos mio," the Latin women said, looking up toward the sky.

"Please tell me he's gonna live. Is he gonna live?" asked Chase.

"Papi pray. You got to pray," she said, clasping her hands together.

A huge crowd was gathering around the truck. Suddenly flashing red lights were everywhere. Patrol cars from 109th precinct came to a screeching halt. Cops jumped out of their vehicles with their guns pointed at QB's truck. They slowly approached the riddled Escalade. One of the officer's yelled, "Don't move. Everybody put your hands where we can see them. Put your hands in the air!"

Chase turned to them and yelled, "What the hell are you doing? We need help!"

Another officer cut him off. "Get your hands in the air!"

Both Chase and the Latina, who cradled Torry's head in her lap did what they were told. She began speaking in Spanish, "Hijo de la gran puta."

Chase knew from her tone that she was cursing them out. As police rushed the truck they realized they needed an ambulance and radioed in for one. Fortunately one was already on its way. An officer instructed Chase to get out of the vehicle first. Chase began climbing out. Once he was standing outside the truck, he was ordered to lay on the ground with his legs and arms spread apart.

He did as he was told. In his 'hood, police were known to get away with killing young black men. The scene reminded him of the night when all of Queens felt the storm of the fifty shots that police rained down on Sean Bell and his friends the night before his wedding. After they searched Chase he was handcuffed and forced to sit in the back of a police cruiser. Two officers interviewed him, while the others secured the crime scene, tended to QB and Torry, and interviewed the Hispanic woman.

Chase knew not to say much. Where he was from, talking to the cops was out of the question. In neighborhoods across America the youth followed a similar version of the Mafia code of *Omertá*. The last thing a young person wanted is to be labeled a snitch. Outside of those Gino Green Global T-shirt's, the next best-selling shirt in the 'hood was one that read, "Stop Snitching".

"I don't know what happened. All I saw was three or four guys with hoodies surround us and begin firing." Chase knew he was saying too much, but he wanted to give them a little something so they would un-cuff him. There was no way he was giving up any names. Looking out the back window of the police cruiser, Chase asked, "Are they gonna live?"

The cop ignored him and then fired off what seemed like a hundred questions, "Where did the shooters come from? What were they wearing? What kind of car? How many shooters did you say there were? Where did you say you were headed? What gang are you in? What set do you claim?" The questions came faster than a boy's first sexual encounter.

Young Adult

UNDER PRESSURE

"I never said I was in a gang," Chase barked. "What the hell are you talkin' 'bout? Why am I handcuffed? I didn't do jack, and I don't know anything, so you can stop wasting your time and let me go."

Turning red, the officer blurted out, "Listen punk, I'll decide when and if you can leave. Until then, you should be counting your blessings that you didn't end up like your buddies. You think we don't know y'all are in a gang. How did y'all get that truck? You sell drugs? We should just take you down, put you in prison, and throw away the key."

Chase eye-screwed the young, white officer and thought about those times when QB had explained to him and the other students about the metaphorical rock that they will be fated to push uphill. The rock was related to the myth of Sisyphus. It was a story about how the gods had condemned this Greek man to ceaselessly roll a rock to the top of a mountain; however, the stone would fall back because of its heavy weight and Sisyphus would have to begin all over again. In this myth, the gods had thought with some reason that there would have been no more dreadful punishment than futile and hopeless labor. However, Sisyphus, refused condemnation by becoming conscious and finding happiness in the everyday task of rolling this rock up the hill. Chase looked toward QB as he thought about how he always provided the students with African proverbs, a Biblical passage, or stories about Greek Gods. It amazed Chase how these sayings always found a way to unfold in their lives.

Like Sisyphus, Chase knew this cop was his own personal metaphorical rock to roll uphill, so he wouldn't allow the police officer to get under his skin. He wouldn't allow the officer to trap him by feeding into his accusations, nor would he dare voice what he was feeling and make matters worse. He was dealing with an officer who was trying to move up in rank and looking for his big case to solve. He smirked at the officer and decided to just put his head down and let the pieces fall where they may.

What Chase did want was for them to get QB and Torry to the hospital. Two ambulances finally showed up, and the medics went right to work. They had QB and Torry out the Escalade and ready to go in record time. Chase then heard some commotion and the medics all rushed toward Torry. Chase's heart momentarily stopped. He looked at the medics place shock pads to Torry's chest. He said out loud, "Don't die on me, Torry."

"One, two, three, clear. One, two, three, clear," a medic yelled.

Chase watched as the pads sent an electrical current through Torry's body in an attempt to restart his heart. Torry's body jumped in response. Chase closed his eyes and prayed for his friend...his brother. When he opened his eyes Chase noticed the ambulance doors shut and speed off with Torry inside. After he saw the medics put QB in another ambulance, he watched the older of the medics head over to where he was at. When he approached the police cruiser the officer stopped him and questioned him about what he was doing. He told him he needed to check up on all the occupants of the vehicle.

As soon as he stuck his head in the back of the police cruiser, Chase asked desperately, "What's up with my brother? Is he gonna live?"

"He's a strong young man. If I had to bet, I'll put my money on him surviving. What about you, are you all right? Do you have any wounds? Do you need any kind of medical attention?"

Chase knew the cops were going to try to interrogate him if he stayed with them, so he exaggerated his injuries. "I have a few cuts on my arms and hands," he said, trying to turn and twist his body so the medic could see. He furthered his act by saying, "Plus I feel like I'm gonna pass out." The medic, knowing what time it was, turned to the officer, "I need you to take these handcuffs off of him so I can properly examine him. "

"Let me see if that's possible," the young officer said as he made his way over to the Sergeant who was in charge.

Young Adult

Both the medic and Chase watched the young officer approach an older officer on the scene. After their brief conference, he came back over and took the handcuffs off. The medic immediately grabbed him by the arm and led him toward the ambulance that QB was in and began checking his vitals.

Chase really went into his act. "Ahh," he screamed when touched. It was as if something was hurting him internally.

With a wink at Chase, the medic approached the older officer who appeared to be in charge and explained that Chase needed medical attention. He told the officer that if he was not under arrest they needed to get him to a hospital as well. After a few minutes, both QB and Chase were on their way to Booth Memorial hospital.

Chase took one last glance at the scene through the back window of the ambulance. He was amazed that he escaped being shot. QB's truck looked like a bullet riddled Humvee abandoned somewhere on the Gaza strip. Yellow tape prevented the growing crowd of spectator's from interfering with the crime scene. There were many small orange cones that marked the spots where the spent shells landed on the streets. As tears filled Chase's eyes, the guilt of Showtyme's ambush weighed heavily on him.

***

As Showtyme drove out to Kennedy airport, he received the call that he was waiting for. "What's good B?"

"It's all good, Showtyme. That lame Chase is done," B said.

"Where them gunners at?"

"At Sherwood Village feeling themselves right now," B said.

"How did it go down?"

"They washed them up at a stop light on Northern. They jumped out and unloaded everything they had on the truck. Then we got up outta there before one-time came through."

"Is that dude Chase wearing a toe-tag or what?" asked Showtyme.

"One-time was in motion so we didn't have time to check for pulses or see if they were breathing," B said nervously.

"Listen B, Chase better be a statistic or you can bet you'll be next," Showtyme shouted. It seemed like every time he gave B something to do there was always some kind of problem.

B was getting more nervous by the second. "Remember when I told you Chase called me and said he was with Torry at the game. Well, when we got to the stadium we were just cruising through the parking lot at Shea and lucked up when we saw them birds coming out early. It was three of them and they got into a White Escalade," he explained.

"Who was the third cat? You told me it was him and Torry," said Showtyme.

"Nobody knows. But none of them could have survived that barrage. Those young gunners unleashed everything they had," he stammered. "I'll see what the streets are saying then get back at you."

"Listen, my dude, make sure you holla at me as soon as you find out what time it is," Showtyme said, abruptly ending the call.

B hung up the phone and took a deep breath, cursing himself for setting up Chase. He closed his eyes and prayed that this wouldn't come back to haunt him. He had a funny feeling that Showtyme was going to flip on him as well. Showtyme was unpredictable. B knew he got himself in too deep, and hoped he could weather this storm. Especially knowing he came from a place where gunshots settled disagreements.

B sat back in his stolen Charger and closed his eyes. He couldn't believe how he got caught up in this mess, but more importantly, he was thinking about how he was going to get out. Taking some purple haze out of his pocket, he rolled a blunt. Smoking weed always unlocked the doors of his mind, or at least that's what he thought. After inhaling, he exhaled what he thought were strategies for getting through this drama successfully. What was scary was that success in his case was a matter of life and death.

***

Young Adult

UNDER PRESSURE

The ambulances raced through the streets of Flushing. Drivers, hearing the sirens and seeing the flashing red lights pulled over like they hit pit stops during a Nascar race. The ambulance carrying Torry arrived at the hospital five minutes before the one carrying QB and Chase. Torry was rushed right into surgery, where doctors removed two bullets. One was stuck in his shoulder, and the other, unfortunately, was lodged in his lower back, possibly damaging his spine. The other two slugs that shattered his leg exited out the side of his thigh without hitting any major arteries.

By the time the ambulance carrying Chase and QB arrived, a team of doctors and technicians with a gurney were on hand. They rushed QB into surgery; his wounds were not as life-threatening as Torry's, but dangerous nonetheless. He was hit in the bottom of his foot, which shattered his ankle. One bullet ripped through his stomach, causing him to have his spleen removed. The long gash on the side of his head would forever remind him where the third bullet grazed his skull. A fraction of an inch more and the bullet would've made Reyna a widow. It was the loss of blood that had caused QB to pass out.

Chase, on the other hand could've walked in the hospital under his own power, but was made to get in a wheelchair. He was treated with a couple of stitches, but no doctor could heal the wound in his heart. The pain of knowing he was the reason QB and Torry was hanging onto life by a thread, killed him inside. His earlier conversation with B kept rewinding itself over and over in his head and made him repeatedly ask himself why he didn't see it coming. *I have to call Torry's mom, Naysia, and Mrs. Banks*, he thought. He reached for his Blackberry and then realized he must've left it in the truck. His head began to hurt; he didn't know what he was going to say to them. He grabbed a nurse and asked if she could wheel him out to the phone booths so he could contact his family. She explained that he was under observation and that he couldn't be moved until seen and released by the doctor. After minutes of negotiating, she agreed to make the calls for him with the understanding that she was only going to tell them that they should come to the hospital. When the nurse confirmed that she talked to both Reyna and Torry's mom, he sat back and thought about how much he was going to tell them. He then closed his eyes and asked God to help pull his boys through.

<u>FOUR</u>

Torrence Harris, aka Torry was full of promise and bursting with potential. Yet, like many young men, Torry felt that his life had been unfair, so he refused to play by the rules. Torry's father had died from cancer when he was nine years old. His mother did all she could to be both a mom and a dad. She used love to shield him from the streets, but it seemed she couldn't do enough. While Torry yearned for his mother to come to his basketball games, she was busy juggling two jobs. She wanted to support him in all his extra-curricular activities, but the reality was that she had to put food on the table and two-hundred dollar Lebron James' sneakers on her son's feet. She was taught by her mother that a parent should always put the needs of their children before their very own needs. To Ms. Harris, it was about sacrifice, putting her life on hold for her only son.

Unfortunately, it was a struggle. As much as she tried, Ms. Lisa Harris could not fill the role of his father. Conversations about girls were brief and rare. She couldn't teach Torry to defend himself in the streets, nor against the real enemy which was often unseen. Ms. Harris didn't know how to show her son ways to confront adversity, or how to navigate through streets that were eating the young boys alive by the day. She had long ago admitted that she couldn't teach him to be a man, but she could teach him to be responsible.

Torry learned the realities of life before ever seeing the possibilities of life. Figuring out what kind of man he wanted to be was not only a challenge, but a mystery. After realizing that spoiling him was not doing the job, his mother began to think she could make things better by finding a nice man. She ended up in and out of useless relationships with men who emotionally and sometimes physically abused her. Torry didn't understand his mother's motives and resented her for what appeared to be her weakness. Too young to understand that older eyes had wider vision, there were some things as a young man he would never understand.

Unfortunately, his resentment led to an anger that caused him to act out at home and in school. He and his mother began to argue daily about the way he dressed, what time he came home, and his chores. Everything seemed to turn into an argument. Although his mother was older in years, she struggled with her pain just as much as her son. Torry didn't make things any better; even though he was an "A" student when he went to school, he traded in his books for an allegiance to kids who specialized in trouble. Torry eventually succumbed to peer pressure, smoking weed, drinking, and hanging out all hours of the night.

Finally, in order to help her son, his mother knew she had to break out of her own prison of pain and confusion. She didn't know what to do with him. It was much too late to become a disciplinarian. She had threatened to kick him out of their apartment numerous times, but inside she knew that was something she could never really do. So she decided to quit with the empty threats and allow him to make his own decisions and mistakes. However, she sat him down one night to explain to him the consequences of dropping out of school and hanging out in the streets. She didn't give up, but decided to give in and did what most mothers in the 'hood do when things began to fall apart; she got on her knees and prayed the streets didn't swallow her only son alive.

Torry's whirlwind of chaos and bad decisions ended when God placed Naysia in his life. From their very first encounter his world

Young Adult

changed. Things started making sense. All the lessons his mother were trying to instill in him about manhood, respect, and determination were not only being reiterated, but suddenly becoming clearer. Naysia let it be known that she was not getting together with any man who dropped out of school and smoked weed all day. He didn't understand how, but she made him see things about himself that he never saw before. She was opening doors within him that had been bolted shut for years. He would never forget the day they met. She was in the park playing chess with her father. Like him, she grew up in LeFrak City, but later moved to St. Albans. During those days it was strange to see a father spending time with his child. In fact, it was what we would call a Kodak moment, since there was an extreme amount of dead-beat dads in the town. Naysia's father was the exception. He always seemed to be with her. He supported and schooled her about the ups and downs of life. On that day, Torry was checking them out from a distance, missing the father he never had. He stood there until he finally got up the nerve to approach them. When he reached them, he pretended to be interested in the chess match.

After observing the battle in silence for a few minutes, her father asked, "Do you know how to play, young man?"

"Ye -yeah. I know how to play," Torry stammered.

"In that case play my baby while I run upstairs for a second." He then got up, looking straight into the eyes of the tall, skinny young man. He watched many boys in the projects drool over his daughter. However, his daughter had proven to be able to handle herself. He had schooled her well. "Is that okay, Princess?"

Naysia rolled her eyes at Torry. "Yes Daddy, I'm good."

Her father said, "I'll be right back."

As her father left, Torry sat across from Naysia staring into her cute face. Her uniqueness is what attracted him to her. She was that Keyshia Cole, down-to-earth type of young lady. One that hung out with boys and was into sports, but was drop dead gorgeous. Her brown skin glistened as she sat there with her hands folded across her chest. "Who makes the first move, you or me?" Torry asked.

"Your first move might be to set up your pieces," she said, setting the boundaries right off the bat.

All Torry could say was, "Oh, my bad." He picked up a piece from the board, looked at it, and then tried to mirror Naysia as she put her pieces in place. He dropped one, and when he bent down to retrieve it, he noticed her well-developed chocolate legs.

He placed the piece back on the table. "I thought you knew how to play," she said.

"That depends on what you're talkin' 'bout," Torry said, flashing what he thought was his irresistible smile. "To be honest I just wanted to vibe with you, to get to know you better. I've been checking you out and I—"

She cut him off. "I know who you are, Torry, and all about your little crew. I watch all of you running around here messing with these jump-offs, filling their heads up with ghetto dreams. So before you waste your time, know that I am not the one nor am I interested in any of your games."

"Whoa, hold up now," Torry said, dropping his chess piece and putting up his hands in defense. "You're getting way ahead of yourself. I just want to get to know you. I'm not looking for marriage, children, and a white picket fence around a three bedroom house."

She laughed at his silliness. "I thought you wanted to play chess."

"I do," he said, looking into her eyes.

She grabbed some of his pieces. "Then let me show you a thing or two." Setting up his men, she added, "Chess is like the game of life. You have to know when to attack and when to defend. Your success in the game depends on how well you maneuver your pieces. Do you understand what I'm saying?"

He looked at her, reached out and grabbed her hand. "Yeah, I know just what you're saying," he answered.

Young Adult

"I hope you do," Naysia said as she withdrew her hand from his grasp.

Torry's heart beat fast. He knew from the feelings of that surreal moment that he had stumbled across love.

***

Reyna was the first to arrive at the hospital. Her locks were wrapped in a black head scarf and her eyes were red and swollen from crying. Nervously, she approached the nurse's station in the emergency room. "My name is Reyna Banks and my husband, Quentin Banks was admitted to this hospital. Can you give me some information, anything concerning him."

The nurse could see the worry written on Reyna's face, but she had very little information about what happened.

"Is my husband alive?" Reyna questioned with pleading eyes.

The nurse could only imagine the pain of what Reyna was going through. She checked her chart, hating this part of her job. Witnessing the pain etched in the faces of mothers, wives, girlfriends, and daughters, as their sons, husbands, boyfriends, and brothers fought for their lives because of the senseless violence in the streets sometimes got the best of her. "Mrs. Banks your husband was admitted about forty minutes ago and taken directly into surgery. He's in the Trauma Unit as we speak, there's not much more that I can provide you with at—"

Frantically, Reyna cut her off. "Excuse me, but that's my husband in there." Reyna slapped her hand on the counter which separated her from the nurse, "I need to know what the hell is going on."

"By policy I'm not able to—" the nurse began, but was cut off again.

"I don't want to hear about policy. I want to know the status of my husband. If you can't provide me with any information I suggest you get somebody out here that can," Reyna said, trying to hold back her tears.

Passing Reyna some tissue, the nurse said, "Listen Mrs. Banks, off the record …" She looked up to make sure no one could hear her. "…

your husband was shot numerous times. He came in along with two other young men."

"Who, Torry and Chase?" Reyna questioned.

"Let's see," she said, flipping her chart. "We have a Torrence Harris and a Sean Matthews. I don't have much information as of now, but as soon as I do you'll be the first to know."

Reyna could see the sincerity in her eyes, but still asked, "Is he going to be all right? Please tell me he's going to live."

"Right now I have very little information, Mrs. Banks, but I can tell you he has one of the best surgeons operating on him and when the doctor comes out I'll make sure you are the first person he speaks to."

"What about Torry and Chase, I mean Sean? Where are they?" asked Reyna.

"Well, one of the young men is in surgery and the other is in observation. He only had a few cuts that required some stitches. However, he was shook up emotionally. I'll see if I can get him for you. Maybe he can fill you in on what happened," said the nurse as she picked up her phone to call the area where Chase was located.

A stress vibe rose from Reyna's body like a heat wave emanating from the hot asphalt on a blazing, hot summer day. While pacing back and forth Naysia and Torry's mom came rushing into the emergency room asking for Torry. The nurse reiterated everything to them that she said to Reyna. When she finished, Reyna approached them and introduced herself. They hugged each other. Reyna then went on to explain everything she was told. Both Ms. Harris and Naysia knew QB, but this was the first time they'd met his wife.

About ten minutes later, a nursed wheeled Chase into the waiting room where the ladies were sitting.

Naysia jumped up and ran toward him. "Chase, what happened? Is Torry all right?"

Chase looked around. Doctors were rushing back and forth. A team of nurses rushed a man on a gurney into the operating room. Chase felt like he was in a nightmare, but this was far from a nightmare … this was as real as it gets.

"Chase. Chase, do you hear me? Can you tell us what happened?" Naysia repeated.

The moment hung around him like a fog. Hearing Naysia's voice lifted him out of the fog. He looked up into the faces of all three women and went on to explain what unfolded, not leaving anything out except the details of the conversation between B and himself.

When he finished they all had tears in their eyes.

Ms. Harris hugged him. "Everything is going to work itself out, let us all pray," she said.

They formed a circle, held hands, and prayed in the middle of the waiting room. Torry's mom felt prayer was the answer to everything. Chase hoped this was true, because he had prayed more in the last few hours than he probably had prayed in his entire life. He hoped God would finally hear his words. In the dark theatre of his mind he needed QB and Torry to make it. If not, he knew he would struggle to live with himself.

FIVE

ll his life people told Sean "Chase" Matthews that he was just like his father, Big S; a chip off the old block. His father, who was known as Big S, got down for his crown. A ruthless gambler, who, on bad nights when he lost, there was no telling what would happen. Rumor had it that on numerous occasions when Big S lost a bet and decided that he was not going to pay because of one reason or the other, he simply made up a reason to pound out the cat he owed. A tiny man with the mean streak of a jackal, Big S was known for his itchy trigger finger.

Sean's mother died from an overdose of heroin when he was eleven. His father went on the run a year later after shooting two men in a bar, leaving Sean to live with his grandmother. It wasn't long before he learned that black families were nothing like the Cosby's, nor would kids from the 'hood get sent to any Bel Air mansion for the summer. The families he knew triggered powerful, angry emotions in the youth that eventually were unleashed in the streets. Home was not a place of comfort for him; he didn't have fun at home. He and his boys always compared what went on in their homes, at least the stuff that they were not embarrassed by. It affected them all in different ways; they were pissed off at their parents for one reason or another. Sean dreaded his

Young Adult

mother for choosing heroin over his life and hated his father for choosing a life of crime instead of him.

As Sean played the bad hand that life dealt him, he found himself contemplating suicide on many occasions. Fortunately, he couldn't bring himself to do it. Somehow through the love of his grandmother, he came to the conclusion that it was his parents' loss for not wanting to be in his life. Sean never again wanted to speak to his father. He couldn't care less if he ever laid eyes on him again.

In his world of darkness his grandmother was his only source of light. Unfortunately, the power of her love was not enough to keep him from the streets. As with many kids in the 'hood, Sean had problems defining who he was. When he was with his boys he was a thug. When kicking it with the young ladies around the way he was one hundred percent player. When he was around grandmother he was the little, respectful, good kid.

Sean was scared to let anyone get close to him and see who he truly was. He didn't like what he saw in the mirror, so he felt other people wouldn't like what they saw in him either. This caused him to become a loner, but keeping to himself seemed to attract nothing but trouble. Fights at school became routine because trying to figure out why other kids picked on him or how to fit in with them took too much energy. Like his father, he had a reputation to get busy with his hands, but unlike his old man he didn't like to fight.

During eighth grade two older bullies took Sean's silence as a weakness and began pressing him for money. At first, Sean tried to compromise by meeting them half way, giving up a quarter of what he had and hiding the rest in his sneakers. He had hoped that this would slow them down. Instead they pushed, making it worse by telling everybody he was setting it out. The straw that broke the camel's back came when they took his brand new Jordans while he was getting dressed in the locker room after his gym class.

Here was a young man being forced to discover what you can do when you're pushed to the brink and finally make the decision to push back. While shopping with his grandmother at Home Depot, he spotted the solution to his problem—an orange box cutter. As they walked down the aisle, he grabbed one and slid it into his pocket while his grandmother wasn't looking. As he pushed the cart he had one hand in his pocket taking the cutter out of its package. When his grandmother began looking at kitchen tiles, he threw the wrapper behind some paint cans while simultaneously looking around to make sure he wasn't seen by an employee.

When he got home, he headed straight to his room, pulled out the cutter, and raised the blade up and down, listening to its clicking sounds. While his grandmother was in the kitchen visualizing her new kitchen floor, he went into her room and confiscated one of her Styrofoam mannequin heads that she sat her wigs on and headed back to his room. He made a makeshift man by impaling the head on top of a broomstick. Day and night he began practicing how to use the box cutter, practicing with both his left and right hand. He felt like he was in boot camp; a young man preparing for war. After a week he reached the point where he could pull out the chopper and slice the makeshift man from any angle. After a few weeks of practice he was so confident in his ability to do damage that he literally yearned for someone to violate him. Sean, unlike, many young men in his 'hood, didn't look for trouble, but now he welcomed the drama.

One morning, as Sean got ready to go to school, he could feel inside that something was going to pop-off. It was the intuition of a hunter—the predators would become the hunted.

As Sean walked along his usual route to I.S. 61, he could see the normal crowd standing at the bodega on 99th Street. This is where most students from LeFrak hung out before heading off to class. On this day there were more than just the usual faces. Sean scanned the area. His eyes stopped on one kid who appeared older than nearly everybody

there. The kid stood there looking cooler than a breath mint. Sean noticed how most of the girls were feeling him.

"What's up, Showtyme?" Puerto Rican Lana said in her sexy, flirtatious voice.

The 6'2" charcoal-black brother acknowledged her with a mere nod as he leaned on a black 745 BMW. He stood there like a model in *GQ* magazine. *Homie is definitely doing him*, Sean thought.

Showtyme had on a pair of black and white Chucks, with a black Polo fitted T-shirt, black G-star jeans, and a black bandana wrapped around his shoulder length braids. He looked menacing. His self-confidence and swagger told Sean that he was a street-baller without hoop dreams.

His thoughts were interrupted when he heard someone say, "Yo, Sean."

When Sean turned around he saw the two kids that insisted on pushing up on him. A feeling similar to rage moved across every nerve in his body and he could feel it in his vocal chords as he opened his mouth to say, "What's up?"

"What's up? You know what time it is. Don't stand there acting like you don't know what it is. What you got for us today?" the taller of the two asked. The shorter one was mad-dogging Sean like he wanted to get busy.

Sean felt both nervous and scared. He slid his hand in his front pocket, feeling the familiarity of his box-cutter. Strangely it gave him some courage. Taking a deep breath, he began walking straight toward the two thugs. "Nothing. I don't have anything for you two," he barked. "Not today, or any other day. You got that?"

From the gathering crowd, a voice boomed, "Little man ain't havin' it."

That remark only added fuel to the fire. It was too late for Sean to be worried. Time for him to handle his business. One of the bullies pointed his finger directly in Sean's face. "You know what it is. Don't make me give you the business out here in front of all these people," he said.

The crowd increased by the second. Showtyme was laying in the cut awaiting Sean's response to the threat. His initial thought was that Sean was going to get beat down or run.

With Zab Judah speed, Sean smacked the taller bully across his face. The kid didn't see or feel the cut Sean caused. He started to charge, not believing Sean had hit him. He took two steps when his face parted like a C-section. The wound opened from his left eye to the bottom of his right cheek. The crowd couldn't believe what they were witnessing. Somebody yelled, "Ooooh, little homie did him dirty."

"Damn, you could see his teeth through his cheek," said a girl, clutching a knock-off Coach bag. The bully immediately tried to hold his face together as blood gushed from the side of his face like a newly found oil discovery. The bully ran into the Bodega screaming for help.

Sean turned his attention to the second bully, who froze in disbelief. Catching the fire in Sean's eyes as he approached, he turned and hauled ass. Sean gave chase. In fact, every time Sean saw the kid he went after him, earning the handle "Chase."

Showtyme immediately recruited Chase into the Five Seven Henchmen. He offered protection, money, and most importantly a sense of family, something Chase had always wanted. Unfortunately, what he didn't know or understand was that this kind of family came with a tremendous price tag.

***

The newly formed Gang Intelligence Unit at 109th precinct was headed by a hard-nosed lieutenant named Mitch Delaney, an Irish American who came from a long line of law enforcement.

Delaney arrived at the crime scene and was immediately briefed by his partner, Dale Hudson about the shooting. Hudson was an ex-Marine. He stood about 6'3 and weighed well over two hundred forty pounds. He resembled a linebacker who had been through his share of gridiron wars. Like Delaney, Hudson moved up in rank quickly. They both worked out of the 109th precinct. They became friends a few years ago when they both were assigned to a case in which they brought down a biker gang. When Delaney was promoted to lieutenant and chose to head G.I.U. he made sure his partner came along.

"Hudson, what do we got?" asked Delaney.

"It wasn't a drive by. According to witnesses the truck was waiting for the light to turn green, when a dark colored car, unclear of the make and model, cut the truck off. Three individuals supposedly jumped out the vehicle dressed in hooded sweaters and did this," Hudson said, pointing to QB's truck and the area where the spent shells landed. He gave Delaney time to take in the scene then continued. "All the occupants of the truck are at Booth Memorial, I've already sent somebody down there. I will head over there when I leave here to see what I can get from those guys. As of now, we only know one of the occupants of this truck, a Sean Matthews, who …" he looked down at his notes, then continued, "… was not directly hit, but needed some kind of medical attention. He gave an initial statement which didn't amount to much. The uniform that took his statement said he felt he knew more than he was willing to give up."

Delaney was taking everything in, viewing the scene with calculating eyes. He turned to Hudson. "Any descriptions on the shooters?"

"We got three shooters with hoodies and darkies that covered their eyes. One guy said he noticed the perpetrators had on black bandanas under the hoods. Definitely gang related, most likely Five Seven Henchmen. It's consistent with their modus operandi (M.O). Everybody else said they took cover immediately and from the looks of things, who can blame them." He looked at all the shells that covered the pavement. Then added, "Mitch, this is becoming a damn war zone out here. The only difference from here and the Middle East is the bombs and those I.E.D.'s, and who knows, these kids may eventually start strapping explosives to their damn bodies and walk into each other's hood and blow their own self up." He looked at the grimness of the crime scene and then wondered, *What happened to the good old fist fight?* He sighed, took a deep breath, and uttered to no one in particular, "I don't really think I can do this anymore."

Delaney patted his partner on the shoulder. "I know how you feel, Dale. We're both getting too old for this. Retirement does sound good right now, but if we don't do this, who will?" He paused to light a cigarette. "I'm going to head over. Give me a few minutes."

SIX

Reyna stood in the doorway of the hospital room hurting and wiping tears from her face. She took a deep breath and just stared at the tubes flowing in and out of what seemed like every part of her husband's body. His head was wrapped in gauze. His left leg, from the foot to a little below the knee had a cast on it. He was in a hospital gown looking weak and vulnerable. She made a mental note to bring him his own robe, knowing he would be uncomfortable walking around with his backside exposed.

The doctor convinced Reyna that QB was going to be fine. In spite of losing his spleen and a few feet of intestines he came through in a remarkable fashion. In the recesses of her mind, she struggled with the thought of losing QB. The thought made her shiver. Watching the love of her life plugged into those machines caused a piercing in her heart which penetrated her soul like the bullets that invaded his body. "I love you," she whispered, hoping he would hear her. She smiled when she noticed his 'Gunz's,' as QB liked to call his chiseled arms. Five nights at the gym kept QB in better shape than most athletes. She couldn't believe she was standing there thinking how good her 'Boo' looked, even after being shot.

Reyna stepped into the room and quietly walked to the edge of QB's bed, afraid her footsteps would somehow add to the pain she assumed he was feeling. She ran her fingers along the tubes that carried the fluid from the IV bag to QB's arm. Surprisingly, it was ice cold. She jerked her hand away, and then looked up at the heart monitor connected to her husband. The reverberation of the beeps signaled the rhythm of his heart. It vibrated throughout the room.

"Oh, my God," she gasped. Covering her mouth with her hand she shook her head no when she noticed the colostomy bag attached to QB. She made a mental note to ask the doctor what was the purpose of the bag and does it mean that he would need it for the rest of his life. When she got the nerve, she ran her fingers through his curly hair then along the sharp, handsome features of his face. "How are you doing, baby?" she asked, not caring whether he heard her or not. A tear descended from her cheek in what seemed like slow motion and fell toward QB.

In the spirit of an alarm clock, the moment her tears touched his body QB opened his eyes. Her intake of breath was sudden and loud. QB blinked his eyes trying to get focused. He smiled and his nickel size dimples came to life. Reyna was momentarily paralyzed. QB struggled to speak. It took effort to move his lips because his mouth was dry. Everything hurt, but the look on his face spoke volumes. He was relieved to see his Reyna ... his everything.

"Hey baby," she said as she bent down and kissed him. "You better had came back to me," she said, laughing and crying at the same time. "How are you feeling?"

Drowsy from the medication and with a low scratchy voice, QB mumbled, "My head hurts like hell, but other than that, I'm fine. Where's Nia?"

Reyna smiled knowing their daughter would be the first person he'd asked for. She couldn't have asked for a better man, or father for their child. "She's at mom's house." She then added, "Let me get the doctor."

"Hold up. Where's Torry and Chase?"

"They're both fine. Torry needed surgery but like you he made it through, however the doctor decided to medically induce him into a coma and…"

QB cut her off. "And what?"

Young Adult

Reyna looked down at her husband. "The doctor said Torry may never walk again."

"What did you say?"

Reyna instantly regretted telling him about Torry. She ran her hand over his arm and said, "Both Torry and Chase are alive, that's what's important. Baby, we'll talk about this later. Don't worry yourself right now. Let me get your doctor to make sure you are all right."

Looking up at Reyna, he said, "Did you say Torry is in a coma and may never walk again?"

"Yes Q," she said, as a tear began to trickle down her face again.

Fury filled QB's eyes and a feeling spread through him like venom. The muscles in his jaw tightened. He was trying to sort things out. His grip tightened around her hand. "Where's Chase?"

She didn't answer.

"I don't want to get into it with you, baby, but do me a favor. Call my brother and tell him what happened. Tell him, I need to see him immediately. Also, tell him I said to bring Ramel and Zeus with him."

She sighed. "Listen, Quentin ..." He knew what he was going to say. Reyna only referred to him by his full name when they were either making love or when she was upset and wanted to make a point. "Chase is outside with Torry's mom and girl. I'm asking you not to try to sort all this out right now. Everybody is upset and trying their best to deal with what is happening. What's important is that we get you back up and running." Her statement was more of a demand than a request. "We don't need any drama right now. I will call Amari and whoever else you want me to call, but I'm telling you now and I'm going to tell Ramel and Zeus, I don't want any crap happening up here in this hospital. I know how they are. We don't need any more people getting shot. You're not twenty-one, Quentin. The last time you called Ramel, he came up in our house like it was some damn military brigade. Not this time. I'm not going through that again."

QB closed his eyes, thinking, *Here's Reyna taking charge.* QB knew he had no wins with her. The last thing he wanted to do was to get into an argument with his wife. He knew she would never understand the rules he lived by. She was a good-girl who took a risk on loving him. He noticed the pain blanketing her pretty face. He would rather face death than risk hurting Reyna. He pulled her toward him with what little bit of strength he had. "I love me some you," he said. Although she was putting up a strong front, QB knew inside that this ordeal had to be killing her softly. Yet, he also knew that somebody violated, and his family-man status didn't stop him from getting busy. Most people saw him as a responsible person, but QB had a team that stayed around hammers like construction workers at a construction site.

***

The following morning QB woke to the sound of visitors moving around in his room. When he looked up he knew exactly who they were. He thought to himself, *I'm not ready to deal with this.* Nineteen-year-old flashbacks of crooked cops and intimidating interrogations tactics began to plague him.

"Good morning, Mr. Banks. I'm Lieutenant Delaney and this is my partner, Detective Hudson." The detectives flashed their gold badges and sneaky smirks. They then added. "We're from the 109th precinct. We're sorry to barge in on you like this. We tried to get here yesterday, but with all the paperwork and you being in surgery we felt it best that we showed up this morning. Of course you understand that we're here to ask you a few routine questions as to what happened yesterday. We understand that you just came out of surgery and need your rest, but the quicker we obtain the facts the more successful we'll be in our investigation, and the more likely we will find the suspect or suspects."

QB nodded, understanding the procedures and the techniques. He looked around the room for Reyna. He needed her to call his lawyer just in case the questioning got out of line. QB knew that an individual like himself could easily go from victim to suspect. He asked the detectives

Young Adult

to let him use the bathroom before they got started. When they agreed to that, he pressed the button to get the attention of the nurse at their station. The nurse responded immediately. The detectives excused themselves as she helped QB change his colostomy bag with minimum embarrassment.

QB was not comfortable with anybody seeing him like this, but he welcomed the nurse that morning. Before she left, he asked her to contact his wife and explain that detectives were in his room and for her to get to the hospital immediately.

The nurse made the call as soon as she returned to her station. This was the first time QB had any interaction with the police since coming home from prison. He had avoided them because he had parole stipulations which stated that any police contact can result in a parole violation. However, these were different circumstances. He wasn't sure how he should handle this and realized that a part of him was still held hostage by certain codes of the streets. QB have never cooperated with the police and after doing fifteen years in the pen he had made a pact with himself that he would never wish prison on his worst enemy.

Lieutenant Delaney came back into his room a few minutes later. This time he took his suit jacket off and draped it across the empty chair in the corner of the room. QB looked at the medium built, five-foot-eleven, pale face man. His nose looked like it has been through one too many bar brawls. He had graying hair, but still appeared to be in shape. When his blue eyes turned toward QB's he quickly looked the other way. QB wondered how he was going to deal with this situation. A cautionary silence filled the room as both QB and the Lieutenant set the stage for a mental showdown.

QB thought about his parole officer. *Damn, I have to contact him and let him know what happened.* He made a note to tell Reyna to call his P.O. later on that day. He wished he didn't have to deal with any of these people. He knew that no matter which branch, law enforcement was never satisfied; police, parole, the courts, the system in general. No matter how well a brother is doing, after he has a felony on his record, especially for murder, it appeared like they would always be out to demonize him.

QB recalled how his parole officer from their first meeting showed bias even though he claimed to support him. QB had come home and put the pieces of his life back together with unusual ease. Believing this irked his parole officer and made QB skeptical about his so-called support, QB compared him to a germ, just waiting in the cut to violate him. Reyna thought his P.O. was jealous because QB came home and made such a difference in the community and to top it off his salary, which was much more than his parole officer had to piss him off. So QB made sure he did everything right. He made sure that he didn't leave any room for himself to slip through the cracks. However, getting shot was turning out to be more than a crack; it was beginning to feel like his whole foundation was being shattered.

QB's thoughts were interrupted by Detective Hudson struggling to get into the room, while trying to balance what smelled like coffee and cinnamon rolls on a tray, "Give me a damn hand, Mitch," he said to his partner.

QB looked at them and thought, *things will never change. We'll always be the one who has to go fetch something.*

"Would you like some coffee and rolls, Mr. Banks?" asked Hudson.

Even though it smelled good, QB declined.

"Then shall we get started?" asked Delaney.

QB shook his head, "Yeah, let's get this over with."

***

When B answered the door at the Sherwood apartment, Showtyme shoved the hammer in his face. He backed him up into the middle of the living room and commenced to hitting him viciously with the butt of his gun. The first blow knocked B's two front teeth loose. B's mouth filled with blood as he attempted to spit out the tooth fragments. Showtyme had told him the last time he messed up that if he ever failed him again

Young Adult

he would kill his punk behind. Everybody in the apartment, in a matter of seconds came down off their high. Showtyme's violent outburst had the tendency to sober everybody up. Like most predators, Showtyme was comfortable with only brief periods of inaction. He loved the drama.

On the leather sofa a few feet away, Nitty and Banger sat frozen. They were not sure if they were next, or if they should make a move for their heat. They knew one misstep could cost them their lives. Showtyme wouldn't hesitate to put something hot in both of them. On the other hand, if they didn't make a move they could be on their way to a better world. They looked at each other and decided to hold tight. They nonchalantly took a sip of the Patron they were drinking, acting as if fear was foreign to them. They knew Showtyme fed off other's fear. They learned a lot from Showtyme and even though they had a lot of respect for him, they both knew he was cold-blooded. Yet, he also showed them love like no one had ever before. This combination is what made Showtyme powerful and influential. He understood the importance of ruling with an iron palm, but also knew when to put on that velvet glove.

Both Nitty and Banger were thinking to themselves that something must've gone wrong. They couldn't understand how, especially after they dumped every slug they had into that truck. Banger turned to Nitty. "We should of put one in each of their heads."

Nitty nodded while shifting nervously in his seat as Showtyme pounded B out. In their line of work mistakes were not tolerated. Punishment for slip-ups was inevitable. Showtyme had B hemmed up by the front of his bloody shirt in between the sectional. His hand was covered in B's blood. Both Nitty and Banger winced as the hard steel of the .357 smashed into B's face. B was trying to shield the blows while simultaneously begging for his life.

"I should kill your sorry behind. Why is it every time I give you something to do … you drop the ball?" asked Showtyme. As he began to get tired, Showtyme weighed whether or not he should kill him. He understood that if he let him live B would be grateful to him for giving him a second chance. Showtyme couldn't think of nothing that deserved more loyalty than to have someone spare your life. Yet, it was just as important for Showtyme to keep all those around him suspended in terror. He knew Nitty and Banger was looking and showing mercy was something that could make him look weak, but it also had the potential to make them respect him even more.

He learned these things while he did a stint in the Feds. He studied everything concerning warfare, reading the likes of Che Guevara, Sun Tzu's *Art of War*, and Robert Greene's *48 Laws of Power*. He had a firm grasp on tactics and strategies, or at least this is what he thought. He didn't worry about B seeking revenge. He thought he was a coward, so he let him live.

By the time Showtyme stopped, B's face swelled up like yeast. He spat globs of blood out of his mouth while trying to stop the bleeding from the gashes spewing blood from his face and head. He managed to say, "C'mon, Showtyme, I thought we were partners. I'm a soldier for life, Henchmen to the end. Just give me a chance; I will wash him up myself."

Banger looked over to him. He couldn't believe he was pleading like that. *Damn, his grill is messed up*, he thought.

Showtyme stepped back and began cleaning off his Magnum with a bandana. Everybody thought he was going to kill B. Instead he just stood there, thinking to himself, *I have no partners; this fool actually thinks he is my equal.* "This is your last shot, B. Don't drop the ball because if you do I will not only send you to a better place, but I just may send your twin sister, too." He then turned to Nitty and Banger. "Get y'all stuff and let's ride."

As they rode the elevator down to the lobby, Nitty turned to Showtyme and said, "You know a snake that's injured, but left alive will eventually rise up and try to bite you with a double dose of venom, Show.

Showtyme smiled. "I see you've been reading those books I gave you, my dude."

Nitty swelled with pride. "Yeah, B is like a half-dead snake that will eventually heal."

Showtyme looked at Nitty with admiration. He liked the up and coming soldier. "I know, my dude, but that lame won't be around much longer—I'm going to kill two birds with one bullet."

SEVEN

QB lay in the hospital bed struggling. He had a terrible headache caused by the bullets that riddled his body. However, figuring out how he was going to deal with the detectives who hovered above him in the brightly lit hospital room caused his head to hurt more.

Lieutenant Delaney and Detective Hudson were disappointed when QB finished his statement. They didn't believe the incredulity of his story.

"So that's your story, Quentin? I can call you Quentin, right?" asked Hudson.

"No, that's not my story detective. That's what actually happened and I would much rather you call me Mr. Banks," QB said, setting the boundaries as to how he'd be treated.

Delaney cut in. "Mr. Banks we're not here to try to bust your balls. We have a possible gang shooting on our hands. If you don't know, there is a full-fledge war going on in those streets. Now, if we seem a bit frustrated, it's because we are." He inhaled and let out a deep breath. "Innocent people are dying. A ten-year-old girl was shot two weeks ago because she happened to come out of a store at the wrong time. Can you imagine what it looks like to see a little girl laying in a pool of blood with a hole the size of a bagel in the middle of her chest while still

clutching a bag of potato chips?" He paused as he looked into QB's eyes. "I hope that is something you never have to witness."

The detective's words opened up a bank of memories for QB. *My child would be eighteen going on nineteen if that animal would have just left after he took the chain*, he thought. "I can do more than imagine, detective. My child was murdered in the streets nineteen years ago. So I know first hand what it is to experience something as tragic as that. On top of that, I work with teenagers, so I'm very familiar with what is unfolding in the streets. However, that does not mean I can tell you more than what I have already told you. I would love to provide you with more information, but that is what took place." QB was beginning to sweat even though it was air-conditioned cool in his room. He knew he was making the detectives' job difficult by not revealing everything he knew about Chase being in a gang and wanting to get out, but he was committed to the well-being of his students and refused to put them in the line of fire. QB, at the very least wanted to speak to them first. He was a symbol of strength and integrity to youth who had very little trust in adults. QB stood firm to his commitment to the young and to a neighborhood that lived on its knees. He understood he was treading a thin line between what he could do and what he should do.

Aggravated, Hudson walked closer to QB's bed, placing his hands on the silver bed rails that prevented QB from rolling out of bed. "You know if parole gets involved, Mr. Banks, you just may get violated. You seem, at least on the surface, to have gotten your life together. I don't know why you would want to throw that all away on the account of a couple of gang-bangers. Moreover, you should be worried about your family. Do you think it ends here? Do you think whoever did this to you is going to stop coming after you once they find out who you are and that you're still alive?" He paused so his words could sink in, and then added, "Who knows, next time your family may be in the car with you."

Before QB could respond, Reyna walked into the hospital room in her grey pinstriped Chanel skirt and Jimmy Choo mules. Coach frames hid the rage in her eyes from hearing the detective's last statement. Detective Hudson froze, as his eyes were transfixed by Reyna's confidence and beauty. He zoomed in on her thin waist, wide hips, and long beautiful legs.

Reyna's full lips parted to reveal a perfect smile. Her locks were pulled back, excluding a few that hung loose, which framed her picture-perfect face. She looked at Hudson and said, "Don't worry about our family, detective. If that happens, together we will find a way to get through it."

Delaney looked down, upset that she heard his partner's last statement. He looked at her hand and noticed the pink diamond ring on a well-manicured finger. He tried to regain his composure before anyone else noticed his lust.

QB smiled, marveled at Reyna's ability to draw the attention of everybody in a room whenever she walked in. Her effect on men was ridiculous. A mixture of her sex appeal and professional persona made men weak in their knees. However, when someone got on her wrong side, her words definitely became her sword. She had no problem verbally abusing someone who deserved it.

Placing her briefcase on the table, she turned to her husband. "Quentin, are you all right?"

QB looked at her. "I'm fine, baby. These gentlemen just finished taking my statement and were just wrapping up."

"Yes, we were, and you are?" Delaney said, getting up.

"My name is Reyna Banks and our lawyer is on his way here if you want to know anything else about me or my husband," she said, looking the detective directly in his eyes.

"There will be no need for that, Mrs. Banks. As your husband stated, we were just finishing up. Here's our card, Mr. Banks if you think of anything else," he said, extending his hand to QB.

Reyna peered at them as they made their way out of the room. Hudson scowled at QB as he exited. He stuck his head back in the door

Young Adult

to say one last thing. "Get well, Mr. Banks. We'll be back to see you in a few days and remember what I said about the family."

"I thought you would never get here," QB said when they finally were gone.

"I had to drop Nia off at SKU," said Reyna.

"Where?"

"SKU, Smart Kidz University."

"I forgot our little baby started Kiddie College. How does she like it?"

"She loves it. This is only her third day, but the first two days she came home telling me how much she loves her school. She can't wait to tell you about it. It's all she talks about. Are you really fine? How were they treating you?"

"Like the usual suspect. But I'm cool, I can handle myself … Baby, I just never want to ever go back to prison."

Sitting on his bed tracing his face with her fingers, she said, "Don't worry, boo, you're not going anywhere." She leaned down and hugged him.

QB thought, *Damn she smells good.* He never wanted to let her go. Yet, his mind was on those things that the detectives said to him. It was more than the subtle threats. It was the questions that the detectives had so casually thrown out there that haunted QB. Do you think your family is in danger? Don't you understand they will get the closest ones to you? Can you protect your wife and daughter? QB knew better than most, the lethal nature of his enemies. He had watched gangs swallow the youth in his community whole. They had no conscience. They killed mothers, children, wives, and anybody in their way. The rules had changed. QB was uncertain whether or not he could play by their rules. He had watched the tide of violence swell over the last fifteen years, ravishing 'hoods across the nation like Hurricane Katrina did to New Orleans. It was what actually motivated QB to work for U-Turn. He knew the cries for intervention within the 'hoods fell on deaf ears. It was up to brothers like him to step up to the plate and give back to a situation that they, at one time, took so much from.

Young Adult

<u>EIGHT</u>

Torry felt numb and sluggish, as if he was climbing out of a cloud of thick smoke. Like a deep sleep, deeper than any sleep he had ever experienced. He had no idea where he was. Attempting to move, a sharp pain beginning at his shoulder sent electricity through his entire body. He tried to look at what was causing him such agony, but couldn't move realizing his right arm had a cast on it. The cast was designed to immobilize his movements, to prevent further damage to his shoulder. The doctors had to reconstruct his shoulder. Like QB, when he came through, Torry had trouble understanding his surroundings. As his vision came into focus, he looked around the room filled with balloons, candy, cards, and flowers. There was a huge banner on the wall directly in front of his bed that read, "GET WELL—WE'RE RIDING WITH YOU! U-TURN." There had to be at least a hundred signatures and messages written all over the banner.

He noticed the open closet with clothes hanging up. He saw a sweater that resembled one Naysia owned. *Damn*, he thought. *I was supposed to meet Nay at her ...* Then it hit him. It all came spiraling back. The shooting, bullets flying, three cats with Mac's. Him ducking, people screaming, windows exploding, the heat of the slugs tearing into his flesh, the pieces were all coming back together. Chase and QB. *Where's Chase and QB?* he thought.

He looked around again and finally figured out he was in a hospital. He wondered, *How long have I been here? Where's everybody?* As he tried to get up a second time, a nurse came into the room. She took one look at him and rushed to his bedside. "Mr. Harris. Oh my God, you're back. How long have you been up? How are you feeling?" the nurse questioned while picking up the chart at the end of Torry's bed and jotting something down. She then grabbed a thermometer out of her jacket pocket and placed it in Torry's mouth and took his pulse. She was working and talking at the same time.

Torry was trying to figure out what was going on. The nurse then pressed the button near his bed which sent a signal to the nurse's station. Another nurse entered the room. Like the first nurse she was all smiles. "Look at what we have here. You finally came back to us, sweetie."

Torry thought, *What the hell is going on? Where have I been?*

"Let me get your family," the second nurse said excitedly.

My family is here? thought Torry, looking at all the commotion these two women were causing. He didn't know what to say.

It had been sixteen days since the shooting. The doctor's had been optimistic about Torry's recovery. His family, along with QB, Reyna, and Chase stood on prayer. There were complications during surgery. The hollow point bullets caused some serious damage. Like the opening of an umbrella, the slugs spread open upon impact tearing flesh and breaking bones as they ripped through the body. Torry was lucky he was alive. He came out of surgery breathing with the help of a ventilator. The doctor's made the decision to medically induce him into a coma in order to prevent him from causing more harm to his already injured spine. If not neutralized, they were afraid that his paralysis may become permanent.

Naysia and his mother stood by his bedside day and night taking shifts as if this was a second job. QB, healing rather quickly, wheeled himself into Torry's room every day. He and Chase watched the Knicks

Young Adult

rookie pre-camp games while in Torry's room, hoping the sounds of basketball would somehow pull Torry out of that coma. QB had heard stories of people doing things, playing music, reading or simply talking to their loved ones until they eventually responded. This incident made QB realize just how attached he was to all his students at U-Turn. Seeing the students support Torry and his family throughout the ordeal made him extremely proud to be doing the work that he does. They visited Torry so much that the administration had to put a stop to all the traffic. They asked QB to speak to students when they found out they were sneaking in, using delivery person schemes, and putting on hospital attire, faking like they were orderlies or patients. One student even tried to act like he was a doctor, stethoscope and the whole nine. They were going to hold their boy down one way or the other.

Ms. Harris couldn't believe all the love her son got from his friends. They had nothing but good things to say about her boy and their presence definitely helped her get through these trying days.

"Torry," Naysia screamed as she came running into his room.

Startled, the nurse turned around. With a smile she put her fingers to her lips, reminding Naysia she was in a hospital. His mother and Chase came in next. Ms. Harris had tears in her eyes and began thanking God immediately upon seeing her son's big smile. Reyna, pushing QB in his wheelchair came in a few minutes later. The doctors had ordered QB to stay in his bed. He was moving around way too much. However, there was nothing that could've kept him in his bed; he had to see Torry.

Torry could feel the love flowing throughout the room as he saw the faces of his loved ones. Between his mother, Chase, and Naysia he couldn't get a word in. He didn't mind. He understood their happiness. The nurse had already explained to him that he had been in a coma for two weeks. What he couldn't understand was why he was having trouble moving. He reasoned that it was muscle fatigue. *Hell, I've been in a coma for two whole weeks*, he thought. He wanted some water. Naysia took some crushed ice the nurse provided and slowly fed it to him.

Reyna pushed QB to the side of his bed. "What's up, little bruh? How you feeling?" QB asked.

He struggled to turn his head toward QB. "I'm good. I feel tired though. How are you? I see you pushing a new whip," he said.

QB grabbed hold of Reyna's hand. "Yeah, this is my new ride. I gotta put some D's on this mutha …" Reyna popped him upside his head.

They all laughed, including Torry's mom who had no idea what was so funny. "The doctor said I can't do too much walking until these wounds heal. He doesn't want me on my feet. But I'm feeling much better. I'm ready to get up out of here. The food sucks and I can't get used to wearing these gowns with my money hangin' all out in the back," QB said.

"Sweetie, those buns of yours sho' look good," said Ms. Harris, making QB blush and everybody laugh.

"I may be checking out in a few days," QB said, not believing Ms. Harris had seen his buns.

"That's what's up," Torry said happily. He and QB stared at each other, knowing there was so much more to say, but now was not the right time.

The doctor entered the room. "Hello, everybody." They all turned to look at him. "If you all don't mind, I need a few minutes with this strong, young man. I have to check a couple of things, and then I'll let you all get back to showing him some love," he said as he winked at Torry.

They backed up to give the doctor some room. He grabbed Torry's left arm and began moving it in different directions. He poked him in his upper body with a cold metal instrument, and he kept asking Torry if he felt the contact. Torry kept saying he did. Everybody in the room tensed up. No one had mentioned anything about the partial paralysis. The doctor then moved down toward the lower half of his body and suddenly Torry couldn't feel a thing. It didn't register that something was terribly wrong. It is remarkable how time slows in moments like this and how the neurons in our brain appear to hesitate in providing information to a person in such a sad situation. When the doctor grabbed his leg Torry wondered, *Why the hell don't I feel him?*

"Doc, I can't feel anything," Torry said, looking down at his leg.

The doctor scratched the bottom of his right foot. "Do you feel this?" he asked.

Torry waited a few seconds, hoping he would feel something. When he didn't he said, "Nah, I don't feel anything." He then looked toward his mother who was crying. He looked at Naysia, QB, and Reyna.

"What's wrong?" he asked, seeing the expressions on their faces. He could tell something was up. Everybody stood there with a deep sadness in their eyes. His mother and QB moved toward him at the same time. QB, seeing his mother, stopped and allowed her to tell him the initial diagnosis.

She wiped her eyes. "Baby, you're partially paralyzed," she said, reaching out to hold his hand. "But don't worry, God has a plan for you. He has a plan for us all."

Placing his hand on Torry's mother shoulder, the doctor intervened. "Let me." He then went on to explain what happened medically. Bullet fragments were lodged in his lower spinal area. He explained the procedure of the surgery, and why he was placed in a medically induced coma. Most importantly, he explained the importance of his rehabilitation, and added that there is a fifty percent chance with medical technology that he will be able to one day walk again.

By the time he finished explaining, Torry was in a daze. Hearing but not really listening. He didn't know what to do or how he should respond to this kind of news. He thought, *Should I cry? Should I be mad?* He was confused as to how he should feel. Everybody in the room had tears in their eyes, except him, the doctor, and QB. Torry turned toward Chase with a 'why me?' look. He wanted to scream, to say something, anything, but he just couldn't get the words out. Naysia came over and hugged him. He hugged her back thinking, *What am I going to do if I can't walk?*

***

The following days were filled with valleys and peaks. The students from U-Turn began coming back through the hospital at all hours of the day. In between the tests the doctors were running on Torry and QB, the boys sat for hours discussing what happened. Chase finally told him everything. From the conversation he had with B at the stadium to Showtyme putting a hit out on him. He explained that he never thought the hit would actually happen. He thought he would be able to get out with nothing more than a few guys jumping him.

QB was livid that Chase only now told him about this. "Why the hell didn't you explain all this to me?" When the words left his mouth he realized he'd made a mistake. Now was not the time to get on Chase's case. Chase was silent, feeling lower than any other time he felt in his life. QB said, "We'll figure this all out. Have the police spoken to you two yet?"

"I spoke to them at the scene, but I haven't seen them since. To be honest, I'm not trying to see them."

"What about you, Torry?"

"Mom told me they came by a few times, but I was out. I'm sure they'll be back any day."

QB thought about how the detectives were constantly coming to the hospital, hoping he would come up with something else that could assist them in their investigation. On top of that, his parole officer made it clear that if QB did anything that would enable him to violate him, he would. The detectives were looking for Chase. They visited his home and tried to catch him at the hospital on numerous occasions. Chase moved in and out of the hospital with stealth. There were so many people visiting both Torry and QB that it was difficult for the detectives to pin down Chase.

UNDER PRESSURE

QB, feeling vulnerable, had finally phoned his lawyer to explain what had taken place and how they were now being treated like suspects. The detectives who found out about Chase's involvement in the Henchmen, automatically assumed that all three of them were tied to the gang, and determined that the shooting was somehow connected to that fact.

While locked up, Amari had turned QB on to a lawyer named William Kingsley to perfect his appeal. Over the years they became very close, and shared a great level of respect for one another. Kingsley even volunteered to come to U-Turn to speak to the students every so often. He was the hottest criminal attorney on the east coast since the unexpected passing of Johnny Cochran. Once he got involved, the detectives had to contact him before speaking with QB, which made their job that much more difficult.

This is not what QB wanted, however, he knew that if he fully cooperated with the detectives they would force Chase and Torry in a corner where they would be made to testify against other gang members and possibly end up in a witness protection program—a program that surely would not protect two young black kids for the rest of their lives.

Instead, QB asked his brother to allow Chase to lay low at his house until he got out of the hospital. QB didn't want Chase to think he had to do something and retaliate for what happened to him and Torry. He understood that Chase, like most youth, was mainlining on violence. Whether it was in movies, video games, music, or on the streets, most of them felt that violence was the solution to all their problems. QB didn't want Chase to be killed or end up killing someone else and then having to spend the rest of his life in prison. New York State had zero tolerance for gangs and senseless violence. He had explained to Chase how on April 28, 2004, the 108th Congress quietly passed a bill destined to have a damaging effect on the youth. A bill known as the Anti Gang Act, with laws structured so that our youth, once determined to be a part of a gang, if convicted, will more than likely be given anywhere between 20 years and a life sentence.

***

Torry finally came apart. It was a month and two days since they'd been in the hospital. Snow had unexpectedly blanketed New York. Torry stared out the window, watching the flakes fall. He had been unusually quiet since being told about his paralysis. His emotions had finally taken him to a place where the air was thin and breathing took too much effort. He felt as if he was stuck somewhere in-between insanity and hopelessness. Most of his days were filled with thoughts of ways to exact revenge. While other days he wallowed in pity, tired of everybody telling him it was going to be all right. What he wanted to do is tell them, *Hello, I'm freakin' paralyzed*. He wondered why they acted like they didn't get it.

That evening, Naysia, Reyna, Nia, QB and Chase were in his room. QB and Chase were watching television. Reyna was busy with Nia. Torry's mom was home getting some much needed rest. They'd finally convinced her to take a break. Naysia was sitting on the bed with Torry, definitely doing her part. She made sure Torry was being taken care of, and even began doing the nurse's job. It was rare to see such a young lady who was that responsible. Torry's mom had joked about hooking up with her father because he had raised such a beautiful daughter. Neither one of them wanted to see that happen; they couldn't imagine double dating with their parents. Reyna liked Naysia as well and was going to keep in contact with her when this was all over.

Naysia was contemplating if she should tell Torry about her pregnancy. She and Torry had discussed having a child on numerous occasions. They both wanted a planned pregnancy, in fact, they both wanted to wait until after they graduated from college. However, fate wouldn't have it that way. Naysia was on birth control and yet she still ended up pregnant. How, was unexplainable. She had heard of cases where women got pregnant while on birth control, but she never

Young Adult

imagined it would happen to her. She had already told her father, who surprisingly, wasn't that upset. He was disappointed that this would put off her plans to start college, but he assured her that he would be there for her and Torry. However, they spoke about her buckling down and handling her responsibilities because the life of a child is precious and serious business. Her father told her that it was the most difficult and rewarding job in the world, and for a nineteen year old it's even that much more challenging.

"What's wrong, Torry?" she asked, trying to entice him to speak. Naysia, like everybody else was becoming concerned about his prolonged silence.

Torry turned his head toward her. "What you think is wrong, Nay?" he asked.

She leaned toward him, touching his face softly. "Baby, I know how you feel. Everything is going to be fine. Trust me, together we will get through this. We just gotta pray," she said.

Pulling the sheet up on his chest, Torry looked at her like she was crazy. "Naysia, do me a favor?"

"What's that, baby?

"Stop talking about that prayer stuff. I don't wanna hear that anymore," Torry said, staring into her eyes.

"What do you mean ... God will get us through this," she said lovingly.

"God! Naysia, God doesn't even exist. Not in the 'hood, and definitely not in my life. I'm tired of you and my mother always telling me to put something in God's hands. God's hands are too clean to hold a nigga like me. I'm tired of hearing that."

This got everybody's attention. They all turned toward him.

Torry added, "Look at me, Nay. I'm paralyzed. I can't move. You know what I've been asking myself these last few days? Where was God? Can you tell me, Naysia? Where's God?" He paused then looked around the room. "Can anybody in here tell me where's God?" Naysia reached out to touch him, but Torry recoiled, pulling back his arm like her touch was repulsive. "If it wasn't for those doctors I would've been dead. Where was God then? Better yet, where was God when those cowards shot up the damn truck? Where was God then?"

"Chill soldier," said Chase.

"Chill?" he questioned Chase as if he had some nerve. "Well, since nobody has an answer, let me tell y'all about your God. He never comes around when I need him," he said.

Nia started crying. Reyna began walking around the room with her. Torry, with tears streaming down his face added, "God should've shielded us from those bullets. Where was his punk behind then? You know where he was, Nay? He was probably was ducking behind a cloud or something. So please don't come at me with that God bull. God don't do jack for people like me. Those doctors saved me, not God." Torry wiped his eyes, took a deep breath, and slowly repeated, "I can't walk. Look at me; I'm nineteen years old and I cannot move my legs." He stopped for a second. "If God is real, Nay, tell him to let me walk again."

The room was quiet. Reyna was expecting QB to intervene, but he just stood there not saying anything. He understood that Torry needed to vent. Noticing he wasn't going to say anything, Reyna handed Nia to QB and went to Naysia and gave her a hug. She was literally shaking in Reyna's arms.

Turning his head toward the window Torry stared at the falling snow. When the silence became too much for him, he said in a low but sad tone, "Reality is my savior, and you know what he tells me? He tells me when it all hits the fan in the 'hood, God is nowhere to be found. I hope you will one day wake up and see things for what they really are and snap out of that Jesus walked on water bull."

Naysia completely lost it and began crying louder causing Nia to start back up. Naysia buried her face in Reyna's chest. Each of Torry's words tore a piece of her heart out.

Young Adult

Reyna looked at Torry and said, "That's enough, Torry. You shouldn't take your frustrations out on Naysia. She didn't do anything to you."

Torry looked away, knowing there was some truth to what she was saying.

Chase approached Torry to let him know he understood what he was feeling. Nia, holding her daddy around his neck, was wondering what all the big people were fussing about. No one had anything to say. Everybody was in deep thought. QB wondered why this had to happen to them. Chase wanted to put in some work.

Naysia calmed down as Reyna held her. Reyna looked at Torry thinking how his words just may destroy the love and strength they all needed to get through this situation. *What if his words had the same effect on them as paralysis is having on him? What a terrible fate paralysis must be if it could kill the God in man,* she thought.

After awhile, Naysia sat up. Her eyes were swollen and bloodshot red. She carried hurt, disappointment, and fate in the lines of her face as others did on their palms. She turned to Torry and said, "I'm pregnant."

NINE

C hase was nowhere to be found. Nobody had seen or heard from him during the past week. Everybody, including Torry, was trying to figure out where he was. They called Amari's house every day. QB was upset at his brother for letting Chase just run the streets. Of course, Amari let QB know that he wasn't in the business of babysitting no grown-ass man. Reyna tried to keep everyone from stressing, reminding them that Chase could hold his own in the streets, and probably knew how to function in the dark much better than any of them. QB hoped she was right.

***

Four days later, Chase strolled into the hospital with a slight Chocolate Thai buzz, a backpack strapped over his shoulder, his cell phone in one hand, and Lexi holding his other. The pressure of living life in the fast lane was taking a toll on him. He hardly got any sleep since the shooting. The streets were buzzing with rumors and talking about the inevitable showdown between Showtyme and him.

So when he ran into Lexi, it was a welcomed relief. At first she ignored his attempt to speak to her when they saw each other in the mall. She had called him on numerous occasions since they met that day at Shea Stadium, but he never returned her calls. So the heck with him, she thought when they spotted each other in Macys. When she gave in and allowed him to explain himself, she couldn't believe it. She felt so

Young Adult

bad for him, and for the next couple of days they spent every waking moment together, going to the movies, shopping, and she even invited him to her house in East Elmhurst. He had met her parents. They seemed cool, though her father made sure to let him know he wanted to vibe with him man to man. He knew what that meant.

Lexi and Chase were really checking for one another. They sat in her basement the night of the get together kickin' it 'till the sun came up. Chase couldn't believe how easy it was for him to pour out his soul to this young lady. Her ability to listen without being judgmental was what cut through his defenses. He told her about his involvement with the Henchmen, showed her his tattoos, and explained to her what had unfolded the day they left the ballgame. It sounded like a movie to her, but she said nothing. Instead she just held his hand as he let it all out. He told her that he would understand if she wanted nothing to do with him, but he wanted her to know before she made that decision that he was doing everything to get out of the Henchmen. Lexi, like most young ladies liked the bad-boy streak in him. He reminded her of her father, but she explained that they can only see each other as long as he promised to do whatever it took to get out of that gang.

Chase couldn't remember when he had a better four day stretch. Unfortunately, reality soon set back in. He was still at war, and he refused to let his guard down. He explained to Lexi that he was not coming around the next day because he had to go check on QB and Torry. She insisted that he take her with him. At first he resisted, but then gave in and decided to take her with him.

***

Over the past week Chase had learned most of the truth to what really went down. The third shooter was still a mystery, but he knew it was only a matter of time before he found out. He had a few people who were still loyal to him on the inside of the Henchmen. This gave him an unexpected advantage in his plan to serve up that cold dish called revenge. He learned that Showtyme put a hit on him, and that the snake,

B drove the car. Right after B hung up the phone with him on the day at Shea Stadium he called Showtyme. Two of the three shooters were up and coming Henchmen named Nitty and Banger, who were eager to show they were willing to put in that work. Chase understood that. He himself had road-tripped on many occasions coming up, doing things he later regretted. Sometimes doing things he really didn't want to do, but did because he was not man enough to say no. He, like most young men, was more comfortable showing that he was capable of letting his gun clap when ordered, than to simply say, "No, that's not right." However, as he thought about what he'd done in the past his conscience began tearing him apart.

With his thoughts now on revenge, he failed to notice the big, brawny detective pretending as if he was talking on the phone as Lexi and he waited for the elevator. She got on first. Chase looked casually over his shoulder to make sure there were no potential gunners following them. He knew that funerals and hospitals were places where the second wave of gunplay could happen if necessary. Everything seemed in order. He stepped on the elevator.

As the doors closed shut, Hudson immediately radioed upstairs letting another partner from the Unit, Detective Powell, know that the evasive Sean "Chase" Matthews was on his way up.

They'd been in the hospital for two days monitoring who visited both Torry and QB. They took notes, compared photos, and patiently waited on Chase to show. One of their many informants had finally provided a photo of Chase. What's ironic is that they were actually about to call off the surveillance when he showed up.

While on the elevator, Chase handed his backpack to Lexi so he could bend down to tie his Uptowns. The doors opened just as he finished making sure his jeans fell right on his kicks. They stepped off the elevator, turned left and headed towards Torry's room. He was about to retrieve his backpack from Lexi when he spotted a nice-looking sister heading in their direction. She was tall, and had on slacks with Air

Young Adult

Max's, which seemed unusual. One of many things he learned from the streets was to spot the strange, those things that seemed out of place. To top it off, it appeared she was intentionally trying to avoid looking at them.

Feeling the presence of something wrong, something misplaced, something staged, Chase looked around, assessing his situation. Lexi grabbed his hand as the distance between them was eaten up quickly by the long strides of the undercover detective. As the detective passed them, Chase steered Lexi into Torry's room on their right. He watched from the door as the lady continued walking down the corridor without looking back.

"Maybe you should go get directions to her heart," Lexi said, mimicking the now famous line he threw at her the first time they met.

Chase looked at Lexi. "It's not like that. I'm just making sure all is good. Making sure that she's not down with the Henchmen or Police. I never saw her on this floor before. She's not a nurse, and since I've been coming here I have seen most of the faces of those that visit their people, and she's not a regular. I'm just making sure—"

He was cut off by Torry. "What's up, Chase?"

"It's all good, soldier," Chase said, closing the door. He ignored his instincts for the sake of Lexi. He didn't want to lose her for any reason. "What's up, Daddy-O? Lexi, did I tell you my boy is going to be a father?"

"Nooo," she said excitedly, and then added, "Congratulations Torry. Do you remember me?"

"How can I forget, Miss 'get your popcorn, peanuts, soda and cracker jacks.' You look so much different outside of that uniform."

They laughed. Lexi said, "I see you got jokes."

It's good to see my soldier smiling again, Chase thought. He wasn't sure whether or not his boy was going to make it after hearing him break down the other day. All week he tried to imagine what it must feel like to be suddenly paralyzed from the waist down. He still felt guilty about the whole ordeal. He knew Torry blamed him for everything, even if he never said so.

Interrupting his thoughts, Lexi said, "Yeah that's me, gotta get my hustle on." She added, "Of course I look better now, but I was hot enough for your boy to want directions."

"Now that's real talk. I'm glad you hooked up with him. He needs a good girl in his life," said Torry. He looked at Chase then added, "Make sure you take care of him and if he gives you any trouble, just holla."

"Yeah, he's a'ight. We've been kickin' it for a few days now and when he starts acting up, I'll be sure to let you know," she said as she winked at Chase. She turned back to Torry. "But what about you—how are you doing? I was so sorry to hear about ..." She paused, looking for the right words. "... about what happened."

"It's all good. I have my ups and downs. But I refuse to lay here and complain about how my life rocks. I'm gonna come up out this a better man," said Torry. He then turned to Chase. "Where the hell you been? Everybody has been worrying about you."

"I had to clear my head, soldier. I'm trying to put all the pieces to this puzzle together. I heard this lame B was the driver and now he is the one supposed to be coming at the kid. This lame got some nerve. He's not built like that. I will never underestimate any of them punk behind cats again. I went out to my cousin's house in Hollis to lay low for a few and then ran into cutie here at the mall and she has been blowing up my cell ever since. So being the playa that I am, I had to check her for a few days."

"Yeah right, big head," Lexi said, playfully swinging at him for telling false stories about her. He dipped her slow punch and threw her into a hug. He looked her in the eyes. "Nah, I'm only playing, kid. She has been there for me, holding me down like a Queen should. Something I really need." He added, "Speaking of being held down—where's that little private nurse of yours? I want them two to meet each other."

"She'll be here in a few. I had to force her and my moms to take a break. To go home and get some rest. They were acting like they were going to move up in here. Look in that closet; it's packed with their clothes, shoes, and all types of stuff."

"Naysia is a good woman, Torry. You're not going to find too many made of what she's made of. You better wife that as soon as you rise up out of this hospital. Plus her old King is going to be on your back about marrying her now that she is pregnant."

"That's the plan, kid. I was ready to marry her anyway. Her pops is supposed to be coming through tomorrow. I got to get these legs working again so I can walk down that aisle."

"Don't worry, kid. That's just a matter of time," Chase said, not wanting to appear pessimistic. "Yo, let me go check QB. Lexi, you can chill here if you want to. I'll bring QB back down here."

"All right, boobie. Maybe I can get the real four-one-one on you," she said, smiling.

"Here, let me get that," he said, reaching for his backpack. She handed it to him, realizing for the first time how heavy it felt as she swung it to him. He took it and put it in the closet. "Damn, you were right. Look at all these damn shoes and clothes. He took his cell out the backpack and then put it all the way in the back of the closet. As soon as he stood up and closed the door to the closet, the door to the room opened and Detective Hudson and Powell stepped in waving their badges. Chase looked at them and thought, *I knew it.*

"Are you Sean Matthews?" the male detective asked, blocking the door to the corridor.

Chase didn't miss a beat. "Nah, that's not me." He turned to Lexi and said, "Are you Sean Matthews?"

"No," she blurted out not catching his sarcasm.

"Listen, Mr. Matthews we could do this the hard way or the easy way. That's up to you. We're only conducting an investigation as of now, but for some reason you've been avoiding us, giving us reason to believe there is much more to the story than you're willing to share. You're not a suspect at this time, but your running is giving us second thoughts." The detective stepped toward Chase. "Now, you could come down with us voluntarily, or we could simply arrest you for interfering with an ongoing investigation."

Chase's mind was in fifth gear. He looked at the female. *I knew something was up with that chick. A damn co. I need to get up out this room.* He glanced toward the window even though they were on the twelfth floor. Detective Powell followed his eye movements, read his thoughts, and immediately moved toward the window.

Torry turned toward Chase. "Listen homie, both QB and I gave statements. We told them what we saw, and that's it."

"Man, I'm not with that. I already gave my statement to a police officer the day this all went down. There's nothing new," he said, looking at the door, weighing whether or not he could get past the detective.

"Listen, Mr. Matthews, or can I call you Chase?"

"Who?" said Chase, looking around trying to figure out who the hell the detective was referring to.

"Okay, Mr. Matthews, all we want to do is have you look at some photos and give us an official statement, that's all. We know you were in the passenger seat of the vehicle that was struck. We're not trying to put nothing on you, just come down to the station with us and we'll have you back here in no time."

Chase knew they were trying to spin him, but he was thinking about the hammer in his backpack. He needed to get them out of this room as quick as possible, so he decided to go. He would tell them the same thing he told the officer who took his statement at the scene. "Torry, tell QB I came through, but was taken down to the precinct by ..." He looked at the detectives wanting to know his name

"I'm detective Hudson."

"… by detective Hudson." He then walked over to Lexi. "I'm sorry, baby. I didn't know this was going to happen. You can stay here with Torry. If I'm not back in an hour or so then—"

Torry interjected, "I got her, Sean. If you're not back soon, I'll get Nay to take her home."

"A'ight, I'm out." He began to let go of her hand, when suddenly Lexi grabbed him and hugged him tight and then kissed him unexpectedly on his lips.

She looked at him with her pretty self and said, "Hurry up back, and don't worry, if you're not back in an hour we will be down at that precinct to see what's going on."

Chase, feeling a new wave of confidence turned to the detectives. "Okay, let's go." They flanked him on each side, and proceeded out of the room.

Torry sent Lexi to get QB as soon as the detectives and Chase left. She wheeled him in five minutes later. Torry explained everything that took place.

QB was upset that they didn't think to get him earlier while the detectives were there. He then turned to Lexi and asked if he could use her cell phone. He placed a call to his lawyer, who immediately got on the case.

TEN

Winter time was the best time of the year to recruit. Showtyme, knowing this, roamed the projects scouting his first round draft pick—the next soldier to put in work for the Five Seven Henchmen. There was something about cold weather that transformed young men into wolves.

Face was thirteen years old, and destined to run red lights. His mother was twenty-nine, single and living a second childhood. She ended up having to raise Face on her own because his father, who was a major player in his time, was in Elmira's maximum security prison doing a twenty-five to life bid for murder. She struggled with employment because when Face's father was home he took care of all the finances. Instead of encouraging her to go to college so she could be prepared to make it on her own in case something ever happened to him, he insisted that his woman stay home and raise their child. To her young eyes, this appeared to be good. However, she didn't anticipate her man going to prison, and now, here she was struggling to keep her head above the poverty line. Their apartment often lacked electricity and water because she was more concerned with how she looked instead of paying her utility bills. This irresponsibility caused rips in their relationship. Face had very little respect for how his mother moved. They argued constantly and it always ended up with her kicking him out of the apartment. They lived on the first floor in their building and sometimes

Young Adult

the sewage that flooded their entire floor was as raw as his young personality.

Like most young brothers in the 'hood, all Face wanted to be was a Five Seven Henchmen. Just like his mother, whenever he saw Showtyme he would go out of his way to impress him. Every so often Showtyme would promise him that he would give him a shot to become one of his many soldiers. His mother inadvertently introduced him to Showtyme when she was sexing him and allowed Showtyme to spend the night at their home.

Today was Face's day. Showtyme was finally giving him a chance to become a part of the Henchmen. Face was eager and ready to put in some work. When Showtyme told the youngin' to meet him that evening at around six, Face couldn't believe it. He spent the whole day trying to keep his composure, but the anticipation was killing him.

When the time arrived, Showtyme was laying in the cut in a Nissan 350 Z. He watched Face as he showed up at the designated spot. By the way he suspiciously looked around he could tell Face was nervous. Most of the kids he recruited were scared, but tried their best to mask it. Initially, they all put on that false sense of bravado, but Showtyme knew better. He, at one time, went through the same process.

Watching from a distance gave Showtyme the opportunity to get a better picture of the recruit's toughness. He knew you could always learn more about a person when they didn't think anybody was watching. It was one of the many tactics he used to keep him ahead of the others. But this initiation meant a little bit more to him. This was personal and he wanted to see it go down. He sparked a blunt of that sour diesel, watched and waited.

Face had heard many of the rumors about what others did to get into the Henchmen. He didn't care what he had to do. Whatever it was, it was going to get done, even if that meant he had to body something. He was ready to put in that work. Showtyme used to just brush the youngster off, knowing the kid never killed anybody and was just doing a lot of talking. However, over the years he watched him, and now felt that Face was finally ready. He admired the fact that Face had heart and no problem shooting on command—the essence of a true soldier.

Showtyme was the first to notice Murder pull up in a black Yukon. When he stopped on the corner of 99th Street, Showtyme thought to himself, *Now we'll see just how 'too good' you are for me.* He eased back in his Recarro racing leather seats to watch the movie about to unfold.

Face stepped out of the shadows of the building when he spotted the truck. He hopped in the back seat. The bass-line of Waka Flocka Flame's "Oh Let's Do It," caused the ground to shake and the truck to vibrate. Face could hardly hear himself think. He leaned up towards the front, "Son, turn that down." When the driver turned it down, he asked "Where's Showtyme?"

A little dark-skinned kid in the passenger seat, said, "You'll see him soon enough. Right now you need to get your head right and get ready to put in this work. The mark will be coming through in a minute."

Looking out the tinted windows, Face replied, "Don't worry about me, my dude, I'm ready."

"What's your name, youngin'?" the kid in the passenger seat asked.

"Face. What's yours, soldier?"

"They call me Bodyshop, and that's Murder," he said, pointing to the driver.

Peering at Face through the rearview mirror, Murder said, "Listen, my dude. On the floor next to you is a cooler. Inside it is a glass container filled with sulfuric acid. You gotta be real careful handling it. In fact, there should be some rubber gloves somewhere back there. Make sure you put them on." Face nodded. Murder continued. "This is what it is: There's going to be this chick coming up this way within the next hour. She'll be getting off the bus. You're going to throw that acid right in her face. You can't miss because you will only get one chance. You got that?"

Face didn't expect that. He didn't like the idea of having to hurt a lady, but he was not turning back now. He had waited a long time to be down with Henchmen. "You already know, just point this broad out."

"When you get out, make sure you pull your fitted low and take this and wrap it around your face. You don't want anybody to I.D. you." Bodyshop handed him a bandana. "When we see the bus pull up, you're going to be over there in the cut," he said, pointing to an underground passage on 99th Street. "Once you handle your business, just turn around and walk slowly to the truck and get in. If anybody tries to play hero, I will pop 'em."

"I got this, my dude," said Face with a lot of aggression.

Both Murder and Bodyshop had seen their share of young cats come through, who at the last minute could not go through with what was demanded of them. Murder turned the music back up and gave Face a blunt. "Here, youngin', spark this up," he said.

Face took the cigar packed with marijuana and put some fire to it. He inhaled until his lungs were full to capacity. He sank in the butter soft leather seat, held the smoke as long as he could, and then released the smoke into the air. He did this two more times then passed the blunt up to Bodyshop. Face immediately felt the buzz. He reached down, opened the cooler, and looked at the glass receptacle that sat there. He had never done anything like this and didn't know what to expect.

"There's a bus!" Murder said, snapping him out of his thoughts

Face pulled his fitted down on his head and tied the bandana around the lower half of his face. He was about to step out the truck when Murder said, "Hold up, I don't think she got off that bus." He looked purposefully at the crowd of people heading their way. Monica was not among them. Face tried to relax because he could feel his heart beating uncontrollably. Murder looked at him through the rearview mirror. "It will be another fifteen minutes for the next bus. You want to hit this again, my dude?" he said, passing back the blunt.

Face took it and blew some more of the blunt, hoping to calm himself down. He was watching the coming and goings of people on 99th Street. He lived close by and started worrying that somebody might recognize him. After a couple more hits, he was good. The diesel did the job of calming his nerves. He was ready to get this over with, and hoped the chick would be on the next bus.

Meanwhile, across the street Showtyme was on his cell talking to Cherokee. Like Face, he was getting impatient, but no matter how long it took, he was going to wait and see this done. He was telling Cherokee how he needed to put Monica in her place. As soon as he ended the call with Cherokee, another bus pulled up. He started his car and watched as passengers exited the bus. Then he saw her.

In the truck, Murder was looking down the block as well. He spotted the target. "Okay, soldier, its game time. You see the girl in the brown pants suit, and white shirt?"

Face eased up on the seat so he could get a better look through the front window. "Yeah, I got her."

"That's her. Handle your business and remember, walk to the truck, don't run. Running causes too much heat."

Face didn't say anything else. He reached down and grabbed the receptacle of acid, then walked to the underground passage and stepped in. The young thug made up his mind that he was going to let her walk by, come up from behind and splash her from the back. Bodyshop was looking at Face from the truck. When Monica, followed by two other women and a Chinese guy, was about twenty-five yards away, Murder started the truck and eased it out of the parking spot.

Showtyme watched everything unfold. Fifteen yards, ten yards, nine … and counting. Showtyme looked at Face as he bent down to tie his sneaker. *What the hell is he doing?* Showtyme thought.

Face wasn't really tying his kicks; he kneeled so the target couldn't see him. When the woman walked past, he got up, grabbed the glass and walked behind her. He picked up his pace—three feet, two feet, and one. He brought his arm up, put his face down and said, "Excuse me, Miss."

As soon as she turned, the acid hit her square in the face and immediately began melting her skin. Everything seemed to slow down. Monica instinctively tried to shield her face, but it was too late. The burning sensation caused her to scream a guttural sound that Face had never heard in his life. Thick and full of pain, her shrieking caused Face to look at the damage he caused. The flesh on her face seemed to be coming off. It was almost unrecognizable. Face couldn't make out all of her features, but in that split second a sense of familiarity overcame him. He looked one more time. Suddenly his eyes got wide, like a frightened deer in headlights, but he kept it moving toward the truck. A wave of nausea came over him. At first, the pedestrians on the block didn't know what happened. By the time they turned and responded to the girl who fell to the ground, Face got into the truck and Murder hit the gas, getting up outta there before police arrived.

Satisfied, Showtyme, eased up out of his spot when he saw that Face got it done.

Face sat in the back of the truck stunned, trying to convince himself that what he just did-did not actually happen. *It couldn't have been Monica,* he thought. But there was a big part of him telling him that it was Monica. As Murder put distance between them and the crime scene, Face turned and looked out the back window, noticing people running to the spot where Monica lay. The air in the truck seemed to dissipate as the knot in his stomach tightened.

"You did that broad dirty, soldier," Bodyshop said as Face turned back around.

Looking straight ahead, Face didn't say anything. His words were stuck in his throat.

"You a'ight?" asked Murder.

Face looked up. "Yeah, I'm good."

Bodyshop turned around from the passenger seat and handed Face a bottle of Patron. "Here, drink some of this."

Face took it and turned the bottle up to his lips, taking a long gulp. It burned going down his throat, but not enough to take his thoughts off what he just did. He took another long gulp and then said, "Where we headed?"

Murder was just about to get on the Brooklyn Queens Expressway. "Be easy, we're going to see Showtyme. You did good, li'l homie, and now comes the after party."

Even though he knew better, he asked, "My dudes, do you know who that chick was?"

Bodyshop and Murder glanced at each other. Murder didn't see the harm in his question. "It was some broad that violated the big homie. I think her name is Monica. She supposedly told Showtyme when he was trying to holla that she was too good to be with him."

"You serious, my dude?" asked Face.

"Yeah, soldier. I was there when she fronted on the big homie. Showtyme wanted to shoot her right then and there, but there were way too many witnesses."

Face could not believe what he was hearing. It was Monica.

Stunned, he hollered up front to Bodyshop. "Turn up the music, my dude." A sharp, stabbing pain shot through Face's chest. He grabbed it, *I'm too young to be having a heart attack*, he thought. He put his head down so neither Bodyshop nor Murder could see the water in his eyes well up. It was hard for him to process what he'd just done. Monica lived two floors above him and used to be his babysitter when he was younger. She was like his family, someone who he had a crush on for as long as he could remember.

Murder looked at Face through the rearview mirror, tapped Bodyshop, and signaled him to check the youngin' out. When Bodyshop turned around Face was bent over with his face in his hands. "You okay, my dude?"

Face slowly looked up and put on as much of a front as he could. "Yeah, I'm good. That weed got my head beating that's all. He looked around. "How long before we reach our destination?"

"About ten minutes," said Murder.

Face sat back and wondered about Monica. Was she all right? Did he cause irreparable damage? These thoughts rained down on him. Face smelled his shirt; it seemed he couldn't get the stench of the acid out of his nostrils. He looked out the window at the cars they passed. He didn't want his eyes to reveal to Bodyshop or Murder the sadness and hurt he felt inside. Feeling himself slipping into that crazy place where he didn't care anymore, he wondered if Showtyme knew that Monica was once his babysitter. The guilt of violating the girl he played doctor with, had fake weddings with—the girl he dreamed of marrying was something that would forever be impaled on his conscience. Monica was closer to him than his own mother. The thought of him throwing acid in her beautiful face made him want to throw up. He cracked his window just in case it actually happened. *What did I do?* he silently questioned. He pressed himself in his seat and just thought about her.

Monica was a promising eighteen-year-old girl. He recalled her telling him a few weeks ago that she was accepted to Seton Hall's Dental program. She dreamed of becoming a dentist. She even used to examine Face's mouth when they played doctor. These thoughts immobilized Face as he struggled with his feelings. He kept trying to convince himself that if Monica could have escaped harm, he wouldn't join the Henchmen. But he knew there was very little chance of that. He replayed exactly what he did over and over in his mind.

Her terrifying screams, the image of her reaching up to her face in attempt to stop the unbearable pain, every second of the act was etched in his memory.

"We here, soldier," Bodyshop said, abruptly interrupting him out of his own nightmare.

Face looked up and noticed they were getting off the highway. He had to regain his composure because he didn't want to lead on that he knew Monica. He needed to hear what Showtyme had to say. *If he intentionally had me run down on Monica, knowing how close we were, then--*Face forced the thought out of his mind.

They traveled for another five minutes before they pulled into a driveway of a nice home in Lakeview, Long Island. Showtyme owned the house and the one directly next to it. Nobody except Shawnee and Cherokee knew about him owning the house next door or the tunnel that connected both homes. The girls knew because they were the ones who stayed with the workers when Showtyme had it done. He had it built in the event he needed a quick escape. He got the idea from a documentary he saw on the Mexican drug cartel. They had tunnels that allowed them to ship countless amounts of drugs without detection, from the countryside of Mexico across the borders and into America.

Face put on his game face. Having never been to Long Island, he had no idea where they were. He couldn't believe Showtyme was living like this.

Murder shut off the engine and stepped out the truck. He looked at Face who was still sitting in the back seat, "You a'ight soldier?" When Face nodded his head yes, he added, "Then let's roll out."

Face stepped out the truck and followed both Murder and Bodyshop to the back of the house where they went in through the back door. The inside of the house was dimly lit. A mixture of incense and weed hovered in the air. At first glance Face calculated at least twenty-five Henchmen running throughout the house. He looked around thinking, *This must be their honeycomb hideout.*

Females were running around half-naked while Young Jeezy's "Vacation" was being blasted through the sound system like they were in a club. The girls were checking him out, looking him up and down like he was fresh meat. Face took everything in enjoying the attention. *I'm gonna be G'd up in this spot one day, runnin' all of this.*

Young Adult

Gangsters were stretched out all over the place, paying him very little attention. Weed was being smoked, cats were playing dominoes, and others were involved in intense competition with the video games. *It's a gangster's paradise*, thought Face. He leaned up against the wall as the whole scene slowly made him forget about Monica. It's unfortunate, but the reality is that violence has become so normalized in our communities that one minute a young person could literally kill someone and the next he could be playing a video game like nothing ever happened. Face was checking out how the Henchmen were rockin' their signature black bandanas. Some had them tied to the bottom half of their faces like bandits in a western flick, while others had them in their back pockets. One dude had his tied around his baldie like he was Bishop in the movie *Juice*. Everyone rocked a black rag and was throwing up signs. *These cats are bangin' for real*, thought Face. *How will I rock my rag?* He thought about it for a few minutes and then decided, *I'm gonna tie mines on my biceps like Rambo.* He was jarred out his thoughts by a brolic kid, who looked like he'd just finished doing twenty hard years up North, screwing him. Face looked away, not really wanting to get in any kind of staring match with homie. The kid had his shirt off, looking like he had overdosed on steroids. The blast on his face spoke volumes about why he was sitting there acting like he was angry at the whole damn world. When Face turned back he noticed the nickel-plated Trey-pound that sat on his lap. The kid looked like someone who could be very hazardous to Face's health.

Face refused to show any weakness. If dude was going to continue to stare at him he felt he had to give it back. The kid sat between the legs of one of the sexiest girls in the house while she braided his hair. Face couldn't stop staring at her, wondering if she was his girl. When she looked at him, Face smiled. The girl suddenly yanked homie's head, telling him to stop moving. In their exchange, Face learned that the brute's name was Tank. He stored that in his memory.

He decided not to press his luck, so he moved to another part of the house. He didn't know where, he just walked. As he passed different groups of soldiers, he received some terrifying looks. Everywhere he turned dudes were ice-grillin' him, testing his mettle. Face refused to back down, so he put on his cold killer face and gave it right back to whoever dared to look at him.

He was about to peep into one of the many bedrooms when Showtyme came strolling down the stairs with a Cuban cigar in his mouth like he was Fidel Castro himself. Face looked at him with mixed feelings as he stood there checking out his swag. Showtyme rocked a blue and gray Nautica sweat suit. Two bad chicks followed him.

Showtyme entered the living room with an air of arrogance. He walked up to Face. "What's the deal soldier? I heard you handled your business like a real G."

With that statement, the wave of guilt and sadness that Face felt came rushing back. "Yeah, I put it in, but ..." Face was about to question how he could have ordered him to do something like that, but decided against it. Instead he stood there contemplating whether or not it was really worth being in the Henchmen.

Showtyme looked around the spot and yelled, "Somebody come take care of our newest soldier. The dudes hollered and the girls blushed. "Which girl you want, my dude?"

"I'm good," Face said, looking around somewhat embarrassed.

"Let me find out you're a virgin." The entire room erupted in laughter.

Face, who was actually a virgin, lied and said, "You crazy, my dude. Me a virgin, never that."

Somebody yelled, "Yeah right."

"Who you want soldier, take your pick," Showtyme insisted.

He was forcing Face's hand. Face was in too deep to fold. He looked around the room, checking out every girl in the building. When he came

Young Adult

eye to eye with the girl who was braiding Tank's hair he pointed and said, "I'll take her."

"I see you got some good taste, soldier." Showtyme looked at the chick and said, "Kema, come take him downstairs and welcome him into the Henchmen."

Kema felt a way but didn't show it. She simply walked over to Showtyme and Face, grabbed Face's hand, and led him down to the basement. There were catcalls coming from everywhere. Face was nervous, trying to remember what he saw on the many porno videos he had watched.

B was in the background checking out the whole scene. He felt sorry for Face. The entire scenario reminded him of when he first was initiated into the Henchmen. He recalled how he had to cut a chick of a rival gang five times and an innocent dude seven times. He wondered if Face knew what he was getting into. B had been laying low ever since Showtyme popped off on him. He had been under a tremendous amount of stress; everybody was waiting to see if he was going to lay down Chase. Everybody knew Chase was official when it came to the gun game. As Face and Kema descended the stairs B glanced at Showtyme and thought, *Your day is going to come.*

****

When Kema and Face were alone she immediately turned to him and asked, "Why did you choose me?"

Face already felt extremely guilty. "We don't have to do anything. I just picked you because I thought you were the baddest chick up there," he replied.

Kema blushed. Like Face, she was young and naïve. She had run away from home seven months ago, and the Henchmen took her in and became her family. But being a part of the Henchmen was nothing like she expected. She regretted ever becoming a part of them, but it was too late to turn back. She felt trapped and just lived with it. Over the next hour she explained how she felt to Face. They sat on the bed in the basement and talked about everything. Kema told him her story and Face told her how he felt about what he did to Monica. By the time he finished they both had tears running down their faces.

Kema shocked Face and told him everything. Through the tears, she explained all that she heard. "I overheard Showtyme telling Murder and Tank how he was going to make you handle her because you knew her. I guess he felt that if you had no problem running down on her then you wouldn't hesitate to put it in when it came to a stranger."

Face couldn't believe his ears. Anger stormed him like a blizzard. His mind was tumbling downward. He looked at Kema and said, "Forget this, I don't want to be a Henchmen."

Face stood up. Kema looked surprised. "What are you going to do?"

Anger scorched his chest muscles. His eyes clenched, and he felt like he was going to pass out. Face sat back down and grabbed the side of the bed to steady himself. He looked at Kema and said, "Stay here."

Face ran upstairs. The basement door led directly into the kitchen of the house. Showtyme sat at the table counting money. Everybody turned toward Face when the door opened. Two people were at the stove cooking crack. He noticed a rubber grip shotgun lying on the counter. With deliberate steps, Face moved toward Showtyme.

Showtyme, not sensing any threat said, "I know you're not finished already, my dude?"

Face said nothing. He walked past the counter, snatched up the shotgun, and pointed it right at Showtyme. "Why you make me throw acid in Monica's face?"

Not really knowing what he was doing, Face fired a shot that reverberated throughout the house like a car bomb. The recoil of the shotgun, and Showtyme's instinctual reflexes allowed him to escape death—again. Face tried to pump another round into the chamber, but before he could his chest exploded in crimson red. Tank, who came up from behind, fired two shots from his trey-pound hitting him in his upper back. The bullets ripped through his upper torso and exited his

Young Adult

chest. Face's eyes rolled to the back of his head. His body flew forward hitting the table. Henchmen, with guns drawn, came running from every part of the house. What they saw surprised most of them. Face lay over the table with a mannequin gaze. Death had opened its arms.

Showtyme stood up, looked down at Face, and then kicked his body off the table. With a loud thud, it hit the floor. He shook his head wondering what made Face come at him. He looked at Tank and said, "Come with me."

An hour later, Showtyme had Banger and Bodyshop get rid of both Face and Kema's corpse. The cops found them three days later and just added them to the long list of senseless deaths in the 'hood.

ELEVEN

Six weeks and three days after the shooting, QB, Reyna, Chase, and Amari left the hospital together. The morning he was to be released, QB wheeled himself into Torry's room. "What's up, partner?"

"Ain't nothing, QB. I heard you're breaking out on me today?" Torry said.

"Yeah, a brother got his walking papers. I'll be back to check you though. The doctor wants me to come back through to get this cast off next week, so I'll see you then." He paused, knowing Torry was upset that he had to remain in the hospital. "You okay?"

Torry grabbed the remote and pressed mute on the television in front of his bed. "It's all good, QB. Just tired of laying up. I'm ready to get up outta here and get on my grind, especially with this seed on the way." He pulled himself up in the bed and looked at QB. "I'm scared . . . I have no idea how things are goin' to turn out with me being in this wheel chair and having a child. How can I be a father when I'm in a wheel chair?"

QB moved closer to his bed. "Listen Torry, I'm not gonna sit here and tell you I understand what you're going through ... I can only imagine. However, what I do know is that there are going to be some days where you feel scared and that's normal. When Reyna first told me

Young Adult

about her pregnancy with Nia, I must admit I was scared to death and I wasn't in a wheel chair."

"You … scared? Get out of here, QB. Stop beating me in the head."

"Yeah me. What? You think I don't get scared? Men have fears, Torry. It's just that most of us like to front and act like we don't. Remember when I told y'all about me doing time in prison?"

"Yeah."

"Well, that was a very difficult time for me. Losing a child has to be the heaviest burden a parent can carry." He turned away from Torry and looked out the window. "In fact, I still carry that weight around. I think about it all the time. How old he or she would be? What he or she would've looked like, talked like? Would she be in college? Those things still haunt me, know what I mean? When Reyna first told me about her being pregnant, I was afraid of losing another child; frightened of not being able to protect my family, and terrified of letting them down."

Torry listened intently. He never saw QB like this. When he looked closer, QB had tears in his eyes. He took a deep breath. "What you need to understand, little bruh is that none of us is immune to struggle. With change comes fear, and having a baby definitely involves change." QB smiled, thinking of having to get up all times of night to change diapers. With the back of his hand he wiped the tears running down his face. "Little bruh, no family is perfect. Even the family that you think looks perfect has its own share of struggles and challenges. So being scared is normal, and talking about it is …" He looked out the window searching for the right words, "… is all right. Actually, it's cool. Most men think we can't show our fears, but that's a bunch of bull. Real men are not afraid to show their emotions, Torry. Your feelings are legit, and you shouldn't ever feel you have to hide what you feel inside. This is something I wish I would've understood as a young man."

QB looked back out the window then turned back to Torry. "Anyway, I don't want to sound like Dr. Phil, but know that Reyna and I will be here for you and Naysia. Right now, what's important is that you

get your recovery on. It's time to put the self-pity mess behind you. Do away with those 'what if' scenarios, the excuses, it's now about reasons, and you have one hell of a reason to move forward. You feel me?"

"Yeah, I feel you. Let me ask you one last thing."

"What's that?"

Torry looked at QB. "I want you to be the Godfather of our child."

"You sure about that? Have you talked to Naysia about this?" QB answered.

"Yeah, we talked about it. She's a'ight with it."

"What about Chase? Now you know he's going to feel a way!"

"Nah, we talked too, and he's cool with being an uncle."

In his best Marlon Brando impression QB said, "In that case, son, it will be an honor to be named the Godfather." They both laughed, and then they gave each other a pound. They held their grip, connecting on another level.

QB realized at that moment that the bond between them couldn't get any stronger. *It's amazing how tragedy brings people together*, thought QB.

The rest of the morning they spoke about his recovery, his relationship, forgiveness and his ability to see light in the midst of darkness. QB wanted to make sure that he pursued his dreams in spite of what he was going through. They both made promises to one another that they intended to honor and keep. By the time QB was ready to leave, they both had tears in their eyes.

As Torry watched QB roll out, he thought, *Without brother's like QB, the youth in the 'hood would never get noticed for anything other than going to jail or dying.*

***

QB wanted to walk out of the hospital under his own power, but Reyna wasn't having it. She held his crutches as Chase pushed his wheelchair out to Amari's Lincoln Navigator. It was nice out. The sun

Young Adult

was shaking her hot, yellow behind for everyone in NYC. QB was ecstatic, yearning to use his own bathroom and lay in his own bed.

The nurses, with whom he'd exchanged so much with during the past six weeks, hovered by his side, making sure they irritated him one last time. QB learned a lot about nurses and people in general, particularly all those that had put up with his nonsense. As a patient, he had no choice but to become intimate with those who cared for him. Until this incident he never realized how nurses learned all your vulnerabilities when you are admitted to a hospital. QB had to admit he was going to miss them, but not the experience of being a patient. He would never get used to having someone help wash his body. He had never felt so vulnerable in his life; it reminded him of when he used to get stripped searched while in prison. He would never forget having to get naked, then lifting his member, having to turn around and bend over at the waist for another man to look in his body cavity all because he dared to have a visit.

As they exited the hospital, there were a lot of hugs, and QB's promise of eating right and getting rest. Amari and Chase then helped him into the truck. Because of the cast on his leg, he had to stretch out. Reyna sat up front in the passenger's seat. QB could tell that she really missed him. She kept telling him how much she loved him. He looked at her and thought, *If I had died, I hope she would've buried me knowing that my heart belonged to her.*

Once settled into his seat, QB checked out his brother's truck. It was the first time he was in it since QB drove him to purchase it. QB turned on the TV monitors mounted into the leather headrest of each seat. "What the hell is all this?" he asked. There was a stereo system that QB estimated to cost at least ten G's. "This is house money, Amari."

Amari looked at QB through his rearview mirror. *Hold up. This dude still thinks he's the older brother or better yet, my father.* "We only live once, QB, and I'm gonna live it to the fullest."

Chase, who sat next to QB, was feeling the truck. He told QB that Amari's truck was hotter than his. QB looked at him and sarcastically reminded him that he no longer had a truck. That it was somehow caught up in a shooting. Chase immediately felt guilty. Reyna turned around. "That wasn't nice," she mouthed. QB was still upset at Chase for not coming clean with him about the situation. He couldn't help but take that shot at him, even though he knew he was wrong. Seeing how bad he made Chase feel, QB turned to him, "Man that's my bad-I don't blame you for my truck or any of this. You didn't pull the trigger, you simply was trying to do what's right."

Chase nodded at him wondering, *Do you really mean that?*

Reyna saw QB clearing the air between him and Chase so she turned back around, put some music on and allowed them to talk.

When QB saw that, he tapped Chase on the leg and whispered, "What's up with this cat Showtyme? Have you heard anything that I should know?"

Chase was not going to make the same mistake twice. He peered up front and then back at QB. He then told him everything his homegirl Shawnee had told him about the initiation of Face, the throwing acid in Monica's face, and how the police found both Face and Kema in the trunk of a car a few days later in the Queen's Mall.

After hearing that, QB sat back thinking about how Showtyme tried to kill him. There was no way he was going to give him another shot. QB understood the nature of the beast and this time around he intended on positioning himself to keep Showtyme in his sights.

QB didn't talk much during the rest of the ride home. Reyna had noticed the silence, but she let him be. He was struggling with his feelings about what he should do. Easing into his seat, he tried to shake the rumbling in the pit of his stomach, but couldn't. Unfortunately, the rumbling always reared its ugly head when it came to drama. As much as he tried to block it out, his mind replayed the scene over and over again.

Young Adult

Cats just rolling up and opening fire ... What if Reyna and Nia were in the truck?

No matter how far he thought he put the streets behind him, he couldn't shake the pull of the 'hood. QB understood how sudden tears could occur in one's life, those deep knife wounds that slash through your flesh. Where your life is one thing, then it is shredded into another. It was happening again to him and this time it was taking a whole different kind of toll on him.

He looked out the window and thought about his comrade Jamal. How they used to exchange jewels with one another while they were doing time in Elmira. Jamal, who thought he was the greatest General Harlem produced, would always tell him, "In the middle of war, make sure you calculate the odds, then recalculate, and then recalculate again. And when it's all said and done, and if you're still not sure what to do, then just go with your instincts." He smiled at his man's words, thinking, *If only he knew that his advice would come to play a major role in his life.* For this is what he planned to do.

They pulled up to their Victorian style house in Uniondale, Long Island. . . As Amari pulled up in the driveway, QB noticed all the different vehicles on and around his property. He looked at Reyna, who was sitting there acting naïve. QB gave her that 'guilty as charged' look.

She smiled and then leaned over and gave him a kiss.

"You didn't have to do this, beautiful," said QB.

"Do what?" Reyna said, still trying to hide the welcome home party she had planned for him during the past week and a half.

As they exited the truck, Nia came sprinting out of the house screaming, "Daddy, daddy, daddy. My daddy's home!"

QB bent down to her level as she ran and leaped into his arms. She didn't care about the cast on his leg, or any injuries that he may have had, she simply missed him, and trusted that her daddy would catch her.

QB wrapped his big arms around her and called her by her pet name. "Hey Ladybug, I missed you, sweetie."

"I smish you too, Daddy. Give me Esh-ki-mo," Nia said, sticking her nose out toward her father's face.

QB turned toward her and they rubbed noses like seals. It was their little ritual shared only between them. Even Reyna was off limits to Eskimos.

Reyna watched QB plant kisses all over Nia's face and blow kisses into her neck, tickling her uncontrollably until she couldn't take it anymore. They were all over each other like cologne.

As they made their way into the house, QB's sister ran up to him. "What's up Fiddy Cent?" she asked.

"Why I gotta be Fifty Cents?" asked QB.

"Aren't you the one out there runnin' the streets gettin' shot and stuff?"

"I hear you, big head." QB smiled. "And you're going to be in my next video Buffy," he said, looking her up and down, checking out the way she was dressed. "You look just like one of these video vixens whose claim to fame is letting some young rapper degrade her by swiping a credit card through her bubble."

"I gotsa bubble, daddy," said Nia.

"Oh no you don't, sweetheart. Not that kind of bubble," said QB.

"That's right, Nia. You got a bubble like your auntie, and you gotta shake what your aunite gave ya," Shai said, gyrating her hips.

"Nia, don't listen to auntie Shai. She's crazy, she fell on her head when she was a little girl, okay?"

"Kay, daddy."

QB made his way to the basement where Ramel, Easy, Zeus, and True, the modern day Rat Pack, were in the corner playing poker.

QB stood back and looked at his team. He smiled. Amari headed directly over to them, flashing big faces. Of course they had a seat reserved just for him. They all raised their fist at QB, and gave him a "yeah, what's up" wave. They were there to gamble, eat, and try to bed one of Reyna's friends. After those things, they would sit down and work out the details as to how they were going to deal with who shot QB...in that order.

Easy yelled across the room, "QB, make sure you limp your butt over here when you finish getting all your hugs and kisses. You know how we do, money over stitches." The fellas laughed at Easy's silly comment. QB shrugged them off. He really didn't want to begin with them. They would want to talk about nothing but payback. Still unsure how he was going to handle the situation; one thing he did know was that he wasn't going to allow his boys to get caught up in this drama.

He and his boys had come a long way, overcoming a lot of odds. Growing up, they were known to get busy. In fact, when it came to the get busy meter, their team tilted far to the right. QB looked around, overwhelmed by all the love. He put Nia down, took in everything, and simply enjoyed the moment.

Reyna was mingling with her girlfriends. They were clowning and dancing to the neo-soul lyrics of Jill Scott. QB looked around and for a split second thought that all was good, but the harsh truth was that when it comes to gangs and gunplay, necessity was the mother of invention. QB knew he had to be extremely cautious, but more importantly prepared. He prayed he didn't have to resort to violence and risk losing all of what he had here in his home. *This is what life is truly about*, he thought.

***

By eleven, Reyna was literally pushing everybody out the house. The party was over. Shai stayed to help clean up. QB's boys finally finished gambling. True was the big winner, he got QB for a hundred and twenty. There was no telling how much Zeus lost, but from the look on his face, no one dared to ask. Because they gambled the whole day and night away they made arrangements to meet up that Friday to iron out what needed to be done. QB briefly heard each of them out during the poker game. He disagreed with all of them, but he didn't want to get into it

while Reyna and company were around. Reyna definitely had her antennae's up.

After Shai left, Reyna locked the door and punched in the alarm code. She waited for the green light, which signaled its activation and then turned around and leaned against the oak door and sighed. She looked at her husband who was sitting in his butter soft leather recliner and said, "I thought I would never get them out."

QB smiled and patted his seat, signaling her to sit down next to him. As Reyna walked over to QB she smiled, "Baby I hope you know how empty my life has been since you were gone. All I kept thinking about is what life would be like for us without you. You have to promise me that you'll never leave us again."

"I promise Queen with all that I am."

Reyna's heart picked up its pace after hearing those words. "And I promise after we take our shower I will show my king just how much I miss him." Reyna hadn't felt this good for days.

Nia was resting comfortably for the first time in weeks. She missed her father tucking her in at night and reading her favorite bedtime story. When Reyna went to check on her, it looked like she had fallen asleep with a smile on her face. Things couldn't be better.

They sat there for an hour and discussed everything that unfolded. Reyna reiterated the importance of putting his family first. She knew QB was planning to get some get-back. She made sure he knew that neither Nia nor she could go on without him. Reyna worked his paternal emotions like a potter with clay. QB listened to her every word, yet, he knew he couldn't ignore Showtyme, especially after hearing about his latest antics. QB drifted off.

Reyna snapped him out of his thoughts, "Did you hear me, QB?"

"What's that, beautiful?

"I was saying I'm going upstairs to take my shower now."

"All right, I'll be right up. I want to check to make sure the house is secured."

Young Adult

In a seductive voice she said, "Okay baby, I'll be waiting."

QB followed her with his eyes as she made her way up the stairs to their bedroom. QB grabbed the glasses and started to make them both another drink, but then decided what the hell, might as well take the whole bottle upstairs. Before he went up he went to the basement where his wall-safe was hidden. He unlocked it and pulled out his P89, loaded it, and then starting with the basement checked all the windows and doors. He knew that no matter how much he tried to make sense of all that unfolded; he knew it was not going to end until he stopped Showtyme in his tracks.

***

QB walked into their bedroom as Reyna stepped out the shower. He sat down the bottle and their glasses and jumped into the shower as she came out. By the time he got out, Reyna had a drink prepared for him, a pair of his silk boxers laid out over his chair, and some Jagged Edge playing softly on the surround sound. She was wrapped in a towel looking delicious. She walked over to him and kissed him on the lips and then helped him over to his favorite chair where he liked to get dressed. Their bedroom was exotic, something out of a magazine display. There were no electrical lights, except for the one in the walk-in closet. They had a sky roof in their bedroom, so at night the room was either lit by the moon or by candles. QB missed the intoxicating scent of the strawberry-banana candles a welcome relief compared to the antiseptic smell of a hospital.

QB sat on the bed looking at his wife as she pulled her locks into a ponytail and twisted them with both hands. The water cascaded from her locks down her smooth brown skin.

Reyna cast a sexy glance over her shoulder. "I'm going to bed. Are you going to sit there and just stare at me or would you like to join me?" she asked, keeping her back to him and letting the towel drop.

Her body was breathtaking. Needing no more encouragement, he set his drink down and followed her onto their king-size bed. He left his boxers on his chair, knowing he wouldn't need them. His eyes never left her body. Reyna grabbed some Carol's Daughter ecstasy body-oil off the armoire and lay on the bed, inviting her husband to take her to that place that no one else could, but him.

Young Adult

TWELVE

If it wasn't for bad luck, he would have none, thought QB. The week started off good. He had the cast taken off and was back at work. Yet, here he was standing outside his parole officer's office, scared at the possibility of being violated. He fought back his fears and made his way up to his office.

When QB sat across from his parole officer he noticed handcuffs sitting on the desk. The P.O. acted busy, he was looking down at some paperwork, intentionally taking his time. The silence was killing QB. After a few minutes QB watched his parole officer open up his desk drawer, grabbed a pen, and finally turned his attention to QB.

"Mr. Banks, do you know that one of the conditions of your parole is no police contact?"

"Yes, I do Mr. White, but….."

His parole officer cut him off. "If it was up to me, you'd be back in a cell. You're lucky it's not my call. But, I'm telling you I will be looking for a reason to do just that. And when I do—I promise you that I will escort you back to jail myself. Am I clear?"

"Mr. White, I want you to…" Again he cut QB off.

"Mr. Banks, I don't care what you have to say. I have the police report right here. What you need to know is that there will be no more breaks. You are back on bi-weekly until further notice. Do you understand?"

Biting his lip, to refrain from saying something that would send him straight to jail, QB looked at his P.O. and said "Yes I understand you clearly."

"Good! Now take this and give me some urine."

As QB made his way to the bathroom, he thought about the message his P.O. was sending. That he would always be guilty in his eyes. After providing the urine, QB left. Once outside, QB stood on the sidewalk, in the middle of the chilling December air and thought, *No matter what I do, if it's positive, it will never be etched in the memory of others with nearly the same permanence as doing something wrong. My past is always going to haunt me.*

Many of the kids at U-turn used the same rationale as to why trouble always seemed to follow them. Most of them believed they failed because those around them didn't nurture the good in them. Instead, they only pointed out the bad. So the popular thinking among the youth became forget it, I might as well do this. It's expected of me.

QB shook his head as he made his way to the replacement truck that the dealership had provided. He abruptly stopped, noticing another one of those signs posted all over NY, on billboards, buses and overpasses telling people to: "Report any possible terrorist activity—if you see something, say something!" QB knew that the message was a result of 9/11, but applied even more to the young, local, so-called black terrorist. Before he opened the truck's door, QB looked up to the sky and noticed a dark cloud hovering directly over him. *How fitting*, QB thought as he jumped in and went to meet his boys.

***

"Son, make sure you keep your eyes on the entrance, I know the boy, Chase is in there. I got a call from one of my chicks who goes to this wack program," B said to his little man, Pitch. They were sitting across

Young Adult

the street from U-Turn in a stolen black Mazda RX7. B had his burner on his lap as he rolled a blunt.

"Yo, I'm gonna hit Banger and Nitty on their cell just in case these lames try to mob-up," said Pitch.

As he sealed the dutch, B said, "I got this. I'm pushing this dude's cap back. It's time for me to show y'all how to do this. Because Banger and Nitty messed up the first hit, I have to put in this work. All I need you to do is make sure no one creeps up on me from behind. Can you handle that?"

"I got you, my dude."

B passed him the blunt. "Here get your head right."

After they blew the blunt, B looked and scanned the area making sure the police were not in sight. About twenty minutes later, Pitch furiously began tapping B on his side. "My dude, look! There go that lame, Chase, right there," he said, pointing across the street.

B snapped out of his high. "Where?" he said.

"Right there," Pitch pointed to a kid who was standing in front of a red brick building. Two other guys were with him. "Look, he's the one with the black fitted."

"I see him, my dude," B said. Thinking about escaping, again he looked around trying to calculate how many people were actually strolling back and forth. Picking up his glock nine-millimeter and cocking it, he said, "You ready to run down on these lames?"

"You already know soldier," said Pitch, gripping his own nine.

As they stepped out the car, B pulled down his skully and tied his bandana around his face. B's look told Pitch to move in the direction that would allow him to come up on Chase's blind side. Queens Boulevard was an eight lane traffic nightmare, four lanes in each direction. Yellow cabs weaved in and out of traffic recklessly. B needed to time his crossing just right. The last thing he wanted to do was to alarm Chase before he was in range.

As the trio stood in front of U-Turn, Chase's cell phone rang. He flipped the phone opened and just when he raised it to his ear, before he even said hello, he saw a figure coming at him with a raised gun. Pushing his friend closest to him out of the way, the burner exploded, sending slugs screaming past their bodies. Chase instinctively reached for his hammer but realized he didn't have it. QB made sure they all knew if they brought any weapons to U-Turn it was grounds for instant dismissal.

Chase and his two classmates ran low back into U-Turn. B followed them into the building. Pitch ran behind B. He cursed B out under his breath because he didn't allow him to get off a shot. *B started shooting too early*, he thought.

Chase was yelling for everybody to get down. Students, seeing them retreat back into the building, began scrambling for cover. Most of them heard the shots, and then saw B and Pitch enter the building pointing their guns. The girls screamed. The guys, seeing their friends in danger, automatically began scheming on how they could help their boys. Chaos erupted. Teachers and counselors were scared. Many were shocked by the gunplay. Chase and his friends split up once inside the building. The positive energy of U-Turn suddenly turned dark. A teacher immediately called 9-1-1 and reported what was happening.

B told Pitch to check the room in the opposite direction. He walked down the other end of the hallway, pointing his hammer at everything that moved. He was upset at himself for missing Chase the first time. They searched a few rooms, looking under desks, and inside closets, turning over everything not nailed down.

When B realized they'd been in there too long he turned around and screamed at Pitch, "Yo, let's roll out."

The students spotted Pitch making his way out the door. These were Chase and Torry's road-dogs, and they were wired, hyped, and itching to pop off. They felt compelled to act. It was a pull stronger than gravity. Raised in 'hoods that told them to never let others violate. It was all about pride. And for them, even though they were beginning to get their lives back on track, U-Turn was their territory and Torry and Chase were their homies. Their inability to back down was unchangeable as their skin color. If one of their boys was in trouble, then they were all in trouble.

As Pitch backed up toward the doors, he looked around. Students were emerging from their hiding place. Chase was in the cut waiting for a chance to leap into action. One of the students beat him to the punch. Brick, who stood about six foot two, crept up behind Pitch and dead armed him. Pitch's head hit the concrete wall from the impact of the punch. His gun flew from his grip as he fell to the ground. The rest of the students pounced. After witnessing the beating they were handing out, a few of the female students began yelling, "That's enough." They were kicking his face like soccer players shooting penalty shots in the World Cup. Pitch's blood was all over the floor and wall. One of the students picked up the gun and said, "Let's shoot this fool." The only thing that stopped them was Ms. Franklin, the G.E.D. teacher. She was well-respected among the students.

"That's enough. Please stop! I'm begging you," she pleaded. They were giving him an old-fashion beat-down. Pitch's face swelled up as if he had hives. He had a long gash on his forehead. His mouth was bleeding and his lips were swollen. Ms. Franklin flung herself directly into the melee. Diving on top of Pitch, praying they wouldn't kick her.

Seeing this, Chase immediately intervened. He pulled Brick off the kid and told the rest of the students to be easy. Pitch lay on the floor leaking. He looked dead. His hands lay at his sides. He was knocked out. The only sign of him being alive was that his chest slightly rose up and down. Ms. Franklin literally saved his life. She looked up at her students, and then locked eyes with Chase who started to explain how Pitch came up in U-Turn with a gun.

Ms. Franklin cut him off, "I was here Mr. Matthews. I saw what happened." She shook her head. "This has got to stop. You young men are doing nothing but killing your own selves. Can't you all see the big picture? This is what they want . . . they want you all to kill one another." She paused looking down at Pitch. When she looked back up she continued, "We talk about this all the time, but you all choose to continue to put yourself in positions to become statistics, collateral damage. What's wrong with y'all?" she asked with a pleading tone.

Chase looked down at the ground, embarrassed by the sadness etched on Ms. Franklin's face, her sadness made him feel extremely guilty. He knew she was right. Yet, he was caught up; it felt like he was literally being pushed into the arms of violence. Being in a gang had him in a chokehold that he couldn't escape from. Chase walked over to the student who snatched up the gun that belonged to Pitch and took it. Chase wiped it down with his shirt and slid it into his waist.

The sounds of police sirens pulling up outside fueled Chase's desire to run, he looked down at Ms. Franklin who was cradling Pitch. He walked over to her and pulled out the gun, making sure he got all his fingerprints off, he handed it to her. She took it from him. They exchange knowing looks and then she told him to take Brick and get out of there. When they broke out, the other students began straightening out the mess that B and Pitch caused.

Outside, B was struggling to get across Queens Boulevard. It was just his luck that cars were zooming back and forth on both sides of the street. Flashing lights were not lighting up the place. Police seemed to be everywhere. Cops were pulling up by the second. As he slowly jogged across the boulevard, B thought, Pitch better hurry up. He turned back just in time to see someone from U-Turn pointing him out to a police officer. He noticed the officer grab a hand held radio and say something into it. B started to run full speed. A white Volkswagen came to a screeching halt. The driver had to slam on the brakes to avoid hitting him when he ran directly in front of her car. Horns blared as B continued across the street. With about fifteen feet to go, a SUV had to swerve hard to the right to avoid smashing him head on. The truck left

Young Adult

tire marks on the boulevard that was at least fourteen feet long. When the vehicle finally came to a stop, the man sitting in the passenger seat leaned out the window and yelled at B. Enraged, B spun and pointed his gun at the man. Both occupants of the SUV immediately ducked.

B made it to the Mazda just as detective Powell pulled up on the scene. She noticed the commotion on the opposite side of the boulevard, spotting the passengers of the SUV looking toward the black male who had just hopped into a car. Detective Powell instantly jumped out her vehicle and headed toward the commotion. Her instincts told her everything she needed to know. She pulled out her police-issued nine millimeter and ran full sprint toward the possible suspect.

B panicked because he couldn't find the screwdriver needed to start up the car. He reached under the seat, felt the tip of it, but couldn't grab it. He jumped out the car so he could retrieve it, but when he hopped out he noticed a female cop sprinting toward him with her gun drawn. Without hesitation, B immediately took off.

Uniformed police had cordoned off both ends of the block. B noticed squad cars everywhere. He couldn't believe this was going down; he couldn't go to jail. His adrenaline mixed with his fear caused him to run even faster. Seeing cops at the end of the block, B decided to cut between restaurants and head for the fence.

Detective Powell was on his back, a former high school track star, who prided herself on her ability to catch assailants. She radioed in her location and where she thought the suspect was heading.

Two blocks away from the scene Detective Hudson turned his Dodge Charger down the back streets anticipating the escape route of the suspect. B kept turning around trying to gauge the distance between him and Detective Powell. He didn't realize that every time he turned around she gained another step on him. He thought about dumping on her, but then reality set in, and he realized he was not ready for a cop body. The thought alone made him throw down his gun. As luck would have it, it landed in a place where the cops would never find it.

Detective Hudson spotted somebody running to his left. He backed up the Charger, and thought, *That's him*. He was not jumping out chasing him. He hated running, plus he had bad knees. He spun his vehicle toward B. The engine roared as he floored the gas. He then radioed in his location. Detective Powell hearing his call headed in that direction on foot. She had guessed wrong at the last backyard B ran through.

B saw the oncoming charger a split second too late. Hudson side swiped him, causing B to fly a few feet in the air and fall to the ground. Amazingly, B tumbled over a few times, but got right back up and took off. Hudson thought, *I can't believe this*. He slammed his gears into park, threw open the door, and gave chase. B hit the back yards, gaining at least a twenty yard lead on the detective. Hudson could feel the rust in his knees. If he had any chance of apprehending the suspect he needed them to warm up in a hurry.

B hit another backyard, running through a pile of raked leaves and headed toward a tall wooden fence that separated two homes. B leapt over the fence like a cat. Hudson thought, *Aah man*. He considered barreling right through the wooden separation, but decided to give the leap a try. Picking up speed he clumsily jumped up, hooked his beefy paw on top, and swung his leg over. His own agility surprised him. He jumped down just in time to see B leap over another wooden fence and head into another backyard. He took off across the yard, but this time he knew there was no way he would be able to jump over, so he put his shoulder down and ran right through the wooden divider. The impact caused a lot of noise, alarming the owners of the surrounding homes. They immediately called the police. The detective hit the fence so hard he was unable to keep his balance and fell. As he rolled over, he instinctively snatched his gun from his holster. Hudson surveyed the yard. He saw no one, but sensed the suspect was there hiding. Bent down, and with his gun outstretched, Hudson moved in a circular motion scanning everything. He noticed the garage, a barbeque grill; car

Young Adult

in the driveway; a swing set; and three Rubbermaid garbage containers. Hudson stood up. His senses heightened. Pointing his gun toward the containers, he inched closer and kicked the bottom of each one. He then backed up, positioned himself and said, "Come up out of that garbage container before I send these slugs in there to get you."

B couldn't believe it, *Why did I stop and hide?* he thought. He heard Detective Hudson tell him a second time to come up out of the container. B quickly rationalized with himself that he didn't do anything. He had no weapon on him, no one at U-Turn saw his face, and if they did, what could they actually say? *That I turned over a few tables. I'm good*, he thought.

A woman opened her back door, and the detective waved her back in. He showed her his shield. She immediately slammed the door shut and ducked behind her kitchen counter.

"Don't make me tell you again. Get out of that container!" Hudson knew he was in there. He had a good police eye and noticed things that were out of place, and one of the containers was missing the black plastic Hefty bag that spilled under the top of the other green containers. As Hudson started inching toward the containers the top of the first container began to slowly rise.

"That's it, move slowly. Put your hands in the air. I want to see both of them," the detective yelled. B stood with his hands fully extended toward the sky. "Now turn around and place your hands on the side of the house nice and slow. There you go." When B placed his hands flat on the wall, Hudson came up behind him and put his arm flat against the suspect's back. He grabbed one of his arms and pulled it behind his back and into his cuffs and then he followed with the second. Once secured, Hudson yanked B from out of the container, and made him lay on the floor face down, spread his legs, and then he searched him for weapons. Finding none on his person, he searched the containers. During the search he heard squad cars pull up out front. When the patrol officers entered the backyard, he produced his shield and then instructed them to comb the back yard and surrounding area for a possible discarded weapon.

***

Smiling, Hudson strolled into the Unit's headquarters with B in handcuffs. He was walking with that 'I got the big catch' grin on his face. He looked like he'd won the lottery. Detective Powell watched Hudson from her desk, not believing he had the nerve to swagger in there like he caught the suspect all by himself.

Hudson shoved B pass dozens of black and white wanted posters of gang members that hung on the wall in the office.

Byron Williams, better known as B, was nervous and scared. He had heard all about the things the Unit did during their interrogations. He didn't know what to expect, but the one thing he did know, he had no Sammy the Bull in him.

Because B proved to have some rabbit in him, Hudson had requested full jewelry; handcuffs, and shackles with a chain that connected him to a ring mounted to the floor. The interrogation room was dreary. An old wooden desk sat in the center of the room with an outdated computer on a desk in the corner next to some old file cabinets. B stared at the two-way mirrored window, wondering who was looking at him on the other side. He had yet to request an attorney, giving the detectives all the leeway they needed. B, like most criminals, knew very little about his constitutional rights, which made law enforcement jobs that much easier. And even though he had been told numerous times by the OG's that ignorance of the law is no excuse in the game, he knew the best thing for him was simply to shut up. If truth be told, the police, the courts, and all those paid to protect society understood that most suspects were unaware of their rights, and laws. The truth of the matter, a lot of the success of the system depends largely on a criminal's ignorance.

Lieutenant Delaney, along with Hudson, and Powell watched B squirm through the two-way mirror. They were confident that it wouldn't take them long to make him cave in and spill the beans. They were counting on it, for this was another shot for them to penetrate the Henchmen. They wanted Showtyme, and had been investigating his street-army for months. They were piling evidence in all the shootings, killings and drug activity that he was involved in. Unfortunately, Showtyme managed to stay outside their reach. Most of the soldiers in his army would rather face death than testify against him. The fear he instilled in the Henchmen was unprecedented. This came as a surprise to the Unit because most gang members couldn't wait to talk. After the latest incident involving the acid thrown in a girl's face and the double murder of the young kids', Face and Kema, the Unit was committed to bringing him down. He had become their primary target. Confidential informants were helping them with some things, but to make a case against him that would stick and put him away for his natural life, they needed more.

For the first hour, Delaney played the role of the bad cop. Hudson took the second hour and he played the race card; black cop, and the one that was going to look out for the little brother. By hour number three both Delaney and Hudson were pissed off with a capital P.

This little piece of crap thinks he's America's biggest gangster, thought Delaney.

After three consecutive hours in the dimly lit interrogation room, B was proving to be a tough nut to crack. He was given fifteen-minute breaks between sessions, escorted to the bathroom, and even offered something to eat and smoke. Delaney smacked him upside his head during the third trip to the bathroom. Roughing up suspects was an unwritten tactic many officers relied on to get confessions. Most officers reasoned that it was much better to violate the criminal's right instead of letting him out and he goes and commits more crime. By the fourth hour detective Powell asked Delaney to let her get a shot at the suspect. She really wanted to be the one to get the confession, especially after Hudson's little performance earlier.

"What do we have on him now?" asked the Lieutenant.

Hudson, waving his arms in frustration said, "We got crap. Absolutely nothing, nada." He looked at Detective Powell. "A criminal trespass, at best a stolen vehicle and the fact he took off running. We cannot find the gun he discarded … some kid probably picked it up and will accidentally shoot himself in the coming weeks. Nobody at U-Turn could identify him from the photo arrays, so we have jack, Mitch."

"Give me a shot, Lieutenant?" repeated Powell.

Delaney sighed, threw his pad on his cluttered desk, and nodded to Powell, "Work your magic. Get us something."

Detective Amanni Powell was a woman who looked like she belonged on Tyra Banks' America's Next Top Model instead of in a Gang Intelligence Unit. She had joined the police force six years ago and already made detective. Delaney had pulled her aboard the Unit because of her toughness, but most importantly because of her smarts. Detective Powell was one of the brightest detectives in his Unit. He also knew her thick hips, full lips, and perky breasts played a major role in her ability to get suspects to talk. Like her fellow officers, most suspects were male, and when she walked into the room the only thing they saw were tits and butt, a major mistake.

She stepped into the interrogation room, and stood behind the chair opposite B. Giving a fake yawn, she then stretched her arms wide, feeling the tension and frustration in the small room. Looking at B slumped in his chair, she thought, *I'm going to make you crack.*

He straightened up when he saw Powell staring at him. He thought to himself, *They're sending a woman in here to do the job that they couldn't do. This is a joke.* He knew the game, and was going to play it until he completed what he needed to do. Already he had made up his mind as to what he was going to do, something that should've been done a long time ago.

She pulled out the seat and sat across from him, remaining silent as he undressed her with his eyes. After a few minutes she said, "As you can see I'm different, I'm not your typical cop."

B smiling at her. "That's real talk; you're definitely better looking than them two clowns who were just in here," B said.

"I certainly hope that's true. But they look at me different around here because I don't pee standing up." She picked up her pen and began twirling it in her hand. "Like you, I have to work twice as hard in order to get any props."

B was thinking to himself, *Listen to this chicken head, she really thinks she could spin a fella with this woe is me bull crap* He looked at her and said, "I hear you."

She took notice of his cavalier attitude. "I'm really tired Mr. Williams and I don't want to draw this out. I really need to get home so I can get in the shower and get some much needed rest. Know what I'm sayin'?" she said, needing B to see her as a woman more than a cop.

After twenty minutes of questioning, it didn't seem to be working, other than the lust filled looks he shot at her. B said as little to her as he did to Delaney and Hudson. *It's time to plan-b him*, she thought, reaching back, pushing her breasts out as she scratched her back, giving Delaney the signal.

The lieutenant came charging in the room red-faced and angry. "It's my turn. I got this Detective Powell. Your time is up."

Turning toward Delaney, and placing one hand on her hip, Powell asked, "Are you crazy, lieutenant? He doesn't want to talk to you."

"What the hell do I care what he wants?" Delaney asked. "We got a dead ten-year-old girl, an eighteen year-old young lady who was disfigured from acid, two thirteen-year-olds who were shot dead and a gang war that are taking lives with each passing hour. You think I care what this piece of crap wants. His behind is going away for the rest of his life just like the rest of them."

B jolted forward, causing the cuffs to rip into his wrist. "That's bull. I don't know nothing about any of that stuff you're talkin' 'bout."

The lieutenant hauled off and smacked him like a pimp upset because his broad came up short. B would have flown over the desk if he were not shackled to the ring in the floor. He tasted the blood that now trickled from his mouth. He puffed up his chest, and then smiled.

Detective Powell raised her voice. "You're interrupting me, Lieutenant. B and I aren't through here," she said, using his street handle. Until that moment, she had only called him Mr. Williams. The idea was for her to develop a rapport with him and isolate both Delaney and Hudson as far away as possible. She turned to B, "Are you okay, B? Do you mind if I call you B?"

He looked up at her and nodded no.

"If B wants to talk to you instead . . ." She intentionally left her remark hanging there.

B took the bait and jumped right in. "Nah, I don't have anything to say to him," he said.

"There you go," Powell said to Delaney. She then walked over toward the door. "Can you excuse us—you'll have to just wait your turn."

"Come on, Powell, you're not going to get nothing out of him. Let me have a few more moments with him. I sense B and I are on our way to some real progress," Delaney said, rubbing his fist and peering at B.

"I doubt that, Lieutenant, there's the door if you don't mind." She glanced at B who was now grinning. *Right where I want him*, she thought.

To all their surprise, two hours later they fingerprinted and hauled B's butt off to Central booking in Kew Gardens. The detectives were frustrated; they couldn't believe he didn't crack. As much as they hated to, they had to give B some props, a little respect. A suspect who stuck to the code of silence was rare. They knew it was far from over. They still had the courts. They would keep trying to apply pressure on Mr.

Williams, but until then, Delaney told his partners to go home and get some rest. Later that evening, he and Hudson found themselves making their fifth pot of coffee while debating as to whether or not the stop snitching campaign was actually working.

THIRTEEN

QB pulled up to Nautica Mile off Merrick Boulevard in Freeport, Long Island. It was Reyna and his favorite chill-out spot. He was meeting his team there to discuss what they needed to do with Showtyme. As he walked into the restaurant he noticed Zeus with an array of fish dishes spread out before him. Easy and Amari were gambling at the miniature basketball game. They were up to their usual, betting on who can make the most shots. Ramel had a blond, blue-eyed snow bunny posted up kicking game to her like he was David Beckham. From the look on her face she was just eating it all up.

QB approached Zeus and gave him a pound as his cell began ringing. It was his assistant Ashanti calling from U-Turn. She explained everything that had unfolded. QB couldn't believe how things were falling apart. His facial expression and his part of the conversation told Zeus and the rest of his team that what was being said on the phone was serious. He flipped his phone shut and just gazed out at the boats in the water along the pier. The whole crew stood around him waiting for him to say something; they could see the stress eating away at their boy.

Images of having to take a life momentarily flashed through QB's mind. He immediately pushed the thought out of his head. "Check it, I have to head back to my job. Something happened there and I'm needed, so can we meet tonight at my place around ten?" asked QB.

"What about Reyna?" True asked.

QB didn't bother to comment. He just looked at True. They all knew Reyna was a no-press. QB then turned to Easy. "E, I need you to come with me. I'll see the rest of you tonight.

Zeus said, "Q, this bull crap has to end. Either we're going to shut this cat down or ..."

"Zeus, let's talk tonight—all right? Right now I have to get back to my office."

They looked at him and Easy head out the door. All of them were ready to deal with Showtyme. Tonight, they would definitely make that clear.

***

Showtyme was relaxing inside one of his many apartments in LeFrak. He was holed up with Cherokee, a Puerto Rican beauty, with long, straight hair that reached the middle of her back. To most dudes she was more than a dime, she was a dub. Her body made J-Lo look anorexic. Shawnee, who was also with him, was considered Showtyme's ride or die chick. She was a brown-skinned pigeon-toed diva packed in a 5'2' inch frame and resembled Trina. Most people on first glance perceived these women as nothing more than eye candy, but they were more dangerous than a poisonous snake in the Garden of Eden.

They were getting their freak on. Sweat glistened off their bodies, as they slithered all over each other like circus contortionist in the small shower space of the master bedroom. To Showtyme, all the women in the Henchmen belonged to him. Out of necessity, they all accepted that position. Showtyme, like most of the Henchmen, viewed women as nothing more than sexual objects for their pleasuring. Cherokee and Shawnee, however, were more than that; they happened to be his most loyal soldiers. Showtyme jumped out of the shower when he heard someone banging on the front door. He slid into his sweats lying next to a .357 Magnum that Cherokee snatched up and quickly loaded. Cherokee was known to clap something without hesitation. The chick had heart. Showtyme grabbed a Mac-11 semi-automatic, sub-machine gun from under the mattress as he made his way to the front door. Cherokee and Shawnee, with water still dripping off their bodies were right on his heels, ready to shoot and kill. Showtyme's apartments, no matter what it was used for was neatly furnished and equipped with expensive gadgets. They each took a strategic position in front of the door. Cherokee stood on one side and Showtyme on the other.

He nodded at Shawnee who then asked in a sinless voice, "Who is it?"

"Yo, where's Showtyme?"

"Who?" Shawnee said, feigning ignorance.

"It's Banger. Open the damn door! It's a blackout. I need to see Showtyme." Black out was a code name for major heat from the police.

Shawnee looked at Showtyme for further instructions. He nodded and she began unlocking the door. Banger charged into the spot and was greeted by heavy artillery.

Startled, Banger said, "What the hell is this?"

Showtyme lowered his Mac. "Why you banging down my door like you're crazy? And how did you know I was here, soldier?"

Banger didn't answer because he was stuck looking at Cherokee standing there in front of him bow-legged and naked. She had the .357 Magnum aimed at the center of his chest. He thought to himself, *This is the second time this crazy broad fronted on me. I gotta check her.* He turned to Showtyme. "Tell Pocahontas to put that hammer down, before I smack her silly."

Showtyme motioned to Cherokee. She lowered the weapon to her side. She stared at Banger with hatred. Her legs were still spread apart drawing his attention. Banger blew her a kiss and then turned to Showtyme and explained what went down with B and Pitch.

Showtyme showed very little emotion, but inside he was steaming, boiling beyond the point of no return. Fed up, he looked at Banger and said, "Where the hell are those fools?"

"Pitch is at St. Johns, and B is at the 109th."

"Listen up, if they are placed under arrest I want them both bailed out immediately. In fact, Shawnee, go with Banger down to Shapiro's office and give him this," he said, digging into his pockets and coming out with stacks of cash. The stacks consisted of all big face hundreds. He handed Banger about five stacks and then added, "I'll call him when I get a chance. But for now, Shawnee, you do the talking. Banger, you fill her in on all that you know about what this clown did. Then I want you to round up the generals and meet me at the trap house at nine. You got that? When Banger shook his head yes, Showtyme turned and walked back into the bedroom.

Cherokee was the only one that followed him. He sat on the edge of the bed in deep thought. She threw the trey-pound down and crawled up on the bed, kneeling behind him and started massaging the tension from his shoulders.

Even though it felt good, Showtyme took the clip out of his Mac. He looked down at the gun and then slammed the clip back in the weapon. This caused Cherokee to jump. He got up and told her to get dressed. Though surprised, she complied without question. Showtyme had never done that before. He was no longer in the mood. All that was on his mind is the fact that the time had come to deal with both B and Chase, once and for all. It was time for them both to come up missing.

***

An hour and half after leaving Nautica Mile, QB stormed into U-Turn. He had Easy take the truck around the back of the building and wait for him there. QB made his way up to his office. His assistant, Ashanti was waiting for him. QB was Nike'd out and Ashanti's eyes widened, surprised to see him dressed like that. Usually, QB came to work suited and booted. He stayed in tailored-made suits, getting his Steve Harvey on.

Ashanti didn't question him; the questionable look she gave asked, *Where are you coming from?* As he made his way into his office, Ashanti began reading off what seemed like a hundred messages. She followed him, reminding him of his deadlines, the proposals that were due, and the upcoming budget that he needed to look over. She then explained the latest news in regards to what unfolded a few hours ago, and how Ms. Franklin didn't report Chase, or any of the students to the police. She told him that Ms. Franklin got rid of the gun the kid, Pitch had on him before he was taken to the hospital, and as a result he was only arrested for trespassing and assault. She did let him know that he got the crap beaten out him.

QB made a mental note to talk to Ms. Franklin about everything. He looked at Ashanti and was amazed at how organized she was. He didn't know what he would do without her. He was definitely going to give her a raise during the next budget.

QB took out his phone and gave it to her telling her to place all his meetings and deadlines into his phone for him. "Where's Mr. Casey?" he asked.

"He's in his office. He told me to call him as soon as you get in. He's furious, he's called four or five times in the last hour."

Okay, I will call him in a second. Right now I need you to do me a favor. First, I want you to go down to the gym by yourself ... I need you to help Easy put the stuff I have out back inside of the gym. Don't get anybody to help you; he knows exactly how I want it. When you two have everything set up, I want you to bring all the students into the gym. Is Chase still here?"

"Yeah, he never left, he hid upstairs."

"All right, I want every last one of them in the gym in fifteen minutes. If any of the teachers or counselors has problems with that tell them to two-way me." QB paused and looked down at Ashanti's high-heeled shoes, "Ashanti, if you have your flats or sneakers, you better put them on. You're going to need them."

She looked at him with squinted eyes. "What are you up to Mr. Banks?"

"Please, I just need you to help Easy out while I go see Casey."

"I got you, Mr. Banks."

"And don't forget, I want every student in that gym in fifteen minutes."

In an attempt to lighten the mood, she clicked her heels, saluted him and said, "Sir, yes, sir."

With a stern expression of frustration, he said "Listen, this is not the time for games, Ashanti."

"Daaanng, Mr. Banks, loosen up. We're all upset at what's happening. Don't take it out on me," she said as she turned to go meet Easy.

QB sat behind his desk. He grabbed his two-way, took a deep breath, and then headed to his supervisors' office.

***

By the time QB walked into the gym, it was buzzing with curiosity and nervousness. The students were lined up in six rows of twelve. They were standing in line like they were in boot camp. QB scanned the entire gym, particularly paying attention to where Easy was standing. Because next to him, sitting there on the floor was something covered up with mover blankets. *Whatever it is, it's big,* thought, one of the teachers. QB nodded to Easy and then walked over to the teachers. He whispered something to them and they exchanged a few words. He smiled and then he turned his attention to the students.

He walked over to Ashanti who was standing near Easy, looking exhausted. He knew she was going to kill him for having her do what he asked of her. He saluted her, and then winked. As mad as she was with him, she couldn't help but smile. She knew QB was apologizing for snapping at her earlier.

All eyes in the gym were on QB as he made his way to the head of the lines. The way he gritted his teeth and looked out at the students, let them know that he was beyond upset. The students knew when he was like that someone was getting kicked out of the program. QB pulled his T-shirt from out of his sweatpants, and then bent down to tie his

Marbury's. He stood up and took a step toward the students, looking at the sea of black and brown faces. Then slowly he began walking down each row. Most of the students refused to make eye contact with him. When he got to Chase, QB stopped. "Mr. Matthews, step out," he requested. With a 'what's up' look on his face, Chase stepped out of line. He looked QB in his eyes for a second, and then put his head down. Some of the students began whispering among themselves. QB looked around, and then yelled, "Did I tell any of you to speak?"

QB then turned his attention back to Chase. "Come with me, Mr. Matthews." Chase followed QB to the front of the gym. He watched QB snatch the blankets off what they all discovered were two caskets. With the help of Easy he separated them by a few feet. They sat parallel to one another. Chase stood off to the side not knowing what to do. QB opened the top to both caskets. "Mr. Matthews, get in. Let's see how one of these caskets look on you." he said.

"What?" Chase asked, not knowing what else to say.

QB stepped right up to Chase, looked directly into his eyes that glinted like fire coals. "Did I ask you to speak, Mr. Matthews? What I want you to do …" He paused as he walked over to one of the caskets. "… is get in this casket."

Chase didn't move. A struggle between whether he should do it or not was unfolding in his head. Unfortunately, his ego defeated his sense of reasoning. He felt QB was trying to punk him in front of everyone. "Why you trying to play me, Mr. Banks?"

"Mr. Matthews, I'm telling you for the last time, get in that casket!" QB said with a booming voice.

Chase looked at QB and stood there not really thinking about the situation in its entirety. "No. I'm not getting in a casket until I'm dead," he said.

"No?" QB stared at him, giving him a chance to change his mind.

"Mr. Matthews, get your property, get out, and don't come back without my permission. QB grabbed his two-way and radioed for security in case he needed an escort.

Chase took a few steps, and then stopped. He turned and looked at QB and was about to say something then thought better of it. He knew better to challenge him out in the open, yet he still felt the need to get in one last word. "I'm out, you can take this program and shove it."

"An ego trip will get you nowhere, Mr. Matthews except on a bus headed up-north." As he exited the gym, everybody followed Chase with their eyes.

Ms. Franklin wiped tears from her own eyes. She hated losing any of the kids. The tension in the gym was on high. QB watched Chase walk away. It hurt to have to kick him out the program, but the group was much more than any one individual.

QB now had the student's undivided attention. "Mr. Cameron, step out." One of QB's many rules were to address each student in the program by their last name. Since the students had to refer to staff by their last names, he felt it would only be right if it went both ways. So he and all staff addressed the kids by their last names as well. Plus, he wanted the kids to know what it felt like to be addressed in a professional manner, something other than their street-names or street-tags. QB knew life was about an image, and constantly reminded them that, in the real world, they would more than likely be addressed by their last names, especially if they were to become successful.

Brick stepped out of formation. QB walked over to him, stopped, and then said, "Go get in one of the caskets."

Brick looked around to see what kind of response he would get from his boys. He paused momentarily.

"Mr. Cameron, what's the matter, you scared?" Those five words had gotten more youth in trouble than any other words in the entire dictionary. QB knew those words would propel him to move, to either get in, or get out. Like Chase, he had to make a decision. "You weren't scared to punch a man who was armed with a gun, but you're scared to get in a casket. That doesn't make sense to me, it just don't add up. Now, either get in the casket or walk out them doors."

Brick looked at QB and then headed to the casket. He hesitated, and then got in and laid down.

QB, pleased with Brick, spun and continued walking up and down the rows of students. A nervous energy was traveling with each step that QB took. "Ms. Ramirez, step out." Everybody looked at her.

She put her hand to her mouth, looked at QB, and said in her Dominican accent, "What did I do?"

Since you found something funny, I want you to go get in the other casket. She pointed to her newly done Shirley Temple hairstyle. "What about my hair, Mr. Banks? I just got it done, I don't want to mess it—"

QB cut her off. "I don't care about your hair, Ms. Ramirez. I'm concerned about your life."

Ms. Ramirez rolled her eyes, and then headed to the casket. She wasn't going to front; she couldn't afford to get kicked out of the program. Playing with QB was the last thing she was going to do. "Trust me, you're going to be just as beautiful when you get out as when you get in," QB said for good measure. Everybody let out a much needed laugh.

Then QB walked up to the caskets and stood in the middle of both. He made sure both students were tucked in nice and neat and then he closed the tops. The counselors and teachers looked at QB like he was crazy. QB paid them no mind and faced the rest of the students. He wiped sweat from his forehead. "I now want everybody to put your hands out in front of you, palms up." He waited until he saw the student's arms outstretched. "Now, I want you to look down at your hands and tell me what you see?"

Nobody said anything at first. QB repeated, "What do you all see?"

"Skin," one of the students yelled.

"Yes, there's skin. What else?" asked QB.

Another student shouted, "Nothing."

One kid said, "Dirt."

QB looked at him. "Then you need to wash your hands, Mr. Peterson." This got another laugh, breaking the ice forming within the gym. "Ms. Francis, what do you see?" asked QB.

Somebody yelled out, "That she needs some lotion for her ashy hands."

She turned to the kid and said, "I see this,"—and gave him her middle finger.

"Ms. Francis, I asked you ... what do you see? Don't pay anybody else any mind," said QB.

"Lines, Mr. Banks, I see a bunch of lines, and that I need to get my nails done."

"That's cute, Ms. Francis." QB began walking back and forth, row to row. "What you should see . . ." He stopped and let the thought linger in the air. "... is your future, a future that you control. However..." He paused, searching for exactly the right words to say. "... a future that can come to an abrupt end if you continue to make stupid decisions." He walked in between the rows, and then added, "Mr. Harris is, at this very moment laid up in the hospital partially paralyzed from bullets that were not meant for him." He stopped dead in his tracks so the seriousness of his words could resonate in their minds. QB suddenly walked back to the front of the students, peeled off his T-shirt, and threw it to Easy. The females gasped at seeing the scar that remained from his operation. All eyes were glued to the wound that ran from his chest to the bottom of his stomach. The scar was dark and ugly, like a train track embedded in his skin. He walked back and forth, making sure everybody got a good look at it. He showed them the bullet holes as well, and then pointed to the doors. "It's real out in those streets. The guns are real, the bullets are real. The prisons are real," He yelled. Walking over to the caskets, he added, "The funerals are real."

The students could see the pain as well as the genuine concern on his face as he spoke. "Now you could go out there and "Do you," as you all like to say. But know ..." He paused so they could follow his every word. "... know that none of you are bulletproof, nor are any of you immune from going to prison. Look at me, these are real bullet holes from young men who obviously had very little regard for human life. And if you're under the impression that prison is some sort of rite of passage, then you are sadly mistaken. Prison is a big business, people. A business where you are its number one commodity, its product."

QB shook his head, his emotions rising. "Either you're going to continue to feed into this street image, or you're going to dare to be different and dance to your own music. You have to be leaders, trendsetters, individuals who are not afraid to say I'm not getting down with that ... I know right from wrong. Prisons are full of young people who cannot think for themselves. Trust me on this, I was once a young person who allowed others to dictate my actions, and guess what happened?" he asked rhetorically. "I ended up doing fifteen years in prison. I've been stabbed, shot, and everything in between. Now, if you think you're built for that kind of life, then by all means let the door hit ya where God split ya—leave. Follow Mr. Matthews and let's see where that gets you." QB exhaled, wishing he knew the magic words to get the students to understand how important their decision-making is.

QB walked up to one of the students and looked down at him. "And for those of you who want to run in a gang, I caution you that the Anti-Gang Act has placed you in the cross-hairs of a cold and highly proficient sniper, one that is armed with the law and backed by a gang far more ruthless than you can imagine. Through his scope he sees neither red nor blue, nor soldier or OG, he sees only one target—inner city youth! You are the hunted, and for that reason alone you should be smart enough to get out. I'm telling you, if you just slow down and think about the consequences of your decisions, and if you allow that inner voice of yours to help you make right choices, you'll never find yourself

Young Adult

in these kind of situations. However, if you choose to do otherwise, you'll notice the police in your rearview mirror are closer than they appear. Do you understand this, Mr. Stevens?"

The young man looked up at QB. "Yes," he said.

"Do you realize that life is not a rehearsal? That there is no sequel to this, Mr. Stevens?"

"Yeah, I know there's no coming back," the young man said.

"That's right, there is no coming back, no second chance," QB barked. He walked up the row of students looking back and forth at each one of them. "If you all didn't know, U-Turn is an alternative school program that is in the business of empowering the youth. We are here to give you an opportunity to make something of yourself." He walked around making sure they were paying attention. "Now, if you're looking for something different, then they have what prisoners call gladiator school, a place where you can go to see just how tough you are. Have any of you heard of Clinton?" He slowed down his talk as he reminisced about the ugliness of that place. "The prison where Tupac did his time. In fact, I was there with him in 1995. Clinton is a place where one learns how to fight like you never fought before; where one learns the true meaning of the words, 'blood on my knife.' A place where I personally witnessed a person get killed over two packs of cigarettes. A place where I saw a man plunge a pair of shear scissors through another man's chest just because he thought he was being disrespected by mere words."

QB walked around, letting his words sink in. "Now, I'm not going to stand up here and tell you I got all the answers, because I don't. However, like you, I am from the streets. I know what it means to show others that I'm not the one to be messed with. I know what it means to get gangster with it, to pop off. I know the value of having a name, a reputation for being willing to get busy, versus what it means to be seen as an individual who operates on punk time. I know all these things. But I also know what it means to take a life, and most importantly, what it means to lose a loved one to senseless violence. I've been on both sides of the fence. I used to tightrope across that hypocritical line and what happened is that I almost threw my entire life away … all because of a split second decision which I made because I thought I was being disrespected." He walked to the coffins. "Now, I want you all to take a good look at these. Come touch them, feel the red-grained wood, touch these pipes, because this is what those streets have to offer." He bent down and opened each coffin. He looked at Brick and Maria, who, if it weren't for the sweat that soaked their faces, both looked dead. They laid there still, with their eyes closed and arms folded across their body, trapped with nothing but thoughts of regrets and future plans of survival.

"Mr. Cameron … Ms. Ramirez, you can both get up now."

With smiles on their faces to mask their fear, they sat up and then jumped out of the coffins. They both looked shaken. "Look at them … In fact, take a good look at them, because today they're fortunate." Once again he let his words hang in the air as he began pacing back and forth again. "You know why?"

Nobody answered.

"This time they were able to get up out of these pine-boxes. Next time, they won't! There will be no rising from the dead, and if you all continue living according to these silly codes in these streets, trust me, neither will you. So if you don't care about your life, then go up there and jump in one of those caskets. See if they look good on you." He paused to see if anybody moved. As he walked to the front of the students, QB exploded. "Here they are, come up here and get in them. Stop wasting our time. If you want to mainline on violence then go right ahead. I'm sure there are other young people out there who would really like to take advantage of this program, who would appreciate interacting with a few people that care," he said, pointing to his staff. QB stared at the students with a menacing, but pleading look. He felt as if he was ready to breakdown; these students were like his little brothers and sisters. He hated the feeling of possibly losing them to the streets.

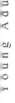

Young Adult

He turned toward the coffins and slammed their tops shut, and then motioned for the faculty to follow him out the gym. There wasn't a dry eye in the building. However, he knew this wasn't a time to pamper them. It was time for the students to make some tough decisions— whether they wanted to be in this program or run the streets. As they exited the gym some spoke in a hushed tone, while others comforted one another. It seemed everyone feared glancing at the two coffins which awaited the next two bodies. Many of them realized this was truly a matter of life and death.

FOURTEEN

Bglared at the big mouth Spanish kid with a sharp stare more piercing than a dentist needle. He wondered how this cat knew his name. After a few minutes, he realized that dude was calling everybody B. He shook his head and thought, *If the judge hears this fool and confuses me with him, I'm gonna eat his face.* Trying to ignore papi, B scanned the courtroom. The public defender looked tired and weak. B quickly assessed that he was the type who wasn't going to fight for him, or any poor kid from the 'hood. His clothes looked disheveled and cheap. The suit jacket he had on was missing a button and when the attorney took it off, sweat circled under his arms. B knew that he was in a no-win situation. He shook his head knowing that Rikers Island was inevitable. The district attorney, on the other hand, looked confident and in control. He was standing there tall and cocky in a suit personally tailored. The DA was as sharp as a paper cut. He was standing there dangling a Mont Blanc pen in between his fingers looking like he was just waiting for the opportunity to sign away the lives of every one of the accused.

The judge was an elderly, white woman, who looked powerful in her black robe. She had little beady eyes that peeked out over her square-framed glasses at the defendants. The court officers were strategically placed throughout the courtroom making sure they put to rest any ideas of escape.

Young Adult

B took a deep breath and then closed his eyes for a second, hoping when he opened them that his current situation would be nothing but a dream. Hearing his name called affirmed that it wasn't, but instead, let him know that he was in the middle of a living nightmare.

"Williams—docket number zero-seven-four-six-two."

B stood up; yanking the Latin guy shackled to him to his feet as one of the Court Officers came over and unlocked him. He then cuffed B's hands together in front of him and led him to the defendant's table. The overworked public defender was looking down into a folder with B's government name written on top. B rubbed his sweaty palms together, and then turned to the public defender. "Can you get me a ROR?"

An ROR is short for Released on your Own Recognizance. The attorney's head remained downcast as if he was actually reading over the facts of his case. He then muttered, "Mr. Williams, let me do my job, I'll do the talking, make sure you don't say anything."

B shook his head, hoping the lawyer could get him released. Unfortunately, the public defender was just going through the motions. He had no intentions of putting up any kind of argument for B's release. Even worse, the judge had no intentions of letting B go anyway, at least not today.

"Mr. Byron Williams?" asked the judge.

"Yes, Your Honor," replied B, trying to sound innocent and respectful.

She looked at him, then toward the District Attorney and nodded her head for him to begin. The District Attorney looked up from his papers spread out on his portion of the table. "Your Honor, we have possession of stolen property, I believe a stolen vehicle and an ahh …"

He was cut off by an attorney rushing into the courtroom, who, in a loud voice said, "Your Honor, I'm sorry I'm late. My name is Peter Shapiro, the attorney for the defendant Byron Williams."

Everybody, except the judge who was sitting facing the door, spun around and looked at the sharply dressed legal beagle as he eased his way down the aisle of the courtroom. The man strolled in with an air of confidence. His black alligator shoes echoed loudly off the shiny floor, as he made his way to the defendants' table. His gray suit matched the color of his eyes. His canary yellow tie was clearly as bright as the gold Rolex on his left wrist.

B thought, *Who the hell is this cat?* There was no way he was going to question him, because he definitely looked more competent than the Legal Aid attorney standing next to him.

As he made his way to the defendant's table he looked up at the judge. "Your Honor, please excuse my lateness. Unfortunately, I got caught in traffic. If you can give me a couple of minutes with my client it would be truly appreciated."

She stared down at him with her mouth open, and brow raised. "I'm going to give you exactly five minutes Mr. Ah ..." the judge said, trying to remember his name.

Looking up at her smiling, the attorney said, "Shapiro, Your Honor, Peter Shapiro."

"Yes, Mr. Shapiro," said the judge. She then added, "I hope this will never happen again. I do not like attorneys that are late in my courtroom. Do we understand each other?"

"Yes we do, Your Honor, and five minutes would be more than enough." He said, laying on his charm.

The judge stood and retreated to her chamber as the public defender gathered his paperwork from the defense table. He gave Shapiro what little paperwork he had in reference to B's case. "Good luck."

"Thank you," Shapiro said and quickly looked through the pending charges and B's rap sheet. He then spoke briefly with B. When they finished, he told the judge's clerk that he was ready to proceed. By the end of the arraignment, B was given a fifty-thousand-dollar bail, which everybody thought was extreme, especially for the charges. However, the cards were stacked against Byron Williams. The district attorney had

Young Adult

already asked the judge to remand B because they needed to infiltrate the Henchmen, and felt that if they could keep him in jail for a few weeks then they could get him to break. The judge was against these kinds of tactics, but after the DA explained all that was at stake, she felt the ends justified the means. She understood her role was just as critical as anybody's when it came to cleaning up the streets of their community.

For public appearance only, during arraignment the DA painted a picture that screamed escape risk and this was all he needed to get B a high bail. The icing on the cake came when the district attorney made the judge aware that B tried to flee the cops when being arrested. Shapiro put up a good counter-argument, but the judge wasn't trying to hear it. Shapiro knew there was much more to the case. He knew what was taking place, and understood his part in all this. He would play it all out to an early retirement.

"Next case," the judge announced as she slammed down her gavel.

Shapiro gathered his papers, and then leaned down and whispered into B's ear that he would have him out before the Rikers Island bus came to pick them up. B couldn't believe what he was hearing. He smiled. *Showtyme came through. Maybe I had him figured out wrong*, B thought.

***

B rolled down the passenger's window in Shapiro's Lexus Coupe; he couldn't believe his luck. He looked at the dashboard; the clock read ten minutes to one. An hour ago he was on his way to jail, standing in front of a judge who never thought in her wildest dreams, he would be able to come up with the kind of bail she gave him. *That'll show her punk behind*, thought B.

They were headed to Shapiro's office where Showtyme was supposed to meet them. B was trying to figure out why Showtyme wanted to meet him there. He was willing to find out until Shapiro took that last phone call. After hearing Shapiro's half of the heated conversation, B could tell that something wasn't right. B noticed Shapiro's responses getting shorter. Yes and no answers. Second thoughts rushed through B's mind. He was having visions of walking into the attorney's office and finding himself standing over some thick plastic, which he knew meant that Tony Soprano type of drama—death.

B looked at Shapiro. "Yo, pull over." It wasn't a request it was a demand.

Shapiro glanced at him. "We'll be there in a second. Showtyme ..."

B didn't let him get the rest of his words out his mouth. "Listen lame, pull this goddamn car over 'fore I kick your face right through that window." B turned toward Shapiro like he was actually measuring the distance between the attorney's face and his ACG's.

Shapiro pulled over immediately. The look he gave B confirmed to the young thug exactly what he had suspected was true. It was a set up. B hopped out as soon as he pulled over. Shapiro watched him walk down the block until he lost him among the pedestrians. The attorney sat there for a second thinking about how he was getting tired of Showtyme and his illusions of being untouchable. *Don't these silly behind kids see that the government is the biggest gang in the world-not the Five Seven Henchmen, not the bloods, Crips, or MS13's, it was the good old U.S. of A.* Shapiro smiled to himself. The attorney shook his head not really understanding the thought process of the young kids of today.

Shapiro, scandalous in his own way, began actually questioning his relationship with Showtyme. He knew he was moving the line of ethics, pushing it further away from that point that he had once refused to cross. He knew it was time for him to make some moral decisions when it comes to the kind of people who he was going to defend. Although he was getting tired of Showtyme, on the other hand, he loved the tax-free cash-money. Shapiro picked up a bottle of valium and tossed a few into his mouth. He sat back in the leather seat and let the prescription drug take effect. After a few minutes he began feeling a little better. He looked in the mirror and thought, *I could put up with this eggplant's bull crap for a little longer. At least until I get enough money to go on a nice European vacation.* Shapiro smiled, and then said to no one in particular, "It's just a matter of time before he goes down anyway."

B made his way down into the subway station. He glanced around to see if Shapiro or anybody else was following him. The transit cop assigned to the station noticed the nervousness on B's face. He watched the thug as he swiped his Metro card and made his way down further into the station.

Twenty minutes later B was standing in front of his apartment loading two guns and putting on his vest. Shapiro, meanwhile, was arguing with Showtyme about what unfolded. Showtyme was verbally abusing Shapiro like he was the attorney's boss. After they ended the call, Shapiro laughed out loud and decided that he was really going to take this joker for all his money.

***

Chase took off his beef and broccoli Field Boots and plopped down on the chair that sat in the corner of Torry's hospital room. He picked up the remote and flipped through the channels hoping to see that new Jay-Z video. Torry was in physical therapy. As Chase sat there watching videos, he was also figuring out his next moves. He knew he needed to holler at his ex-girlfriend. It had been a few days since they'd spoke. He knew he had so much to do; he'd been meaning to check exactly what Showtyme was up to and straighten things out with QB. He felt like it was him against the world. Chase laughed to himself to keep from crying. .

"Let me find out you going crazy on me?" Torry said, looking at Chase strangely while being wheeled back into his room.

Chase jumped. "What's up, my dude?"

"Who the hell you in here talkin' to?" Torry asked.

Chase made his way over to Torry. "Nobody man. I was just thinking about the crap that happened with me and QB yesterday," he said, reaching out to help Torry get in the bed.

Torry smacked his hand. "What I tell you about that? I got this. Don't come up in here treating me like I'm handicap."

Chase smiled, and threw his hands up at Torry. "You got that, my dude, but watch your hands. I might catch a flashback and put these all up in your area," he said, waving his fists in Torry's face.

Balancing himself between his bed and the wheelchair, Torry threw his fists up, and shot three consecutive jabs toward Chase's face. "What? You think I can't keep you on the end of this jab? My moves is still quicker than your eyes."

"That's enough you two ..." the motherly looking nurse said. She stepped between them like she was a referee and helped Torry onto the bed. "Make sure y'all don't make a mistake and hit Big Momma or else I'm gonna show you both what it means to drop it like it's hot."

They put their hands down and laughed; neither one of them was going to test those waters.

The nurse got Torry into bed and then covered him up with his sheets. She left the boys to their business. "I don't want any horse-playing up in this room. Do y'all hear me?"

"A'ight," they both said in unison.

When the door closed behind her, Torry turned toward Chase. "So what happened between you and QB?"

***

Surrounded by the kind of cars that suggested a hard working community, B was sweating nervously. He was stressing while sitting down behind a Toyota Avalon. The exhaust fumes from the garage added to B's confusion. The dim lights prevented him from seeing the oil stains on the floor. He sat there second-guessing his decision, yet the liquor provided the necessary courage for him to believe he could pull this off. From where he was sitting he could see both cars that

Showtyme owned. They were parked about ten feet from where he hid. His sweaty hands kept palming the two 40 cal's in his lap.

The sound of the mechanical door startled B. With caution, B watched as a resident entered the garage and parked her car. The woman gathered her belongings, locked the doors of her vehicle, and headed into the building. As residents came in and out, he wondered, *What the hell happened to my life?*

He took a big gulp of liquor and watched an elderly man make his way out of the garage. *A working life has to be better than this,* he thought. After sitting there for over an hour, familiar voices raised the hairs on B's skin and caused his heart rate to accelerate. The surrounding vehicles offered visual cover, but not protection. B jumped into a crouching position, almost knocking the half-empty bottle of liquor over. He snatched it just before it tumbled and hit the floor, wondering whether or not they heard him. His heart beat like it was on a drum-line. He leaned his back against the side of the car, closed his eyes, and said a thug's prayer.

When B opened his eyes, Showtyme was less than forty yards away. B looked at him and Nitty making their way to Showtyme's car. *I didn't expect that little dude to be with him*, B thought. He was looking for any sign that they may have heard the noise that he made. B had to time his drop perfectly; one mistake could cost him his life. A drop is when you draw your gun first. He had no doubt that both Showtyme and Nitty were armed.

Still crouching, B circled to the passenger side of the Avalon, making sure he wasn't seen. Looking down at his twin burners, he braced himself for the encounter. He took a deep breath, trying to stop the beating of his heart as he inhaled as quietly as possible and then made his move.

As Showtyme and Nitty approached their car, B raised up stealthily with both hammers aimed at their chests. Nitty spotted B first and immediately reached for his burner.

"Don't think about it—both of you put your hands where I can see them."

This has to be some kind of joke, thought Showtyme. He couldn't believe he let another one of his own dudes from his camp creep up on him. As he raised his hands in the air, he saw B shift slightly, a nervous twitch. Showtyme was thinking how he could use B's obvious fear to his advantage. "What's up B, you gonna stand there and pull your heat out on me after I bailed your sorry behind out?" Showtyme said, taking a few steps back. *With some space one of us can make a move.* In Showtyme's quick appraisal of the situation he had to admit it looked like B was ready to pull the trigger. Trying to remain cool, Showtyme said, "Listen Soldier, I know you're under a lot of stress. Because of that I'm gonna give you a pass and let this ride … we all can act like none of this happened."

B chuckled, then responded, "Shut-up coward. You wasn't trying to make a deal when you ran down on me at Sherwood was you? I'm tired of you, and if you move again I'm goin' to …"

What happened next took a fraction of a second. Time seemed to pause. Instinctively, Showtyme dove over the hood of his car. Shots! Rhino bullets tore into the hood of the car as Nitty hit the floor at the familiar roar. Showtyme ended up sliding head first onto the floor of the garage. An instant later, he heard B cry out, and felt the wet spray of blood, brain matter, and skull fragments on the top of his head. When the ringing in his ears calmed down, Showtyme checked his body for bullet holes. He didn't feel any wounds. He flung his hand over the top of the car, pulled himself up to see B lying face-down on the hood of the car. He had a hole in his head and no life in his body. Blood was flowing off the car like syrup poured over pancakes. B's eyes were wide open as if he were frozen in shock.

Shawnee stood behind B with her arms still outstretched, holding a smoking cannon. Both Nitty and Showtyme looked at her in amazement.

Young Adult

Neither one of them had seen her sneak up behind B. Showtyme wiped B's brain off his face. "Where the hell you come from?" he asked.

Shawnee lowered her gun and reached into her pocket. "You left your cell upstairs. I ran down here to catch you before you left." She looked at B sprawled across the hood of the car. "Lucky I did."

Showtyme grabbed his phone, looked around the garage, and then hugged her. "I love your gangsta self," he whispered in her ear. He backed up and just stared at her, knowing she had saved his life.

Nitty looked at them two. "Let's get the hell outta here, Bonnie and Clyde, before somebody comes through."

"Let me get my shoes," said Shawnee as she ran to the entrance of the garage.

Both Nitty and Showtyme watched her run barefoot to get her shoes. They pulled B off Showtyme's car, and wiped off some of the blood and matter from the hood. They then wiped down anything that they may have touched. Nitty then bent down and grabbed the two .40-calibers from B's hands, hopped in the car, and then pulled off. Nitty, who was in the back seat looked at Shawnee from behind and thought, *I got to keep my eye on this chick*.

***

"That's what happened . . . do you think I was wrong?" asked Chase

Torry looked at him. "Yeah, you was wrong. You know QB wasn't trying to play you. He was making a point. You know how he do."

"I knew you were going to say that." Chase looked out the window, a rush of uneasy energy surged through him. "You're probably right." Chase paused to check out Nikki Minaj's latest video on 106 and Park. At the end of the video Chase turned to Torry. "I'll call him in a couple of days. But he shouldn't have come at me like that, he knows what it is."

"I hear you. So what's up with Showtyme?" Torry asked.

Chase turned around. "I don't know. I need to link with my shorty." Torry looked at him. "What's her name again?"

"Shawnee," said Chase. He then added, "I was supposed to link up with her the other day, and see who this fool has coming at me now."

Torry looked at Chase, and then looked down at his legs. "Do you see what dude did to me, homie? This faggot got me laid up in a hospital paralyzed." With his voice beginning to break up, he added, "He tried to lay me down, well actually he tried to lay you down … and I …" He looked away. "I just happened to be there."

Chase suddenly felt the room getting smaller. He didn't know how he should respond to Torry. Torry sighed, turned toward Chase and spoke through clenched teeth. "I know you're not trying to just let this slide. I want you to put a bullet in his head so that we'll forever be on his mind." He looked at Chase, who avoided his stare. "Let me find out you are on some bull right now."

Hearing those words Chase looked up. "Forget you, Torry."

"Forget me? Forget you, Chase. I'm the one that can't walk and you up in here poppin' bull to me. I took these slugs because of you. You're the one that got me in this mess. You need to handle your business!" said Torry.

Chase was overwhelmed with guilt so he said the only thing he could say. "Come on, Torry, you know I didn't mean for none of this to happen."

Torry looked down at his legs. "But it did. Now I can't walk because of you. What happened to all that bull talk about you getting busy like midtown? Well, it's time to get busy." He and Chase stared at each other. Torry added, "But if you don't want to mess with it, then don't. But do me a favor, stop coming up in here frontin' like you G'd up. In fact you can stop coming up in here period. I don't even wanna mess with a dude who can't keep it one hundred with me, let alone himself."

Chase felt a chill run down his spine. "So that's how you want it to be? You want me to go out there and run up in his spot with my guns blazin'?" Chase paused when Torry didn't respond. Slowly, Chase moved toward his bed. "Is that what you want me to do, Torry?"

Young Adult

Torry looked at him, speaking with a sarcastic edge, and a throwing down of the gauntlet. "Yeah soldier, that's what I want you to do."

Chase's heart dropped like the temperature. He turned and walked toward the chair where his belongings were. "You got that, and after it's done, you don't have to worry about me one way or the other. Like I said, forget you, Torry." With a deadly look Chase put on his Timberlands, and with a heavier burden on his back, he stood up to leave. He almost ran right into Naysia who stood at the door with her mouth wide open, shocked by everything she heard.

"Hold up, Chase," she said.

Without even acknowledging her, he pushed passed her. He didn't bother to wait for the elevator; instead he took two steps at a time down the staircase. As he exited the hospital, his lungs burned and his heart cried. He felt as if he was caught in a strong current of raging emotions finally taking him over the edge of sanity.

FIFTEEN

At 9:30 P.M., Reyna and Nia were watching *The Lion King* for what seemed like the millionth time. QB was in the basement waiting for his boys when he heard the doorbell chime. As always, Ramel was the first one to arrive. Reyna answered the door.

"What's up, Ray Ray, where's Q?" Ramel asked. At six foot three with a physique like a NFL wide receiver, he bent down so he wouldn't bump his head on the door frame. Brown-skinned with looks that most women adored. He loved to dress and stayed with a pair of Cartier frames. Although graduating from college with a master's in marketing, at thirty-six, he still wasn't sure what he wanted to do when it came to a career choice.

Reyna rolled her eyes, knowing Ramel would be one of QB's friends to push the issue of getting back at whoever shot him. "He's in the basement." She didn't mean to be rude; she liked QB's friends. They looked out for one another like brothers, but she knew Ramel wasn't here to keep the peace. She'd spoke about it with QB earlier and let him know that she wasn't comfortable at all with what he was contemplating on doing.

Zeus pulled up just before she closed the door. He exited the truck quickly and ran toward the door. A massive man of six-six and over three hundred pounds, he looked like a grizzly bear. "What's up, sis?" he

Young Adult

said as he entered the house and bent down to give her a kiss on her cheek.

"They're in the basement."

"Where's my girl?" Zeus asked.

"She's in the den watching television," she said.

"I think I'll go chill with her for a little while. What you cook? I'm hungry as hell. Look out for your brother."

"I'll see what I can do." Reyna liked Zeus. She knew that he was the most serious of all QB's friends. Behind his humble appearance lay a hideous depravity. Zeus would zone out when the people he considered family were threatened. Reyna went to the cabinets and withdrew an extra plate. Her gaze shifted toward the heavens, she closed her eyes and murmured, "God, please watch over them."

True and Easy arrived a few minutes later. Zeus opened the door for them and Easy headed straight for the bathroom, singing the hit "Move, Get Out the Way" by Ludacris. Easy was the pretty boy of the team who grew up in the South Bronx. His mom, calling herself trying to save her only child before he fell victim to the streets, sent him to the Navy. It backfired. In the service he became the epitome of the term bad-boy. Thanks to the Navy, he turned into a one-man army, a weapon.

"Open the window in there," Reyna shouted when she heard him grunting.

True hugged Reyna, then stuck his head in the den and stuck his tongue out at Nia. She returned the gesture but called herself topping him by rolling her eyes. True laughed and blew her a kiss to make up. Then he ran down stairs to see his boys. Reyna told Zeus to come and eat his food.

"A'ight," he responded.

Zeus ate his food in less than ten minutes. Nia sat next to him and watched in amazement at how her uncle devoured all that food so quickly. *He didn't chew his food slowly, like mommy always taught me and Daddy*, she thought.

Growing impatient, QB yelled up the stairs for Zeus and Easy.

Reyna grabbed Nia. "Come on, baby it's getting late. Let's go say goodnight to Daddy and then go run your water for your bubble bath. Then we can watch some more movies," she said.

"Okay Mommy." She turned to Zeus and asked, "Uncle Sheus, you wanna watch movie with me and Mommy?"

"Let me check out your daddy first, and then I'll come hang out with you and mommy, a'ight sweetie? Come here, give me a big hug."

Reyna put her down and she ran around the table to him. He scooped her up in his huge hands. She looked like a kitten in his arms. He was kissing and biting on her stomach, making her laugh uncontrollably.

"Okay, okay, okay, stop uncle Sheus," Nia yelled as she twisted and turned, trying to escape his attack.

Reyna jumped in to save her baby from peeing on herself. She popped Zeus upside his head and said, "What I tell you about doing that to her?"

Laughing, Zeus put her down. "I'll see you later, okay?"

"Okay."

As soon as Zeus had gone down to the basement, the doorbell rang again. This time Amari stood on the other side of the door.

"Hey 'Mari."

"What's up, Reyna? Where's everybody?"

"They're in the basement."

"What's up, Nia? Come here, give Uncle 'Mari some love. He reached out, revving her right back up as she ran into his arms. He reached into his pockets and pulled out some money. "Here you go ma-ma, this is for you."

Nia's face lit up. *She's too spoiled*, thought Reyna.

"Look what I got, Mommy," Nia said, holding out a bunch of bills in her tiny hands.

Reyna smiled. "What do you say?"

Young Adult

"Thank you, Uncle 'Mari. I put it in my bank," said Nia, putting her arm around his neck and giving him a kiss on his cheek.

That's right, princess, stack that cheddar, baby girl," he said and headed for the basement door with Nia in his arms. Reyna followed them. Before going down the stairs, Reyna stopped him.

"'Mari, do me a favor?"

"What's up, Ray?"

"I need you to make sure nothing happens to Q?"

He put Nia down and looked Reyna in her eyes. "Don't worry sis, nothing is going to happen to him. This is going to be handled without anybody getting hurt."

Reyna closed her eyes. "I hope so. We cannot ..." She stopped in mid-sentence realizing that Nia was looking up at them.

Amari understood what she was going to say. He reached out and hugged her. Nia, feeling left out, hugged her mommy's leg. "Trust me, Ray. We got this," he said, wiping the tears that were beginning to water in her eyes.

QB frowned as Easy and Amari made their way down the stairs. Looking at his watch, he started to curse them out until he noticed Reyna and Nia trailing behind them. "What's up, baby?"

"Nia wanted to say goodnight," Reyna said, handing Nia to her father. QB gave his daughter an Eskimo, and promised to take her to the park the following day. He then put her down so she could say goodnight to all her uncles.

When she was on her feet, she dug in her pocket, pulled out her money, and said, "Look what I got, daddy."

"Wow, where did you get all that?"

"Uncle 'Mari," Nia said, lighting up the dim basement with her big smile.

Amari yelled out, "That's right. Your favorite uncle always looks out for you, right Nia?"

She looked at him and smiled, but didn't answer his question. It was as if she knew better to put one above the other. *She got men eating out of the palms of her hand already*, thought QB.

Predictably, seeing this, Ramel, Zeus, True and Easy all dug in their wallets for money to give their niece. Like kids in junior high school fighting for the attention of a girl, they all competed for the 'Favorite Uncle' title. They shouted, "Here you go, Nia." Reaching out to give her hands full of cash, Nia's eyes were as big as the cue ball on the pool-table which sat in the middle of the basement.

Reyna tried to step in, "What are y'all doing? She doesn't need all that money. You all need to stop spoiling her like that."

None of them were trying to hear that, this was much bigger than Reyna. QB came up behind Reyna, grabbed his wife by the waist and whispered in her ear, "Leave her. Let my baby get that dough. Hell, I might let her stay up during our poker nights so I won't lose so much."

Reyna softly elbowed him in the stomach, "You're not right."

As Nia grabbed all the money, QB kissed Reyna on her neck, knowing that was one of her many hot spots. She playfully hit him again, and then turned toward him. "How long are you going to be?"

"Why? You got something sweet for me?"

"Maybe," she said, looking up into his eyes.

"Well, since you put it like that, not long. Give me an hour," he said.

She continued looking in his eyes, but said nothing. Her look pleaded with him to think about his family. She rose up on her pretty toes like a ballerina and kissed him gently on his lips, reminding him of what was truly important. With that, Reyna called Nia, who was busy counting all her money. Hearing her mother's call she began stuffing all the bills in her pocket, then kissed all her uncles, her father, and then headed up the stairs following her mother, happier than a kid in a candy store. QB and the team waited until they heard the door close shut before they got down to business.

***

Chase got home a little after seven in the evening. The weather was beginning to flip. That cold January air was beginning to creep up on New York. He was still reeling at the exchange between him and Torry. He had called Lexi at her job and convinced her to come over after work. She was the one person he could really harmonize with; there was just something about her that made him feel comfortable in expressing and exposing his feelings.

He rushed into the apartment he shared with his grandmother, hoping that she'd left for church. Tonight was either choir rehearsal, or Bible study. His grandmother stayed up in the House of the Lord. He opened the door, "Grandma. Grandma," he called out.

When he got no response, he thought, *Cool*. He then went to his room to clean it up. He had about twenty minutes before Lexi was supposed to be there. He threw his keys on his dresser, hit a switch on the wall, and watched as the entire room came to life. Chase looked around and rushed to the corner of his room and snatched up a pile of clothes piled there for God knows how long. He smelled them and threw them into his closet. Pulling out some sour diesel, rolling it in a dutch, he sparked it. Ten minutes later, he then lit some incense and put on Little Wayne's hit song, "Loyalty." Chase pulled off his button down shirt, and threw himself on his bed. He rewound the conversation he had with Torry. A part of him understood why Torry felt the way he did, but another part felt like he should've never challenged him like that. In his mind, Torry crossed the line. They were supposed to be brothers who had a bond stronger than blood. *I guess not*, Chase thought.

The weed was easing the stress, or so he thought. He looked at the dutch blunt and said, "This is some good stuff." Suddenly he jumped up and went back to the closet, flung open the door, and started rambling inside. He pulled up a panel hidden in the floor of the closet and pulled out an MP-5 automatic sub-machine gun. He lucked up on the weapon when he met a girl whose brother was in the military. The brother was stealing artillery from the Army and was showing off his stash. Chase sat there acting like he didn't care nothing about guns, but it wasn't even a week later that Chase found a reason to break up with his sister and a better reason to break into their home.

Chase took one last pull on the dutch and then clipped it. He put it in the ashtray, and then turned toward the mirror hanging on the back of the closet door. Standing there for a second looking at his reflection felt like he was looking at a stranger. He closed his eyes. When he opened them he heard a voice say, "You don't have to do this, Chase." He spun around as if someone else were in the room with him. But nobody was there.

Then another voice said, "C'mon, my dude, man-up. You're nice with a gun. You get busy, kid. Get off that bull and handle your damn business." Again, Chase looked around, making sure no one else was in the room with him. He looked in the mirror and said, "This is tha bomb weed, this diez got a fella hearing voices." What he was hearing was his own conscience, that self-accusing spirit that all humans have. Unfortunately, most young people ignore their internal voice; the voice of right and wrong. Chase was no different. He refused to listen to his own alarm system. With bloodshot eyes and the weight of the world on his shoulders, he raised the MP-5 toward the mirror. He pulled the trigger and said, "I'm gonna pop this thing off like I'm wheelin' a bike."

He lowered the gun, reached into the hidden compartment of the closet, and grabbed his Kelvar vest and the only two cartridges he had for the gun. He put the vest on and then loaded the weapon. Running his fingers along the stock of his gun, he thought about the potential destructiveness of the weapon. It actually scared Chase to think about what he could do with it. He said out loud, "You want drama, Showtyme, well here comes a true soldier."

His thoughts were interrupted by knocks at the door. He threw the gun behind him onto the bed, sprayed some air freshener, threw on his fitted and ran to the door. Chase looked through the peephole and saw

Young Adult

Lexi standing there looking sweeter than cotton candy. He opened the door. "What's good, beautiful?"

She smiled. "Hi baby," she said. Chase stood there speechless, staring at her with a silly look on his face. She looked at him. "Are you going to invite me in?" Lexi asked.

"Oh, my bad," he said, moving to the side to let her enter the apartment. He closed the door behind her and made sure it was locked. Chase then turned toward Lexi, leaned down, and gave her a brief kiss, after which he led her to his bedroom.

On the way there, Lexi noticed how over-furnished the apartment was. She smiled inside because she understood how the elders got down. Her grandmother did the same thing—saving everything. Her grandma's house resembled a museum, minus the skeletal bones of pre-historic animals. In the hallway, Lexi noticed the classic Martin Luther King and Malcolm X portraits peering down at her. Her grandmother had the same exact ones. She looked around for the infamous Jesus portrait most African American families hung up in their homes.

When they reached Chase's room it was like stepping from one world into another—a shift in time—from the 1970's to 2010. It was crazy. Chase had all kind of devices, while the rest of the apartment looked like something out of the TV show *Good Times*. Lexi noticed the flat screen television mounted on a wall next to a wall unit filled with CD's, an iPod, a Sidekick, DVD's, with other expensive gadgets.

"When you finish checking out my kingdom you can sit any where you want," said Chase.

When Lexi finished looking around she sat down on the bed. She shifted around to get comfortable, when she noticed the big, black gun lying there like it was just another normal piece of furniture. She looked at Chase, noticing for the first time that he was wearing a vest. She asked, "Chase, is everything all right?"

He smiled at her, "I'm good, ma. Why you ask?"

She looked toward the gun and then back at him. "Hello ... you got a bullet proof vest on like you're heading to Afghanistan and what about this big gun just laying here next to me like it's a stuffed animal or something?"

He rushed over to the bed and grabbed the gun. "This ain't nothing. A fella just making sure I'm safe in the 'hood, that's all."

She sucked her teeth, and curled up her pretty lips. "Chase, don't play with me. What's going on?"

He put the gun back in the closet, then turned toward her and just stared. She crossed her legs, sending him a clear message. She wanted an explanation as to why he looked like the Black Rambo. He sighed and told her everything that took place. He explained how it felt like he was in a vacuum; that he was being sucked into a danger zone, a place where he felt pressed, stressed out, and desperate. How it had come to the point where it was either bite or be bitten. He turned to her and said, "It's time that I handle my business, Lexi. The bottom line is I have to take care of this or you may be coming to my funeral."

"Why don't you go to the police?" she asked.

He stood up. "I'm not going to the cops." He shook his head, then added, "We don't do police, Lexi."

"We don't do police. Who is 'we,' Chase? Didn't you tell me you were leaving that street mess alone? I don't know about you ... but I took that to mean that you were leaving those stupid principles of the streets alone as well." She looked into his face, hungry for a response.

He put his head down. "Yeah, I told you that, baby. But going to the cops isn't what I meant. I wish I could make this all go away but—"

She cut him off. "I don't believe you. I really don't. I can't believe you are willing to throw your life away like this. Look at Torry, he's paralyzed, struggling to come to terms with possibly never walking again, and you want to go out there and just add fuel to a burning fire. Do you have to end up like him for you to understand that it's not worth it?"

Young Adult

Chase walked toward her. "That's just it, Lexi—he's paralyzed because of me." Momentarily lost for words, he then added, "That's why I have to do what I gotta do." He tried to justify his decision by explaining how street drama was handled a certain way and he hoped that she would understand. When she looked away, he reached down and gently lifted her face by her chin. She was crying. He sat down next to her, unsure of what he should do. So he moved in to hug her. She pulled back, recoiled like he was too dangerous to touch.

She wiped her eyes. "I'm ready to go home," she said.

He looked confused. "What?" he asked.

Trying to mask the hurt she was feeling, she stood, wiping away the tears that managed to escape her eyes. "I said I'm ready to leave. Can you please let me out?"

He stood, his eyes pleading with her not to leave. But she was firm in her stance. "I want to go home."

"So that's how it is? You're on some bull too—huh?"

As they walked to the front door, Lexi maintained her position, "Listen. I told you we weren't getting together if you were going to be throwing up signs, fighting over blocks, and all that other crap y'all are out there fighting over. To me, that is some little boy crap. I'm trying to come up in this world. It's hard enough for us out there without all the complications of being in a gang. I don't have time for that, Chase. I've been down that road before, and I know what it's all about. I'm just not with it, I'm sorry." She stopped at the front door and finished by saying, "I was just beginning to trust in you, in us. When you get your life together then contact me. I do believe we can have a future together, but there is no way I'm getting involved with someone who is going through the drama of being in a gang. What kind of life is that?" Lexi looked at him not really expecting an answer, but hoping he would tell her he was finished.

When he didn't, she said, "Call me when you grow up."

He looked at her, and opened the door. Lexi stepped out and turned around to face him. Chase slammed the door in her face. He stood there for a second, leaning against the inside of the door. Sliding down to the floor, he cupped his face in his hands, hoping she would knock, begging him to let her back in. She didn't. After about five minutes, he got up and looked through the peep hole to see if she was there.

Lexi was gone. He kicked the door, leaving a sneaker print on it. He then stormed into his room, slamming the bedroom door, rattling everything in the house. He sat on the edge of his bed, grabbed the half of blunt out of the ashtray and said out loud, "To hell with her, forget everybody." He picked up his phone and called his ex-girl, Shawnee.

SIXTEEN

Eyebrows went up around the glass table in the basement.
"What you talkin' 'bout? Let me get this straight. You want to set up a meeting with this cat, but you don't want us to pack heat?" Ramel looked around at the rest of the team. He couldn't believe QB. He turned back to him. "Are you crazy? What type of mess is that? Are you telling me you want us to walk up into a spot with killers who don't give a damn about anything, holding up peace signs?" asked Ramel.

"No!" QB said while staring directly back at Ramel. He turned his attention to the rest of his boys. "That's not what I want you to do. I want to meet with this cat to see if I can stalemate this. I'm not trying to go back to prison for one of these little punks out here trying to get a name. We're not eighteen years old anymore, this is not a high school beef, and our reps for getting busy no longer matter to these young cats. They don't give a damn about what we used to do, so I'm just trying to avoid…"

Ramel cut him off. "Hold up, QB, this has nothing to do with our reputations, nobody in here is living off their past. This has to do with someone shootin' your behind up like you're a dope fiend. What the hell is wrong with you wanting to give this fool a pass?" He sighed. "I say either you go to the police and file a report or get on your Pat Riley and get back to handling the heat. That's the bottom line!"

Zeus, who drained the last of his drink, set the glass down on the table in front of him. "You know what? Let us take care of him. You don't have to do nothing." He looked at QB. "Ramel is right, this nigga shot you all up and now you want to talk. I don't know what's gotten into you, but these young dudes are out there laying it down. They're not trying to talk." He looked around to see if anybody disagreed with him.

True, Easy, and Ramel nodded in agreement. Amari didn't lean either way.

Ramel added, "Yeah, let us handle this. You can pull back."

QB picked up his drink, took a sip, hoping to hide the shame he was beginning to feel. He didn't want them to feel as if he was trying to get them to do his dirty work.

True jumped in and spoke his piece. "I agree with them, QB, we can't give dude a pass. You know I'm not with that black on black violence, but sometimes we got to do what we got to do, especially when this punk is out there going around dumping on innocent people. To me, it's like we're doing the community a favor." True stood up and began circling the pool table. He was what you called blue-black and he rocked a blowout that looked as smooth as mink. He believed himself to be a revolutionary; a man of iron principles and convictions. He loved to debate, the type of person who always argued that there were no gun factories in Harlem or cocaine fields in Brooklyn. He spent many days trying to show younger brothers that selling drugs only destroyed their own 'hood, and created crime, which in turn created jobs for lawyers, judges, correctional officers, and allowed the system to build prisons in rural communities that very few black folks reside in. However, he knew his talks went in one ear and out the other because nobody was offering alternative ways for them to make money. It's hard to tell young people who are hungry, to put down a gun or stop selling drugs.

QB looked at him, hoping he would understand his position and be the one who would back him up. True and QB were the closest,

Young Adult

intellectually. They shared books, discussed politics, strategies, wars, racism, reparations and devised methods to get people out to vote. They wanted to leave their mark in the world, to bring about change. The difference between the two is that QB felt the vessel to do this was through education, and True felt it was through the barrel of a gun. His idea of education was teaching the youth how to assemble a gun in the dark; take it apart, clean it, and then put it back together in under ninety seconds. He felt white America would never respect black people until they showed that they were willing to die for their natural rights. His motto was similar to Patrick Henry, who coined the phrase "Give me liberty, or give me death." The irony in this was that Patrick Henry was a white man.

True stopped, reached down, and grabbed the eight ball. He looked at QB, then rolled it across the table into the corner pocket. "So ... I agree with Ra and Zeus. I say we rid the 'hood of this problem!"

Amari was unusually silent as he watched his brother calculating everything being said. Amari understood both point of views, but felt it was QB's call. He knew his brother wasn't the type to send others into a fire that he was unwilling to put out himself. Even though QB was younger, he admired a lot of things about him. QB was always the first one out of them two to want to pop off. Not only did he possess a relentless drive to survive the physical abuse in their home, but he survived a fifteen year prison sentence, and the loss of a child. He had handled all of life's obstacles up to that point, without complaint. Amari always felt that QB had a determination to live life as if it was a book that would hold its reader to the last word. Yet, at the moment, Amari could see a look of worry all over his face. Whatever his brother decided, he was going to support. He hoped that if they were pushed into the flames of this fire, that they would be able to put them out without getting burned.

Everybody was in deep thought when QB spoke up. "I want to set up a meeting with this kid. I'm not letting y'all do anything without me, so cut that bull out. I have to do this my way. I got a family now and I cannot be out there fighting these young cats who are trying to come up at the expense of another brother's blood." He turned to his brother, "Mari, I want you to see if you can get me a meeting with this Showtyme. Can you do that?"

If the streets were a chicken coup, Amari was definitely a fox. During his run in the streets, while others merely absorbed the codes, he devoured them with the appetite for destruction. He earned his stripes hustling. While most hustlers ended up with life bids or dead, he was one of the few hustlers who were able to get in and out the game with nothing more than a few scratches. After holding down QB and witnessing what he went through during his bid, Amari realized that life was too short to be spending time in prison. So he got out of the game, invested his money in real estate, among other ventures, which actually brought him in a good salary and more importantly, peace of mind.

During his run, he learned valuable lessons, and made life-long connects that would come in handy. So when QB asked could he set up a meeting with the Five Seven Henchmen, no one questioned Amari.

Amari looked around. "Yeah, I could do that."

Zeus stood up and put on his jacket, then started walking toward the stairs. Before he climbed the stairs, he turned around and said, "I hope you know what you're doing, QB. Call me with the details. I'm there."

No one tried to stop him. They knew he was not feeling the decision to have a sit-down with a dude that had more bodies than a clown car.

QB stared at his back as he walked up the stairs of the basement. Easy was looking at the floor, thinking, and slowly shaking his head. He understood QB's reasoning, and realized how thin a tightrope QB was walking. Between U-Turn, his friends, family, his values, and his need for revenge, QB was under a lot of pressure. Like Amari, Easy was going to ride, but he was going to let QB drive the car. Each of them had much to lose. For the first time in his life he questioned whether or not he was

Young Adult

beginning to get soft or was it a matter of maturity. He hoped it was the latter because he knew being soft and violent was not a good combination when dealing with street gangs.

QB made himself another drink and swallowed it straight, trying to resist the gut feeling urging him to attack. A big part of him wanted to go after Showtyme. He knew Zeus and Ramel had made some valid points. Yet, instead of giving in to their opinions he decided to follow his instincts. He took a deep breath, and looked at his brothers. When no one said anything, QB started to speak, but then decided against it and sat back and thought, *This is one of those decisions that will either be looked back on as smart and gutsy or just plain stupid. Like a football coach deciding to go for it on fourth down rather than kick a field goal. The wisdom of such a decision is always dependent on the success of the gamble.*

***

Showtyme sat at the bar in the basement of the trap house where Face and Kema were killed. There was nothing in the house that remained from that day besides the bar. Everything was replaced, repainted, even the floors were redone. Getting rid of all possible evidence was key to staying out of prison. Showtyme was very meticulous when it came to things like that. It was one of the many habits that kept Showtyme out the reach of the law.

Pulling out some weed he began constructing a blunt, somewhat shaken by the fact that Face and B had gotten the drop on him. Showtyme knew he was extremely lucky. He listened to the ruckus being made by his soldiers and thought, *I have to slow down and start watching every one of these cats. I'm giving them way too much room to operate.* He leaned back and blew the dutch until it was gone, and then headed upstairs with menacing red eyes that matched his temper. He walked into the living room and yelled "G's up."

About twenty pair of eyes shot up, immediately stopping whatever it was they were doing. Showtyme didn't bother to hide the stress on his hardened face. He explained what B attempted to pull off, even though many of them already knew about it. He was looking for reactions, something that might tip him off to who actually knew about it. He understood that many of them were gunning for his position, and made sure to emphasize how B's brains got blown all over the pavement. Many soldiers looked at him with surprised looks. He looked at them knowing there were backstabbers among them just waiting for their opportunity to get the top-spot. Showtyme told them that he was going away, and then gave them instructions on what he expected of them in his absence.

He didn't tell them where he was going and no one dared to ask. Timing, silence, and unpredictability played a major part in his success of the so-called game. One thing he tried to teach his soldiers was that a lot of them got knocked because they were only part time gangstas. They wanted to make money for eight hours a day, and then party for another eight, and then go home to sleep. Whereas detectives, on the other hand, were on their job twenty-four hours a day. When one detective went home, another came on and picked up the case that they were slowly building on them. He explained to the Henchmen that real soldiers never slept. If you slept you were setting yourself up for a fall. He explained that the rapper Nas said it best when he said "Sleep is the cousin of death."

Showtyme never slept. He took power-naps, and it was little things like that which he thought kept him above the rest. Showtyme actually thought he had psychic powers. He literally thought he could sense when danger was lurking or when police were closing in. He could feel it now; this is why he instructed every one of his generals to close shop and to go underground for a minute.

Tank yelled out, "What about that punk Chase?"

Showtyme looked at him and every other soldier in the room. "He gets washed up on sight."

Getting rid of him was now top priority. His presence was something weighing heavily on the entire army. Showtyme looked around at his Henchmen then nodded at Cherokee, Banger, Nitty and Shawnee, signaling them to follow him into the basement. Some of the soldiers threw up their sign, while others were scheming, laying in the cut. They were beginning to see a chink in Showtyme's armor. The vultures were beginning to smell weakness, or at least that is what they thought.

SEVENTEEN

I t was one thirty in the morning by the time QB walked into his bedroom. Reyna was surprisingly still up reading a book titled *Spirit of a Man*, by Iyanla Vanzant. A book she had been begging QB to read.

"You're still up?"

"Yeah, I'm finishing up this book."

"I thought you finished that already, and wanted me to read it."

"I do, and I think it would be good if you order it for your students. Young black men need to read this. It's an analogy of the flaws of black men from a female perspective.

"Oh yeah ... when did she become an expert on being a black man?"

Rolling her eyes, Reyna placed the book on the nightstand. "No one said she was an expert. She simply is giving her opinion. Before you start, you should read it, maybe it will help you figure out what is truly important to you."

QB sighed, and walked into their closet hoping to avoid an argument. He could feel it coming. He knew Reyna waited up just to fight. It surely wasn't for sex because she had on her I'm not in the mood pajamas. Reyna had a bloodhound's nose for trouble. She smelled drama in the air. "QB, can you do me a favor?"

"What's that, baby?" he answered from the back of the closet.

"Now I don't want to argue about this, but I'm asking that you put us first when it comes to whatever decision you make in regards to this Showtyme."

"Don't I always put you first, beautiful?" he asked, trying to ease the tension.

"Yes, but now I'm asking that you not go out there and fight a battle that you cannot win. You have too much to lose, and on top of that Nia needs you."

QB calmly stepped out the closet. "Reyna, stop using Nia as a needle to puncture my conscience. You don't have to do that, I'm very much aware of what's at stake. You cannot push hard enough to puncture my conscience anymore than I have already punctured it myself. So please, baby, trust me, and let me handle this."

Getting up from the bed, Reyna tried to subdue the anger in her voice, but failed. Her words were coated with serious attitude. "What the hell do you mean let you handle it, Quentin? You know something ... there are times when I feel you're only acting out a positive character. Look at you—you still feel as if you have to live according to some tough guy standard." She put her hand on her hip. "In fact, Quentin, I'm beginning to believe that there is very little difference between you and your students."

QB's brown eyes smoldered with hurt. The pent-up anger from all that unfolded thus far almost erupted. But he caught himself. *Do not argue,* he thought. "Pardon my insensitivity, Reyna, but I really don't want to get into this right now. However, I don't know how many times I have to prove to you that I'm not going to do anything to jeopardize my freedom, or what we share." He paused to take off his shoes. Reyna started to say something but he cut her off. "Tell me what I got to do Reyna, because you're starting to make me feel as if you doubt me."

Raising her voice slightly, Reyna moved toward QB. "Stop, Quentin. Knock it off, don't stand here and insult my intelligence. You know damn well that's not what this is about."

"Then what is it about, Ray?"

She rolled her eyes at him. "It's about you and your brothers meeting in our basement like it's the Oval office, and this is an issue of National Security." Narrowing her eyes, she added, "It has nothing to do with my doubts. It's about you putting our future up for adoption."

QB couldn't find the words to respond to that. He had to admit there was validity to Reyna's argument.

Seeing that her husband had nothing to say, Reyna continued, "What you need to do, Quentin, is stop trying to define yourself to me with false definitions of survival." She looked him up and down. "Aren't you the one who's supposed to teach the youth about alternative ways to deal with conflict and adversity out there in the streets? Yet, here you are wanting to go out into those same streets and take revenge." Feeling like she was about to cry, Reyna lowered her head, and tried to gather her emotions. When she felt she had her feelings under control she looked back up at him. "I am really scared, Quentin. Can't you see what this is doing to me, to us? I'm so tired of training my tears to crawl back into my eyes."

QB shifted his weight as he felt guilt overtake him. It felt like his soul was being divided between his love for his wife and the pull of his past. "Reyna, I don't understand how you can stand here and say that. However, I refuse to argue with you. What I need from you is to trust me, to know that I'll take care of this without jeopardizing what we have."

She bit her bottom lip, contemplating whether or not she should push. "Quentin, people can't just do what they want in this world. You can't go out into these streets and act like some damn vigilante. What you need to do is to learn how to swallow your pride."

Reyna was really beginning to piss QB off. With a smirk on his face, and a touch of sarcasm, he replied, "Unfortunately Reyna, my pride is not edible." He then turned and walked away from her.

She was not going to let him escape though. Knowing she was successfully pushing his buttons, she lowered her voice. "Baby, all I'm saying is that you can't take this matter into your own hands. Sometimes you simply have to let other people help you, even if that means the police." She walked over to him and wrapped her arms around his neck. "You know something, Quentin? Since we met, you have not only been struggling with how to love yourself and embrace what it means to give and take in a relationship, but for whatever reason, you feel you have to deal with your fears all by yourself. That tells me you still have doubts about me, and I'm supposed to be your wife." She gently rubbed her hand along the contours of his face. "You have to do something with your fears Q, the non-trust, and the ghosts that have been programmed in your psyche from your past experiences. We all have a past, sweetheart, and voices inside of us telling us what we need to do to protect ourselves from making the same mistakes over and over again. Yet, we have to master these voices, baby. All your past experiences, the bid, your ex, the loss of your child, are things that you have to learn to break free from. Don't you see the pain from these events are holding you back, and causing you to make decisions that will only hurt you … hurt us?"

QB grabbed Reyna by her waist, looked into her eyes with serious conviction. "This is an Oprah moment if I ever heard one." She playfully slapped him upside his head. He pulled her closer and grabbed her tighter. "Reyna, seriously, let me ask you something. How would you like your life's work reduced to the stupidest thing you've ever done?" There was a pregnant pause before he spoke again. "You know, everybody expects some kind of reaction from me based on my past. My parole officer and even my friends are expecting me to respond in the typical fashion. As much as I try to fight the feeling of needing to seek revenge, there is a part of me that is screaming for me to run out there and take this dude out. It's crazy, because I thought that part of me no longer existed. But here it is—armed and ready. And you know what, beautiful? To be totally honest, it's really pulling me." He let out a little laugh. "My students tell me all the time that I don't understand the pull of the streets. Unfortunately, I do, and when it comes to being shot, the pull of revenge is stronger than the pull of gravity."

Reyna stood there speechless, but he wasn't looking for an answer. "Reyna, sometimes I think I function better in the dark. It's crazy, but you know I'm beginning to think responsibility is way too complicated," said QB.

"Not if you're out there shooting people, Quentin. Then it will be simple, so maybe sometimes complicated is better," said Reyna.

He smiled, "You're not going to let me win this one are you?"

"No, I'm not. Losing you is not an option for me."

"Promise?" asked QB.

She looked into his brown eyes. "With all that I am."

He bent down and gently kissed her forehead. She leaned her head on his chest, feeling the beat of his heart against her face. "Quentin, I want you to be able to trust me without reservation. I need to know what's going on at all times. I promise I won't ask for details, but please, baby, keep me in the loop," she said.

QB patted her on her butt. "So I guess you want to know what was said tonight?"

She smiled. "Yep."

"If it will make you feel any better, I asked Amari to set up a sit down with this Showtyme character to see if we can end this without anybody getting hurt, killed, or going to jail."

"Do you think that's best?"

"I don't know, but it beats having to go out there and holding court in the streets."

"Just promise me you'll take care of yourself, Quentin."

"I promise. With all that I am."

UNDER PRESSURE

She leaned up and kissed him passionately. He immediately began peeling off her I'm not in the mood pajamas, turning the night completely around.

EIGHTEEN

Torry was hyped because he was finally going home. Everybody was there except Chase. As good as he felt about going home, there was still an empty space inside of him created by his dispute with his boy. After speaking with both Naysia and QB, he realized that he was out of line for pressuring Chase to do something that might actually get him killed or sent to prison for the rest of his life.

While spending his last moments in the hospital room, he sat in his wheelchair looking out the window; his face was as blank as a starter's pistol. He was thinking about Chase. Torry had tried calling him every day since their exchange of words. He left countless messages, but Chase didn't return any of his calls. He hoped nothing had happened to him. For the past couple of days he kept pushing the troubled feelings he was having aside. You can call it intuition, but Torry felt something was terribly wrong.

With her round belly, Naysia came up beside him, "What's up, baby, you okay?"

"Yeah, I'm just sitting here thinking 'bout Chase."

She ran her fingers over his waves. "He's fine, I'm sure. He's just mad at you right now, but he'll come around. You two always go through this."

Young Adult

Torry reached down to adjust his leg. "Not like this, Nay. I played myself this time."

"Don't be so hard on yourself, baby. You heard QB. He said he was going to find him." She bent down and fixed his Gino Green button down.

Torry looked into her glowing face, smiled and ran his hand across her belly. "What's up with my little man?"

Naysia tilted her head to the side. "What makes you think it's a boy?"

"I can tell by the way he kicks."

She slapped his hand away. "I'm telling you it's a girl, and I started buying all these cute pink outfits, so if it is a boy he is going to be rockin' pink like Cam'ron."

"Not my little man," said Torry. "Queens Cats don't do pink. That's that Harlem swag, so you better keep the receipts." Nay smiled and began pushing him toward the exit of the hospital.

***

Showtyme, Nitty and Banger were waiting in the suite of their hotel for the girls to come back from shopping. They had been in Miami for two days. They were meeting the new connect tonight. Even though Showtyme had come down there to relax, he used the opportunity to meet his new partners and cop some bricks at a cheaper price. His Columbian connect was playing hardball when it came to prices. Showtyme had been dealing with them for over two years, and felt it was time they gave him a play, a little break on the prices. Hell, they were in a recession. When they refused, Showtyme hooked up with some Haitian kids who were willing to provide bricks for two grand cheaper.

Showtyme was chilling on the couch thinking about B and all the loose ends he had to tie up back in New York. Nitty and Banger were in the next room counting money, making sure everything was correct for the drop-off. Showtyme was getting impatient with Shawnee and Cherokee. He flipped open his Sidekick and was about to call Cherokee when he heard them coming through the door of the suite. "Didn't I tell you two I was meeting these dudes at nine? Where the hell you been?"

"Oh Daddy, wait 'till you see what we got you. You know we had to cop you something before we left that mall. You know Shawnee and I have different taste, so we got a little caught up trying to decide what we wanted for our Papi," Cherokee said, throwing her shopping bags on the floor.

Shawnee just walked by and blew him a kiss. When she reached the dining table suite, she turned back to Showtyme and said, "You know we had to have you lookin' gangsta when you meet with these Miami cats." She reached in the bags and pulled out a pair of olive green ostrich closed-toe sandals, some egg-shell white linen drawstring pants, and white and olive striped tight-fitted shirt to show off his physique. She held it all up so he could see and then started singing Rick Ross's anthem, "Every day I'm hustlin', hustlin', hustling."

Showtyme laughed and thought, *I love these silly behind broads.* If nothing else, they knew how to treat their Mack. "That's what's up, but we have to get ready. These dudes will be here in less than an hour." They grabbed the rest of the bags and headed to the bedroom to get ready for the exchange.

An hour and forty minutes later they were still waiting. The Haitians were already thirty minutes late. Showtyme, who didn't like to wait on anybody, refused to blow his cool. He knew he had to keep his composure especially since they were giving him a play on them birds. They went over what they had to do in the event the Haitians tried to cross them. Showtyme always prepared for the worst. He knew how greed could get the best of people.

Nitty finally hit Showtyme up to let him know the Haitians had arrived. He watched from the lobby as they entered the hotel. Five of them—three dudes and two chicks. Nitty checked out the surrounding area to make sure there was not a back up team with them. He strolled back and forth to make sure all was safe.

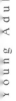

Young Adult

Showtyme closed his cell. "They're here," he announced.

Everybody moved into position. Even though no one expected anything to pop off, they all had their hammers within reach. They heard the knock on the door. Shawnee waited for Showtyme to signal her. Once he did, she opened the door with a bright smile and an itchy trigger finger. She stepped aside to let them in. *These are some ugly mofos, the chicks, on the other hand, are fly, she thought.* Again, she wondered, *What the hell they see in these cats?* As soon as the answer registered, she knew it was all about that paper. As she closed the door and went to the bar. *What's the difference between them and me?* she asked herself.

After making sure all was clear, Nitty made his way back upstairs. He checked the staircase, the hallway, and then entered the room next door to the suite that Showtyme occupied. Grabbing the knapsack with the cash, he ran back down to the parking lot and hit the valet attendant with a c-note. In turn he was allowed access to the parking area where the Haitian's Tahoe was parked. Nitty opened the driver's side door, threw the knapsack onto the floor in front of the passenger seat, and then just waited.

Showtyme, as usual, made a grand entrance, exiting the bedroom looking like new money. He shook everybody's hand like a damn politician, and then asked the Haitian named Notch to follow him out onto the balcony. As they conducted business, the suite filled with a nervous tension. Everybody's eyes moved back and forth like they were secret servicemen there to protect their man. After about a half an hour of negotiation, Showtyme and Notch leaned over the balcony, and Showtyme pointed to Notch's truck. Nitty opened the door, looked up, and then displayed the knapsack. Then he threw it back inside the truck, locked the doors, and then pressed the button which activated the alarm. The deal was sealed. The Henchmen had a new connect. Showtyme and Notch hugged one another, and then walked back into the suite where a sigh of relief was heard throughout the room.

Notch then yelled, "It's time to party M-I-A style. We should hang out tonight and celebrate."

"No doubt, but let's have a few drinks and be easy for a second," Showtyme replied. He didn't like showing up anywhere too early or too late. He always had to be the center of attention.

The music was turned on. Bottles of Ace of Spades were being popped open, and that potent Miami smoke was being lit and filled the air. Nitty came through the front door, threw the keys to the truck to Notch, and joined the party. An hour later they were sitting around enjoying the buzz, and vibing about Barack Obama's presidency.

Shawnee and the girls were vibing as well, talking about places to shop. They were ready to go to the club. Notch approached Shawnee and said, "Before the night is over I want us to get together. What do you say?" Shawnee looked past Notch and toward Showtyme, who smiled at her. Her stomach turned. She wondered, *Did Showtyme tell this fool I was available for his pleasuring.* Showtyme was known to do this. She looked at Notch with an attitude. "Give me a second," she said.

Shawnee headed directly over to Showtyme, who was flanked by both Cuban chicks. They were giggling like he was some kind of comedian. Shawnee thought, *I know he don't think this is some kind of swap party.* "Excuse me, Show, can I speak to you?"

Showtyme looked up at her then nudged the Cuban chick to his left over. He patted the seat for Shawnee to sit next to him. "What's up, baby? Talk to me."

Shawnee looked him in his eyes. "You told this bama' that him and I can get together?"

Showtyme looked at her like she had lost her damn mind. "Nah, I didn't tell him that, but if his country behind wants to get with you, then you get your butt over there and get with him. This is about business and you better not ever mess up my business. Do you understand me?"

She couldn't believe what she was hearing. Shawnee sucked her teeth and was about to storm off when Showtyme grabbed her by the arm. "Don't you ever suck your damn teeth at me again. Next time you do some mess like that I will knock them down your damn throat. Now if he wants to be with you, then you better go in there and show him a good time. You understand?" he whispered.

"Yes," she answered.

He then smacked her on her butt and watched her make her way back over to Notch. She turned back to glance at Showtyme, hoping he would stop her from having to be with this man. But he was back to business as usual, sliding his hands up the skirt of one of the Cuban ladies. Shawnee felt sick to her stomach. As she entered the bedroom her soul left her body.

NINETEEN

Chase slammed his phone shut. Stressed out after listening to Shawnee explain what happened in Miami, he tried to get her to just bounce like him, but she was not ready to deal with all the drama that came with getting out of the Henchmen. Chase had listened to her complain. *This can't wait any longer, it's time I lay this faggot down.* It felt like he was in no man's land. *Forget it … I'm doing this today,* he decided.

Chase got dressed, put on his vest, threw his *Glock*, cell, and other accessories in his back pack in order to meet Shawnee at Queens Mall. Heading out the front door he grabbed a green apple off the kitchen table. As he opened his front door, he realized he didn't have his keys and ran back to his room to get them. While looking for them, he noticed the scalpel sitting on his wall unit. He didn't know why, but something told him to grab and stash it on his person. *You never know,* he thought. He checked the hoodie he wore the day before and found his keys. Before he closed the closet door, he checked himself out in the mirror. Inside he felt like a true street soldier, unfortunately the foxhole he was in, kept getting deeper and deeper. Like most young men, he pushed his fears aside. *No time to be struggling with emotions during crunch time. Ready or not here I come. It's show time,* he thought.

As he made his way out of the apartment, his ability to see tomorrow was vanishing with each step he took. He pushed the button for the elevator. When the elevator opened, the staircase door slowly cracked open. Because he was focused on what he had to do, Chase did not see the eyes that peeked at him. The men who were posted on the staircase immediately raced down the stairs and radioed to their partners that Chase was coming their way. Chase pulled out his iPod and threw on his ear-plugs as he descended to the lobby. When the elevator door opened, Ms. Turner was standing there waiting to get on. Chase said hello and held the door open for her. Once she was on, he headed out the building. Focusing hard on Showtyme, and feeling the weight of his gun, Chase slung his backpack over his shoulder. He pushed the door open and stepped out into the fresh air. Suddenly things seemed to slow down, yet, there was a lot of movement around him. He felt like he was caught in some kind of matrix. He reached inside his backpack, but it was too late.

Four men ran up on him with their guns pointed directly at him. They were yelling, "Don't do it! Get your hands in the air!"

As Chase wrapped his fingers around his gun he noticed the badges hanging from the necks of the men. This stopped him dead in his tracks. He slowly removed his fingers from around his burner, knowing the police had no problem killing him if he dared brandish a gun. He looked around at all the weapons sighted on him. He was both mad and scared. Mad for getting caught slipping and scared that one of these cops just might let off. Slowly, he lifted his hand out of his backpack, snatched the headphones off his ears, and then raised his arms into the air.

"Get on the floor!" one of the detectives yelled.

Chase heard him, but his feet felt glued to the ground. When the second order was given for him to get on the ground, he smartly eased to the cold concrete. A crowd was now gathering, and he noticed people looking out of their windows and off their terraces.

Someone yelled out, "Make sure you don't do anything to that boy. We're watching you."

The detective placing Chase in handcuffs looked up at the older gentleman who made the comment. "Sir, he'll be fine," he said. After they put the restraints on, they searched Chase and found the nine-millimeter and an extra clip. The same officer asked, "Where you get the vest from?"

Chase said, "The Gap. They have a sale going on."

The officer passed the gun to his partner, who held it up for the residents to see what the police were dealing with. He made sure to look up at the elderly man who was still looking from his balcony. "Maybe you need to be worried about the boy doing something to us."

The old man just shook his head, and watched the detectives pull Chase off the ground and placed him in the back of a police car.

Chase went through the usual interrogation procedures. Of course, he held fast to the street code. He went to the arraignment the following morning and was remanded without bail. This was expected because he was not only caught with a loaded firearm, but a vest. He was lucky the Feds didn't pick up the case. His legal aid did say he would get a bail hearing within the next three weeks. When he reached Rikers Island, he immediately called QB. Of course QB was disappointed in him, but instead of reading him the riot act, he assured Chase that he would let his grandmother know and he would be out to the Island as soon as possible to visit. They ended the call with each trying to figure out how things fell apart so quickly.

Chase set the receiver down. When he turned around, the other inmates were mad-dogging him from every corner of the dorm. He reached into his pocket and felt his scalpel, glad that he had checked it when he left his house. He was ready for whatever, and like a lion in the jungle Chase stepped to them to mark his territory.

***

Amari pulled up to U-Turn. He stepped out his truck and hit QB up on his cell. He didn't want to go into the building. He knew a short visit would turn into QB having him lecture the youth about coming up in the streets. He always did that to him, so now he simply called him from outside the building. January was slipping into February bringing with it

Young Adult

a chill that wasn't to Amari's liking. He pulled his hoodie over his head as he waited for his brother.

QB came out the building five minutes later. "You should've just come up, 'Mari. Why you standing out in the cold?"

Amari walked to the driver's side. "Get in," he said. Once they settled into the truck, they wasted no time with small talk. Amari turned to him and said, "The meeting is a go." He looked in his rearview mirror. "He agreed to meet with us Friday night."

QB glanced out the passenger window. "Where at?" he asked.

"He said it will have to be in his 'hood, on his terms. In LeFrak, section two's garage, second level. He didn't say at what time. He wanted to wait until I confirmed the meeting with you and then he said he would let me know." He paused, getting lost in his thoughts. "I told him I would get back at him once we've talked. Q, this dude is crazy. We have to be careful dealing with him."

"Why you say that?"

"It's just the way this dude was talking to me. He's a loose cannon. You should have heard this cat telling me how the meeting place was not negotiable, either Friday or never. I was looking at this kid like who the hell do you think you are?"

"Listen 'Mari, tell the kid it's a go. In fact, call him now."

Amari took out his cell and called him. While the phone was ringing he let out one of those silent, deadly farts. After a few seconds QB literally started gagging. He hopped out Amari's truck cursing his brother out. People on the street were looking at him like he was crazy. Amari smiled at his brother, as he listened to what Showtyme was telling him. After QB caught his breath, he looked back in the truck to see Amari yelling into the phone. He could tell they were going back and forth with whatever they were talking about. Amari finally hung up. He waved for QB to come back in the truck. QB waved for him to get out. Amari jumped out the truck. "This punk thinks he's a shot-caller. He wants to meet Friday night, second level of the garage at three in the damn morning. On top of that, he had the audacity to tell me that we cannot bring more than four people with us. I asked that fool is he crazy? You know what he said?"

"What?"

He said, "Yeah I'm crazy, a rage against the machine kind of nigga." I wanted to jump through that phone and gun that fool down."

"At least he's honest, Amari. You need to keep your cool," said QB. They both looked at two passing young ladies. "What you think?" QB asked.

"I think we can hit them both over lunch and ..."

QB looked at Amari who was still looking at the junk in the trunk of the two ladies that walked past them. "I'm not talking about them, idiot. I'm speaking about Showtyme."

He leaned back on the side of the truck. "I don't know how you do it, little bruh. You should've never gotten married. I mean Reyna is cool and all, but damn. Anyway, I think Zeus was right, Q. There is no reasoning with this dude. Our best bet is to just give him the business."

"'Mari, I can't take that risk right now. I'm not trying to go back to prison unless it's for my family, and to be truthful, if someone violates Reyna, I may just snatch this fool up and then give her the burner and make her pull the trigger. They won't give her too much time." They both laughed.

"I hear you; I don't want anything to do with prison either, especially after seeing what you went through." They both got lost in their thoughts for a second. "So what's our next move?" Amari then asked.

"I'll call Zeus, but I need you to contact the rest of the team and tell them what happened. We'll meet Wednesday night at my spot."

"What's up with all these damn meetings?"

"I want to make sure we're all on the same page. So we can come up out of this with the best hand. Another thing ... I need you to take care of the hardware."

Young Adult

"Now that's what I'm talking 'bout," Amari said as he gave him a pound.

They broke their embrace. "One more thing. Go get your insides checked out," QB said.

"What?"

"You smell like roadkill." QB laughed as he walked back to the entrance to his job. "Hit me up on the cell if anything else comes up."

***

After speaking with Amari, Showtyme laughed to himself as he hung up his phone. He was in Hardbody's shopping for rims for his new truck. He couldn't believe he was being asked to meet with these lames. He refused at first, but Riv insisted. Showtyme knew better than to defy the OG. It was Riv who actually handed over the keys to the Henchmen to him two years ago. Showtyme knew it would've been a sign of disrespect to the OG if he refused. Now was not a good time to make mistakes, he had too much on his plate. After hooking up with the Haitians the Columbians had been making threats because he stopped doing business with them. It was just a matter of time before they tried to make a move on him. After deciding on the rims he wanted he flipped open his phone and called Tank to explain to him exactly what he needed him to do for their meeting with QB.

***

Wednesday night came quicker than QB expected. Reyna had one of her girlfriends over. QB forgot to tell Reyna about his expected company, but he reasoned that as long as her girlfriend was there it would be cool.

Nia, hearing her father come in the front door came running to get her usual hug, kiss, and Eskimo. With Nia in his arms, he made his way into the kitchen where Reyna and her best friend, Tiffany were busy yapping away. "What's up, beautiful?" QB said as he kissed Reyna.

"Hey baby, how was your day?"

"Work is work. What's up, Tiff?"

She waved at him nonchalantly, like he had some nerve interrupting their gossip session. QB looked at his wife's friend, who could have passed for Serena Williams twin, like she was crazy. He told his wife that he was expecting company in a few, and asked would she mind sending them downstairs when they arrived. Reyna didn't bother asking who, she knew it was nobody else but his brothers. QB never invited anyone else to their home.

"Who's coming over ... Ramel?" Tiffany asked as she chopped up some celery.

QB looked at her. "Why? You feeling my boy or something?"

She placed her hand on her hip and twisted up her lips. "Who said that?" she asked.

QB laughed. "The stupid look of anticipation on your face is telling me that."

"Forget you, Q. Is he coming or what?"

Reyna said, "Yeah Tiff, he's coming."

"Here Ray, finish chopping up this salad, I have to get my stuff together," said Tiffany as she smoothed out her skirt.

"Yeah, you're feeling my boy," said QB.

"He's a'ight. The only problem I got with him is he keep coming at me with some wack lines."

"Like what?" asked Reyna.

"The other day I saw his butt at Cosco and you know what this fool said to me?" She bent down to scratch the side of her leg. "He comes up behind me and says, 'Miss, if I could see you naked, I'd die happy.' I looked at this fool and said, 'If I saw you naked, I'd probably die laughing.'" She reached out to give Reyna some dap. "You know I got some comebacks for his crazy behind."

They broke out laughing. QB said, "Y'all are not going to be shootin' at my boy."

"Then tell him to come at me on a grown man tip and ask me out," said Tiffany.

Young Adult

QB turned to her. "Why don't you ask him out?"

Tiff looked at him like he was crazy.

"That's the problem with women. You all act like the whole process of getting together is something that's relegated to men. Trust me, that's no easy task, it's way too much pressure," said QB.

"Daddy, that's not nice word," said Nia.

"That's right, princess. Daddy is sorry. But back to y'all. Like I said that is way too much pressure to be putting on us."

Reyna and Tiff were not trying to hear that. They both started going at him with what they perceived the man's role should be. QB knew he had no wins, but he couldn't resist taking a shot at his wife. "Reyna did you tell Tiffany how you were sweating me when we first met. How you somehow arranged to accidentally meet me in the deli every single day for lunch."

Reyna threw the dish-rag at him, which missed by inches. "Q, you must be out of your mind. You were damn near stalking me ... I started to call the cops on you. Let's see, you sent a bouquet of flowers to my job for five straight days. If that's not sweating a sister, I don't know what is."

"Yeah, yeah, yeah, I sent you flowers, but you were still sweatin' a brother, so don't be acting up in front of company, you know I don't chase them, I replace them."

"We'll see who'll be chasing what tonight," said Reyna as she turned to Tiffany and gave her a high five.

QB looked at them laughing and knew he was in a danger zone. He decided to stop while he was ahead. The last thing he needed was for Reyna to start holding out on that good loving. He put Nia down and went into the bathroom to handle his business.

***

The boys showed up a little after eight. Zeus carried a stainless steel briefcase like he was out of the *Mission Impossible* movie. Reyna looked at it, but was afraid to even ask, yet, when Amari came through with a big trunk, her antenna shot up. She followed him to the basement and gave QB 'the look.'

He winked and mouthed the words, "Trust me."

Standing with her hands on her waist like she was somebody's mother, Tiffany just had to add fuel to the fire. QB ignored her and made his way to the basement, and closed the door behind him, hoping they got the message.

They wrapped things up about ten o'clock. Everything was set. Tomorrow QB was going to visit Chase. Zeus and Easy were going to check out the parking garage first thing in the morning. Ramel and True had to get the vehicles and Amari had to get the rest of the material that they were going to need. Their success depended on each of them pulling their own weight. They all knew it was time for them to turn the table on this dude; the hunter will now become the hunted.

***

QB's nerves were on edge. Friday night was finally here. Reyna and QB were in their bedroom. She was pleading with him to be careful as he got dressed. She noticed his gun snuggled in its holster, hanging on the closet door. It reminded her of the seriousness of the situation. Reyna's girlfriends were coming over; There was no way she could stay in the house by herself. She needed company until QB got back. She wanted to call the cops and report Showtyme, but knew QB would go ballistic if she did something like that.

Nia was at her grandmother's house for the weekend. There was very little QB could've done to ease Reyna's worries. The bottom line: She was going to be worried until he came back home in one piece.

When he finished dressing, he hugged her and promised that he would be back. He was in another zone, warrior mode. She hugged him tight, but the warmness of her embrace was unable to penetrate the coldness he would need during the confrontation. The doorbell rang, interrupting them, causing them to break their embrace.

Young Adult

UNDER PRESSURE

It was Shai. She gave her brother a kiss, and took one look at Reyna and said, "Girl stop worrying, this boy is going' to be a'ight. He knows how to handle his business." She looked at him and winked. "If not, he's going' to have to worry about me puttin' the beats on him like a MP3."

QB smiled, knowing his little sister was just trying to ease Reyna's fears. He kissed his sister and then Reyna, grabbed his keys, and headed out the door. He refused to look back at Reyna, afraid that her look would change his mind from doing what he knew he had to do!

TWENTY

QB, Zeus, and Amari pulled up to the garage at a quarter to three in the morning. Showtyme, who considered himself a General, had the Henchmen in place since midnight. They had the whole second level of the garage hemmed up. Henchmen were strategically placed throughout the entire garage, even the attendant who worked the entrance of the garage was down with them. QB put his hands in his coat pockets and felt his equalizers. They gave him a bit of assurance, yet, they also made him very nervous.

Zeus was checking out everything. As they made their way through the garage he counted at least thirty dudes. This was no surprise especially since they expected Showtyme to put on a physical display of strength and power. He smiled to himself when he noticed how dark it was. Thanks to Easy and his electrical skills the lights were intentionally put out. As they made their way around the bend of the garage where the elevators were located, four Henchmen stepped out in front of their vehicle just the way Chase said they would. This relaxed QB a little bit as he thought, *Maybe our plan has a chance of working.*

One of the Henchmen held his hand out, signaling Amari to stop the vehicle. Amari said in a low voice, "I should run his silly behind over." Instead he stopped the truck as he was instructed. Each of them looked around, taking in all necessary information, and calculating exactly what had to be done in the event chaos unfolded. They noticed the Henchmen posted up alongside the concrete poles. The scene looked like something out of the movie *Training Day*.

"Y'all ready?" asked QB.

"Let's do this," said Zeus, checking his Taurus's swinging in his holsters. They started to step out of the truck. Before they could close the doors, twenty different types of automatic guns were raised and aimed at them. There was a chorus of guns being cocked. Zeus just smiled. QB looked at him like he was crazy. Amari was busy checking out who he was going to shoot first in the event that it went down. They stood there, no one said anything. The three of them began to slowly spread out as much as they could without drawing attention to themselves. They were trying to strategically position themselves. Everything they spoke about Wednesday night was actually happening like clockwork. You wanted a degree of predictability in situations like this, and along with the help of Chase, thus far, they had nailed down the Henchmen's every move.

"Who told y'all niggas to move?" yelled Nitty.

They glanced at each other with looks that read, *Who the hell is this kid talking to?* QB shook his head thinking, *He can't be no older than fifteen.* However, the AK he was holding definitely made him appear bigger.

"Which one of you is Showtyme?" QB asked.

Standing about 5'6", with a body that reflected he spent too much time eating honey buns, Nitty said, "Showtyme will be here when he gets here."

Zeus let out a breath that signaled his frustration. This irritated Nitty. "You got a problem with something I said big man?"

Zeus stared down at him. "Usually when I have problems with little creatures like you, it's when I come home at night and turn the lights on in my apartment. I usually see the likes of you scattering across my floor and I simply step on you," he   said.

The remark caused Tank to step to Zeus. *Damn, he's just as big as Zeus*, thought QB.

"You think you're tough, my dude?" Tank asked, as he raised his hammer and centered it directly in between Zeus' eyes.

Zeus was cool as a fan. He looked at him. "Nah, I'm far from tough, but I have a feeling you think you are because you got that gun in your hand." He paused for a split second and then added, "I would like to see just how tough you are without one?"

QB tensed up and thought, *Why did I bring Zeus? I knew he was going to push it to the limit.*

The deadly Henchmen were not feelin' the fact that Zeus challenged their boy. Somebody yelled out, "He thinks he can take you, Tank."

Tank is a fitting name, the kid is a beast. He probably was in prison lifting steel for breakfast, lunch, and dinner, thought QB. He looked around, preparing to react if necessary.

Tank pulled off his shirt. Zeus backed up a few steps, twisted his neck like Mike Tyson did before he pounded out his opponents. The Henchmen closed in, forming a circle.

QB, Amari, and Zeus were in the center of the makeshift ring. Amari was not feeling this. QB, always the optimist, thought, *This is going to work to our advantage.* They squared off. Tank was circling Zeus trying to feel him out. QB wanted to say something, but decided against it. He knew that Zeus was going to do this kid dirty. *But not now*, he thought.

Nitty suddenly spun on QB, and pointed an AK 47 at him. "Back it up."

It caused a chain reaction. The theory that it only takes a spark to start a forest fire was about to be tested. QB looked at the faces half-covered with bandanas and wondered if any of them was actually Showtyme.

Zeus and Tank were still circling one another. Neither one wanted to make the wrong move. They both were capable of breaking bones with their bare hands. Zeus decided he was going to shatter his leg, and

Young Adult

then break his neck. Zeus studied martial arts in the military—Krav-Marga was a martial art technique which he learned during his short stay. Unlike Easy, Zeus got kicked out of the Marines for beating up a racist sergeant like he was an African drum. However, while there, he too was a one man dream team who crushed his opponents. He was about to step in and make his move, when a booming voice stopped everyone in their tracks. "What the hell is this?"

The Henchmen spun around, recognizing the voice. It was Showtyme. The ring slowly parted. Showtyme, Banger, Cherokee and Shawnee, stepped into the makeshift ring to see what was going on. Cherokee and Shawnee held the leashes of two pit bulls. The vicious dogs were foaming at the mouth and growling viciously. They were pulling the young ladies like they were going to break free from their grip at any second.

Nitty was the first to speak. "This lame was poppin' smack to Tank. Showtyme looked at Zeus and Tank. He told Tank to put his shirt back on. "Didn't I tell you fools to be easy until I got here?" Nobody said anything. Showtyme was disgusted with them. *I have to get back to the basics, start handling these niggas with an iron fist*, he thought.

He then turned his attention to QB, Amari and Zeus, "Which one of you is QB?"

QB stepped up. "I am." Showtyme smirked while smoking a cigarette. He looked at QB and then flicked his cigarette. It hit the ground and cart-wheeled toward QB, the burning tip breaking apart, showered QB's feet with red sparks. QB looked up slowly, trying his best to conceal his hatred.

QB knew immediately that Showtyme wanted to get inside his head and that the cigarette was nothing but a silly attempt to anger him.

Amari's eyes seemed to darken; he was reading Showtyme like a cashier's scanner reading the bar code of butter. He thought to himself, *Dude is soft. I should blow his head off his shoulders*. Zeus's jaw tightened like it was set in concrete. His nostrils flared, and his eyes changed from a cool brown to a 'kill this nigga red!' He already knew who he was shooting first. He looked over at Tank, playing out in his mind how he was going to put his first shot right through Tank's neck. The tension in the air was thick.

"What you wanna see me for?" Showtyme asked with a look of displeasure.

Caught in the crosshair of emotions, QB didn't trust himself to speak. However, he knew he had to. He took a deep breath. "What can I do in order for you to let Chase live, and forget that this whole thing ever went down?" He looked Showtyme in his eyes for a sign that would tell him whether or not he was pushing the right buttons. "It was my truck that was shot up." He swallowed, fighting to keep his composure. "I was the one who got hit and since I am willing to forget the whole thing, then ... I'm just hoping my ability to forgive can be enough for you to consider letting Chase walk away from your ..." He paused, searching for the right word; he didn't want to offend this punk. "... organization without him having to worry about somebody shooting him."

Showtyme's breathing became short and labored. He blinked. "Let me get this straight. You fools come up in here lookin' square as *Cheez it's*, telling me what you think I should do about one of my own." Showtyme reached down and rubbed the head of one of the pit bulls. He didn't believe what he was hearing. "Let me tell y'all something. I know Chase is on the Island ..." He spit on the ground. "I doubt very seriously he'll make it home in one piece." Rikers Island was notorious when it came to detention centers. It's the largest City jail in the world. Once you entered its buildings, you either had to get busy or be victimized. Showtyme added, "And if he does make it out, there is nothing any of you three can say or do that will save him from getting washed up."

The pit in Cherokee's grasp was beginning to act up. It was itching to attack, causing the other beast that Shawnee held to get riled up.

Young Adult

They both struggled to control the dogs. Everybody's attention was now on the two animals. Amari was inching toward his heat. Zeus had his arms crossed, but kept his hands wrapped around his burners. The tension was about to break. The barking of the dogs was loud and vicious. Amari looked from Showtyme to the dogs and back. Showtyme reached down again and grabbed the pit and spoke to it with soothing words of a trainer. The pit calmed down. He then stepped closer to QB. "You know you got some balls comin' at me with this bull. I respect your courage, but let me tell you what I think you should do." He ran his hand across his face and then continued. "You need to take your punk behind back to U-Turn and worry about the little kids in your program. Because if you ever come at me with this stupid mess again, then the least of your worries would be whether or not Chase is gonna live ... You'll be worrying about your punk behind—do you understand?"

QB said nothing. He slid his hands into the pockets of his field jacket and palmed that which he hoped he wouldn't have to use. He stared at Showtyme, refusing to be the first to break the stare down. QB thought, *This fool is good; he doesn't even blink. Even people with glass eyes blink.*

Showtyme felt disrespected by the eye-screwing and the silence. He looked around at his soldiers, and then cleared his throat gathering a glob of phlegm in his mouth. He looked back at QB and then spit the phlegm directly in his face. Amari and Zeus couldn't take it any longer; they both pulled out their choppers. With their arms outstretched, they each held two big caliber handguns. They were flanking QB, setting their sights on specific individuals. The Henchmen reacted at the same time, a full fledge massacre was about to pop off. All it took was for one person to let off a shot.

QB, who was temporarily paralyzed by the disrespect of being spit on, miraculously remained calm. He allowed the phlegm to slide down his face to his shirt. He didn't move, even though he was boiling inside. He pulled his hand out of his pocket to wipe his face, when suddenly

Cherokee reacted to his movement. She instinctively reached for her gat and let the leash of the red nose pit loose. The dog rushed directly at QB, it leaped but was stopped in its track by one shot. The pit's head exploded in mid-air like a watermelon being hit with an aluminum bat. Everybody was stunned and shocked because nobody heard a shot or saw where it came from. They all turned, the Henchmen could not believe their eyes. Gunmen with night goggles and army fatigues surrounded them. It was eight of … what looked like real soldiers. Nitty thought, *Where did these niggas come from?* Then he realized they came up out of the trunks of the cars parked in the garage.

Showtyme looked around not believing the position he was in. Nobody knew what to do. You could see the confused looks on the faces of the Henchmen. They felt vulnerable. They looked at Showtyme for instructions, but then their mouths slowly dropped open at what they saw next.

Showtyme followed everybody's eyes to his chest. He looked down to see what everybody was looking at. The eight infra-red dots circling his chest scared the hell out of him. Eight M16 high velocity weapons were aimed directly at him. Amari and Zeus chose them because they were very dependable weapons as long as they were kept clean and ready. Ready, meaning a kac suppressor, silencers, and hundred round c-mag double-drum magazines. The way they looked standing there with those weapons sent the message to Showtyme that he was in a no-win situation. For the first time in a long time, he felt powerless. He looked down at Terror, the heaving body of the red pit irritated him. When he moved toward one of his soldiers the red-dots followed. He grabbed the kid's nine, pointed at the body of the pit, and fired one shot to stop the beating of the heart.

QB thought, *This dude is good. He definitely knows how to remain cool under pressure.* Showtyme smiled, trying his best to mask his anger. He realized QB was the only one who didn't pull out a weapon. Yet, when he looked closer, his eyes almost popped out his head. QB was standing there in the midst of all the chaos with a grenade in each one of his hands.

QB was a man who gained control with anger. He could tell Showtyme was beginning to realize that he lost this round. QB could see the indecision and lack of confidence beneath the calmness which he tried to display. Showtyme was now paying serious attention to QB. He could feel the force of his hatred through QB's silence. How the situation got out of hand in a matter of seconds had Showtyme second guessing himself. Though he would never admit it, he did feel some fear. However, he knew how to turn fear into a weapon. When he looked into QB's eyes there was an absence of fear. "You know you messed up? You might as well kill me now, because if you don't, if I walk out of here today ... It's war."

Hearing this, QB became numb with fear, he was not scared of what Showtyme said, but of what he felt like doing. He recognized the feeling from the last time he killed. He tried to calm himself. "You know I thought you were much smarter than you actually are. You got some nerve threatening me. You must have the mental capacity of a puddle. I think I gave you too much credit." QB stopped and looked around at all the young soldiers he had under his control. "You got me mixed up, Showtyme. What kind of name is that? What—you like being under the bright lights?" QB ate up the space between them. "Let me give you some advice. You're messin' with a different kind of soldier now, and if you ever again think about coming after me, Chase, Torry, or anybody I am associated with, I swear ... you'll regret it. I will hunt you down like you have never been hunted before and let you star in my movie." He paused for a second. "Trust me fella you're not in my league."

QB realized his boys were right. He couldn't make sense with a fool who could not get out of his own way. Showtyme just stared at him with a smirk on his face. QB gripped the grenades tightly and could see Showtyme contemplating his options.

They were interrupted by the footsteps echoing off the concrete of the parking lot. It was Riv along with two other men. They approached the group. Riv looked around and said, "I want everybody to put down their toys."

The Henchmen looked at Showtyme, who nodded. The OG's word held more weight, but they still knew to give Showtyme his respect. They lowered their weapons. Riv turned to Amari. "'Mari, tell the Green Beret to put down their weapons. They're beginning to make me nervous." Riv looked around at the situation. "... I thought you told me you just wanted to talk?"

Amari looked at Ramel, who signaled for the rest of the team to lower their weapons. Everybody had lowered their guns except for Zeus, who had both of his burners sighted on Tank. They stared at each other until he slowly holstered his guns. He then blew Tank a kiss, indirectly calling him a punk.

Seeing this, Riv said, "What's up with all the hostility? This is not what this was supposed to be about. I got y'all together to prevent a war, so why is it, I come up in here and you cats is looking like the Navy Seals and Al Qaeida?" He looked around frustrated, and then dismissed the Henchmen. He pointed down at the dog and said, "Make sure you clean this up." He then turned to Amari, "Who's QB?" Amari looked at his brother. Riv then turned to QB and Showtyme. "Let's walk."

Twenty minutes later there was still a stalemate. Showtyme wouldn't bend because he felt disrespected. All QB wanted was for the Henchmen to stay away from U-Turn and for them to let Chase live. He didn't think that was too much to ask for, especially after he was willing to give them a pass for shooting him and paralyzing Torry.

Riv told QB he would handle it from here on out. He didn't want this to become any bigger than it already is. He checked for Amari, that was his man. They went back like old car seats. Like QB, Riv was from the old school, and realized that for these young dudes today, violence was an addiction, and gangs had become the perfect release for their bottled up anger.

He assured QB that U-Turn would be off limits, and told him that if he felt any immediate threat from any of the Henchmen that he should contact him directly. He gave QB his direct contact information, as he looked down at his hands. "I see you like pineapples. You can put them away," he said, referring to the grenades that QB still clutched.

"Not really," QB said, and then put them in his coat pockets.

They parted. QB hopped in Amari's truck, Zeus was the last to get in. He had to walk back over to Tank. "I like your style, youngin', but if you really want to see me, we can meet on our own terms." Tank said nothing; he stood there shooting daggers back at him, knowing that they would, real soon.

Ramel, True, Easy, and the rest of their team hopped into the car that they 'jacked in the box' out of. They pulled out of the garage in one minute intervals, with Amari bringing up the rear. They all headed in different directions. They all knew what they had to do.

QB immediately phoned Reyna. She answered on the first ring. "Hello."

Everything is good, beautiful, I'm on my way home," said QB.

***

Reyna met QB at the door. Her smile said it all, and some. They hugged each other tight. QB's heart was caught in between two extremes: love and war. He felt punch drunk standing there in his wife's arms. As he held her close, he realized she was the one person who brought sanity to his craziness. He prayed it was enough to sustain him through the madness. He couldn't afford to slip through the crevice of irrational decisions. Since coming home from prison, his goals were to alleviate any room to fall through the cracks, build a family, and to avoid recidivism.

They did very little talking, they proceeded upstairs to their bedroom to say all the things that needed to be said.

***

QB and his team met the following afternoon at De'Roche's, a classy restaurant in the city. When QB showed up, Ramel was bragging about how he executed his 'one-shot-one kill' on the pit bull. Unfortunately, what he failed to recognize was that his actions could have set off a reaction that could've gotten all of them killed. Each of them understood that this was far from over. Showtyme was not the type to let something like this go. He was the kind of guy who had road rage driving down an empty street, a thug with a big motor who needed nothing more than a little revving to get started.

During their meeting they decided the best thing for them to do was to wait until they heard from Riv before they planned their next move. Zeus, Amari, and True were still leaning toward just getting rid of Showtyme. However, they knew the stakes were even higher now than before because Showtyme now knew what they all looked like.

Young Adult

TWENTY-ONE

Three' weeks had passed since the meeting with Showtyme and his Henchmen. Things were finally falling back into place. Reyna seemed like her normal, beautiful self. She was not as worried as much as she was prior to QB meeting with Showtyme. QB was getting stronger by the day, working out lightly with the weights, and a lot of cardio. His motto was you had to stay ready, so you don't have to get ready.

Torry was doing well. He sent out his applications to colleges and was putting in major work in therapy. Naysia, who looked like she was going to burst any day now, was making sure she was there to comfort him after those grueling hours of being twisted and turned. Torry didn't make it out to visit Chase yet, but they had resolved their differences, and had been talking on the phone regularly. Torry was kept abreast about Chase's happenings because Lexi had been going up to see him. Naysia had convinced Lexi to give him a second chance after she explained that he was really trying to get his life together.

The District Attorney offered Chase a one to three, and he decided to take it. He could've ended up doing much more time if he went to trial. But QB, among others had pulled what little strings they possessed. Chase was good with his plea. He just wanted one thing, and that was for Torry to accept his diploma on his behalf at the upcoming U-Turn graduation. He also wanted him to read a speech that he prepared. This took some coaxing, but Torry finally agreed.

Life in jail was as bad as Chase expected. He hated being there, was lonely, and missed his grandmother. But he knew the saying, do the crime—do the time. He had a few squabbles since being there. The beefs were nothing he couldn't handle. However, he was trying to avoid them at all cost. He finally realized that Showtyme was not worth him throwing his life away. There were some thorough dudes waiting for Showtyme to come through. He was going to get the business if he ended up on lockdown. Chase knew it was important for him to do his time and get out. He didn't want to get caught up in the madness of cutting and stabbing cats for reputations and props. Some brothers on the Island had and gave out more cuts on faces than a barbershop. When Chase lay on his bunk at night, he reminisced about all the lessons that QB had shared with him and Torry. For reasons unknown, they were finally making sense, becoming clearer. *Maybe it was due to the solitude of a cell*, he thought.

He asked Torry to send him some urban 'hood books. QB gave him some self-introspective books, which he read. Naim Akbar, *Community of Self*, Napoleon Hill, *Think and Grow Rich*, *The Autobiography of Malcom X* by Alex Haley, among others. The books were cool, and he learned a lot about himself and told Torry he should read them as well. But he wanted some entertainment. So Torry promised to get him some books.

Glad that his man was getting his life back in order, it actually inspired Torry to continue moving forward during those times when he was feeling low. Torry desperately needed to speak to QB, and reminded himself to call him later on. He needed to talk about the baby and the whole issue of fatherhood. Naysia was due any day now, and honestly speaking, he was getting more nervous by the minute.

***

It was Reality Week at U-Turn. A time when QB and the staff took the students to morgues, prisons, and other similar places where they taught the students first-hand lessons about the dangers associated with

Young Adult

running the streets. QB had even asked Torry to speak to the students this time around, and he accepted.

Torry reminisced about the time when he had to go through Reality Week, seeing babies in the hospital unit who were born to mothers with HIV as a result of drug usage, visiting prisons, and hearing stories from murderers about the consequences of peer pressure, and making that one bad decision. But it was seeing bodies with bullet holes and knife wounds in them, which reminded Torry of just how precious life really is. He remembered how scared he was during his trip, and how he had made a pact with himself that week to do things the right way, which to him meant distancing himself from the streets.

But look at me, he thought. *Even though I was doing right, things still had a way of coming at me.* He wheeled himself into his living room thinking about QB and all the things he did to pull up everyone around him. Torry promised he was going to be the same way with his son or daughter; he wasn't going to let them fall victim to the streets.

***

Five in the morning, the cloak of darkness was barely hanging on. The heavily armed Gang Intelligence Unit (GIU) was getting prepared to move. They were assembled into four teams of eight, sitting around anxiously waiting for the signal. Delaney, Hudson, and Powell led three of the units. In addition, a young, gung ho detective named Madison led the fourth one.

They would strike simultaneously. The GIU was charged up and not just because of the coffee they'd been drinking for the past two hours. There was a tremendous amount of adrenaline that these type of raids created within a law enforcer. It was the fuel that made these missions successful; successful meaning that no officer comes out injured. If there had to be casualties, they would prefer it be the suspects as opposed to one of their own. Make no mistake about it—each and every one of them was prepared to kill.

They didn't know exactly which apartment Showtyme was in, if any at all. They were going to hit each spot hard and fast. They had the Sherwood Village spot surrounded, and three apartments in LeFrak City under surveillance.

People were beginning to exit the buildings—heading for work. The unit's vehicles blended in well, not alarming the residents at all. They had a moving company truck, Cable Vision Company van, among other well-disguised vehicles. Inside these vehicles, they had the latest technology, and enough artillery to take out a small island. Each member of the Gang Intelligence Unit was deep in thought, nervous, yet prepared to enter the spot full of deadly unpredictable shooters who felt they had nothing to lose.

Hudson sat there hoping that Showtyme would be in the apartment he was assigned to. He hungered for the opportunity to take him out. They had their share of run-ins, and Showtyme had stated many times before, that he would much rather be carried by six than judged by twelve. To Hudson, Showtyme was nothing more than a rabid dog that needed to be euthanized. So Hudson decided that he was going to be the community veterinarian.

His thoughts were interrupted by the order that came across his ear piece. He jumped up and gave his team the signal, "Go! Go! Go!"

The units stormed out of staircases and vacant apartments that they had occupied. They were strapped for war, ambushing apartments like a military brigade. Knocking the front doors off hinges with a ram, awaking neighbors, flash grenades were tossed into each spot. All four apartments were under attack. Delaney's unit was the only unit involved in the exchange of gunfire, but it was all over in under eight minutes, and each spot was secure.

The leading detectives each yelled, "Secure," into their mic when they had their assigned apartments under control.

Two suspects in Delaney's spot were shot—flesh wounds. They were immediately taken to the hospital, where they would be placed under

Young Adult

arrest. The rest of the suspects were handcuffed. Most of them didn't have time to get dressed, so the detectives gave them whatever clothes that were in reach.

Drugs, guns, and money were confiscated from each apartment. As the suspects were led to the awaiting transport vehicle, neighbors were quietly watching from their doors. Kids stood between their mother's legs. Most of the residents had issues with the police, yet, they were, for the most part glad that the GIU finally rounded up the Henchmen. Twenty-three suspects in all were arrested. None of them, unfortunately, was the infamous Showtyme.

***

It didn't take long for the word to spread about the raids. Showtyme immediately went escape mode. He called down stairs, waking Shawnee and Cherokee, then called out for Banger, but realized that he'd dropped him off at the Sherwood Village spot the night before. "Who's here?" he asked Cherokee.

"I don't know. I saw Nitty and Tank before I went to bed. I'll check," she answered.

A few other Henchmen were in the spot at the house where the killing of Face and Kema had occurred.

"Clean up shop and let's roll out," Showtyme yelled to everyone. They were out of the trap house within twenty minutes. Showtyme always prepared for the worse. Shawnee, Cherokee, Tank, and Nitty jumped in the truck with Showtyme. Everyone else was instructed to go underground for a minute. He would get back at them in a few days. He wanted them to keep their ears to the streets and report to him with any information that they hear.

***

Chaotic was an understatement when it came to what was happening at GIU headquarters. Interrogations, statements, and the lineups were all being conducted. The District Attorney was on hand taking video confessions. Delaney, who thought the stop snitching campaign was working, suddenly had a change of heart. These kids were singing like American Idols, some worthwhile, and others just wanted to put on a show.

The Unit made a few more arrests throughout the day based on new information provided by those who were relieved from being under Showtyme's rule and those who were scared to go to jail. "It's a good day for the good guys," yelled Powell.

Hudson was pissed off that Showtyme got away. But they had put a major dent in their operation. They all knew that this was not enough; they wanted to bring the notorious Showtyme down.

***

Chase had Lexi use her three-way to connect him to U-Turn so he could let QB know about the morning raids. Chase didn't know much, but word on the Island was that the Henchmen were coming through by the busloads. Both administration and prisoners were getting ready to welcome them. It was all over the news. Unfortunately, QB missed it taking Nia to his mother-in-law... Hearing about the raids from Chase stirred mixed emotions inside of QB. On one hand he hated the fact that it took prison bids for youth to understand that life was too short to be playing street games. But on the other hand, everyone must be held accountable for their own actions, and if the threat of going to prison can act as a deterrent then so be it. He hoped that these kids would take advantage of the solitude they were about to encounter, and use the time to take a serious, brutal look at their lives and make some real changes. QB made sure to remind Chase of the importance of him being smart, and to not get caught up in anything that will hurt his chances of getting out. Chase promised that he would. After they hung up, QB turned to his daughter who was reading a book while in her car seat. *If only life could be so sweet and easy*, thought QB. He blew a kiss at his daughter. She smiled, touching a place within him reserved strictly for her.

***

LeFrak was swarming with rumors. The residents felt safer because the Henchmen no longer had LeFrak under siege. Fifty Seventh Avenue was finally clear of drug trafficking. How long would it last, no one knew, but most residents felt if it was only for one day, it would be worth it. Mothers who once held their children close to them as they walked in and out of the projects now allowed their children to walk freely, but not too far away from them. They were still cautious. They heard all the rumors of retaliation toward any resident who even thought about cooperating with the police. The last time something like this happened there were at least five shootings, and two innocent victims were hit. Drive-by-shootings were the ultimate deterrent, and for most residents testifying was simply not worth the risk.

The presence of the police, patrolling from 99th Street to Horace Harding Boulevard, made them feel somewhat safe, but they knew their presence was only temporary and would fade in a few days. These were very trying times for the residents of LeFrak. However, if they wanted to take their community back, there was no better opportunity. They had some tough decisions to make, because one of the reasons why their projects had earned the handle Iraq was due in part to the spontaneous use of violence. They hoped this raid didn't set off a rash of shootings and killing of innocent people like its namesake in the Middle East.

TWENTY-TWO

Later that evening, Showtyme was gathering as much information as possible about what had taken place. He finally spoke to Shapiro, who had heard about the raids. He told him that he was on the case. Showtyme assured him that money wasn't a problem. He told Shapiro that he wanted as many Henchmen bailed out as soon as possible. He knew the longer they stayed in jail, the easier it was for the District Attorney to get them to sing. Shapiro had his bail bondsmen on the case. He explained that he would contact the District Attorney to see exactly what they had on Showtyme, and then together, they would decide what was best for him to do.

Showtyme threw his phone on the couch in frustration. The timing couldn't have been worst. His first shipment from his new connect had arrived two days before the raid, so he needed to figure out how he was going to unload this product. He sat in the recliner contemplating his next move. "Cherokee," he called.

"What?" she answered.

"Where is Shawnee? She's been gone for three hours."

"I don't know, she didn't tell me where she was going."

"Hit her up on her cell and tell her I said to get back here."

She sucked her teeth. "A'ight," she said.

Closing his eyes, Showtyme leaned back into the soft leather. His head was pounding. He had to get his thoughts together. *I should go down to Miami by myself and leave everybody here. Nah, I can't do that. My absence may cause everybody to get paranoid and start singin' to the police. A'ight, I gotta stay in Lakeview for a minute, move around at night. During the day Cherokee and Shawnee will have to handle things*, he thought. "Cherokee."

"What's up, Show?"

"Bring me somethin' to smoke!"

"Okay, give me a second?"

Showtyme pulled his Glock from his waist and thought about what needed to be done. He looked around and mumbled, "Pressure bust pipes—not gangstas!"

***

The following two weeks, nine of the twenty-three Henchmen got out, some on bail and others were released on their own recognizance. Those that were let out were looked at with suspicious eyes. Either they were cooperating with the DA, or the DA had very little evidence against them. Exactly who was doing what, was something Showtyme needed to find out. The rest of the Henchmen had parole or probation holds, so they were not getting out. Banger was one of the nine that got out. He lucked up because of his age. He was only fifteen, so he had been released through the court.

When Showtyme spoke to Shapiro again, he found out that there might be some truth to the secret indictment coming down against him. Showtyme had heard this before, but the difference now is that they had been investigating him for the past six months and the raid would've never went down unless there was evidence to substantiate his arrest. Showtyme was pleased with Shapiro and the way he was handling his business. However, he noticed his greed, but Showtyme understood you had to pay the cost to be the boss. While many hustlers went to jail broke because they lived for foreign cars and iced out jewelry,

Showtyme, had that Johnny Cochran, Dream Team money, and would pay anything to stay out of prison.

Shapiro told Showtyme that there were six unidentified individuals willing to testify against him at the grand jury. He assured him he would do his best to find out all the names. Earlier during the day, the District Attorney had contacted Shapiro offering a deal if Showtyme turned himself in. Showtyme laughed and then cursed his attorney out for even relaying such a message. Shapiro explained to him that he was bound by ethics to relay the offer. Showtyme told him to screw ethics, just get him the names of who was supposed to testify.

After hanging up, Showtyme thought, *Don't these fools know that I'm as elusive as smoke on a windy day? I'm the modern day Osama Bin Laden.*

***

Cherokee picked up Banger that evening. When they got to the house in Long Island, Banger was welcomed like he did a ten-year bid. Showtyme had some girls waiting on him, to take care of his sexual needs. Banger was turning out to be Showtyme's most trusted Henchmen. From the moment he was released, he was talking trash like he did some hard time. Showtyme was doggin' him for acting like the two weeks he spent on Rikers Island was an eternity in Attica.

It had been quiet for the last two weeks. In Showtyme's mind things seemed to be coming back together; he felt like he was weathering the latest storm. They had opened three new spots. The Columbians were trying to move into the old spots, but Showtyme wasn't having that. He was waiting for things to cool down and then he would hit them up, and get his old spots back just on general principle. He refused to let anybody push him without pushing back.

It was getting late. Banger and Showtyme both had jump-offs draped all over them. Banger turned to Showtyme and said, "I hear that Chase is supposed to be turning state on you."

Young Adult

"Yeah, that's what I heard, too. In fact, I heard six cheese eating, cock-suckers are supposed to be testifying against me. Shapiro is supposed to get me the names. I cannot see Chase testifying, but we'll see," Showtyme said.

"That's the word on the street, Show. We should've been washed him up."

Showtyme turned to Banger. "Homie, I'm untouchable. Forget Chase, if he testifies against me, he's gonna regret every word that comes out of his mouth. Let me ask you something, do you know where his grandmother lives?"

"Yeah, I know where that old hag lives," replied Banger.

Showtyme stood and walked to the wall unit. He then turned back around. "Do you know where this dude, QB lives?"

"Nah, but you know he works at U-Turn."

"Where's that program at?"

"Queens Boulevard," said Banger.

Showtyme stood there contemplating. "That's good. I got something for these lames."

***

It had been a long weekend for Shapiro, his eyes were red, reflecting the fatigue his body felt. He threw his suit jacket on the back of his office chair, popped a valium in his mouth, and chased it down with some vodka. It was Monday morning, the worst day of the week for him. He was not in his office a half hour when the District Attorney contacted him. His secretary put the call through without warning him. *Damn*, he thought. It was confirmed, Showtyme would be indicted Thursday morning. He explained to Shapiro that this was his client's last opportunity to come in voluntarily or else the hole he was in would become much deeper. Shapiro chuckled, but was willing to play the game. "What kind of deal are we talking about?"

"Rob, you know it's much too early to be negotiating the amount of time ..." He paused to make sure he said the right thing. "However, you and I both know there is no way he's getting less than life. Now it's his choice between twenty-five to life or life without parole. That's what's negotiable, Rob." There was a prolonged silence, until the D.A. asked, "You there?"

"Yes, I'm listening," said Shapiro.

The district attorney continued. "Furthermore, there is also the possibility of us turning the case over to the Feds, and if that happens, Mr. Adams would be tried by them and he'd end up doing life in places like Leavenworth or Marion, as opposed to Sing Sing or Comstock. Now I'm sure he would much rather do his time in the State as oppose to God knows where."

Shapiro wanted to scream, "You've got to be kidding," through the phone. His offer was nothing but a smokescreen, but Shapiro held his tongue. "I'll make sure I relay your offer to my client if he contacts me." Shapiro knew better than to lead on that he and Showtyme were in touch. The last thing he needed was to be followed and harassed by police. "By the way, what makes you so sure he will be indicted?"

"C'mon, Rob, we've got eight people testifying at the grand jury and to be honest with you, more are lining up as if they were waiting to play the lottery. The community wants this animal in a cage. My advice to you is to stay clear of this scum, but if you insist on helping him, the best thing you could do for him at this point is advise him to turn himself in, and maybe we can work out a deal."

Tired of the rhetoric, Shapiro said, "I'll be sure to contact you if I hear from him." He hung up the phone. Shapiro sat at his desk and wondered exactly how he was going to handle the situation. Knowing this just might be his last opportunity to get a nice lump sum of Showtyme's money. He had to make sure he played his cards right. *For now I have to keep him from going to jail*, he thought. He picked up the phone and called Showtyme.

***

Young Adult

UNDER PRESSURE

I got three days to make it happen, thought Showtyme. He had just ended his call with Shapiro who informed him that he was well on his way to being indicted, and that he wouldn't be able to get the names of those scheduled to testify at the grand jury until Thursday. Unfortunately, that was the day it was all supposed to go down.

Showtyme was faced with the choices of running or fighting. Not only with this case, but with the Columbians as well, who were now taking over his spots. Things were really beginning to mount. His money was spread out and in order to successfully go on the run he knew he needed a lot of cash. Shapiro was a whole different issue. He no longer trusted him; he noticed the changes in his behavior recently. It was time for him to take matters into his own hands. He needed to prevent everybody from testifying, and it was his only option.

He picked up the phone and called Banger. When he answered, Showtyme said, "It's a go. Don't screw this up, do you understand? Hit me up if you run into any problems. I will meet you at the trap house at six. One." He clicked off and went to work.

***

Reyna grabbed her bag and hopped in her car and raced toward Smart Kidz University. She was rushing, because her mother had called her at the last minute and told her she couldn't pick up Nia. Because she was in a hurry, Reyna didn't notice the van that was following her.

"Homie, we have to do this now before she hits the main roads. Matter of fact, at the next stop sign I want you to bump into the back of her car. Not too hard, we don't need people coming out their homes, just tap her."

"A'ight, I got this, son."

When Reyna slowed down at the next stop sign, she reached down to change the XM station. Suddenly a van ran into her from behind. Her body jerked forward, her head hit the steering wheel, dazing her a little. "Damn!" she cursed.

Banger jumped out the van, along with Nitty. They went to the driver's side of the car and asked, "Miss, you all right?" Reyna looked up ready to curse somebody out when she noticed the black gun being thrust in her face. She didn't understand what was going on. Shock took over; she was stunned and now frozen. The thug pulled her by her arm, but the seatbelt prevented her from being snatched out the car.

Reyna let out a loud, "What do you want?"

"Shut up," said Banger, "before I shoot you right here." He then reached across her body and unhooked the seatbelt. She hesitated, not sure what she should do. All kind of thoughts were running through her head, *carjack, robbery,* the last thing she thought of was being kidnapped.

"What do you want? Here, take my car," Reyna said, reaching for the keys. Suddenly he snatched her by her shirt. Remembering an episode of Oprah about preventing kidnaps, Reyna began screaming and clawing at Banger. She dug her nails into his eyes trying to gauge them out. She kneed him in his privates and started swinging at him like Barry Bonds going for the home run record. Reyna didn't think about her actions. When your life is on the line you'll be surprised at the courage and strength you may find inside yourself, especially when you have to fight for your very own survival. Reyna was putting up one hell of a fight. *Where's the help? Why hasn't anybody come to my aid? Everything is happening so quickly. What is this?* she wondered.

Suddenly she saw lightning, somebody hit her on the side of her head with what she thought had to be a pipe. Nitty stood there laughing. He had gun-butted Reyna, knocking her completely out. "She was handling you," he said to Banger.

"C'mon, let's get this broad in the van and get out of here," said Banger. They both dragged Reyna to the back of the van and threw her in. Nitty ran and got in Reyna's car and followed the van. He couldn't wait to get on Banger for getting his butt whipped by a female.

Young Adult

Once in the van, Banger hopped in the back with Reyna and bound her wrist and ankles with duct tape. Once he knew she was secured, he hauled off and smacked her until she woke up.

Tank, who was driving yelled to the back, "Yo, what are you doing?"

Looking up, Banger said, "I'm going to beat this broad silly. Look what this hoe did to my face."

"Leave her alone, Banger. Don't get mad at her for fighting back. What the hell you expecting from her? Hell, she raised more ruckus than some of the other lames we snatched up. I'm feeling her, leave her sexy butt alone. You should be counting your blessings that Nitty came to your aid, she might've million-dollar-babied your punk self," said Tank while laughing.

Banger got up off her. *I'm gonna do this chick dirty before it's all over, bet that.*

***

QB's cell was ringing. He searched for it, paper work scattered throughout his office. He made a note to himself to ask Ashanti if she would clean up his office, and of course it would cost him. When he found his phone, the caller's number was unfamiliar. He took the call anyway. "Hello."

"May I speak to Mr. Banks?"

"This is Mr. Banks. Who's calling?"

"This is Chelsea from Smart Kidz University, we have Nia here and it's already after seven. Your wife called about an hour ago and said she was going to be here in a few minutes. We were getting a little worried because we have been calling her, but no one is answering. Since your number was listed as a secondary contact, we decided to call you."

QB, didn't really understand what the lady was saying. "Is Nia all right?" he asked.

"Oh yes, Mr. Banks. Nia is right here, she's fine. It's just that it's so unlike Mrs. Banks to be an hour late. She has never—"

QB cut her off. "I'm on my way. Give me twenty minutes." Grabbing his jacket, QB headed out of his office a bit worried. He attempted to call Reyna, but there was no answer. He called her mother. She explained that she had talked to her earlier when she told her she couldn't pick up Nia. That was about an hour and a half ago. "Is everything all right, Q?"

QB didn't want to alarm her mother. "Yeah everything is fine, I was just trying to call her. Her battery probably died, I'll have her call you when I talk to her okay?" he said.

"You do that."

He hung up, slammed his fist on the dashboard and screamed "No!" He finally reached Nia's school. Nia was busy in the play area talking to another little boy whose parents were probably running late as well. QB apologized to the daycare provider. He offered them money for the inconvenience, but they declined it. He then snuck up on his daughter and said, "Hey Ladybug."

Nia, hearing her father's voice spun around and yelled, "Daddy." She immediately ran and jumped into his arms. They embraced each other in a way that only a father and daughter could. Nia was surprised that her father was there. He never picked her up before, "See my nice school, Daddy?"

"Yeah, I see it. It's real nice. I wish I could go here."

"Daddy, you can't go here, this only for Smart Kidz," Nia said, laughing.

"Daddy's smart."

Nia tilted her head, "Umm hmm, but you're not a kid."

"You know something, you're right." He looked at his baby girl knowing exactly where she got her wits from. He felt a pang of momentary guilt, wondering why this was the first time he had come to his daughter's school. He planned to make sure he picked her up more often. They made their way out to the truck, and headed home. By the

Young Adult

time he got home, Reyna's mom called at least ten times. QB ignored the calls.

Once he got home he immediately phoned Reyna's friends. None of them had heard from her in the past three hours. He called Shai, who told him the same. He asked Shai to come over, and he would explain everything when she got there. He then went and checked on Nia, who was eating a fruit roll-up, and watching one of her favorite cartoons on television.

Fifteen minutes after talking to Shai, his phone rang. He looked at the caller ID, but none showed on the display. He took the call. "Hello."

"Q, I love you, baby," Reyna said frantically.

"Hey baby, where you at?"

"If something happens to me know that ..."

QB heard her cry out in pain. Then he heard a smack that suggested the worst. Caught somewhere between rage and fear QB yelled, "Reyna!" He grabbed the cell tightly, trying to listen to everything that was said. He heard a muffled voice in the background. "Why are you doing this to me?" she yelled. QB could hear the fear coming from her words.

His heart suddenly dropped. "Reyna," he screamed again.

"Chick, if you don't shut the hell up, I'm gonna give you something to scream about."

QB's eyes squinted closed and he balled his fist. "Who the hell is this?" What in the hell do you want?" he yelled into the phone.

The person on the other end said, "You there, QB?"

"Yeah, I'm here. What you got my wife for? Let me speak to Reyna!"

The person on the other end was not listening. He was telling someone else, "If she keeps fighting, knock her teeth out her mouth."

QB ran his hand over his head and began pacing through the kitchen. The doorbell rang. He answered it. It was Shai. He put his finger in front of his lips, signaling her to be quiet. Covering the mouthpiece, he whispered, "I think someone kidnapped Reyna."

"Who?" she questioned.

He put his finger in front of his mouth again and said, 'Go in the room with Nia. Don't let her come out here."

Shai looked at her brother, feeling sorry for what he was going through. As she made her way into Nia's room, she pulled out her cell and called Amari.

"Yeah, I'm here," QB said as he walked into the bathroom. He closed the door and sat on the edge of the tub. He stared into the mirror, noticing the sweat on his face. His throat felt constricted and his mouth dry. His lungs felt like they were losing air. When he tried to speak, he couldn't find the words.

"Listen up, homie, and listen closely. We got your wife," said the person on the other end of the phone line.

"What do you want?" asked QB.

"I do the talking here. You just listen … Now, we know that Chase is due to testify this Thursday against Showtyme at the grand jury …" The caller paused for a second then added, "It's up to you to make sure that doesn't happen. If he testifies, then your wife is done. Do you understand?"

QB was having trouble understanding what was unfolding. "What does my wife have to do with it?"

"Listen, punk, just make sure Chase doesn't testify. He better not go anywhere near that witness stand on Thursday. If Showtyme gets indicted you might as well go buy some skirts 'cause she'll be done off and you'll be playing Mr. Mom. And another thing, if you think about going to the cops she'll definitely be history. If we feel any heat from the pigs, we'll make sure she regrets ever having met you." There was an eerie silence on the line. " … You know what that means, don't you? If not, let me help you out, I will cut off every one of her pretty fingers and toes, and then let my soldiers have their way with her. Do you understand?"

Young Adult

QB threw up his breakfast, missing the toilet. After catching his breath, he said, "Listen, do you want money? Anything you want I'll give you … anything, please just let her go!"

"Did you hear anything I said, you idiot? Now man-up and just make sure that punk Chase don't testify and things will turn out fine."

"Please," QB pleaded.

"Just keep Chase out of that courtroom and we'll be in touch," said the man before ending the call.

"Nooooo," QB yelled.

Shai rushed into the bathroom and hugged her brother. He was on the floor banging the phone against the bathtub. "What happened, Q? Who was that on the phone?"

"Daddy, what's wrong?" asked Nia as she stood outside the bathroom door.

Hearing his baby girl's voice provided him with the strength he needed to get himself together. "Nothing, baby. Daddy just feels a bit sick right now. Go watch TV and I'll be there in a minute, okay?"

"Okay," she said, but didn't move.

QB knew he had to pull himself together for his family's sake. They needed him now, more than ever. Shai helped him up from the floor. Standing in front of the sink, QB splashed water on his face and then rinsed his mouth. His head was spinning. When he looked into the mirror he saw a desperate man. He felt overwhelmed, and the apprehension that contained him a few weeks ago seemed to be going straight down the drain following the running water. He was ready to road trip, the line between what's right and what's wrong had become so blurred, that his well-being was no longer a concern. It was all about his wife's safety. If he lost her, nothing else would matter, but then again that's not true, because he had Nia. But without Reyna, the trinity of their love would be fractured. Like steam forming in a pot as water boiled, there was rage building up inside him. Out of his peripheral he noticed Nia looking up at him in confusion. They locked eyes. QB was at a loss for words.

How do you tell your two-year-old daughter her mother has been abducted? he thought. Shai reached down to pick up her niece. "C'mon Nia. Let's go watch TV while Daddy gets himself together," Shai said

Nia climbed into her auntie's arms. "Kay auntie," she answered.

QB watched them as they made their way to her room. Nia turned back to look at her father right before they turned into her room. Father and daughter locked eyes. QB's heart dropped like the temperature on a February.

Tears poured from QB's eyes. He needed time to sort things out. He rewound the conversation with Reyna's kidnappers. Looking into the mirror and then wiping his face again, QB stopped and wondered if Reyna had heard the threats her captives made to him on the phone. How they promised to cut off her fingers and toes and then … he couldn't get the words out, they were stuck in his throat …

… Rape her!

As he stared at his reflection, he imagined his wife bound in some dark room being smacked up, touched in unimaginable ways, having things done to her that would probably scar her in ways that she could never recover from. Vengeance muffled his thinking. His life was shattering into a million different pieces, a fractured madness that ignited in him a desire to go after Showtyme. Nothing mattered. He had finally reached a point where virtually anything is justifiable, up to and including murder, just like nineteen years ago with his unborn child. He threw more water on his face, and then went downstairs and retrieved his P89. Showtyme had finally shattered what QB thought was his unreachable window.

Zeus and Amari both rushed over to QB's when they heard what took place. QB asked Shai to take Nia to her house. This was too much for her to be around. He knew he had to do everything right, and understood from experience that a mistake could cost him everything.

Young Adult

This was one of those moments when one wrong move could cause his life to quickly unravel. Similar to when a loose thread is pulled and a seam gives way, the change is slow at first, nearly imperceptible. For Quentin Banks the unraveling began with that phone call.

***

Zeus was making calls on his cell-phone, putting the word out on the street. In the 'hood the streets did more than whisper, they talked, and the message read: If Reyna was touched or harmed in any way, nothing less than the lives of those responsible could satisfy their thirst for revenge. If anything happened to Reyna the heat would be turned up to a level that they were not prepared for. Reyna was a part of their team, the first lady of their faculty, and they were going to do whatever it took to get her back, unharmed.

After hearing about the phone call, Amari immediately left the house, saying nothing more than that he'll be back. By midnight, the whole team, along with Reyna's girlfriends was there. Reyna's father was there as well. QB was a nervous wreck. There had been no contact since the call.

QB convinced Reyna's dad not to call the police. To give him time to get her back. Reluctantly, he agreed to give him twenty-four hours. He understood what was at stake.

What scared QB was that if he went to the police and Showtyme had someone on the inside feeding him information, what would actually happen to Reyna. The other thing was that if he told the police they were likely to work against the demands. They could possibly get Reyna killed because of their policy of not negotiating with kidnappers, especially street soldiers. Reyna's father said he would keep his wife from making contact, but pleaded with QB to get his daughter back. He even told him he was ready to bear arms with them to go get his daughter back.

***

Doubt was beginning to embrace Reyna. She was sitting in the dark, mad at herself. QB's voice was ringing in her ears; she could hear him encouraging her to be strong. She knew that she could count on her husband. Besides her father, QB was the most reliable man she'd ever known. When it came to reliability, Reyna knew that she could set her watch to her husband; he was always on time. She had no doubt that he was going to tear New York upside down looking for her.

Reyna rubbed her throbbing, aching head—the lump on her head reminded her of the seriousness of the situation, and the young punk who gun-butted her. She realized just how lucky she was that nothing more tragic happened; she could've been killed. The thought of death sent chills down her spine. *Why did I do something so stupid?* she thought. She smiled at her own craziness, then closed her eyes and silently hoped she gouged out the eye of the young thug.

She suddenly stilled herself in order to listen to the sounds of her captors. She couldn't make sense of the conversations; they seemed too far away. However, she could tell by the way they operated that they were young and not too bright. The hoodies and bandanas made them appear more dangerous. Reyna could hear them laughing and joking. She didn't find anything amusing about being tied up in somebody's basement. She wondered whether or not their un-professionalism could be used to her advantage.

She didn't want to think about the worst, so she drifted back to the argument between QB and herself. He wanted to deal with these people his way, but calling herself protecting her king, she just had to intervene. *I should've let him handle his business*, she thought. She knew what her husband was capable of, and she understood that he did some things in the past that most women would run from. But not her, she married QB knowing that he had a dark past. There were parts of QB that she would never understand, parts of his soul that could never be figured out. Reyna had gone with her gut when she decided to marry him. She ignored the advice and opinions of her family and friends. She

Young Adult

understood their apprehension, but knew QB was more than what happened in his past. She was turned on by all that she did not understand about him. There was an edge to him that she loved, and she felt blessed that he chose her to hold his hand in marriage, to be his Queen. If others wanted to judge him because he would do anything to protect his family, then so be it. No matter what they thought, she would always stand by her husband's side ... until the bitter end!

Sitting there bound in the dark, Reyna held onto her sanity knowing that QB would take those aspects of his past and form them into a weapon to be used against every voice she heard up those stairs laughing. She admitted to herself that he was right on this one. These people only respect one thing ... Violence!

Pulling at her arms, trying to break free from the bindings that held her down, a vague damp smell pinched her nostrils. It smelled as if wet clothes were left out to dry. . She couldn't see ten inches in front of her in the dark basement, and wondered what time of the day it was. Bound to a metal chair, she was beginning to get cold. Her arms were numb with pain, as if the ties were cutting into her wrist, and her shoulders felt as if they were going to pop out of the sockets. After the first couple of hours of trying to break free she decided to stop. Reyna didn't want to tire herself out. She needed to preserve all her energy, because the last thing she was going to do was allow any of these animals to violate her. She would die fighting before she let anybody rape her. Hearing what they said to QB scared the hell out of her. Reyna closed her eyes and prayed that she'd make it out of here alive.

TWENTY-THREE

Dark clouds cast a cold shadow not only over the sky, but QB's heart. It was as if his world had been tilted and everything that wasn't tightly screwed down had slid into chaos. He pressed his right elbow reassuringly against the P89 handgun holstered beneath his shirt.

QB kept checking his cell phone, making sure it was on. Everybody was waiting to hear from the kidnappers. By two in the morning, the storm was still pounding incessantly upon the roof of the house. Sleep avoided QB. He was laid back on his bed looking up into the skylight. He was watching the violent storm and thought, *How sometimes the best climate for growth has nothing to do with sun and rain ... but everything with struggle and pain.* He knew if he dared to give himself entirely to the thoughts of revenge he would go to pieces. By the time the sun rose, he was feeling fragile so he got up, showered, and decided to go visit Chase.

The rest of his team had hit the streets trying to gather all the information they could. By the time QB entered C74's visiting room it was two in the afternoon. As QB walked toward the row of colorful chairs and little tables, an overbearing officer instructed him to his seat. While waiting for Chase he scanned the entire room. He watched women cuddling with their men. It brought back memories of his time

Young Adult

spent on lock down. Approximately twenty minutes after his arrival, eight inmates wearing grey jumpsuits and slippers were escorted from behind a sliding steel door. Chase noticed QB and smiled brightly. His mood quickly changed when he noticed the stress etched on QB's face. As Chase walked to the table all the flags of fear, both rational and irrational were raised high in his mind.

"What's good, QB?"

QB looked at him, but remained silent. He didn't trust what was going to come out his mouth just yet. He nodded, gesturing for him to sit.

Chase sat down noticing the seriousness of his mood. "What's good, QB?" he repeated.

QB sighed and came straight out and told him, "You got Reyna kidnapped."

Chase looked at him with shock. "What you talkin' 'bout?"

If looks could kill, then Chase would've been Elvis. "Your decision to testify against Showtyme got my wife snatched up. Why didn't you ..."

Chase didn't allow him to get the rest of the statement out of his mouth. "Testify against Showtyme? Where you get that from?"

QB looked around to make sure nobody was listening to them. "That's the word on the street, Chase. I got a call from somebody yesterday who I suspect was Showtyme, and he told me that if you showed up to the grand jury ..." QB paused and gave Chase a caustic look. "... then Reyna will be tortured, raped, and God knows what else."

For a moment, Chase looked as if the aftertaste of what QB said was going to make him throw up. He took a deep breath. "C'mon, QB, you know me better than that. I'm not testifying against anybody." Chase's breathing seemed labored, like he was drowning in his own guilt. His muscles tightened and his palms became moist. He put his head down feeling bad about dragging QB and now his wife into his mess. It made

him feel like crap. "QB, let me see what I can find out. I'm gonna make a few calls to see where Reyna's at."

Hearing those words made QB's stomach constrict. Sweat was beginning to trickle down his face; he swallowed hard, and then leaned in close so no one could hear what he had to say. "Listen Chase, they got my wife." Lowering his eyes, he sat there imagining the worst. He looked back up. "Chase, whatever happens you cannot testify! Under any other circumstance I would advise you to do what's right, but I need you to do me this one favor. I may be wrong for saying this, but this is how it has to be." He took a deep breath in an attempt to slow down his pulse. "I have to get Reyna back safe, and I don't have much time. I need you to find out what you can and call me at the house. I'll tell whoever is there to accept the call and forward it to me if I'm not home."

Chase knew, if nothing else, getting Reyna caught up in this had definitely changed their relationship. He really messed up; he had hurt the one person that showed him true love. He could see the pain on QB's face. Wanting to get at something, he looked around the visiting room for any of the Henchmen. As much as he wanted to do what was right, hate wouldn't let him, and it was hate and regret that was fueling him now. Suddenly he began feeling the urge to put in some work, but when he looked at QB he knew that was the last thing that he would have wanted him to do, so he pushed it out of his mind.

QB suddenly stood. "I'm out Chase. Make sure you call me if you find out anything." He waited as Chase stood up to embrace him, and then whispered, "No grand jury, Chase!"

***

By the time QB got home from Rikers Island, his mind was running a hundred miles per second. His dark brown eyes smoldered with anguish and pain. He was questioning his decision to not call the police. *Maybe I should,* he thought. The feelings of indecision confused him; he was beginning to feel as if every decision came with the pressure of deactivating a bomb—one wrong move almost certainly meant Reyna's

Young Adult

demise. QB hated to admit it, but his cold, empty eyes were now looking beyond the consequences of his decisions.

***

Showtyme sat on his bed staring at his guns laying out on the comforter. He was beginning to get paranoid, especially after the move they made on the Columbians. Rumor on the streets was that the Henchmen laid down the brother-in-law of the top Columbian named Chino. Showtyme also heard that Chino had put twenty grand on his head, so Showtyme put thirty on his.

Even though the voice in the back of his mind was screaming at him to get the hell out of New York, Showtyme's pride and ignorance wouldn't allow him to budge. He sat back and listened to the chaos in the house; it was much too noisy. He shook his head in disgust at hearing the ruckus coming from downstairs. The constant flow of traffic in and out of the house wasn't a good look. Neighbors were already looking at them suspiciously. This was not the 'hood. Too many young black faces set off alarms. *I got to get these niggas outta here*, he thought. The grand jury proceeding was a day away. Showtyme's thoughts were alternating between holding court in the streets and breaking out. He thought to himself, *Maybe I should leave and set up shop in Arizona like my man from the mid-west has been telling me.* He was also thinking about what Cherokee said to him the night before. That he was slipping and becoming way too paranoid. Little did she know, her words possessed a lot of truth. What she didn't understand was that it was his paranoia keeping him ahead of the game.

He rubbed his temples and thought about what he was going to do with Reyna. *I like that stuck up chick. She probably thinks she's too good for a nigga like me.* Showtyme grabbed his crotch. *I got something for her fine behind*, he thought. Showtyme loathed people who thought their crap didn't stink.

Showtyme sighed, stood up and stretched. He looked around the room, and then snatched up a *Don Diva* magazine lying on the

nightstand. He looked at the cover and thought, *I should be on this*. He threw the magazine on the bed, grabbed his fitted, and headed downstairs. Opening the bedroom door he ran right into Shawnee. "What's up with all the noise in this house?"

She swallowed and looked at him incredulously. "I told you before about having all these people in the house."

Showtyme looked at Shawnee with a "who are you talkin' to" look. "When did you start tellin' me what I should do?"

Shawnee sucked her teeth. Showtyme couldn't believe what he saw and heard. "What are you suckin' your teeth for? You want something to suck?" He didn't give her time to answer; he hauled off and back smacked her. She hit the floor instantly.

She looked up at him with fear. He peered down at her and said, "If you ever speak to me like that again I will kill you. Do you understand me?"

Shawnee looked up at him and said, "Yes."

"Yes what?"

She felt his animosity wash over her like a strong smell. With tears in her eyes, she said, "Yes, Showtyme."

Unfazed by her hurt, he stepped over her and walked down the stairs. Shawnee laid there trembling with an inner rage. She hated what her life had become. Her lips twitched as she rose from the floor. She thought to herself, *I'm gonna kill you, you bastard*.

***

QB was turning into a nervous wreck waiting to hear from Reyna's captors. Watching the evening news, he tried to bring some calmness to his frazzled nerves.

Shai was on her laptop computer absorbed in the numbers she was crunching for her job. Everybody tried to stay busy to keep from worrying. Zeus and Ramel were scrounging for food in the kitchen. QB couldn't eat, he didn't care about nothing but getting Reyna back. However, he knew she would kill him if she found out he allowed his boys to rummage through her kitchen with free reign. The thought of her raising hell made him smile inside. He would give anything to hear her nagging right now, to see his wife kick them all out her house, him included. These thoughts of Reyna allowed him, for the moment, to escape the reality that she was missing.

The moment was short-lived as thoughts of her kidnappers returned. From experience, QB knew that the worst part of kidnappings for criminals was usually the transferring of the money, but in this case it was simply a case of Chase not testifying in court. Being optimistic, he thought, *This should all be over soon.* Yet, there was a part of him which doubted this was going to end peacefully. After visiting Chase, QB felt a little relief. He believed Chase would honor his word and not testify. Although he struggled with the fact that he gave him some bad advice, his biggest concern was how he was going to get Reyna back. *Sometimes the ends does justify the means*, he thought. QB covered his face with his hands, thinking about how life always seemed to present opportunities for him to be cold.

***

At G.I.U. headquarters Detective Hudson was reviewing folders titled Confidential Informants (CI's). The name on the particular file he was reviewing was Nate Hayes, aka Nitty. Nitty had been their ace in the hole for the past six months, reporting directly to Hudson, providing inside information about the Henchmen. It had become obvious to everybody at GIU that the Henchmen needed to be taken down one way or the other. Many within the Unit felt that if the courts were not going to do their part in keeping these maniacs off the streets, then they would. The Unit was tired of these gang-bangers beating the system, they had been told to submit profiles on all their CI's. The Unit was going full-force to take down one of the most notorious street gangs of their time.

Hudson took a sip of coffee from his steaming mug. He was meeting Nitty in their usual contact spot later that evening. He looked at his

partners working at their cubicles, knowing that these men and women had put their lives on hold in order to make the community a better place to live. He thought to himself, *this piece of crap better have some information or I'm going to send his behind right to the Island.* Hudson sighed, closed the folder, stood and headed to see Delaney.

***

Reyna was not only hungry, but she had to pee badly. She'd lost track of time. It had been a little over twenty-eight hours since she had been snatched up. She wondered about Nia, hoping that QB picked her up from school. She wanted to take a shower. Her thoughts were all over the place. She was beginning to think she was losing her mind. She squeezed her legs tightly together in an attempt to stop the urge of having to use the bathroom. *Who was going to prepare food for her family?* She laughed at herself for thinking such thoughts. For Reyna, every passing hour was a roller coaster ride. She didn't really know how she was going to feel from one moment to the next. Being isolated, and not knowing whether or not she'd make it out of there alive, made her realize just how much she took for granted.

Right when she was beginning to feel like she was going to break down, she heard footsteps coming down the stairs. This time there was no mistaking that someone was approaching. When they reached the bottom of the stairs, someone came over and spun her and the chair around. Now facing them, she braced herself. She could barely see. Making out faces was impossible. She only saw silhouettes of people. Reyna struggled to open her mouth, but her lips were sealed shut with duct tape.

Showtyme spoke first. "Hit the lights."

The brightness caused Reyna to squint. She tried to focus her eyes to get a good look at the faces of her captors, but she felt panic take over. Fear was smothering her. The one, who appeared to be calling the shots, looked menacing to her. Another thing she noticed was that they looked so young, and the kid next to the menacing one was the one

Young Adult

from the van. He had a big gun protruding from his waistline. What surprised Reyna were the two females who were standing there. Reyna blinked and attempted to talk. But again was reminded that she couldn't by the strip of the duct tape over her mouth.

With a sarcastic, mocking voice, the menacing one said, "Mrs. Banks."

Reyna looked up into the dark eyes of the thug.

"Take that tape off her mouth," Showtyme said to Banger.

Banger stepped to Reyna, kicked her chair, almost causing her to fall over. Reyna stared at him with a hatred she didn't know she possessed. He grabbed her hair, snatching her head back. He intentionally manhandled her because of what she did to him in the van. He inched a corner of the tape off the corner of her mouth, and then snatched it off with such reckless abandonment that Reyna thought he tore off her lips.

"Damn!" she screamed. She stared at him, and then blurted out, "What do you want with me?"

Showtyme approached her. She caught the scent of weed and liquor on his breath. It was blending with some kind of Muslim oil. He brushed his hands lightly over her locks. "Around here, I do the questioning and people answer to me. Do you understand?"

When Reyna didn't respond he bent down and grabbed her chin between his strong, rough hands. "I said do you understand me, Mrs. Banks?"

Reyna nodded. She hesitated because she didn't want to satisfy his need to be in charge. But if she had any chance of making it out of there alive, she knew she couldn't fight fire with gasoline, she had to fight this fire with water.

Showtyme stepped back, but held her gaze. *She's one bad Chick*, he thought. He nodded toward Banger. "Untie her!" he said.

Banger did as he was told. He took a knife and cut the tape that bound her legs to the bottom of the chair, he then cut the tape that bound her arms to the chair. He left her arms taped together behind her back. He then snatched Reyna by the front of her shirt and pulled her up to her feet.

I want to kill this punk, thought Reyna. She felt disgusted, her clothes were disheveled, and she had already urinated on herself twice. She refused to use the bathroom in front of these thugs. Reyna stared at Banger, and then snatched away from his grip. She didn't want him touching her.

Standing now, she looked into the eyes of the two girls. The Puerto Rican one held a gun in her hand like she was really a gangsta. She eye-screwed Reyna with disgust, as if they were high school rivals. Reyna then looked at the other young lady, who in Reyna's quick assessment, felt that the girl was just as much a prisoner as her. There was something different about her; she looked like she was being held hostage, just without restraints.

Reyna remembered QB telling her how America has had street gangs almost as long as it had streets. However, today's gangs were turning up in more places than ever, including the suburbs, in fact, in their own neighborhood. She remembered him telling her that they were spreading like viruses. But what she found alarming was the surprising number of young females who were joining them. She didn't know why, but at that very moment, Reyna finally realized the importance of her husband's work. Reyna stared at the young black girl. Shawnee's eyes softened, and then she just looked down, not able to look Reyna in her eyes.

Showtyme watched Reyna with preying eyes. He fixed his rag on his face. "In spite of the circumstances you're looking pretty good," he said, moving closer and began inspecting her like a new car. Circling her, he gently touched her, making Reyna cringe. "I may be willing to let you sleep in my room tonight, which may enhance your chances of getting out of here in one piece—what do you think?"

Reyna said nothing. Showtyme now stood directly in front of her. He ran the back of his hand along her cheekbone. He looked at her,

Young Adult

noticing she was holding his gaze, and looking at him with anger. "I want you to freshen up, and eat something, and if you cooperate, everything will turn out just fine, know what I mean?"

Reyna turned her face away from Showtyme's touch.

He smiled and said, "I have to give your husband some credit, he definitely knows how to choose a woman that a brother wouldn't mind waking up to in the morning." Showtyme then ran his hand down across her breast.

Reyna closed her eyes trying to resist the impulse to spit in his face. However, something came over her, from where she didn't know, but she decided to go for broke. She kicked upward sharply, without warning, landing a powerful foot right to Showtyme's jewels.

Showtyme fell backwards with a grunt of pain, as Cherokee jumped on Reyna. She smacked her flush on the side of her head with her gun. Reyna fell to the floor upon impact of the blow. It was the second time she's seen lightning. She tried to cover up as much of her face as possible by curling up into a fetus position. Banger ran up to her and kicked her in the ribs, surely fracturing a few of them, but also setting off the other Henchmen to unleash on her. Reyna desperately tried to shield as much as her body as possible. In their haste to hit her, none of the blows, with the exception of the gun-butt and Banger's kick, hit her flush. Shawnee found herself paralyzed, not able to move. She stood there in awe, wishing she had the courage of Reyna.

Showtyme recovered in a matter of seconds. He stood up. "That's enough. Get her to her feet," he yelled. Everybody stopped. Cherokee snatched her up by her locks. Reyna felt like she had been hit by a car. She felt pain everywhere, and didn't know how she was able to stand.

Showtyme grabbed his crotch, checking out his jewels. He then approached Reyna, looked directly into her eyes and smacked her with such force that she flew into the wall like a screen door in a hurricane.

Crumpling to the floor—again, she thought, *This is the end ... he's going to beat me to death.*

Showtyme pulled her back up to her feet, and then wrapped his calloused hands around her neck, applying just enough pressure so that she had to fight to breathe. She didn't know how she stood there without passing out. Reyna peered back into his eyes when suddenly he slammed her into the wall. Grimacing at the pain that shot through her body, she decided not to give him the satisfaction of showing fear. Her body was actually becoming numb to the searing pain. She looked back up into his eyes with hatred. Showtyme saw the same look of hatred somewhere before.

Then it hit him.

It was the same look of fearlessness that QB had displayed when Showtyme spit in his face in the garage. With what little strength she had left, Reyna attempted to break free from his grasp. However, his grip was too strong for her. Showtyme then reached on his side and pulled his gun from its holster. He shoved the barrel into Reyna's cheek. "Listen, you stupid trick! If you ever put your hands or feet on me again, I will not only kill you and your husband, but I will kill that pretty little daughter of yours. Or better yet, I'll snatch her up and put her on eBay for all the pedophiles out there to bid for her, do you understand me?" he said with clenched teeth.

This got Reyna's attention. She couldn't understand what it was inside of her that kept propelling her to fight, but hearing Showtyme's words about harming Nia extinguished all further thoughts of fighting. She looked at him and meekly said, "Yes ... Please stay away from my daughter." Tears were now running down her bruised face.

"Good," he said. Showtyme stared at her, a predator who understood the influence of fear. He slid his gun back into its holster. He took a half step away from her, deliberately daring her to touch him again. When she put her head down, he pulled her forward and then shoved her back down into the chair.

She whimpered as she landed, almost falling to the floor again.

"Where's the tape?" Showtyme asked.

Young Adult

Banger located it, and then tossed it to him. Showtyme then bent down in front of Reyna and grabbed her left ankle and then roughly taped it to the leg of the chair. He did the same with her right leg, all the while looking into her face. He then slid her dress up to her thighs.

Reyna started, "Please nooo ..."

Showtyme stopped in his tracks and looked up at her. "Didn't I tell you don't say nothing unless I tell you to speak?"

Reyna nodded her head yes.

"Say something else and I will send some of my wolves to pick up your little girl.

"Let me go get her, Showtyme; I'll get that little trick started early," said Banger.

Reyna bit down on her bottom lip, drawing more blood. Showtyme then moved his rough hands up her legs. Reyna tried to close them as much as she could. She closed her eyes, as her spirit searched for strength. His hands continued up her body, he caressed her breast. "Let me tell you something, you stuck up trick. Where I come from we treat hos like you dirty. You better learn to keep your nose outta the air, and if you make it out of here alive make sure your husband stays clear of my business. Do you understand me?"

She nodded yes. He then grabbed her face. "And remember what I said, if you act right, I just might keep my wolves off your fine self, because if I don't, when they finish with some fresh meat like you, trust me, your husband will not want to have anything to do with you."

She felt the coldness of Showtyme's words penetrate her conscience. It felt like a syringe being plunged into her vein, one filled with a deadly poison.

"Are we clear, Mrs. Banks?"

She opened her eyes, but couldn't find the strength to say anything. Showtyme grabbed her around her neck again. "You better answer me when I speak to you!"

Reyna tried looking at him, but couldn't stand the evil she saw in the windows of his soul. "Yes," she said, feeling defeated.

Showtyme had chosen his retaliation well. Mere violence would only have strengthened Reyna, but the thought of being raped by a gang, and having her daughter touched by these animals made her want to comply with everything he said. He was about to leave, when he noticed the heart shaped diamond pendant hangin' on Reyna's neck. He walked back to her, reached down, and raised her chin. He fingered the pendant in his hand, then without warning, snatched it off her neck. Reyna started to protest, but quickly thought better of it. She wanted to fight, but refused to put her daughter's life in jeopardy.

Sensing her displeasure, Showtyme peered into her eyes to see if she had anything to say. When she looked down, he turned toward Shawnee and threw her the chain and diamond pendant. She caught it, looked at Reyna and hesitantly clutched it in her fist. Shawnee knew that Showtyme was giving it to her as a way to apologize for doing what he did to her earlier that morning. He was always like that, feeling sorry after he did something dumb. But Shawnee was through with his abuse. Like Chase, her only objective was getting out of the Henchmen. She didn't look at Showtyme, fearful of what her eyes may have revealed.

As he turned to leave the basement, Showtyme instructed both Cherokee and Shawnee to get Reyna cleaned up. "And if she acts up give her the business."

Cherokee didn't need to hear anything else; she wanted Reyna to do something stupid, just one wrong move or look. *I want to chop this trick*, she thought. She hated the way Showtyme was checking her out. *I'm gonna fix her right up for you, baby*, she thought.

Young Adult

TWENTY-FOUR

A storm of emotions was rolling through QB. He was having trouble pinning down exactly what his next move should be. He was sitting on the edge of his bed trying to make sense of all that was taking place. He couldn't believe how Showtyme had grabbed hold of his world and turned it upside down like an hourglass. QB paced the room thinking how he had worked hard to put the pieces of his life back together. Yes, he had made some poor choices as a young man, but he paid for those decisions. His time in prison was a living hell, but while in prison he promised himself to come home and dedicate his life to giving back to the community. Yet, here he was preparing to walk through the fire—again. He shook his head realizing that it only took a split second for things to fall apart. Yet, he had to convince himself that this was different. This wasn't about revenge, or getting even. Showtyme had violated, taking from him the greatest thing that ever happened to him—his wife.

QB forced himself out of the space where his doubts roamed; he couldn't afford to start second-guessing himself now. When it came to dealing with street drama, he needed to summon the dark side of his being. Most people lacked the ability to bring such inner hate to life, but it was easy for QB. He could literally call on his hate as if it was just a touch a way. This had been something that always scared him. Closing his eyes, he fell back on the bed, and clutched the sheets, squeezing them tightly trying to find little comfort in his shattered world.

Minutes could have passed. Then again—maybe hours, the memories of what his life had once been were fading into the insanity that had filled his mind. As he descended further into the murkiness of his nightmare, he heard ringing. *The phone*, he thought.

Sweating, he jumped up and stared at the phone. He didn't know why, but he was suddenly scared to answer it. A strange feeling embraced him, he could feel something was about to go down. Exactly what, he knew, was on the other end of the telephone. The gloom of the moment was beginning to suffocate him. He forced himself to relax; he took a deep breath, and picked up the phone.

***

Mrs. Mayers, Reyna's mom couldn't take it any longer. She picked up the phone and called the police to report that her daughter was missing. She was connected to the missing person(s) squad, and was told that they would send a pair of detectives to her home.

***

QB seized the phone. "Hello."

"Listen," said the same female from earlier. "If you want your wife back you have to come get her tonight. Remember, you cannot involve the police. He will kill her if you call the cops. He'll find out, he has them on his payroll. Do you understand?"

"Yes," QB said nervously.

"The address is four-eighty-nine Langdon Boulevard in Lakeview. It's a brown and white house. There is a black Denali in the driveway and a statute of a little white man in the front yard. You got that?"

QB repeated the address. He couldn't believe Reyna was being held right there in Long Island.

"You should come early in the morning; he's laying low tonight because of the court date tomorrow. It should be calm around here by four in the morning. What I'll do is leave the back door unlocked." Shawnee then whispered what QB thought was an apology.

"Listen, don't you worry about it. What you're doing now makes up for everything." There was a pause on the phone.

"Exactly where's my wife?" QB asked.

"She's in the basement. If you come through the back door, you'll be in the kitchen. There's a door that leads to the basement from the kitchen. She's down there by herself, but they check up on her every hour or so. There are eleven of us here, and everybody's armed ... so be careful."

"I'll be all right. What about you? You should get out before we get there. Is there any way you can somehow get Reyna and get out the house?" asked QB.

"No, that cannot happen. If I'm not around he will automatically become suspicious. What I'll do is keep him occupied upstairs," said Shawnee.

There was a brief moment of silence between them two when QB said, "All right, Shawnee, when this is over we have to get together—okay?"

"How do you know my name is Shawnee?"

"Chase told me all about you. I wish ..."

She cut him off. "Listen, somebody's coming ... I gotta go. See you tonight." She hung up.

QB hung up the phone and immediately called out to Ramel, "Rah, get everybody over here now. I've located Reyna."

Ramel ran up the stairs to his bedroom not believing what he'd heard. QB reiterated what he needed him to do, and then ushered him out his room. He needed to be alone. His heart was beating, and his adrenaline was on high. He closed his bedroom door, looked around the room noticing the photos of him and his wife. He took a deep breath and then placed a call to his lawyer.

***

His receptionist answered on the first ring. "Cohen and Kingsley," she said.

"May I speak to Mr. Kingsley please?"

"Who's calling?"

"Quentin Banks."

"Hold on, let me see if he's in," she said.

Kingsley was screening his calls, but QB only had to wait a few seconds. "What's up, QB?" said Kingsley.

QB didn't know the proper response for that question. So he got straight to the point. "I found out who kidnapped Reyna."

"What are you talking about? Who kidnapped who?"

Oh snap, I didn't tell him, he thought. "Reyna got kidnapped."

"When? Did you call the police?" asked Kingsley.

"Yesterday and no, I can't call the police ... the low life said he will kill her and I believe he has the police on the take."

"Listen Q, start from the beginning. Tell me everything that happened."

QB did. Kingsley couldn't believe it. "This is some movie crap," he said. "So what are you going to do? Better yet, what can I do for you?" Kingsley asked.

QB was silent for a moment. "I'm gonna get my wife back tonight. What I want from you is to ..." He paused, trying to get the words out of his mouth. "... I want you to meet me at the precinct in the event I get arrested."

"Arrested! Why would they arrest you?"

"Did you hear anything I said? I'm going after my wife tonight, and there's no telling how things are going to turn out."

Kingsley yelled into the phone. "QB, you cannot go out there like some outlaw and take the law into your own hands. You're much smarter than that."

QB walked around his bed. "This has nothing to do with intelligence, Kingsley. They got my wife tied up in some damn basement. Now I know it may be easy for you to sit there and tell me I shouldn't take the law into my hands, but it's my wife they have, not yours. QB sighed, then asked a question that put things in their proper prospective. "What would you do, Kingsley, if it were your wife?"

"What do you mean?"

"What the hell do you think I mean? You're married ... suppose somebody had your wife tied up somewhere, doing God knows what to her ... What would you do?" QB repeated.

Kingsley, unconsciously found himself staring at the photo of him and his wife sitting on his desk. He didn't answer. When he did open his mouth, he said, "Be careful, Q."

"Answer my question ..."

"I can't."

QB was swollen with emotion. "What if he beat or raped her, Kingsley, what would you do?" he asked.

Clutching his pen tightly in his hand, Kingsley looked at the photo again. "Kill him!" he said, surprising himself.

QB smiled at his honesty. "So will you meet me at the precinct if they arrest me?" he asked.

"Yes. Of course I will."

QB then told him everything he knew, leaving out the details of what they planned to do in retrieving Reyna. There was no way he would incriminate his team. He needed to tell Kingsley as much as possible, but at the same time he didn't want to involve his boys anymore than they were already involved. He spoke about his last will and testament and asked Kingsley to be there for Reyna if and when the police questioned her.

Kingsley took it all in, understanding that QB was ready to die for his family. He tried to talk QB out of it one last time, but realized that there was nothing that would stop him from going after his wife. Even though he was his lawyer and was supposed to set certain standards, he knew inside, he would've done the same thing.

They hung up.

QB sat there thinking about everything and nothing. Since coming home from prison, the egregious stupidity of going after someone who had pushed him wouldn't have been an option, for he'd learned the hard way about being a person who simply reacts to situations without thinking. But this was different, he kept telling himself. He wearily accepted the entire incident, from them going to a ballgame to celebrate his students receiving their GED, to ending up shot and now his wife being kidnapped, as further proof that his life, like a shirt with a loose thread was unraveling beyond his control.

Young Adult

TWENTY-FIVE

y ten o'clock QB's stomach was in knots; his nerves were on edge. It was fourteen of them in the basement—the whole team was there except Amari. Nobody had heard from him since he called QB and told him that nobody should do anything until he returned. He had worked out the perfect plan. Zeus was lying on the floor resting. True, Easy, and Ramel were in the basement with the rest of the team trying to relax themselves, but for most of them that was next to impossible. The tension was thick like hot air in a sauna. You could literally feel the fear and apprehension of the team, even Easy, who normally was the one with the cool demeanor, paced around thinking about the possibility of death waiting around the corner. However, each of them was prepared to hold their boy down like gravity.

Amari finally arrived. QB heard his music thumping from his truck as he parked in the driveway. He met him at the front door. Amari stood there with a pock-marked face Columbian. QB looked at him like "what's up?" Amari made introductions. "QB, this is Chino ... Chino, my brother." They shook hands.

Amari looked at his watch. "Where's everybody?"

"In the basement," QB replied.

Amari nodded towards the stairs, "Let us talk before we go downstairs."

They were about to head upstairs when Zeus appeared, "Where y'all going?"

Amari stopped, turned to Zeus, and told him to come with them. Once in the bedroom Amari told them that Riv was nowhere to be found. He then laid out his plan. After going back and forth with the how and when, they finally came to the agreement that it could be pulled off. QB thought the plan was risky. However, it eliminated most of his team from getting their hands dirty. QB told Chino to put it in motion. The success of the plan depended on stealth and timing. Everybody had to be where they were supposed to be and then do what they needed to do in order to get out as quickly as possible. Chino left, and told QB that they would be waiting for his call. After QB saw him out the house, they went down to the basement and explained how things would go down. He then gave everybody an option to back out … nobody did.

***

At three in the morning, five SUV's rolled down the street, enveloped by the silent darkness of the Long Island suburb. QB peered out the window of the truck. He looked at the caravan of vehicles and prayed they were not stopped by the police. He pushed all his other doubts out of his head. There was no turning back now. They were on their way to get his wife. Four of the trucks were full of blood-thirsty Columbians who were armed with dangerous intentions. The last one was driven by Ramel, with Amari in the passenger seat and Zeus and QB in the back. True, Easy, and the rest of the team were on standby in case they needed to storm in with heavier artillery, a second wave so to speak.

It was up to QB and Zeus to get Reyna out of the house. QB wasn't leaving that up to anybody but himself. He lifted his black gloved hand from the rear door panel and ran it across the M16 that lay across his lap. He clicked the magazine back in place and put the firing switch on a two-shot burst. He hoped he wouldn't have to use it, but that seemed impossible now that the Columbians were on board. They were more than pleased when Amari approached them with his offer of delivering Showtyme.

Amari and Chino knew one another from his days of hustling, so when Amari found out that the Henchmen had killed his brother-in-law he knew nothing but blood would satisfy Chino's need for revenge.

***

By the time they located the block where Reyna was being held, QB was numb beyond grief; feeling nothing anymore, but as they drove by the brown and white house he did begin to feel one single emotion—a growing, burning anger. He couldn't predict what was going to happen, but he knew he was going to do whatever it took to get his wife out of there safely. Showtyme had intended to cast a dark shadow over his life, wanted to push, and intimidate him, but instead of running away, QB was running toward them. They wanted war, well now they were going to get it.

They scanned the area as they drove by the house numerous times. Then they parked the truck three blocks away. Everybody in QB's vehicle was silent. There's something about the anticipation of having to kill, or possibly be killed by somebody that helps keep the conversation subdued. Zeus extracted a nine-millimeter Glock automatic from his jacket and quietly screwed a suppressor onto the end of it. They were startled when Chino tapped on their window. How he had snuck up on them they didn't know? QB opened the back door so he could hop in and go over some last minute details. Finally, the team was ready to move and synchronized their watches. They would move in twelve minutes. The Columbians were going to strike first, hard and fast. Sixty seconds later they would be followed by QB and Zeus. Hopefully they would be able to get in and out without confrontation or having to kill someone. Ramel found a house on the farther side of the street that offered a good vantage point for him to pick off any Henchmen that may follow them out of the house. Silently, everybody maneuvered into position. The Denali in the driveway and the naked statue of a white man confirmed that this was the house. QB was surprised that Showtyme didn't have any of his soldiers watching the street.

Inside the house, Shawnee was trying to hide her nervousness. It was that time. Showtyme was watching his pit bull puppies play fight with one another when he heard a loud crash come from somewhere downstairs. Someone had kicked in the back door. It was Chino, he opened fire with a Heckler & Koch nine millimeter and felt the powerful recoil of the gun as he unleashed the thirty round magazine on the faces and chest of three startled Henchmen that were in the living room. The other Columbians fanned out throughout the house, checking the rooms on the main floor. The Henchmen along with Showtyme immediately ran for their artillery. Before anybody knew what was happening there was a full-fledged war, bullets were flying everywhere. Two Columbians began making their way up the stairs when suddenly Cherokee with a cat-like gaze fixated her sight on the two targets. When they reached the top of the stairs she pivoted on the balls of her feet and unloaded four quick shots, two dead. She walked over to the bodies and looked down at them and immediately recognized who they were. She ran back to the room and told Showtyme that it was the Columbians. He finished strapping his armored vest to his body and grabbed an AK 47 and told both Shawnee and Cherokee, "Let's go." He didn't have time to think about how they found out about his hideout spot.

They made their way down the stairs without confrontation, but as they turned into the hallway they saw two henchmen laying dead with vacant faces, their eyes looked beyond everything. Showtyme couldn't believe the Columbians were in his home. As he was making his way to the basement he spotted a Columbian to his left, he spun and squeezed the AK and saw the Columbian's body jerk backwards into the wall. The Columbian's eyes opened wide upon impact as his body slid to the floor—confirming the presence of death. Showtyme continued toward the kitchen when suddenly Chino opened fire on them. Showtyme hit the ground just in time. However, the dum-dum bullets whizzed by him and tore through Cherokee's throat. She was killed instantly. Showtyme looked back at her. She had the face of a mannequin. He had no time to grieve. Shawnee returned fire, making Chino take cover behind a wall. This allowed Showtyme just enough time to roll into one of the bedrooms to his left.

QB and Zeus finally made it through the back door. The scene of carnage was everywhere. Bodies were strewn all over the place. They saw Chino with his back against the wall shielding himself from bullets. Chino looked back and waved for them to hurry down into the basement. QB couldn't believe this was going down, but getting to Reyna was his only concern. He led the way to the basement door. It was locked. Zeus pushed him to the side and kicked the door off the hinges. They immediately ran down the dark stairs, yelling out Reyna's name. Zeus found a light switch along the wall, and flicked it on. The basement lit up, and QB immediately spotted Reyna tied to a chair, and ran to her. He began untying her, hoping the gunshots he heard above didn't follow them down the stairs. Zeus checked the rooms then made sure nobody came downstairs. QB finally got Reyna loose. They hugged each other so tight, it felt as if their bodies became one. The grip of needing each other was so intense that it robbed each of them of their breath. Zeus finally said, "Let's get her out of here—it's been eight minutes, Q."

With Reyna in between them, they began slowly climbing the stairs, making their way out of the basement. When they made it to the backdoor leading them outside, they stepped out into the dark night and picked up their pace. Amari pulled up the truck at the end of the driveway. He hopped out of the vehicle calling for them to hurry up. QB grabbed Reyna's arm and they began running toward the truck. Suddenly Amari's eyes widen and he immediately cried out. It was a long wail of agony. He ran toward them, yelling, "Get down! Q, get down …"

All three hit the ground as Amari raised his weapon and squeezed off a barrage of bullets. The force of the lead that hit Nitty's body drove him back into the backdoor. Nitty's body shook for a moment then laid still. QB grabbed Reyna, and along with Zeus they ran for the truck. Amari turned to retreat when Showtyme suddenly stepped out into the driveway and took aim at him. When QB got Reyna into the truck he turned just in time to see Showtyme pull the trigger. The slugs tore through Amari's back. QB immediately whirled and fired his weapon, driving Showtyme back into the house. QB then ran to Amari. He was bleeding from the holes in his stomach and chest. His breath was slowly dissipating with every effort to find some air. Blood was easing out his body. His fatigues were soaking up the dark blood stains. QB bent down and lifted his brother's head. Amari opened his eyes and with labored breath said, "I guess mom was right ... looks like death has finally claimed your boy." He grabbed QB's arm. "Q, whatever you do man, don't lose your family over this ..." Violent spasms rocked his body—he coughed up blood.

QB clutched him tight to his chest. Reyna ran out the truck and stood behind her husband crying, her hand was covering her mouth in shock. QB felt Amari's life take flight. He knew if heaven had a ghetto it's where he would find Amari. QB stood up; he didn't say anything as Reyna ran into his arms. Sweat was running down QB's face, his body felt as if it was overheating. Zeus came up to him and said, "Q, we have to get out of here."

Feeling a huge void within, he looked Reyna in the eyes hoping to find something in them to fill that space. Killing Showtyme suddenly was no longer a question of morality, it was business. He fought back his tears; he couldn't afford for his emotions to interfere with his reasoning. He knew death was a natural consequence for those who were not focused. His eyes glared with hatred. Reyna had never seen him look like that. She started to say something to him, but he stopped her, grabbed her by the elbow and led her back to the truck She jumped in the back. Zeus, who already knew what it was, hopped in the driver's side. With a heavy heart, QB stared at Reyna for one last second. Reyna usually had

the ability to restrain him from his unreasonable instincts. He had never met a woman who was not only caring, but forceful. The only person who, many times, stopped him from stepping in his own mess. But not this time, his brother was gunned down, and he hoped she wouldn't make a scene. He saw a look of understanding in Reyna's eyes. He looked at Zeus and said, "Pick up Ramel and get her to a hospital." Zeus started to say something, but QB yelled, "I got this! Now get up out of here." His mind was made up. He leaned over and kissed Reyna's forehead. With a stroke of hatred pure as bottled water, he turned and went after Showtyme.

Against Reyna's protests, Zeus pulled off. QB ran back into the house, where he noticed Chino laid out on the kitchen floor, holding his stomach. He had been hit in the gut, and was bleeding profusely. QB grabbed him and dragged him outside where he would be safe. He looked at QB, and gripped his arm. , "Papi, kill that piece of mess," he said.

Upon reentering the house QB looked at the bodies with gaping holes in them, blood was everywhere. He stood still trying to hear anything. Suddenly, he heard something in the basement. A female voice called out, "Showtyme."

Slowly making his way down to the basement, QB listened for more voices. Sliding his hand down his weapon he clicked it on full automatic. He swung his weapon around in a wide arc when he came to the bottom of the stairs. The room was clear. He slowly moved toward the other rooms. Nobody. *Where the hell did they go?* he thought. He heard sirens then he saw it. The floor. Bending down, he pulled on the metal cover, and sure enough, it led somewhere. QB climbed down the steps without hesitation, and thought, *This cat has a tunnel under his crib.* QB raised his gun and then moved out into the tunnel. He picked up his pace, when suddenly he heard three shots. Crotched down, he cautiously moved on. Then he saw them. A female was standing over someone with a gun aimed at a heaving body.

QB called out, "Is that you, Shawnee?" She spun around ready to fire her weapon. She was surprised to see him. He held his gun to his side.

"It's me, QB." She looked at him not really knowing what to say. They stood there facing each other, suspended in reality. QB noticed the tears in her eyes. He never thought about his next step. He moved toward her as she lowered her weapon. When he reached her he hugged her. Shawnee almost collapsed in his embrace. QB thought he could literally feel the burden of her troubles leave her body. "Is that Showtyme?"

She shook her head yes.

"Okay, let me think … We got ourselves a real problem here." Suddenly he heard voices, it was the police. What he did next involved tremendous consequences. He gave Shawnee his gun and told her to run and get out of there. She looked at him with a surprised look, but stood there stuck. He snapped her out of her reverie. "Shawnee, you have to hurry up, the cops are going to be here in a second. Find somewhere safe to go. Get rid of those and I'll be in touch."

The look in her eyes was of disbelief. She couldn't believe he was letting her go, and felt the need to explain why she shot Showtyme. "I … couldn't let him live because ..."

QB cut her off. "Listen, don't worry about that. You need to get out of here now. I will take care of everything here. Now, get going, we'll talk later."

She gave him one last look and then took off. QB watched her exit the tunnel and then approached Showtyme. He was lying face down. QB picked up his wrist, feeling for a pulse. Crimson red flowed from the gaping hole in the center of his torso. Before he bent down to administer CPR, he turned back and yelled for help, the police heard him.

Showtyme's body began twitching. QB could hear the breath of life wheeze out of his body. He rolled Showtyme over and in an attempt to calm the face of death that was staring directly at him, QB gave him mouth to mouth, trying to blow life back into his body. He didn't know how long this lasted, perhaps only a few seconds, maybe minutes. But as he attempted to save the life of the man who had been tearing his life apart, hands clamped down on his shoulders and he was jerked away from Showtyme.

"He's still alive, we can still save ..." QB began.

But before he could finish he was manhandled to the ground. His face was slammed into the dirt, and his arms were snatched behind his back. His nightmare was confirmed. Déjà vu—as handcuffs tightened around his wrist, he heard someone say something about his rights. Flashes of his arrest eighteen years ago exploded like a camera bulb in his mind. After arresting QB, the cops searched the rest of the tunnel. They found no one.

By the time they escorted QB out of the tunnel, the entire block was lit up like a movie production. However, the bloodbath he saw reminded him that this was far from a script. The police led him to a police car, where he sat as detectives, and forensics scrambled around. He sat there for twenty minutes when he noticed Reyna walk up and approach a cop. She stood there with her father and his lawyer. QB was relieved to see them. He could see the officer call out for a detective who took Reyna aside to explain something. The detective then pointed toward QB. Reyna, along with Kingsley looked in his direction. The whole scene felt like Al Pacino's *Scarface*. Columbians, gang members, dead-bodies, and him sitting in the back of a police car.

QB saw Reyna and Kingsley being escorted to another police vehicle. The next time he saw them they were at Homicide headquarters in Mineola.

TWENTY-SIX

The funeral for Amari Banks was held two weeks after the shooting. He was laid to rest on the same plot with his mother and grandmother. The funeral was far from a sad event; it turned out to be a big party. QB looked around and couldn't believe the number of people who showed up to pay their respects. Amari was well-known, a man of many different circles. QB couldn't believe how many type of people showed up. There were hustlers of all kinds: entertainers, sport figures, street legends and about twenty different women who claimed to be the love of his life.

The mood was celebratory, and by the time the reverend said his closing remarks, people were in a giving mood. QB was surprised by how many lives Amari touched. The hustlers approached QB afterwards and handed him envelopes filled with money. QB looked at Reyna with eyes that said, *I can't believe this*, knowing that his brother meant so much to others helped him cope with the fact that his brother was dead.

***

QB felt extremely lucky to be able to attend Amari's funeral. His words fired up the audience as he shared his thoughts and memories of those youthful days he and Amari shared. After his arrest, Kingsley had to pull a lot of strings to get him a bail. His biggest hurdle was to convince the supervisor of the parole division not to put a hold on him, but once he sat him down and explained what happened to QB and his family, the supervisor decided to give him a shot. However, it came with a clause—an ankle bracelet. He was bailed out on a two hundred and

Young Adult

fifty thousand dollars bond. In spite of telling the police most of the truth, including the shooting after the baseball game, the shooting at U-Turn, and Reyna's kidnapping, he was expected to be taken to trial for the murder of Showtyme. Everything added up for the detectives except the death of the thug. QB told the police that he was chasing Showtyme through the tunnel when he heard shots, so he immediately took cover and when he thought it was safe, he moved forward only to discover Showtyme's heaving body. Even the first police officer on the scene gave a statement that when he approached them it appeared as if QB was trying to revive the deceased. But the Nassau County District Attorney was so upset that this went down in his neck of the woods, he decided to still pursue charges against QB. Without much physical evidence and despite the fact that Showtyme was a fearsome gang-banger, who most people believed deserved to die a horrible death. It was close to election time, and for the D A's office this was a case that could guarantee victory.

In the aftermath of everything that took place, QB tried his best to prepare Reyna for the worst. It had been eight months, and a trial date was finally set. For QB, mornings had taken on a terrible sameness. Each passing day had brought with it a fleeting hope that he was finally awakening from the terrible nightmare his life had become. As the warm embrace of sleep released him from its clutches, the hope that he was waking up from a bad dream always slipped away. The scorching burn of fear in his stomach since his indictment burned steadily as he thought about the horror of what tomorrow might bring, the day his trial begins.

The district attorney for the past five days, put on a pretty strong circumstantial case. His final witness was Travis Smith, aka Banger. As he sat at the defendant's table, QB thought about the kid, Banger, the ninth and hopefully final witness to testify against him. He couldn't believe how the Nassau County District Attorney had dressed these thugs up like choirboys and marched them into the courtroom to testify against him. He shook his head, not believing his fate rest in the words of crooks with forked tongues.

The State of New York attempted to paint a picture of QB as a ruthless killer who carefully planned and then killed, vigilante style, a gangster named Darius Adams, also known as, Showtyme.

Judge Barron Hailey, more popularly known as "Hang 'Em High Hailey," looked at the district attorney and then glanced over his thick lenses at the defendant's attorney, William Kingsley III, who sat next to his client, Quentin Banks, aka QB. The pale-faced judge removed his glasses and wiped sweat off his forehead. "Are the people ready?" the judge asked, looking down at the district attorney.

Hang 'Em High sat back in his throne, took a deep breath, and exhaled slowly, bracing himself for another long day in court. Still pissed off from the prior day when some of the spectators and a prosecutor's witness attempted to turn his courtroom into a circus and make a mockery out of the law by getting into a cursing and shoving match. He looked down at his law clerk, who nodded, letting him know that she was ready. This was the fifth day of this murder trial.

The district attorney quickly replied, "Yes, Your Honor."

Judge Hailey turned his attention to the defendant's table. "Mr. Kingsley, is the defendant ready?" he asked.

Kingsley stopped shuffling through his papers and looked up. "Yes, Your Honor, we're ready to proceed."

"Bring in the jurors," the judge instructed his bailiff.

Once the jurors were seated, Judge Hailey addressed everyone in his courtroom. He turned toward the juror box. "Ladies and gentlemen of

the jury, I want to apologize for the outburst that occurred yesterday. I want you to know that this display of behavior will not be tolerated in my courtroom."

The jurors nodded their heads and hoped he would be able to maintain order. There was no doubt that the mostly white jury was scared to death when one of the prosecutor's witnesses took the stand the previous day and spectators from both sides began fighting. The courtroom erupted into a free-for-all. The court-officers had to secure the defendant, rush both the judge and the jurors out of the courtroom during the melee, and then stop an all out brawl. Hang 'Em High assured the jurors that nothing like that would ever happen again. He looked at the spectators in the audience. "If someone dares to interrupt this trial again they will be held in contempt and punished to the fullest extent of the law." Turning back to the jurors, he added, "What I need to know from each of you is whether or not the melee that unfolded yesterday will hinder your ability to be impartial? If so, please approach the bench."

When nobody stood, he looked relieved and then turned to the D.A. "You can call your first witness."

The district attorney stood up. "The State calls Travis Smith."

An electric charge flowed throughout the courtroom. Murmurs echoed between the aisles of spectators. A well-dressed young man approached the witness stand with a confident bop in his step, gangster grillin' the audience like he was auditioning for an *Americas Most Wanted* reenactment. The district attorney straightened his tie as Mr. Smith settled into the witness box. He then approached his witness. "Can you state your name for the court?"

The young man mumbled something, but nobody could hear him. The stenographer, who sat two-feet away asked the witness to speak up.

"Mr. Smith, you have to talk into the microphone," the district attorney reiterated.

Leaning forward, Banger grabbed the microphone as if he was a DJ. "Oh, my bad, testing one—two, testing one—two."

This was received with laughter, which enraged the judge. Hang 'Em High didn't find it funny. "Just answer the question that you're asked, young man. Do you understand?"

He looked up at the judge. "Yeah ..." he said then shifted in his seat. "... My name is Banger."

The DA put his head down wondering, *Why did I put this kid on the stand?* "No, Mr. Smith—we need your real name. What your mother named you."

Banger seemed to be enjoying the attention as his eyes moved back and forth from the jurors to the audience. "Oh, Travis Smith," he said

"Where do you live, Mr. Smith?"

"Iraq."

"Excuse me ... where do you live?" asked the DA, totally baffled by Banger's response.

"LeFrak City. We call it Iraq because we bust our guns and pitch rocks like the Middle East," Banger said.

The District Attorney moved closer to Banger in an attempt to get him to relax. "Who do you live with, Mr. Smith?"

"My moms."

"Do you know a Mr. Darius Adams?" the DA asked while silently praying that their countless hours of rehearsal paid off.

"Yeah, that's my boy."

"That's your friend," the DA repeated, looking at the jurors.

"That's right," Banger responded.

"Were you there the night Mr. Adams was killed?" he asked, looking at the jurors.

"Yeah, I was there."

"Could you tell us what happened?"

"He was murdered."

"Do you know how?" the DA coached.

Young Adult

He stood up and pointed directly at QB. "He hit him up. I would've been with Showtyme, but I got shot in my thigh and couldn't roll with him as he tried to escape. But I saw that dude run after him with this big gun. He didn't see me because I was playing dead," he said.

"Objection, Your Honor. Speculation, the witness is testifying to not seeing what actually happened, but to what he assumed happened," Kingsley said.

"Objection sustained. Strike that from the record. Please be seated, Mr. Smith, and watch your mouth," the judge ordered angrily.

He then turned his attention to the jurors and explained that they were to disregard the statement made by the witness.

The DA continued. "When was the last time you saw Mr. Adams?"

"At the funeral home ... well, I didn't actually see him 'cause they had a closed casket." He noticed the judge shift in his seat so he quickly corrected himself. "I mean, they had it closed because I heard a bullet tore through his neck and his head could not be re-attached."

"Objection. Your Honor, once again hearsay."

"Sustained," said Hang 'Em high, peering down at the district attorney.

"Do you see the man who killed your friend here in this courtroom?" the DA asked.

"Hell yeah, that's that nigga right there," he said, pointing at QB.

The judge was growing more impatient by the second. He looked like he was going to blow a blood vessel. He turned to the witness. "Mr. Smith, I'm going to tell you one last time to watch your language in my courtroom. You are not allowed to use profanity, nor will you use any racial slurs to refer to anybody in my courtroom or you'll be the one going to jail. Do you understand me?"

Banger regained his composure, and then looked up at the judge. "Yeah, a'ight," he said.

QB stared at Banger and thought to himself, *It's a damn shame how these young gang members have the ability to be heartless at will, yet on the other hand, they will do and say anything to save their own behinds. It's crazy how the system takes advantage of these young kids and their ignorance of the law and uses them as pawns in their own political game.*

For QB, this courtroom drama was déjà vu. However, this time around he was not even offered a plea. If he's found guilty they are going to put him in a cage and throw away the key. The thought of coming home in his mid-fifties, possibly sixties, made him sick to his stomach. He knew he could never put his family through a relationship that would be defined by cell bars and prison rules—again. As his trial came to a close he knew he had no choice but to put his faith in a system riddled with more holes than a golf course. This is one of those times when ... even he prayed. His mom used to tell him that prayer had a way to get in places where nothing else could. Well, he hoped his prayers would lead him to victory; justice instead of just-us, meaning just black folks in prison. He turned around toward the first row of the courtroom where his wife sat with his daughter and gave them the best smile he could conjure.

His daughter smiled and waved back, while his wife placed her hand on her heart and mouthed, "I love you." He turned back around and drifted off in thought.

***

In the beginning of banger's testimony QB had seen doubt in the eyes of the jury, but the more the DA coached him, QB noticed the tides were turning. The prosecutor had somehow got the jurors up on the edge of their seats with the tales of what took place in a gang member's life. As with most of the prosecutor's witnesses, his words were cancerous. They were mostly lies and had the potential to ruin QB's life. Fortunately, Kingsley tore each one of the prosecutor's witness testimonies apart, and Banger faired no different. QB looked around, trying to size up the jurors as his lawyer discredited Banger's entire testimony. Kingsley had Banger fidgeting in the witness stand, and trying to retract things he had testified to earlier.

In spite of the jury hearing a lot of testimony about the unbelievable violence that disfigured whole neighborhoods, there was very little evidence that supported the premise that Quentin Banks was any kind of contributor toward that ugliness. However, the district attorney was banking on getting the jurors caught up in the vivid scenes of the bloody massacre in order to squeeze out a conviction. He drew a portrait that this was something that could've possibly unfolded in their communities. This strategy, along with the preponderance of evidence backed up by the District Attorney's theory as to why Quentin Banks wanted Showtyme dead, had QB beginning to doubt his chances of acquittal. The DA promised to show that Mr. Banks on the surface, appeared to be an upstanding citizen, but was nothing more than a vicious, vigilante killer, and when pushed wouldn't hesitate to take matters into his own hands.

QB couldn't get a good read on the jurors. To say he was nervous was an understatement. The fact that there was only one black person out of the twelve jurors had him second guessing his own attorney. He couldn't understand how they dared considered this a jury of his peers. Kingsley, however, thought they were safe. *We better be*, thought QB. He finally brought his cross examination to an end.

QB had to admit, thus far, Kingsley had shredded the prosecutor's case. Things appeared to be going their way. However, the knot in the pit of his stomach told him otherwise. Just twelve months ago his life had a bounce to it like a twelve year old on a trampoline. Now all he could see was the long days of prison. QB wondered if the district attorney knew what losing your freedom truly meant. It was nothing like losing your keys or having a blowout on the highway. You don't just pull onto the shoulder, put on a spare and continue on your way. For QB, the impact was much more complicated and would affect the many moving parts of his life—Reyna would struggle to be faithful, and Nia would grow up without her father, and so much more. He looked at the DA sitting there across from them with his calm, indifferent stare, like he had it all under control and wondered what he would have done if he had to walk in his shoes.

When Kingsley sat down, the district attorney stood and announced that the people rest their case. This meant it was now up to Kingsley to call witnesses to counter the case the gangsters painted for the jurors. Kingsley and QB had previously decided that he wouldn't testify, if he did, his prior conviction could be brought up and that was just too risky. However, Reyna would be the first witness to testify on the defense's behalf, and then Kingsley planned to call some of the students of U-Turn. Kingsley told QB it would be a good way to counter the testimony of thugs that the prosecutor paraded in front of the jurors for the past week. QB wasn't so sure. He didn't know if he trusted the students of U-Turn with his liberty, his life.

The judge dismissed everybody for lunch. QB went outside with Reyna, Nia, and his lawyer. Reyna was trying to calm herself down because she was due up first to testify when the trial resumed. QB noticed how uptight she was, so he asked, "Baby, what's wrong?"

"Nothing Q," she said, but he didn't believe her any more than she believed herself. Each day Reyna and her parents sat side by side in the first row. Every time QB looked at them, they smiled encouragingly as if they thought their own belief in his innocence would somehow be transferred to the jury. What they couldn't see, but QB could, was that the criminal justice system was indeed a business, the only business where the recall of its product is viewed as a success. Meaning, because QB once did time in the system, he would forever be targeted to return. The slogan "Crime does not pay" is false. It pays … just not for the criminal.

Pulling her close, he said, "Baby, things are going to turn out fine."

She looked up into his eyes. "I know, but I cannot understand how after hearing those … people testify, how the judge is allowing this trial to continue," she whispered.

"Beautiful, I know how you feel, but if feelings were allowed to rule our courts, our prisons would be empty. There isn't a man in prison, anywhere in this country, I suspect, who doesn't have a girlfriend, wife, or family members who swears he's innocent," he said, looking into her face.

"You're right, Q. I just don't want to lose you."

Kingsley jumped in. "You're not going to lose him. Now let's go get some lunch, we have less than an hour to be back in the courtroom."

***

When the jury came back from lunch, Reyna took the witness stand. Kingsley stood up. "Can you state your name for the courts and your relationship to the defendant?"

"My name is Reyna Banks, and I'm the wife of Mr. Quentin Banks."

Kingsley then guided her through everything that took place. Reyna described how she was kidnapped, and then beat up numerous times during her captivity. She told the jurors how they threatened to rape her, and worst to snatch up their daughter and sell her on eBay. Reyna's mother had to leave the courtroom during her testimony. Reyna's testimony was electric. She sent a charge down each juror's spine with a detailed description of her experience. By the time Kingsley finished with Reyna, a heavy silence had settled over the courtroom.

The district attorney sat there with his elbows on the table and his fingers folded together, staring straight ahead weighing if he should cross examine Reyna. He decided against it. She was a victim in all of this, and he did not want to seem as if he was attacking her.

The judge said to the prosecutor, "Your witness."

The district attorney stood. "Your Honor, the people have no interest in cross-examining Mrs. Banks. The people understand the unfortunate ordeal that she had to endure and there is no need to rehash that experience."

The judge nodded, he agreed with this.

Kingsley had asked the judge for a recess, claiming to have to make an urgent call. Judge Hailey reluctantly allowed him ten minutes. What Kingsley really needed was time to speak to his next couple of witnesses. Being that the prosecutor decided to make his case by dressing up young gangsters as good kids, Kingsley decided to counter by actually showing the difference between a truly good kid and those that consider themselves gangsters. As Kingsley walked out of the courtroom every eye seemed to be glancing in his direction. The students of U-Turn were his hole card; the case was now in their hands. The judge was eyeing the courtroom clock, he then told the jurors to take a few minutes to stretch if they had to, and then he quickly made his way into his chambers.

Ten minutes later when the judge returned, Kingsley was ready. He was sitting at the defendant's table conversing with QB.

"Are you ready, Mr. Kingsley?"

"Yes, Your Honor."

"Well, call your next witness."

"We call Ms. Maria Ramirez to the stand."

A well dressed Latina walked up to the stand. QB couldn't believe his eyes, Maria was one of his favorite students, but she never exhibited the kind of maturity that showed as she walked up to that stand. She was a feisty young Dominican lady, who had a rough life and no problem letting any and everybody know what she felt about them.

Kingsley stood up. He fixed his tie and walked slowly toward the witness box. "Can you state your name for the court and your association with the defendant, Quentin Banks?"

"My name is Maria Ramirez, and I'm a student at U-Turn where Mr. Banks is the director, counselor, mentor and most importantly, friend." She looked at QB and smiled.

"Wow … a counselor, mentor and friend. What do you mean by that, Ms. Ramirez?" Kingsley asked.

Maria sat straight up in the witness chair, then looked at the jurors. "Mr. Banks is actually much more than that. He's a life saver, the only person who actually believed in me. I mean … I grew up in an environment that was actually a living hell."

"What do you mean by that, Ms. Ramirez?"

Maria shifted in her seat, looked down at her hands that were in her lap. She then looked up at the jurors and then the prosecutor. "I remember when I was twelve years old, coming home from school telling my mother that my teacher told me I would be wasting my time thinking I can actually be a doctor. When I was younger I wanted to be a pediatrician, a doctor for babies. My mom looked at me, and surprisingly said, 'She's right, you need to be smart and just take your butt to nursing school and become a nurse's aide so you can help out with some of these bills.' That was the very day my dreams of becoming someone significant was killed. I never went back to school. I ended up in the street, and got pregnant at sixteen. I had a baby boy, and nowhere to go because my son's father decided to run instead of help me." Tears were now falling down her face.

Kingsley interrupted her. "Would you like some tissue, Ms. Ramirez?"

She nodded, and Kingsley gave her some Kleenex. When she finished wiping her eyes, she sniffled. "I'm so sorry, I didn't mean to cry…"

"That's okay, we understand how hard it is to speak about certain things; especially painful things about ourselves. So you were telling us about your living hell, how the father of your child left you to raise a child on your own at the age of sixteen. Why didn't you go back home to your mother?"

"I tried, but she slammed the door in my face, saying she could not afford me and another child. So I walked the streets during the day and slept at different friends' homes at night. Then one day I walked past U-Turn, and just walked into Mr. Banks office. I sat there with my baby looking pitiful and told him I needed help."

Kingsley walked toward Maria. "Well, what did Mr. Banks do?" he asked.

Maria seemed to swell with pride. "He took me and Chance, that's my son, to lunch and then he gave me a room at U-Turn and began helping me get my GED," she said. "He ... taught me how to dream again." She paused for a second, looking down at QB. "In September I will be going to John Hopkins Medical College. I was recently accepted to a special program for inner city youth to become doctors. In four to six years I will be known as Doctor Maria Ramirez, thanks to Mr. Banks."

Looking at the expressions on the juror's faces, Kingsley knew he was turning the table. "That is wonderful, Ms. Ramirez. Now let me ask you ... do you think Mr. Banks is capable of doing the things that were described by those young men who testified for the prosecutor?"

"No—I know he would never do something like that, he makes sure every one of us walks a straight line. Believe me, he keeps more eyes on us than Al Sharpton does the police department." Several people in the courtroom laughed, the jury, too. Even Judge Hailey put a hand in front of his face to conceal a smile. "Mr. Banks makes sure we don't waste our lives, so I know he wouldn't waste his by doing something like that. As I said, he is a lifesaver not a life taker."

"Thank you, Ms. Ramirez, I have no further questions."

The prosecutor stepped up to question her on cross examination, but there was very little he could say to trip her up. Maria knew very little about the crime, all she knew was that Quentin Banks saved her and her child's life and that's all she testified too.

Kingsley called his next witness. "Your Honor, we call Sean Matthews."

Everybody looked around the courtroom for Chase. However, being that he was incarcerated; the guards couldn't prejudice the jury by

showing that he was locked up. So they kept him in the back until he was needed. When the guards heard his name, keeping a close eye on him, they allowed him to walk to the witness stand. QB really had his doubts about having Chase testify, but Kingsley once again convinced him that it was best.

The prosecutor sat at his table with a pleasant smile on his face, he couldn't believe Kingsley called him to be a witness, especially after Chase had refused to testify for the prosecutor. *I will get my chance to get him after all*, he thought.

"Good afternoon, Mr. Matthews," Kingsley said as he stood up.

"Morning, Mr. Kingsley."

"Can you tell us your current address, Mr. Matthews?"

"My current address is Rikers Island."

"Jail?" the attorney said rhetorically. "So for the jury's sake, you've been convicted of a crime?"

"Yes … I have."

"Can you tell us about it?"

"I recently pled guilty to a gun possession and in exchange received a one to three years sentence."

"So this means you have to go upstate for a minimum of one year and a maximum of three, is that correct?"

"Yes."

"Mr. Matthews, can you tell us the circumstances surrounding why you were carrying a gun?"

Chase looked out into the audience then up at the judge. He took a deep breath. "Well, I was on my way to get at Showtyme when the cops arrested me," he said.

"When you say you were on your way to *get at* Showtyme, you mean Darius Adams. Correct?"

"Yes."

"Can you tell us what you mean when you say you were on your way to get at this Showtyme?"

Chase looked at the jurors and said, "At the time, I was headed to shoot him." Some of the jurors shook their heads in disbelief. Chase noticed one white man looking at him with his lips curled up. "I was going after him because he had put a hit out on me. At that time there were two attempts on my life. The first one was when Mr. Banks was shot, and the second time was at U-Turn."

"Okay, let's slow down a bit, Mr. Matthews so we can get the facts right. You say that the day you were arrested you had decided to go after Showtyme because he had put a price on your head, and up until that point there were two attempts on your life."

"Yes, that's correct."

"Why was there a hit put out on you, Mr. Matthews?"

"Because I wanted to get out of the Henchmen."

"That's a gang? A gang that this Showtyme ran, correct?"

"That's right."

"So you mean to tell us because you wanted out, the price you had to pay was death?"

"Yes, that's right. Being in a gang is supposed to be until death do you part. You're not permitted to leave the Henchmen without paying a tremendous price, and in most cases it's in blood."

"Why did you want to leave, Mr. Matthews?"

"I decided to leave the Henchmen because after I joined U-Turn, I learned that there was more to life than selling drugs. That the measure of a man comes from things besides fighting, stealing, and sexual adventures."

"What exactly did you learn at U-Turn?"

"Well, besides getting my GED, and learning a vocational trade in electricity, it was at U-Turn that I learned that maturity comes with the acceptance of responsibility."

"That's good, Mr. Matthews. Can you tell us how much of a role Mr. Banks played in this transformation of yours?"

Young Adult

Chase looked at QB and smiled. "Well, until I met Mr. Banks I was like water, always following the path of least resistance. At that time, I was easily convinced to be down with any and everything. But when my grandmother told me about U-Turn I was hesitant, I didn't want to go. I had very little confidence in myself in any arena other than the streets. However, because I wanted to make my grandmother proud of me, I gave it a try ..." Chase looked at Kingsley who was shaking his head, giving him just enough silent support for him to continue. "... so I went and when I heard Mr. Banks speak that very first day I knew that he would help me get my life together. I, like most young kids knew that my life was spiraling out of control, but most of the time there is nowhere to turn. The schools don't want us, our parents don't want us, so there is nowhere for us to turn but the streets, or in my case, the gangs. But with QB ... I mean, Mr. Banks, it was different. In the beginning we had our run-ins, because I was hard-headed, but after I began trusting him and the program, I learned how to say no. No to peer pressure, no to drugs, no to being a follower. Mr. Banks taught me that I had choices as to what I could do in life, and to be honest up until that point, I didn't believe that."

"It appears after getting off to a slow start that you have begun to get things together, Mr. Matthews. Do you know exactly what you're going to do when you get out?"

"To be honest, Mr. Kingsley I cannot sit up here and lie and say I got it all together, because I don't. I know what it's like to be part of a thug's world—and I don't like it, can't do it. But I have no idea what it's going to be like once I get back out into the real world. However, I have been studying the books Mr. Banks has been sending me on real estate investment, plus I promised him I would get into college so I plan on fulfilling that promise."

"Well, at least you are on the right path." The rest of Kingsley's questioning was about everything he knew about the case. Chase told all, from the time he joined the gang to the day he was shot at. He turned out to be a very credible witness despite his record and personal flaws. By the time Kingsley finished questioning him QB felt damn proud to be his mentor.

The words coming from each teenager that took the stand for the defense were less a compliment than a revelation. *It was breathtaking to see young people carry themselves in such a way*, thought most of the spectators. However, for QB it was hard, for he loved his invisibility. Yet, because of the testimony of the kids at U-Turn his visibility was never more evident—he touched lives.

The district attorney went after Chase like a skilled hunter. He stood up with his pen in his hand. "Mr. Matthews ... or is it Chase? They do call you Chase, right?"

Just like Mr. Kingsley told him, Chase sat there thinking how he should respond to the DA's question. "Yes, on the streets they call me Chase, but in U-Turn I learned that it is not appropriate to be called by my nickname, so in the real world I would much rather be referred to as Mr. Matthews."

The district attorney turned red as a beet at this response. "Mr. Matthews, that's fine with me. In fact, you're right. This definitely is, as you put it, the real world."

Chase didn't respond. He was told not to say anything if nothing in particular was asked of him. He was becoming more nervous because he knew the district attorney was not going to treat him with kid gloves.

The DA looked at Chase and asked, "How long have you been in the Henchmen, Mr. Matthews?"

"Since I was about ... 13 or 14, which means five years."

"So you've been in a gang for five years, Mr. Matthews?

"Yes."

"Have you ever hurt anybody, Mr. Matthews?

Chase hesitated. He peeped at QB who slightly nodded his head yes. He gazed up at the DA. "Yes. I hurt far too many people, something I truly regret," Chase answered.

"Have you ever killed anybody, Mr. Matthews?"

"No, I have not."

"Do you mean to say, not that you know of?"

"No, I mean exactly what I said. I have never killed anybody."

"But you testified today that you were on your way to kill Showtyme when the cops arrested you."

Kingsley jumped up trying to prevent Chase from digging a hole too big for him to get out of. "Objection, Your Honor, the question is irrelevant because that did not occur and it has absolutely no bearing on this particular case."

The judge glanced at the DA.

"Your Honor, the question is relevant because of Mr. Matthew's testimony on direct. He testified that he was going to get at Darius Adams, which meant either to kill or to inflict very serious bodily harm."

The judge looked at Kingsley and said, "Overruled, I will permit it."

"What I actually said was I was going to shoot him, whether or not he would've been killed is something I do not know. However, it was my intention to shoot him. He had attempted to kill me twice—by that time it was either bite or be bitten."

"Bite or be bitten, is that so, Mr. Matthews? Earlier you testified that you wanted nothing to do with the Henchmen and was trying to distance yourself from them, but here you are telling us it was bite or be bitten. Which is it, Mr. Matthews?" the prosecutor asked.

Kingsley was about to jump up, but QB stopped him. Chase looked at QB and then the District Attorney. He then leaned into the mic and said, "While I don't blame my actions on others, my upbringing did teach me irresponsibility. I sit here today and take full responsibility for all my bad choices. Unfortunately, I grew up around many pathetic role models ... surrounded by those role models I admit I adopted the same lifestyle. And the unlearning of that is going to take some time. However, at that time I felt under pressure, and I attempted to deal with it the best way I knew how. You, as a District Attorney shouldn't be surprised at how quickly it is for young men to accept the unimaginable, especially if one sees it enough. And when I think about it, it was way too easy for me to make the decision to hurt another. In fact, Mr. Banks always tried to talk to me about that."

"I bet he did," said the prosecutor.

The district attorney continued along the same line of questioning, but Chase held up. The district attorney underestimated the intelligence of the young man. Both QB and Kingsley were impressed.

The next witness he called was Ms. Franklin. Her testimony was short and powerful. She testified how under Quentin Banks' tutelage the students at U-Turn reinvented themselves, tearing into that image passed down to them from prior generations. She told stories of how he got them excited about responsibility and the prospect of becoming one of the greatest social weapons a family or community can ever hope to see.

The district attorney knew better than to attack her on cross, so he asked a few formal questions about her job at U-Turn and of course what happened the day when U-Turn was attacked by some of the Henchmen. To everybody's surprise, Ms. Franklin stuck to her story of not seeing much, just a young man laid out on the floor, whom she helped until the cops arrived.

Next, Kingsley called Michelle Francis, another U-Turn student. She testified to how QB taught her how to see herself as something more than she'd ever imagined.

When the district attorney got her on cross examination, he came at her hard because she had a prior, a felony that Kingsley didn't know about. In his attempt to discredit her, he asked, "Ms. Francis, is it true you used to sell your body for money?"

Michelle couldn't believe he was putting her business out there like that. She looked embarrassed; she put her head down, not knowing what to say. She looked up at the judge, hoping he wouldn't make her answer that. But he said, "Answer the question Ms. Francis."

Young Adult

She cleared her throat and said, "Yes, but ..."

"But what, Ms. Francis? Like the other students, you want us to believe you have it all together now."

With tears in her eyes, she said, "No, I don't want you to believe I have it altogether. I was actually forced to sell my body."

"Oh yeah, I bet, Ms. Francis. As uncomfortable as this might be, I venture to say that everyone on this jury, and everyone in this room, has done things that they're ashamed of, and told lies that they regret. But gun possession, drug selling, and now prostitution. Come on, now. How much do you all expect us to really believe?" he asked rhetorically. "Maybe U-Turn isn't turning out so many positive youth at all. Maybe you all are coming out of that program worse than when you went in."

Appearing a bit upset, she said, "That's not it. U-Turn is definitely doing its job. I grew up with my own self-esteem issues. All my life I was told I was nothing; ugly, a ho, a bitch or a whore. But it was Mr. Banks who taught me that I'm not a bitch, or a ho. He taught me that I am a young woman who is pregnant with potential. That I simply had to believe in myself." She wiped her eyes and then pointed at QB. "That man right there was the first to ever tell me that I was a beautiful person; that I was someone's child; someone's dream come true. Someone special, important, in spite of being raped at eight years old. Mr. Banks convinced me that I had a whole life in front of me, that all I had to do is decide to take control of it."

The district attorney decided not to push. He couldn't believe these young men and women were handling themselves in such a manner. Once again the witness recovered, trapping him in a sense. He had to admit, as the trial wound down, he himself was beginning to hope that the jurors found Quentin Banks not guilty.

After Ms. Francis' testimony it seemed as if there was not a dry eye in the courtroom. Reyna and her mother both were wiping tears from their faces.

Kingsley's final witness was Torrence Harris.

When his name was called, everybody turned around to see Torry being wheeled into the courtroom. Yet, instead of being wheeled to the witness stand, he stopped Naysia from pushing him. Then miraculously, he struggled up out of his seat and began walking without assistance to the witness box. Everybody in the courtroom, at least those who knew Torry was opened mouthed. They couldn't believe he was walking; it was a sight to see and this was his way of telling the Henchmen he was back.

QB whispered in Kingsley ear. "Did you stage this?"

"It was his idea," said the attorney. "I couldn't take this moment from him. Just sit back and watch us win this case."

When Torry settled into the witness stand, Kingsley approached slowly. "Good afternoon, Mr. Harris."

"Good afternoon."

"Mr. Harris, can you tell us your relationship with Mr. Banks?"

"He's my mentor, and I'm a recent graduate of U-Turn. I was also in the car with him the day he was shot. I was shot as well. In fact, I was told that I was going to be paralyzed, but as you can see I'm on the road to recovery."

"Yes, we see, and I want to congratulate you on your courage." Kingsley smiled at Torry. "Can you tell us about the day you were shot?"

Torry sat back and explained what took place from the very beginning. How Chase and him joined U-Turn, and once they met QB, soon after they had made a pact to not only get their GED, but to go to college. Basically, to get their lives together. He explained how QB had been there for them; encouraging Chase to get out of the Henchmen, and for him to get out of being lazy.

Kingsley asked him to explain to the jurors how this entire incident affected him. "Well, between those moments of being shot and getting accepted to college, I undertook a journey of emotional discovery; examining my life in painful detail. I had to literally reintroduce myself to myself because there were days where I didn't want to live … not because I was suicidal, but ..." He paused for a second to get his words together. "... because I didn't want to go on living not being able to walk," Torry responded.

Kingsley walked toward the jury box to get a feel of the jurors. "Mr. Harris, can you tell us what made you change your mind?"

Torry looked directly at QB. "It was Mr. Banks. Even in the hospital he would wheel himself in my room at night and speak to me at length about me facing those challenges that seemed insurmountable. By life's standards, I admit, it has always been hard for me to measure up. For the majority of my life I was always told I was too black to do this, or do that. Then this happened and I was told I would never walk. After this, I began thinking I would never be anything, but Mr. Banks didn't allow me to sulk in self-pity. He pushed me until I saw beauty in my struggles. He made me realize that I couldn't ever love myself unless I was ready to look and live beyond myself, and today I am proud to say I will be going to college in the summer, and I will be a father in less than a month. Because of Mr. Banks I live in hope. Hope is a fire that burns deep in my heart even on my most fearful nights."

"Thank you, Mr. Harris. I have no further questions."

It was the district attorney's turn. The jury was still and attentive. He looked around the courtroom and felt the weight of their expectations. "Good afternoon, Mr. Harris."

"Good afternoon."

The prosecutor stepped back toward his table. "Mr. Harris, why did you have to enroll in U-Turn?" he asked.

"Excuse me."

"Why did you enroll at U-Turn as opposed to going to a conventional high school?"

"Pausing, Torry surveyed the jurors. "I was kicked out of school because I was caught selling marijuana."

"Are there any further reasons?" the DA questioned in a flat, unresonant voice.

Torry said, "No."

The DA stood there looking at him silently. He moved closer to Torry. "Mr. Harris, have you ever been to jail?" he asked.

Torry paused and took an audible rumbling breath. "No, I have never been to jail, nor do I plan to … especially not after Mr. Banks shared stories of his experience."

The DA paused, not believing his luck. He finally got one of them to falter; to say something that can actually win him this case. The district attorney attacked. "What experience are you talking about?"

Kingsley jumped out of his seat. "Objection, Your Honor. May counsel approach the bench?"

The judged peered down at him, knowing that this was a pivotal point in the case. Hailey realized that Torry's slip up may have swung the pendulum back in the prosecution's favor. The judge paused. "Make it brief, counsel."

Kingsley and the prosecutor approached the bench where Kingsley objected to the prosecution questioning Mr. Harris about Quentin's conviction. Unfortunately, the rules are the rules, the judge told Kingsley. It was his witness who opened up that can of worms by testifying about listening to stories of Mr. Banks' experience. He told Kingsley the prosecutor had every right to question him about this experience. Kingsley was livid. He nodded and returned to his seat.

QB immediately asked what the judge said. When the attorney told him that Hailey was going to allow Torry to be questioned about the "experience," the blood drained from his face. He sat back up, and as he waited for the final phase of his trial to wind down, he tried to summon up some shred of hope—but couldn't find any.

The DA looked at his notes. "As I asked earlier, Mr. Harris, could you tell us about the experience you were talking about?"

Torry realizing his mistake didn't know exactly what he should do. He looked at Kingsley who nodded slightly. Torry took this as a sign to be truthful. "Well … Mr. Banks has on a few occasions shared with us his experience of being in prison to make sure we understood that prison was not a kind of ..." He searched for the right words "... a rite of passage."

"Do you know what Mr. Banks was in jail for?"

"Objection, Your Honor," Kingsley said from the table.

The jury watched in puzzlement as the judge once again overruled the attorney's objection. "Answer the question, Mr. Harris."

"Torry shifted nervously in his seat. "Yes, I know what he was in jail for."

"Can you tell us, Mr. Harris?"

Torry was quiet for a moment. "He killed ..." He took a deep breath. "... he shot the man who robbed his girlfriend and killed their child."

"Is that what he told you?"

"No, he never went into detail about what he did ..." Torry turned away, and then stared at the floor, He continued in a flat voice. "... he just shared with us his experiences in prison; you know, how his days were and stuff."

"So how did you know Mr. Banks did fifteen years in prison?"

QB looked down at the table with a studied blankness; it was the face of a defendant whose case just sustained damage and who didn't wish the jury to see his dismay. But the jury did.

Torry looked at the prosecutor. "I never said how much time he did in prison."

"Excuse me, how do you know he did any time in prison?"

"The Internet ... I looked up his case on the computer."

"That was smart; we all must know who we're around."

"Objection, Your Honor, the DA is indirectly attempting ..."

Hailey didn't let him finish. "Objection is sustained." He then instructed the jurors to disregard the last statement by the prosecutor, and then admonish the DA.

The district attorney acknowledged his slip, but his point was made. The jurors seemed to be on the edge of their seats. The DA attempted to find out just how much Torry knew, but he held up pretty well. Saying QB only spoke about his incarceration to let the students know that prison is not something they should never look forward to. The prosecutor wrapped up without any further damage, but felt confident that what unfolded was indeed enough.

For Torry it was finally over; he felt bad. But as he made his way out of the witness stand, QB was there waiting for him. He took him by the arm and led him back to his wheelchair. As he helped him into it he told Torry, "You did a good job."

Torry looked up at him. "I hope so," he said.

Once everybody was settled back down, Kingsley turned to QB. "This is it," he said.

QB seemed stunned; his eyes appeared to be unfocused. He looked up at Kingsley. "I think I should testify," he stated.

Kingsley disagreed vehemently. "He didn't get much out of Torry, just the fact that you went to prison for murder. But if you take the stand he will be allowed to probe further; to dig into places that we don't need this jury to hear."

QB started to say something when Kingsley asked for a recess so he can consult with his client. The judge agreed that it was a good time to take a break. "Fifteen minutes everybody," said the judge.

After the jury was escorted out of the courtroom, QB was out of his chair and headed out into the hallway. Reyna and Kingsley followed. They were all huddled in the rotunda of the courthouse. "I think I have to testify," QB repeated.

"I'm sorry, Quentin, but I do not recommend you do that. The district attorney expects that; he believes you have no choice but to testify. So he and his team are back in his office putting together a line of questioning that will no doubt convince the jury to convict." Kingsley looked at Reyna. "I believe we have placed enough doubt in the minds

of the jury. The kids did well, and other than that one slip up, I would put my life on a not guilty verdict. Even with the slip, I still feel we are about seventy-five percent there, and in this County that is good odds."

QB glanced at him in open disbelief. He wanted to believe in his attorney, but something was telling him to testify. He turned to Reyna. "What do you think, baby?"

"I … I don't know. However, I do believe we are winning right now," she said.

QB let out a deep breath as he looked around the giant courthouse. He knew Kingsley was right about Nassau County, seventy-five percent was good. Nassau County was known for their high conviction rate. QB hugged his wife. "All right. Let's rest," he said.

When court resumed, Kingsley stood up and announced that the defense rests their case. QB looked at the prosecutor—a quick glance—then looked back at the judge. He didn't want to get caught staring at him. The prosecutor couldn't believe his ears; he saw things from a totally different angle. He thought he turned the tables, and had decided to take it easy on Mr. Banks, but that was all to no avail now.

The judge announced to the jurors and everybody else in the courtroom that the trial would be postponed until the following morning, when both the people and the defense will present closing arguments, and then the case would be put in the jury's hand. With that, he dismissed everybody for the day.

***

Later that night, QB sat with Reyna and their daughter in the living room of their home. There wasn't much said. QB was lost in his own thoughts of possibly having to go back to prison. He unconsciously placed his hand over Reyna's, his fingers tightening as his emotions yearned to escape. But he restrained himself. He could not afford to have Reyna worrying more than she already was. They spent the evening talking about everything else except the trial. Even though everybody wanted to come over, they told them that they were in no mood for company. Everybody understood. Shai volunteered to pick up Nia and allow her to spend the night over to her condo if they wanted to be alone. But they refused, they needed to be with each other, and that included Nia.

At about three in the morning QB finally fell asleep. Unfortunately, his sleep took him to a place he didn't want to be. He was in a prison cell, this time on death row, trying to convince the reverend, who was standing in front of his cell that he did not kill anyone; that he was innocent. He was pleading, the desperate words tumbling from his dry mouth, but no one was listening. QB screamed, "Listening is an art, people!" He began screaming at the superintendent and other faceless men who were standing there ready to take him to the execution chamber.

As they were leading him away, he turned toward them to make one last pitiful appeal. As he did, the reverend's face suddenly was identical to Showtyme's.

QB, jumped up into a sitting position on the bed. He woke Reyna. He realized he was sweating as he rubbed his eyes. His head was pounding from the intensity of the nightmare.

Reyna asked, "Baby, are you all right?"

QB looked at the bedside digital clock and then at Reyna. "Yeah baby, I had a nightmare about Showtyme," he answered.

She reached out to hug him. Never had something felt so comforting; the feel of her body was like an electrical wire with a strong current passing through it—a warm, loving shock. After a few moments he jumped up and hopped in the shower. He told her to get her sleep and that he would be fine. Reluctantly, she got another hour of sleep. Both she and Nia woke up to a fabulous breakfast that he made. He appeared more upbeat than the night before. QB was trying to be optimistic. He spoke to Kingsley that morning, who assured him that everything was going to be all right. That he was working on something that might guarantee a not guilty verdict. However, he could not, at least at that time show his hand, even to him because it all might backfire. Kingsley told him to keep his spirits up and that he'd see them in court in a few hours.

TWENTY-SEVEN

As everybody made their way into the courtroom, people were approaching QB telling him to keep his head up, giving him words of encouragement. The judge finally entered the courtroom and settled everyone. He then set the stage for the closing arguments.

Taking about forty-five minutes apiece, both attorneys did a good job with their closing remarks. The jury watched each attorney with deep attention. For over a week and a half they had listened to evidence, mostly circumstantial, meaning no real physical evidence linking Quentin Banks to the murder of Showtyme. No DNA, no fingerprints, no weapons, nothing. Unfortunately, a lot of prisons are filled with individuals who have been convicted by circumstantial evidence alone. The evidence in this case was more inferred; the district attorney attempted to inflame the passions of the jury by speculating that once the dots were connected, the story of a black man who failed to escape his past would emerge. That Quentin Banks was the same person that killed before.

Kingsley, on the other hand, closed by speaking about how when mothers and fathers walk in their community they should feel a sense of comfort, not fear and apprehension. How we each need to be the person that the community can turn to, not run from. He showed how

Quentin Banks was—is that person. He also pointed out how Mr. Quentin Banks, in spite of his positive influence in the community, fit a convenient, race-based template that says that when a black man is somehow involved with an investigation, he must be guilty. However, he hoped that this jury would be different, and consider the facts, and weigh the evidence and come back with a not guilty verdict, for anything else would be an injustice.

When Kingsley finished, QB asked him was that what he was working on? The attorney turned to him and told him no. That what he was working on did not pan out. But QB wouldn't allow that news to get the best of him, he felt Kingsley did a good job closing out. When he looked at the jurors he thought he saw not guilty written on their faces. He also noticed that every time the door to the courtroom opened Kingsley would turn around looking for someone.

In the end, both attorneys simply asked for the jury to do justice. With that and the instructions from the judge, the jurors were finally allowed to deliberate. There were a few read-backs. That's when the jury sends out a note requesting to hear testimony of a particular witness, whether it's the police, forensics, or any of the so-called material or character witnesses.

Everybody in the courtroom was antsy; both sides were anticipating a verdict in their favor.

***

The jury deliberated for two long days and on Friday at 4:40 in the afternoon QB and Reyna was at a restaurant eating when Kingsley's secretary reached him on his cell to tell them that the jury had reached a verdict. The wait had stretched QB and his family to their limits. With the verdict finally in, they both were assaulted with feelings of stress. On their way to the courthouse they discussed whether or not the timeliness of the verdict was a good or bad sign. Most people had their opinion on the amount of time it took juries to reach a verdict. Some said the longer they were out, the better for the defendant, while others thought the sooner the better. It really didn't matter either way now, what mattered was they had a verdict, and in less than an hour their future would be determined.

Reyna phoned everybody. By the time they entered the courtroom there was a buzz of expectancy among the spectators. When everybody was in their seats the judge asked, "Ladies and gentlemen, have you reached a verdict?"

The thin dark-skinned foreman answered, "Yes, we have, Your Honor.

"Please stand and read the verdict for the Court."

The foreman glanced at QB, then looked at Judge Hailey. "On the count of Murder in the second degree, we the jurors find the defendant Quentin Banks…" He hesitated for a slight moment then said, "Guilty."

Pandemonium broke out in the courtroom. QB literally felt his knees buckle. As the moment appeared to just hang in the air, Reyna passed out. The court officers rushed to Reyna's aid. When they got her back up in her seat, the judge was banging his gavel loud and hard, trying to regain order so the jury could finish. When he regained order, the foreman cleared his throat. "On the charge Criminal Possession of a weapon in the 1st degree, we the jury, find the defendant Quentin Banks … Guilty." He announced the verdict as if it pained him to say the words guilty. Throughout the chaos, the Court officers made their way to QB's side and was beginning to place his arm behind his back when Shai wailed for them to let her brother go. This set off another round of confusion. QB, knowing he had to do something, turned around and tried to calm everybody, letting them know it would be all right.

The scene was near unmanageable—the officers had to get him out of the courtroom. For QB, the thought of living in a prison cell for the next twenty-five years was something that he just couldn't envision. He didn't know what, but he had to somehow prove his innocence. Just when the officers were tightening the handcuffs on his wrist, Shawnee entered the courtroom. Noticing Kingsley, she immediately walked over

Young Adult

to him. When the attorney saw her, he couldn't believe it. He literally wrapped his arms around her in a warm embrace. He asked her, "Are you here to do what's right?"

Shawnee looked at him and said, "As long as you're my attorney … yes."

Kingsley stood up, not giving her a chance to change her mind, and in a booming voice called, "Your Honor … Your Honor, can I have the attention of the court?"

The Judge, who was about to dismiss the jury, and exit for his chambers sat back down. He immediately picked up his gavel and began banging it in order to quiet the courtroom. Everybody seemed to pause in mid-sentence or whatever it is that they were doing. Facing Kingsley, Judge Hailey asked, "Yes, Mr. Kingsley."

QB looked at his attorney and then noticed Shawnee by his side. *Where did she come from?* he thought. She looked at QB and then it hit him. He knew what she came to do. He stood there somewhat transfixed. Kingsley nodded to the judge.

"Your Honor, I don't know how to say this any other way, but the defense would like to put forth a motion for immediate dismissal based on new pertinent evidence."

Eyes narrowed, Hailey asked, "What evidence is that, Mr. Kingsley?"

QB glanced at the jury, and then at the DA who was standing there poised to object, and then at Kingsley. "I have someone here who says she shot and killed Mr. Darius Adams," Kingsley said.

The judge sat straight up in his chair and looked at the district attorney as he shot up with an objection, "Over-ruled," said the judge. Everybody in the courtroom stood up. The judge instructed the bailiffs to uncuff Mr. Banks, and for everybody to take a seat. Once the courtroom was composed, the judge peered down at Shawnee. "Young lady, do you mind if I ask you a few questions?" he asked.

Shawnee looked up at Kingsley who nodded at her. "Yes, you can."

Hailey leaned up on his desk. "Is what Mr. Kingsley saying true?"

"Yes sir."

"Can you tell the court exactly what happened?"

Shawnee turned to Kingsley. He then interjected, "Your Honor, this is a very peculiar situation … I don't advise Ms. Clarke to openly admit her role in open court. However, if we can meet in the chambers I will be more than willing to advise her on—"

The judge didn't let the attorney get another word out. "Mr. Kingsley, we just had a trial where a jury of Mr. Banks' peers came back with a guilty verdict. And now you stand before the court telling me that you have someone who is admitting to being the shooter of Mr. Adams. I will suggest you advise this young lady to say what she has to say in open court. Once I hear what Ms. …" The judge let it hang in the air.

"Clarke, Ms. Clarke, Your Honor," said Kingsley.

"Once I hear what Ms. Clarke has to say then we will decide exactly where we should go from there."

Shawnee went on to tell the court everything that took place. Her story had everyone's attention. She described in graphic detail how Showtyme killed others, had ordered people killed, and raped women. She spoke about how he abused her and made her sleep with other men. How he ordered the hit on Chase, the day QB and Torry was shot. She finally explained about Reyna being kidnapped and how she called Mr. Banks and explained that he couldn't call the cops because Showtyme had police on the payroll and finally how and why she shot Showtyme in the tunnel leading to the escape house. Her story filled in every blank in the jury's mind. When Shawnee finished, people were sitting in their seats in awe. Most of the jury held their heads down because they had falsely convicted the wrong person. Reyna, Shai, Naysia and Lexi all were wiping tears from their eyes. QB sat there not believing the courage of Shawnee. When she finished, he stood up and walked over to her and hugged her—a tight, caring embrace. They stood there in the middle of the courtroom for what seemed like forever. QB

whispered to Shawnee his appreciation and promised to be there for her no matter what she has to go through.

The judge finally asked for them to be seated. He then spoke to the entire courtroom, explaining that he had a lot to think about. That he was going to take a break, along with both attorneys and come back with a decision. The judge represented law and justice, and had the power of bending the rules to his will, so against the objection of the district attorney's office, he decided to rule on this today.

About an hour later, Judge Hailey stood before the courtroom and announced that the charges against Mr. Quentin Banks were being dismissed. The courtroom erupted. Reyna reached over the rail and hugged her husband. The spectators were overwhelmed with a relieved happiness. Unfortunately, Shawnee was taken into custody. A bittersweet ending for everyone, but as always QB would stick to his word and be a light at the end of her journey.

TWENTY- EIGHT

Two months later, the graduation for U-Turn was a huge success. QB had never been so proud of a group of students, who together, had overcome tremendous obstacles. Torry was accepted to St. Johns University. In fact seventeen of the students received scholarships from numerous colleges throughout the state. Others went on to work for the electrical union, while a few remained at U-Turn and became counselors.

Chase was coming home in thirty-seven days after receiving tremendous support at his first parole board appearance. Shawnee, on the other hand, had taken a deal of four years in exchange for her testimony, especially involving police corruption. A flat sentence for manslaughter, initially she didn't want to take it, but after Kingsley explained that it was a deal in which all her criminal activities would be accounted for, she realized that there would be no better deal. QB was true to his word and had been supporting her. In fact, he started a mentoring program where students at U-Turn adopted a young prisoner and corresponded with him or her in hopes to show them through their own personal journeys, that they themselves could turn their lives around.

Banger ended up getting shot and killed one month after the trial. He lost all street credibility when he testified at the trial, but in his haste

Young Adult

to fill Showtyme's shoes he got caught up in a robbery gone bad and was murdered.

Torry and Naysia were planning to be married. Both attend St. Johns, while raising their son who they named Zaire Harris. Reyna fully recovered from her ordeal, and was contemplating leaving her job to partner with her husband and work with the youth.

The government on the other hand was quietly executing the bill that the 108th Congress quietly passed, a bill designed to have a devastating effect on our younger generation. The bill is known as the Anti Gang Act, a bill that will allow law enforcement to lock up anybody for a mandatory amount of time for simply being associated with a gang.

So the author advises that all youth read the Anti Gang Act Bill, and fully understand exactly what you're getting into. Ignorance of the law is no excuse; you must take control of your life, and know that it's never too late to make a U-Turn, to change the course of your life. Even if you're "Under Pressure," know there is always a better way.

Anti Gang Act Bill
Passed by 108th Congress on April 28, 2004

SEC. 102 CRIMINAL STREET GANGS
(b) PARTICIPATION IN A CRIMINAL STREET GANG.

It shall be unlawful for any person:

1. To do any act with the intent to effect the criminal activities of a street gang.
2. To commit, attempt to commit, aid or abet the commission of or conspire to commit any predicate gang crime ...
(A) In furtherance or in aid of the activities of the street gang;
(B) For the direct or indirect benefit of the criminal street gang, or in association with the street gang;
(C) For the purpose of gaining entrance to, or maintaining or increasing position in, the criminal street gang;
While knowingly being a member of or participating in a criminal street gang
3. To employ, use command, counsel, persuade, induce, entice or coerce any individual to commit any predicate gang crime–
Under the penalty, provisions for the aforementioned crimes the ANTI GANG ACT provides as follows:
4. Whoever violates subsection (b) (2) or (b) (3) shall be fined under this title, imprisoned not more than 20 years or both; except–
(A) Where the predicate gang crime is a serious drug offense, then whoever violates these subsections shall be fined under this title, imprisoned not more than 30 years or both; or

Young Adult

(B) Where the predicate gang crime is a violent gang crime, whoever violates these subsections shall be fined under this title, imprisoned for any term of years or for LIFE, or both.

As you read the words in the comfort of your so-called freedom, the penalties outlined above, some carrying life sentences are probably to you nothing more than mere words on paper. But for many young brothers and sisters sitting in prisons throughout our Nation they mean so much more. Hear their cries, smarten up, do not crumble *Under Pressure*, and lastly, rise up young people, because a better tomorrow depends on you.

READING GROUP DISCUSSION QUESTIONS

1- Do you think Chase should have told Q.B about Showtyme's threats on his life? If so why?

2- Do you think Chase was at fault for the shooting of Torry and QB?

3- What do you think about Torry's confrontation with Chase at the hospital? Do you thing Torry was wrong or do you believe Chase was obligated to react to Torry being shot?

4- What do you thing about Naysia and Lexi and the influence they had on Torry and Chase's growth?

5- How do you feel about the judicial system? Do you think prison is an effective means of punishment/rehabilitation? Why or why not?

6- How do you think gang violence affects the youth in the community?

7- Do you think Chase, QB or Torry should have cooperated with the police? How do you feel about the street campaign of "**Stop Snitching**"?

Young Adult

8- If Shawnee had not stepped forward, do you think QB should have been convicted and possibly gone to prison?

9- Do you believe QB was wrong for putting the kids a U-TURN in the casket to make a point?

10- Is there a gap between youth and adults when it comes to eh understanding the times, if so, how do we bridged the gap?

11- How does peer pressure influence your life?

12- Do you agree with QB's decision when he asked Chase not ot testify at the grand jury? Do you think his persuasion was selfish? Do you think he was promoting the whole "**Stop Snitching**" campaign? Or do you believe his concern was genuinely for the safety of his wife Reyna and Chase?

13- Do you believe Reyna was justified when she questioned QB's loyalty to his family or to wanting to get some getback? Was it fair for her to question his priorities even though the safety of the household was his primary concern?

Bio about the Author:

Rashawn Hughes is the father of two beautiful daughters. He was raised in both Lefrak City Queens and Uniondale Long Island. At the age of twenty-two, he was convicted and sentenced to twenty years in prison for a shooting in a street altercation where a man lost his life. While in prison Mr. Hughes has dedicated himself to being responsible, to showing that life once set on its course can change. He began honing his writing skills in 2000 after taking a brutally honest look at his life and situation. He wanted to create a way to keep the memory of his victim alive and do something that would make his family proud of him. So he decided to pen his first novel. Today Mr. Hughes lives with his regrets but now wants to give back to the situation from which he took so much.

While in prison, Mr. Hughes graduated from both Dutchess Community College and Bard College. He's a certified HIV/AIDS counselor and works with the Youth Assistance Program (YAP), where he lectures youth about the consequences of wrong choices, drug usage, gangs, peer pressure, promiscuity and the importance of education. He has given numerous motivational speeches throughout his twenty years of incarceration. He was interviewed on *60 Minutes* in April 2007 concerning the importance of higher education in prisons, and also quoted in Bill Clinton's best-selling book titled, *Giving,* about his ideas on freedom.

Mr. Hughes has completed his minimum sentence of twenty years and now awaits his release. Until then, he plans on living responsibly and putting out work, which will help the young awaken the potential that exists inside of them.

Mr. Rashawn Hughes
P.O. Box 2000
Dannemora, New York 12929

W·CLARK PUBLISHING
60 Evergreen Place, Suite 904
East Orange New Jersey 07018

ATTENTION:

We are seeking submissions for the
Wahida Clark Presents Young Adult Line.

Submission Guidelines:

✓ No emailed submissions accepted.

✓ Submissions must be typed and double spaced.

✓ No handwritten submissions.

www.wcpyoungadult.com

WAHIDA CLARK PRESENTS

Y.A.
YOUNG ADULT

THE BOY IS MINE!

A WILSON HIGH CONFIDENTIAL

A YOUNG ADULT NOVEL BY

CHARMAINE WHITE

COMING SOON FROM

WAHIDA CLARK PRESENTS
YOUNG ADULT

www.wcpyoungadult.com

WAHIDA CLARK PRESENTS

Y.A.
YOUNG ADULT

NINETY NINE
PROBLEMS

A Young Adult Novel BY
GLORIA DOTSON-LEWIS

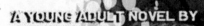